THE FEMALE AMERICAN

broadview editions
series editor: L.W. Conolly

THE FEMALE AMERICAN; OR, THE ADVENTURES OF UNCA ELIZA WINKFIELD

second edition

Anonymous (Unca Eliza Winkfield, pseud.)

edited by Michelle Burnham and James Freitas

broadview editions

Library and Archives Canada Cataloguing in Publication

Winkfield, Unca Eliza
[Female American]
    The female American; or, The adventures of Unca Eliza Winkfield /
Anonymous (Unca Eliza Winkfield, pseud.) ; edited by Michelle
Burnham and James Freitas. — Second edition.

(Broadview editions)
Includes bibliographical references.
ISBN 978-1-55481-096-3 (pbk.)

    I. Burnham, Michelle, editor II. Freitas, James, editor III. Title.
IV. Title: Adventures of Unca Eliza Winkfield. V. Series: Broadview
editions

PS875.W74F45 2014   813'.1   C2014-903572-1

Broadview Editions

The Broadview Editions series represents the ever-changing canon of literature by bringing together texts long regarded as classics with valuable lesser-known works.

Advisory editor for this volume: Betsy Struthers

Broadview Press is an independent, international publishing house, incorporated in 1985.

We welcome comments and suggestions regarding any aspect of our publications—please feel free to contact us at the addresses below or at broadview@broadviewpress.com.

North America
PO Box 1243, Peterborough, Ontario K9J 7H5, Canada
555 Riverwalk Parkway, Tonawanda, NY 14150, USA
Tel: (705) 743-8990; Fax: (705) 743-8353
email: customerservice@broadviewpress.com

UK, Europe, Central Asia, Middle East, Africa, India, and Southeast Asia
Eurospan Group, 3 Henrietta St., London WC2E 8LU, United Kingdom
Tel: 44 (0) 1767 604972; Fax: 44 (0) 1767 601640
email: eurospan@turpin-distribution.com

Australia and New Zealand
NewSouth Books
c/o TL Distribution, 15-23 Helles Ave., Moorebank, NSW 2170, Australia
Tel: (02) 8778 9999; Fax: (02) 8778 9944
email: orders@tldistribution.com.au

www.broadviewpress.com

PRINTED IN CANADA

Contents

Acknowledgements • 7
Introduction • 9
The Female American in Literary Context: A Brief Chronology • 33
A Note on the Text • 39

The Female American • 41

Appendix A: The Colonial Americas and Its Native Peoples • 163
    1. From Thomas Harriot, *A Briefe and True Report of the New Found Land of Virginia* (1590) • 163
    2. From George Percy, "Percy's Discourse of Virginia" (1625) • 167
    3. From John Smith, *The Generall Historie of Virginia* (1624) • 169
    4. From Aphra Behn, *Oroonoko* (1688) • 175

Appendix B: Ibn Tufayl and Autodidactic Castaways • 179
    1. From *The History of Josephus the Indian Prince* (1696) • 179
    2. From George Keith, *The Woman-Preacher of Samaria* (1674) • 185
    3. From Simon Ockley, *The Improvement of Human Reason* (1708) • 187
    4. From *The Life and Surprizing Adventures of Don Juliani de Trezz* (1720) • 194
    5. From *The History of Autonous* (1736) • 203
    6. From John Kirkby, *The Capacity and Extent of the Human Understanding* (1745) • 208

Appendix C: Isolated Castaways • 215
    1. From William Dampier, *New Voyage Round the World* (1697) • 215
    2. From Woodes Rogers, *A Cruising Voyage Round the World* (1712) • 217
    3. From Daniel Defoe, *Robinson Crusoe* (1719) • 220

4. From Daniel Defoe, *Serious Reflections During the Life and Surprising Adventures of Robinson Crusoe* (1720) • 230

5. From Peter Longueville, *The Hermit* (1727) • 231

Appendix D: Castaway Communities • 233

    1. From [Ambrose Evans], *The Adventures and Surprizing Deliverances, of James Dubourdieu, and his Wife* (1719) • 233

    2. From Penelope Aubin, *The Life of Charlotta Du Pont, An English Lady* (1723) • 241

    3. From "A Remarkable Voyage in the South Sea," *Edinburgh Magazine* (1760) • 245

Appendix E: Reviews of *The Female American* • 249

    1. *The Monthly Review* (1767) • 249

    2. *The Critical Review* (1767) • 249

Works Cited and Recommended Reading • 251

Acknowledgements

This second edition of *The Female American* was inspired by the scholarship that has been published on the novel since the first Broadview edition appeared in 2001. In preparing the current volume, we have relied on and been inspired by this work, which has brought to light richer and deeper contexts for the novel. These scholarly debts are acknowledged in the Works Cited and Recommended Reading list at the end of the volume as well as in footnotes throughout the text. We would like here to acknowledge, however, two especially influential works: Matthew Reilly's article on Arabic and Quaker sources for *The Female American*, and Eve Tavor Bannet's book on eighteenth-century stories about transatlantic subaltern migration. Together, these two works helped to set us on a series of paths more fascinating than we could possibly have anticipated, leading us toward a large number of the texts and contexts that are represented in the much expanded appendices to this volume.

We thank the Office of the Provost at Santa Clara University for a Faculty-Student Research Assistance Program grant that supported our collaboration on this new edition. The staffs at Stanford University Special Collections, the Beinecke Library at Yale University, and the Library of Congress helped us to locate and reproduce the images included in this edition. Ashley Barros joined us at a critical moment to provide excellent assistance with organizing and proofreading the appendices.

This volume remains indebted to Paula Backscheider, whose always generous advice and mentorship first helped to see this novel into print for modern readers, scholars, and students. For their assistance, suggestions, and willingness to answer questions, both past and present, we also thank Mary Chapman, Judy Dunbar, Leanna Goodwater, Mark Kamrath, Jody Pinault, Gordon Sayre, and Laura Stevens. We remain grateful to the University of North Carolina Press for permission to reprint selections from *The Complete Works of Captain John Smith, 1580-1631*, edited by Philip L. Barbour, with a foreword by Thad W. Tate. Copyright © 1986 by the University of North Carolina Press. At Broadview Press, Marjorie Mather, Leonard Conolly, and Betsy Struthers have offered exceptionally supportive assistance with this project. We also want to acknowledge the good work Broadview continues to do with its Broadview Editions series by bringing lesser-known or forgotten literary texts into print and making them available and accessible for students, scholars, and general readers. Finally, we thank our families: Chip Cassin, Mara Alice Burnham Cassin, and Jana Ursula Burnham Cassin; and Ken Freitas, Cindy Freitas, and Cara Freitas.

Introduction

When *The Female American; or, the Adventures of Unca Eliza Winkfield* was first published in London in 1767, only two very brief reviews of it appeared, neither of which gave the novel much in the way of either attention or praise (see Appendix E, p. 249). The notice that appeared in *The Monthly Review*, for example, succinctly summarized and evaluated the book in less than 20 words: "a sort of second *Robinson Crusoe*; full of wonders; and well calculated to make one sort of readers *stare*." Just what "sort of readers" are being identified here—and whether their ensuing "stare" might be one of horror, disdain, disbelief, or fascination—remains unspecified. Dominant eighteenth-century reading practices suggest, however, that this review is addressed to educators or parents concerned about the effects of novel-reading on that population believed to be especially susceptible to the dangerous fascinations of novels: young women. A similar concern may well have motivated the critic writing for *The Critical Review*, a periodical published by "A Society of Gentlemen," who sarcastically insists that *The Female American* would have fared better had it been published in America instead of in England, since an American audience of "wild Indians" would probably have greeted the book with "the most judicious and sincere applause" and thus have saved this particular reviewer "six hours very disagreeable employment." This review, too, does not explain precisely what made the novel so disagreeable, but it is likely that the critic objected both to the boldness and to the implausibility of the adventures depicted in it.[1]

When Broadview Press first reissued *The Female American* in 2001, modern critics had bestowed on the novel almost as little attention, and just as little praise, as had its eighteenth-century contemporaries. By 2001, the only critical account devoted solely to *The Female American* had appeared in the

---

1 We have located no reviews of *The Female American* in American periodicals. Essays on novels and novel-reading in late eighteenth-century American periodicals, however, echo English fears about the dangerous effects of novels on young readers especially.

"Unca Eliza Winkfield," engraving from *The Female American; or, the Adventures of Unca Eliza Winkfield* [1800]. Courtesy of the Beinecke Library, Yale University.

inaugural 1929 volume of the journal *American Literature*, where it was introduced in a short essay as an example of "the literary poverty of eighteenth-century America" and where its plot was described as "so preposterous that the book has little intrinsic worth" (McDowell 307, 309). Over the remainder of the twentieth century, *The Female American* received only brief and occasional mention by critics interested in the literary representation of European-Indian contact (see Slotkin) or of America in early English fiction (see Heilman). It otherwise went unnoticed by scholars and students of either British or American literature.

Twenty-first-century scholars and students have by now sharply departed from this reception history by seeing *The Female American* as a crucial addition to literary histories of the Anglo-American novel and as a text characterized by a complex intertexuality layered with political and social critiques.[1] This revised edition takes advantage of recent scholarship on *The Female American* to more richly contextualize its engagement with questions of empire, gender, religion, and race in the eighteenth-century Atlantic world.[2] It continues to consider the ways in which the novel engages with and departs from Daniel Defoe's *Robinson Crusoe*. At the same time, however, this edition aims to situate the novel within a much more extensive literary history of castaway fiction, a history that includes many texts as forgotten or overlooked as *The Female American* once was—beginning with seventeenth-century English translations of a fourteenth-century Arabic text and continuing with a proliferation of eighteenth-century narratives set on islands around the world, in the Indian and Pacific as well as the Atlantic Ocean.

The Female American in Transatlantic Context

The Monthly Review critic writing in 1767 calls *The Female American* a "second *Robinson Crusoe*," since the book appears clearly indebted to Defoe's popular 1719 novel of wanderlust, shipwreck,

---

1   Armstrong and Tennenhouse (196-97) first positioned the genre in transatlantic context when they argued that the "English novel" has "American origins."
2   The Works Cited and Recommended Readings at the end of this volume will point readers toward this recent scholarship.

and adventure. Like Defoe's hero, the protagonist of *The Female American* is cast from a ship during a transatlantic voyage and abandoned on a deserted New World island. In both novels, the central figures endure physical and psychological trials and learn to survive and prosper, first in isolation and later in encounters with the indigenous peoples (and later European arrivals) who visit the island. *The Female American* even seems to borrow a number of quite specific details from *Robinson Crusoe*: both protagonists experience illness soon after their arrival on the island; both survey the island from atop a hill; both are visited by hurricanes and an earthquake; both use the goats that roam the island as a source of meat, milk, and tallow from which to make candles; both ascribe their experiences to Providence; and both introduce European technology and religion to the indigenous peoples who eventually arrive on the island.

But although it resembles *Robinson Crusoe* in outline and mimics some of its details, *The Female American* is otherwise a vastly different kind of story than Defoe's. For one thing, its central character and narrator is a woman. For another, she is biracial, multilingual, and boasts a transnational heritage. Unca Eliza Winkfield—the heroine, narrator, and putative author of the novel—is the daughter of a Native American princess (whose father, a kind of Powhatan figure, is the reigning king in the region named Virginia by the English) and an English settler (whose father is identified as an actual historical figure who was the Virginia colony's first president). Although the heroine's central experience of living on a remote island somewhere in the Atlantic Ocean may be analogous to Crusoe's, *The Female American* revises the narratives of capitalist accumulation, colonial conquest, and political imperialism that have been associated with Defoe's book. Winkfield's story engages instead in fantasies of a feminist utopianism and cross-racial community, both of which are enabled, however, by a specifically religious form of imperialism. This text therefore significantly remodels the Crusoe story in ways that not only make it an intriguing critique of Defoe's work but an important early Anglo-American novel in its own right.

The heroine's very genealogy suggests the ways in which this novel strategically combines in rich and striking ways historical and literary antecedents from both the Old and the New World. The text appears aware of Elizabethan and Jacobean descriptions of Virginia written by travelers such as Thomas Harriot, John Smith, and George Percy (see Appendix A, p. 163) and of the early missionary activity of John Eliot among the New England Indians as well as the eighteenth-century missionary work of Samson Occom in America and England. It is equally engaged with early English novels set in the Atlantic world, such as Aphra Behn's *Oroonoko* (see Appendix A4, p. 175) and Defoe's *Robinson Crusoe* (see Appendix C3, p. 220), as well as eighteenth-century English interest in Egyptology and oracles.[1] The book's depiction of the role of women in the projects of New World colonialism and religious conversion places it among other early modern transatlantic representations of women, race, and empire—including works by Mary Rowlandson, Aphra Behn, Charlotte Lennox, and Susanna Rowson.[2]

Texts such as these moreover challenge the traditional identification of the adventure genre with masculinity, male protagonists, and male writers. Such assumptions allow Martin Green, for example, to dismiss German novels about female castaways as "historical exceptions" to the male genre of the Crusoe adventure story, although these exceptions, he admits, "must be of great interest to feminists" (6). Far from an exception, however, a novel such as *The Female American* belongs to a vibrant and increasingly recognized genre of female adventure fiction that complicates the traditional dichotomy between male adventure and female domesticity.[3] This tradition furthermore challenges the critical privilege given to those novels that confirm the ideology of separate spheres, which genders

---

1 McMurran offers a compelling discussion of the novel in the context of eighteenth-century discourses on oracles.

2 Rowlandson's *The Sovereignty and Goodness of God* narrates her captivity among the New England Indians (1682); Behn's *Oroonoko* (1688) is a novel about slavery and colonialism in Surinam; Lennox's *Harriot Stuart* (1751) is a novelistic romance that takes place in both England and North America; and Rowson's novel *Reuben and Rachel* (1798) tells the story of the descendants of European nobility and Native American royalty. All four depict early modern women in cross-cultural and transnational zones of contact. For a fine study of gender and empire in eighteenth-century English literature, see Brown.

3 For studies of female adventure, see Castiglia, Dugaw, Kolodny, and Owen.

the private realm of the home as female and the public domain as male.[1] The heroines of Samuel Richardson's novels *Pamela* (1740) and *Clarissa* (1747-48), for example, are often identified with immobility, domesticity, and such passive virtues as submission, obedience, and frailty that reflect eighteenth-century social ideals for women (see Brophy). The heroine of *The Female American*, by contrast, represents a radical alternative to dominant novelistic representations of women and to the lives of their readers.

The Female American in Global Context

These features of *The Female American* stand out as remarkable in a literary history limited to the Atlantic and dominated by Defoe's *Robinson Crusoe*. Read in a more global geography and a less canonical literary history, however, *The Female American* emerges as far less idiosyncratic, affiliated with an historically long and geographically wide tradition of narratives about shipwrecks, castaways, and islands. The earliest of these is undoubtedly *Hayy Ibn Yaqzan*, a narrative about an infant abandoned on a deserted island who is nursed by a gazelle before going on to reach exceptional levels of philosophical knowledge and spiritual understanding, despite growing up in solitude as the island's sole human inhabitant.[2] Written in Arabic in the twelfth century by the philosopher Ibn Tufayl, *Hayy Ibn Yaqzan* experienced a minor vogue in England several centuries later when it was translated—first into Latin by the Orientalist scholar Edward Pococke in 1671 and then into English in three separate versions: by the Quaker George Keith in 1674 (see Appendix B2, p. 185), by George Ashwell in 1686, and by the Anglican Simon Ockley in 1708 (see Appendix B3, p. 187). The subtitles of these translations frequently emphasized the protagonist's identity as an autodidact or "self-taught philosopher."

These translations appeared during a time when England was

---

1 For recent discussions of the separate sphere debate in American literary history, see "No More Separate Spheres!"

2 See Reilly for an analysis of *The Female American* in the context of *Hayy Ibn Yaqzan* and its later translation by the Quaker George Keith. As Reilly notes, Keith also published a treatise on women's role in missionary preaching, *The Woman-Preacher of Samaria* (see Appendix B2, p. 185).

receiving not only descriptions from and about the New World by such writers as Harriot, Smith, Percy, and Behn but also news from early privateering voyages that circumnavigated the globe. Both William Dampier and Woodes Rogers, for example, recorded their discovery of an abandoned sailor (a Moskito Indian in the first case and the Scotsman Alexander Selkirk in the second) found living alone on the Pacific island of Juan Fernandez with only goats for companions (see Appendices C1 and C2, pp. 215-19). The English translations of Ibn Tufyal's narrative likely combined with such contemporaneous accounts to launch an extraordinary series of popular castaway stories published over the course of the eighteenth century. These narratives ranged from nearly identical copies to elaborate revisions of their Arabic predecessor and from brief accounts to lengthy and complex novels with multiple intertwined plotlines. Like *The Female American*, the vast majority of these were published anonymously, although the setting of their stories and the national or religious identities of their protagonists could vary widely. Once we recognize *The Female American* as part of this larger global context and more diverse literary history, the novel emerges less as an oddly idiosyncratic text than as one of many contemporary iterations of a popular story that grappled with the practical and imaginative possibilities that attended island isolation and human community.[1]

While many of these castaway narratives featured male protagonists, several—such as Ambrose Evans's *The Adventures and Surprizing Deliverances, of James Dubourdieu, and His Wife* (1719) and Penelope Aubin's *The Life of Charlotta Du Pont* (1723)—offered accounts of female protagonists who were cast adrift, usually with a small community of fellow victims suffering from patriarchal authority, dispossession, poverty, or piracy (see Appendices D1 and D2, pp. 233-45). Novels like these have typically been positioned as descendants of *Robinson Crusoe*, and Jeannine Blackwell has used the term "female Robinsonades"

---

1   The influence of this Arabic source on English literary and philosophical traditions has gone under-recognized, to say the least, by Western scholars. Hassan, however, has reviewed the connections between *Robinson Crusoe* and *Hayy Ibn Yaqzan*, and Russell argues that *Hayy Ibn Yaqzan* influenced the philosophy of John Locke. For recent assessments of the text and its East-West influence, see Attar, Avaramudan, Ben-Zaken, and Baroud.

to categorize novels that put a woman in the place of Defoe's hero. According to Blackwell, at least 26 female Robinsonades appeared in Germany, Holland, France, England, and America in the eighteenth and nineteenth centuries—a number that is certainly an underestimate, if only because it does not include *The Female American*. The term "Robinsonade" itself assumes, however, that *Robinson Crusoe* is a kind of ur-text that spawned imitations throughout Europe, rather than seeing Defoe's novel as one English version of an island survival story with a long history that includes many textual variations and improvisations.[1]

Problems of Truth and Virtue

Making female-centered castaway stories legitimate reading material for an eighteenth-century audience—for whom the novel was still a relatively new, and morally suspect, genre— could nonetheless pose a challenge. Indeed, the first reviews of *The Female American* suggest that this particular attempt did not completely succeed in overcoming those difficulties. In his study of the English novel and its origins, Michael McKeon argues that the novel emerges during an historical period of instability in the interrelated categories of truth and virtue, an instability characterized by a crisis in the ability to determine whether a narrative is telling the truth and whether a person is really virtuous. Novels *represented* such crises in the stories they told, but they also *performed* such crises for their readers, who were themselves left uncertain about whether the text they read was truth or fiction and its characters virtuous or corrupt. Indeed, in the eighteenth century, novels were almost routinely condemned for being both untrue and immoral, and many worried that novel readers drawn into the fictional and intriguing world of a novelistic narrative would be led to desire or imitate the kinds of unrealistic and illicit behavior they encountered in books. In an effort to legitimate their work, novelists almost inevitably attested both to the truthfulness and to the ethical usefulness of their books, insisting that their volume provided moral instruction as well as entertainment to readers. When the novel in question told a

---

1 See Bannet for a study of eighteenth-century transatlantic migration stories that surveys many novels and narratives that formed part of this tradition.

story, however, about the very improbable adventures of a woman living alone on an island somewhere in the Atlantic Ocean and fending for herself among the goats, hurricanes, and Indians, such claims to truth could prove difficult to sustain. Moreover, a text that recounted the rather remarkable freedoms of a solitary and independent young woman was especially subject to criticism by those who feared that readers, by desiring to repeat the experiences of novelistic heroines, might lose their virtue.

The author of *The Female American* was clearly aware of these potential criticisms and attempted to accommodate them in part by attesting to the authenticity and educational value of the narrative. For example, the novel's "editor" claims, in the opening advertisement, that the narrative is "both pleasing and instructive, not unworthy of the most sensible reader; highly fit to be perused by the youth of both sexes, as a rational, moral entertainment; and, as such ... will descend to late posterity, when, most of its contemporaries, founded only in fiction, will have been long forgotten" (p. 43). But the writers of novels like *The Female American* obviously had to do much more than simply assert that their stories were virtuous and true. They also engaged a range of plot devices, modes of characterization, and narrative details that, by creating a logical and moral rationale for the heroine's exploits, anticipated objections about inauthenticity and immorality.

The heroine Unca Eliza Winkfield, for example, is free of many of the weaknesses or limitations that characterize her male castaway counterparts. Whereas Crusoe is a disobedient son who defies his father, Winkfield is devoted to her father. Crusoe takes to the sea in an act of resistance to his father's pleas that he adopt the secure but unexciting "middle station" of life. Winkfield, on the other hand, crosses the Atlantic precisely out of obedience to and affection for her father, whose wishes she is carrying out when she finds herself marooned. Crusoe consequently interprets his shipwreck as providential punishment for his defiance and independence, whereas Winkfield's abandonment appears an unprovoked and undeserved fate. Winkfield generally also avoids having to engage in tasks that require specifically masculine forms of knowledge or that would otherwise be easily dismissed as impossible. Thus, while Crusoe spends years fashioning and fortifying several residences for himself on the island, Winkfield fortuitously finds an immense dwelling already existing on the island and locates a manuscript left by a hermit that offers her instructions on how to survive there.

In spite of such attempts to attain a kind of plausibility, the narrator also makes clear from the very beginning of the novel that her experiences can only be classified as extraordinary,[1] particularly when they are compared to the rather repetitive and mundane lives of most women. She implies that it is her uniquely non-domestic existence that has made available to her the opportunities for adventure and mobility typically enjoyed only by men when she notes that "The lives of women being commonly domestick, the occurrences of them are generally pretty nearly of the same kind; whilst those of men, frequently more vagrant, subject them often to experience greater vicissitudes, many times wonderful and strange. Though a woman, it has been my lot to have experienced much of the latter" (p. 45). On the one hand, this remarkable passage aims to minimize the narrative's more illicit and fantastic dimensions by making them more believable: if her adventures seem implausible, it is only because women are not given the opportunity for more mobility and thus more "wonderful and strange" experiences. But this passage, by drawing attention precisely to the transgressive elements in her story, announces its "dangers" even as it minimizes them. This double-voiced strategy, which can be seen to work throughout the novel, at once appeals to and diminishes the unauthorized desires of readers.

Winkfield, Crusoe, and Eighteenth-Century Castaways

The discussion above suggests that many of the variations on Defoe's narrative in *The Female American* attempt to render the actions of a female protagonist realistically possible, if not believable. But many of these changes constitute differences that also carry a significant cultural and political charge. We have seen, for example, that Crusoe interprets his series of disasters at sea and his eventual shipwreck as providential punishment for his disobedience to his father. Winkfield's seagoing misfortune, on the other hand, is represented as a cruel and unwarranted response to her refusal to consent to an unwanted marriage.

---

1   In fact, the word *extraordinary* appears with remarkable frequency in *The Female American*, and the two nineteenth-century American editions of the novel in 1800 and 1814 both add the word to its title: *The Female American; or, the Extraordinary Adventures of Unca Eliza Winkfield*.

She is abandoned on a remote island by the captain of her ship because she refuses to sign a contract that would bind her to marry his son upon their arrival in England—making her safe arrival dependent on her submission to patriarchal tyranny and the sacrifice of her own desires. As Blackwell notes, many other "female Robinsonades" use this plot device of resistance to an unwanted marriage in order to land their heroines on deserted islands where they typically find themselves living in a utopic environment and practicing sometimes radical forms of independence and power.[1] But this dilemma actually puts these heroines in good company with the vast majority of early eighteenth-century castaways, who tend either to be women escaping from or trapped within coerced marriages or the children of such women who were put to sea as infants by mothers hoping to save them from political or patriarchal violence.[2] Like other such texts, *The Female American* critiques the helplessness of women within a coercive marriage market, and it goes on to offer an alternative fantasy to typical female roles within dominant culture.

Such plot elements suggest not only an attempt to fashion a heroine who can participate in unlikely adventures without compromising her virtue but an attempt to fashion a feminist revision of Defoe's earlier tale by drawing on a long and lively literary tradition that begins before *Robinson Crusoe* and continues alongside it. One of the primary engines that enables these differences in *The Female American* is the specifically "American" identity of Unca Eliza Winkfield. Winkfield's Native American cultural upbringing and status as the daughter of an Indian princess enable her to engage in activities and to fashion an identity that would be unavailable to an ordinary English heroine. Her excuse for rejecting a string of marriage offers from a host of interested suitors, for example, is that none of these men are able to shoot a bow and arrow as effectively as she, a skill developed in the context of her mother's culture. Those actions and abilities that seem most unusual or surprising for a female are invariably explained and

---

1 These include, for example, the German narrative *Der wegen besonderer Schönheit und seltener Tugend liebenswürdigen Mariana* (1752) and the British text by Penelope Aubin, *The Life of Charlotta Du Pont* (1723) (see Appendix D2, p. 241).

2 See, for instance, *The History of Josephus* (Appendix B1, p. 179), *The Life and Surprizing Adventures of Don Juliani* (Appendix B4, p. 194), and *The Life of Charlotta Du Pont* (see Appendix D2, p. 241).

legitimized by her status as a female *American*, an identity that strategically allows her to indulge in what would otherwise be, for an *English* woman, transgressive acts and adventures.

But although Winkfield is represented as extraordinary by virtue of her birth, this novel is also the story of her subsequent development into a powerful and influential religious leader. While her bicultural identity sets the stage for her achievement of this end, it is her experience on the island itself that allows her to arrive there. Upon being deposited on the island, she undergoes a series of difficulties and transformations that add up to a kind of rebirth. She is at first so overwhelmed by her abandonment and isolation that she faints, becomes almost paralyzed with fear, and refuses to explore the island because she "was not fond of rambling" (p. 69). An illness brought on by anxiety over her condition reduces her to a state of near-death. She must literally crawl, like an infant, in order to reach water and shelter. After undergoing a kind of inadvertent baptism in the island's river, she recovers her strength by nursing from the dugs of a she-goat. As her health returns and she regains the ability to walk, Winkfield is figuratively reborn. But that rebirth also increasingly resembles something more like a resurrection.

Winkfield begins, in the wake of her cure, not only to adopt a much more fearless relationship to the island but to take on the persona of a prophetess. Whereas before the idea of "wandering alone was terrifying" (p. 69), she now spends days "rambling about the island" (p. 115), exploring it with pleasure. Like a naturalist, she even records descriptions of the flora and fauna she discovers, including one strange animal whose very physiology might be read as an allegory of exploitative colonialist relations. She descends into the underground chambers of the extensive temple in which she has been living and discovers the coffins of Indian priests and virgins, as well as evidence of the sun worship that is practiced on the island. She adorns herself with the bracelets and jewels worn by the high priests of this solar religion and determines to convert the Indians to Christianity by speaking to them in their tongue from within the hollow idol that they visit the island to worship. In the process of inhabiting this idol, Winkfield becomes "entombed alive" (p. 96) during an earthquake and, in an attempt to emerge from her premature burial, wounds and bloodies the palms of her hands (p. 96). It would seem that Winkfield's earlier reminder to herself to "imitate Jesus" (p. 78) becomes at this point almost literally realized, for following this experience she ultimately takes up a position among the Indians of a female apostle whose gender, racial, and class identity all facilitate their acceptance of her and her spiritual teachings.[1]

Critics of *Robinson Crusoe* have long been divided over the religious and economic dimensions of Defoe's novel. Ian Watt, following Karl Marx, argued that Crusoe exemplifies economic individualism and represents a capitalist hero whose narrative is organized by profit, exploitation, and accumulation. For Watt, Crusoe's story celebrates capitalist and imperialist agendas: "discover an island that is desert only because it is barren of owners or competitors, and there build your personal Empire with the help of a Man Friday who needs no wages and makes it much easier to support the white man's burden" (87). Other critics, including Maximilian Novak and J. Paul Hunter, have challenged Watt's emphasis on capitalist economics by fore-grounding instead the novel's Puritan elements, insisting that it is best understood as a spiritual autobiography in the tradition of Bunyan's *Pilgrim's Progress*, organized by providences and the experience of conversion.[2] More recently, critics have focused on the ways in which Crusoe's story plays out a colonialist fantasy in its attitudes toward race and culture as well as in its religious and economic assumptions (see Hulme, Dharwadker, and Weaver-Hightower).

The Female American, however, is difficult to read as either a capitalist lesson plan or a spiritual autobiography, largely because its narrative is less concerned with accumulation—of either wealth or piety—than it is with the fantasy of female power exercised within and by means of a Christian colonialist utopia. After becoming shipwrecked on the island, Crusoe begins to stockpile economic wealth and spiritual status, eventually returning to England both rich and converted. As an only child and the niece of a minister who has guided her early religious instruction, Winkfield is already wealthy and pious when she lands on the island. In both cases, of course, the New World is robbed of its

---

1 Ockley's translation of Ibn Tufayl's narrative includes appendices that argue against the existence of any modern-day prophets. This context suggests that *The Female American* may have been responding to such a position. See Appendix B3, p. 187.

2 See also White for an anti-economic reading of *Robinson Crusoe*. Hulme provides an insightful summary of the economic and religious strands of criticism of Defoe's novel (177-79).

resources: most of the riches that she inherits from her Indian mother have already been removed from America to England by her father, and these are further supplemented by the additional treasure she discovers in the tombs beneath the island's temple. This treasure certainly enriches those Winkfields back in England to whom she sends it, but it does not enrich Winkfield herself. While these choices distinguish Winkfield from Crusoe, they significantly align her with his Arabic predecessor, Hayy Ibn Yaqzan—and many of the subsequent figures modeled on him—who finally returns to human civilization after living alone on an island for decades, only to choose to return to his island isolation after discovering how hopeless his efforts are to bring spiritual awakening to a fundamentally materialist society.

Like Crusoe, Winkfield vacillates between doubt and conviction and gains respect and influence through her religious instruction to the Indians. But instead of undergoing a fundamental spiritual change herself, Winkfield undergoes a change in power gained by proselytizing the spirit to others. In order to retain that power, she must forsake England and remain on the island, because it is only on the island and among the Indians that her power as a female apostle remains viable. Whereas Robinson Crusoe sustains, throughout his 28 years on the island, an insistent desire to escape, Winkfield quickly loses any desires she first entertained of leaving her newfound utopia. The sense of confinement and isolation she endures becomes in time the very means by which she escapes European limitations on cross-racial exchange and female liberty. For such reasons, it is not surprising that she is not interested in leaving the island even when a rescue party arrives for her. Like those European women who elected to remain with the Indians who had taken them captive rather than return to their home culture, Winkfield locates cultural possibilities among the Indians that would be unavailable to her in England.[1] *The Female American* gives an early novelistic account therefore not of an economic man who practices venture capitalism and

---

1   The two best-known accounts of women adopted into and remaining among Indian tribes are those of Eunice Williams, who was taken captive in 1704 (see Demos) and Mary Jemison, whose story was published in 1824 (see Seaver). See also studies of female cross-cultural captivity by Burnham and Castiglia.

political colonialism in order to make of a New World island a small England but of an apostolic woman who practices missionary zeal and religious colonialism to make of a New World island a cross-racial Christian utopia that remains deliberately isolated from Europe. Indeed, the binary opposition between European and Other that underpins *Robinson Crusoe* can hardly be so easily maintained in a book whose protagonist's hybrid identity upsets that very opposition.

The novel's representations of colonialism and slavery are, however, ambivalent at best. At times, both English and Indian characters condemn those practices. Winkfield's clergyman uncle warns his brother William, her father, that "We have no right to invade the country of another" (p. 47), and when William is later taken captive by the inhabitants of the country he has invaded, the Indian king asks, "we know you not, and have never offended you; why then have you taken possession of our lands, ate our fruits, and made our countrymen prisoners? Had you no lands of your own?" (p. 48). Unlike Crusoe, who gains a kind of monarchic power on his island precisely by enslaving the indigenous peoples there, Winkfield pointedly rejects the Indians' offer to become their queen and even speaks out against slavery (although she of course boards the ship with Indian slaves of her own) when she compares her abandoned condition on the island to "those consigned to slavery for life! forced to bear with accumulated evils" and "slaves to a tyrant, and the subjects of unrelenting cruelty!" (p. 78). But although it seems at such moments to critique *Robinson Crusoe*'s account of the enslavement, exploitation, and conquest of America's indigenous peoples, this text articulates its own forms of imperialist violence.

Even if the narrative pattern of *The Female American* subordinates personal accumulation and geopolitical expansion to personal divestment and geopolitical isolation, Winkfield still benefits both economically and spiritually from her island experience just as Crusoe does. And the Indians suffer the loss of both their native resources and their native religion as a result of her arrival. Rather than a mutually beneficial spiritual exchange between Europe and the Americas, the novel depicts the religious conquest of Indian society; Winkfield even goes so far as to order the sun idol destroyed to ensure that the Indians will never be tempted to worship it again. One might also argue that it is the heroine's religious imperialism, much more than the insistence on her virtue and believability, that serves as the novel's most effective alibi against potential criticisms of her vanity and self-indulgence.

The utopian feminist elements of *The Female American* are compromised not just by its Christian imperialism but by its conclusion with a traditional marriage plot that threatens to erase the fantasy of unrestricted female freedom in which the novel otherwise indulges. This conclusion also complicates the novel's formal qualities. In its last chapters, narrative agency slides from the heroine to her cousin and would-be rescuer John Winkfield Jr., who—despite continued resistance from and an explicit lack of interest on the part of the heroine—succeeds in becoming her husband. As this development takes place in the plot, the narrative voice begins to slip inconsistently and unexpectedly between speakers and between the singular and plural first person (from "I" to "we"), as if its author were no longer sure who is telling the heroine's story. At the same time, the narrative recounted in the final chapter is often being told at second, third, or even fourth remove; for instance, in explaining to her how he discovered her whereabouts, Winkfield's cousin tells a story he and his father were told by a merchant captain, who is in turn repeating the story told to him by a reformed pirate named Captain Shore, who had earlier encountered the captain of the ship that left her on the island. The resulting confusion between speakers, voices, and direct and indirect discourse is, as Blackwell notes (15), common enough in other female castaway fiction and in early novels and prose fiction generally. But more importantly to our understanding of this particular novel, these narrative confusions reflect the difficulties of representing female voice. Here as elsewhere in the text, the narrative voice of Unca Eliza Winkfield might be seen to speak, quite strategically, through the mouths of others—including the imagined words of her preacher uncle urging her to take on the project of conversion, and of course the mouth of the idol itself through which she speaks to the Indians. This practice of narrative ventriloquism dislocates the voice of the heroine from her body and makes it seem as if that voice—while clearly identified as hers—is nevertheless issuing from the lips of male figures who are invested with social and religious authority. This strategy enables the heroine to express sentiments and to engage in vocal performances that, if spoken more directly, might be far more open to censure. It may be that the anonymous author of *The Female American* is similarly speaking through Defoe and the novelistic apparatus of *Robinson Crusoe*. But the larger textual universe to which *The Female American* belongs also suggests that scholars have perhaps granted Defoe and his novel a kind of excessive authority and voice that has drowned out a literary tradition of castaway stories more far-reaching and diverse than many have recognized.

Problems of Authorship and Identity

The title page of *The Female American* indicates that its narrative chronicling the "Adventures of Unca Eliza Winkfield" was "Compiled by Herself," just as the title page of *Robinson Crusoe* and of countless eighteenth-century castaway stories claimed to be written by their eponymous heroes and heroines. While Unca Eliza Winkfield is clearly a pseudonym, the author who used that pseudonym remains unidentified, as is the case with many other such texts. Although a number of critics have made the assumption that the author was American, no evidence exists to substantiate that claim, and we do not know whether the author lived in England or in the American colonies. The publication history of the novel cannot resolve this question either. While its first printing in London might suggest an English author, it does not exclude an American one. The only reference within the text itself to its publication seems almost deliberately to muddle the question of its national origins, for the narrator notes that "if ever [her account] should be published *in any country*" (p. 113; emphasis added), it would surely inspire later imitations by male writers.[1]

If the author were in fact a colonial American, *The Female American* would undoubtedly be the first American novel, pre-

---

1   The preface to *The Life and Surprizing Adventures of Don Juliani de Trezz* similarly insists that both Ockley's *Improvement of Human Reason* and Defoe's *Robinson Crusoe* are thefts of this anonymous tale (see Appendix B4, p. 194–95). The repetition of this claim in *The Female American* suggests that its author was familiar with *Don Juliani* as well as with the Defoe and Ockley texts.

ceding by over two decades most other competitors for that title. Recent attempts to redefine the category of "American literature," however, suggest that it is unnecessary and fruitless to engage in such unsupportable speculations. If we follow William Spengemann (21-24) in defining American literature not by the identity of authors but by the contents, concerns, and language of the texts themselves, then certainly *The Female American* (1767) is an American novel, though not the first one (that claim would still go, as Spengemann argues, to Aphra Behn's 1688 *Oroonoko*, set in the West Indies).

The only two subsequent editions were both published in New England, the first circa 1800 in Newburyport, Massachusetts and the second in Vergennes, Vermont in 1814. This later publishing history may shed no further light on the author's identity, but it does shed a great deal of light on the cultural appeal of the novel, for it indicates that *The Female American* continued to find interested readers and even gained some popularity among a specifically post-colonial, early national *American* audience.[1] When the dismissive critic writing for *The Critical Review* in 1767 sarcastically suggested, therefore, that the novel would find a more appreciative audience in America, he was, in a sense, correct—although not in the way he intended.

These difficulties of establishing the author's national identity are just as insolvable, and perhaps even more frustrating, in relation to the question of gender. Here, too, critics have tended to suppose that *The Female American* was written by a woman. In her discussion of the large percentage of pseudonymous or anonymous female Robinsonades whose authors' real names have not been discovered, Blackwell says (17) that it is tempting to assume these texts were written by unknown women authors. But she goes on to note that such conclusions cannot be supported without evidence, particularly since there are female Robinsonades—such as Charles Dibdin's *Hannah Hewit; or, The Female Crusoe* (1792)—that were written by men.

But as disappointing or frustrating as this lack of information may be, it is critical to recognize that *The Female American* is important for reasons other than who its author may or may not have been. Whether female or male, American or British, the

---

1 Reilly suggests that a Quaker audience in New England may have been especially receptive to the novel (271).

author of *The Female American* articulated for readers on both sides of the Atlantic an often radical vision of race and gender through an account of a biracial heroine who is able to indulge in a kind of "rambling" mobility and "extraordinary" adventure precisely because she is, as the title declares, an American female. As we have seen, the freedom and power that she experiences is largely legitimized by the novel's religious imperialism and its use of strategic narrative devices. But this heroine's exploits are in the end enabled as well by her identity as a "female American." And *The Female American* is, finally, a book about the potentially extraordinary possibilities of being both female and American.

Further Sources and Contexts

Although information about the real author of *The Female American* has, thus far, been impossible to come by, the text created by that author reveals a great deal about the literary and historical sources he or she may have used to fashion the novel. While the appendices to this edition of *The Female American* make no effort to be exhaustive, they do include selections from among the most relevant of the sources and literary contexts for the novel. The heroine Unca Eliza Winkfield, for instance, is the fictional granddaughter of an actual historical figure. The early part of the novel, which recounts the history of the heroine's family and its relationship to America, declares that her grandfather was Edward Maria Winkfield. Edward Maria Wingfield (which was alternately spelled Winkfield) was the first president of the Virginia colony and the author of "A Discourse on Virginia," a tract that describes the first attempts to establish a settlement at Jamestown and that defends Wingfield from the discredit that had been cast on him by John Smith and others.

Although Wingfield's "Discourse" did not appear in print until 1845, various accounts of the establishment of the Virginia colony and of Wingfield's role in it were available much earlier in narratives by George Percy, John Smith, and others. Both Percy's "Discourse on Virginia" (Appendix A2, p. 167) and much of Smith's writings, for example, were included in Samuel Purchas's *Hakluytus Posthumous; or Purchas His Pilgrimes* (1625) a massive multi-volume compendium of travel narratives that followed the project begun by Richard Hakluyt in his *Principall Navigations* (1589). *Purchas His Pilgrimes* included not only works by Smith and Percy but also accounts, such as Thomas Harriot's *Brief and True Report* (Appendix A1, p. 163), that Smith borrowed from and reproduced in his *Generall History of Virginia* (Appendix A3, p. 169), a text that is best known for a brief anecdote about Pocahontas that has since become Smith's most famous and most mythologized exploit. *The Female American*'s author was certainly familiar with this episode, since the first few chapters of the novel offer an informed retelling and intriguing elaboration of the Pocahontas legend. William Winkfield, the heroine's father and the son of Edward Maria Winkfield,[1] is a figure who is modeled after both John Smith and John Rolfe. Like John Smith, William Winkfield is taken captive in Virginia by Indians, where he is saved from death by the intervention of the Indian princess, Unca Eliza's mother. Like John Rolfe, William Winkfield marries this Indian princess and has a child with her—thereby giving birth to the heroine of *The Female American*.

The narratives by Harriot, Percy, and Smith are also likely sources for the novel's characterization of the Indians who come to visit and worship on the island, since each of these earlier narratives describe the Indians' practice of sun worship. Just as often, however, the Indians of *The Female American* resemble ancient Egyptians or even the Aztecs rather more than they do the southern Algonquin people encountered by Percy and Smith or even the Indians of Surinam described in such Edenic terms by Aphra Behn in her fictional *Oroonoko* (Appendix A4, p. 175). The depictions of the Indians' ancient temple and idol of the sun, the embalmed remains of priests and the ashes of virgins, and the hermit's solitary monastic cell are probably influenced as well by accounts, whether classical or more contemporary, of ancient pagan and Coptic Egypt. Like the early American materials that inform this novel, such tales of ancient Egypt sometimes contained examples of powerful female figures, including goddesses, prophetesses, and women who took vows of absolute solitude and lived alone, like the anchorite hermits of Coptic Egypt, in the desert. The excerpts included in Appendix A suggest the complexities of English interactions with and perceptions of New World indigenous peoples, including dependence, misrecognition, violence, and idealization. Selected engravings by Theodore de Bry, based on the original watercolors of John White,

---

1 The real Edward Maria Wingfield had no children. See Jocelyn R. Wingfield.

from Harriot's 1590 edition, provide some visual evidence of these perceptions.

Even if the author of *The Female American* was not familiar with the writings of John Eliot, who was called the "Apostle to the Indians," he or she ascribed to the heroine Unca Eliza Winkfield Eliot's famous achievement of translating the Bible into the Indian language. Eliot and others also wrote a number of tracts, published for the Society for the Propagation of the Gospel in New England, that were largely made up of question and answer dialogues between English missionaries and the Indians. These dialogues, which provided evidence to English readers of the Indians' interest in and conversion to Christianity, look very much like the exchanges between Winkfield and the Indians whom she instructs. This missionary context must also include the work and writings of Samson Occom, the Mohegan convert and preacher who was on a well-publicized speaking tour of England precisely at the time that *The Female American* appeared in print.[1]

In 1674, the Quaker George Keith published a tract called *The Woman-Preacher of Samaria* whose argument on behalf of allowing women to preach is another likely source of the depiction of Unca Eliza Winkfield. Appendix B2 (p. 185) includes selections from this tract, which appeared in print the same year as Keith's translation of *Hayy Ibn Yaqzan*. It was likely, however, the 1686 translation—titled *The History of Hai Eb'n Yockdan, an Indian Prince, Or, the Self-Taught Philosopher* and attributed to a George Ashwell—that provided the source for the tale *The History of Josephus, the Indian Prince* (Appendix B1, p. 179), set like its predecessors in the Indian Ocean world. The latter appeared bound together with a text by Robert Greene in 1696 and made few changes beyond condensing the narrative and transforming the characters' names from Arabic to Latinate form, a critical change that both Occidentalized the text's more foreign elements and novelized its more philosophical elements. While Keith's 1674 translation emphasized the elements of Hayy's story that coincided with Quaker spirituality, these were directly challenged in the 1708 translation by Simon Ockley (Appendix B3, p. 187), whose edition included an extensive apparatus designed to persuade readers away from such a reading.

---

1 See Bannet (158-85) for an excellent analysis of *The Female American* in the context of Occom's writing and tour.

Despite their differences, these accounts all feature island narratives about autodidact castaways who survive and thrive as self-taught individuals despite their isolation from other humans. Only at the narrative's end is the solitary protagonist of these tales met by one or more humans, with whom he shares his newfound experience and knowledge. Later versions of this plot in *The Life and Pleasant Adventures of Don Juliani* (1720; Appendix B4, p. 194) and *The Life and Surprizing Adventures of Don Antonio de Trezzanio* (1761) foreground the marriage and family conflicts within the story. Further elaborations in *The History of Autonous* (1736; Appendix B5, p. 203) and Kirkby's *The Capacity and Extent of the Human Understanding: Exemplified in the Extraordinary Case of Automathes* (1745; Appendix B6, p. 208) add fascinating science fictional and romance elements to this plot, while also acknowledging debts to the philosophy of John Locke, whose 1690 *Essay Concerning Human Understanding* is deliberately echoed in the latter title.[1]

This plot of the isolated castaway also characterizes, of course, Daniel Defoe's 1719 *Robinson Crusoe*, the central text to which *The Female American* is usually compared and which has generally been supposed to be its central source. Appendix C (p. 215) includes relevant excerpts not only from *Robinson Crusoe* but also from earlier sources detailing the discovery by the English privateers William Dampier and Woodes Rogers of abandoned sailors found living alone on the island of Juan Fernandez in the Pacific. Excerpts from Defoe's sequel novel, *Serious Reflections During the Life and Surprising Adventures of Robinson Crusoe*, are also included, along with selections from Peter Longueville's 1727 *The Hermit*, one of the better known and more popular imitations of Defoe's novel. These so-called "Robinsonades" circulated alongside the varied versions of the Hayy Ibn Yaqzan story described above, suggesting that these two traditions should be read together as part of a longer and more global literary and cultural tradition.

But this already more complex genealogy for the Unca Eliza Winkfield story must expand even further to include the parallel literary tradition of eighteenth-century castaway stories that

---

1 Russell has argued that Ibn Tufayl's work was a source for Locke's philosophy. Reilly (271-73) points out that the naming of the character "Mr. Lock" in *The Female American* suggests the novel's awareness of and engagement with this tradition.

emphasize a community-oriented plot over that of an isolated castaway. These novels typically differ in form as well as content, for their stories of island castaways tend to include an interconnected series of overlapping narratives, usually involving a multiplication of shipwrecks, storms, and abandonments amid intersecting romance and adventure plots. Appendix D (p. 233) includes three of these, beginning with Ambrose Evans's narrative of James Dubourdieu, the titular figure whose wife, Martha Rattenberg, emerges as the text's narrator and central character. This novel was published the same year as *Robinson Crusoe*, suggesting that it is less an imitation of Defoe than a complementary or competing branch of castaway fiction (along with W.R. Chetwood's popular novel *The Voyages and Adventures of Captain Boyle*, which was printed together with *The Voyages, Shipwreck, and Miraculous Escape of Richard Castelman* in 1726). Penelope Aubin's novels *The Strange Adventures of the Count de Vinevil and His Family* (1721) and *The Life of Charlotta Du Pont, an English Lady* (1723) likewise belong to this tradition. Both of these feature female heroines, while the latter also includes a subplot involving interracial and interreligious marriage that seems a world away from the treatment of race and religion by Defoe. Some of these texts are set in the Indian Ocean and others in the Atlantic Ocean, while one 1760 serialized narrative, set in the sixteenth-century Pacific Ocean, recounts the island adventures of Spaniards whose voyage from Panama goes off course. Finally, Appendix E (p. 249) contains the two 1767 reviews of the novel discussed in the first section of this introduction.

It bears remembering that the European sixteenth- and seventeenth-century accounts of America and its Indians represented here underwent transformation by eighteenth-century reconceptions of the Indians as noble savages. Rousseau may be the writer best known for deploying the trope of the noble savage, but several texts printed in the year or two prior to the publication of *The Female American* are of particular interest because they fashioned models of American identity out of Indian figures, much as this novel does. Two such titles—William Smith's 1765 *Historical Account of the Expedition Against the Ohio Indians* and Robert Rogers's 1766 play *Ponteach, or the Savages of America*— are notable for their depiction of Indians as heroic exemplars of the specifically American-identified virtues of independence, patriotism, and love of freedom, despite the fact that both texts were far more popular in England than in America (see Slotkin and Sayre).

Shifting relations between England and its American colonies are also a means of accounting for this novel's representation of the colonization of the Americas. When *The Female American* was first published in 1767, the French and Indian wars in America were in their final phase and the Stamp Act had just been passed. England's colonial presence in America was, therefore, far more complicated and far more contested than it had been even when *Robinson Crusoe* first appeared some 50 years earlier. Likewise, interest within the Anglican Church and the Society for the Propagation of the Gospel in furthering American missionary efforts increased over the first half of the eighteenth century (see Cross), and that interest might be seen reflected in this novel.

The Female American ought additionally to be considered within the extraordinary transnational tradition of early eighteenth-century fiction produced about America and its social and cultural possibilities, a tradition that would include such other overlooked texts as the German and Dutch Robinsonades[1] and Alain-René Lesage's 1732 *Aventures du Chevalier de Beuchêne,* which incorporates an American Indian utopia and the character of a female missionary and which was translated into English and printed in London in 1745.[2] If studies of women in the novel have so often been dominated by discussions of the domestic, it is texts like these that demand our attention if we want to uncover and understand this fascinating counter-tradition of anti-domestic female adventure which unfolded across a global landscape of oceans and islands.

---

1 See Blackwell for at least a partial listing of these texts.
2 For a study of Lesage's and other contemporary French novels, see Marouby.

The Female American *in Literary Context: A Brief Chronology*

1160s   Ibn Tufayl's *Hayy Ibn Yaqzan* is written in Arabic. Often called a "philosophical romance," this tale chronicles the life and metaphysical journey of Hayy as he grows up in solitude on a desert island in the equinoctial Indian Ocean.

1349   *Hayy Ibn Yaqzan* is translated into Hebrew by Moses of Narbonne.

1492   *Hayy Ibn Yaqzan* is translated into Latin from the Hebrew by Pico della Mirandola.

1516   Thomas More's *Utopia* is published, describing the discovery of an idealistic island society.

1588   Thomas Harriot's *A Briefe and True Report of the New Found Land of Virginia* describes the landscape and peoples of early Virginia. The text was reprinted in 1590 with illustrations by Theodore de Bry.

1606   George Percy's "Discourse of Virginia" describes the hardships and encounters of early settlers under the leadership of Edward Maria Wingfield in Virginia. Percy's text was included in the widely circulated collection of travel writings, *Hakluytus Posthumous or Purchas His Pilgrimes* (1625).

1624   John Smith's *A Generall Historie of Virginia* contains the famous Pocahontas story as well as descriptions of Algonquian culture, politics, and religion.

1651   Baltasar Grácian's *El Criticón* published in Spanish. The book's character Adrenio grows up without hearing human conversation and may have been based upon the figure of Hayy.

1660s   The scientist Robert Boyle drafts a utopian story, "The Aspiring Naturalist," featuring a self-taught central character named Authades who lives on an island in the "southern ocean."

1663   The New England Puritan and missionary John Eliot translates the Bible into Algonguian.

1671   Edward Pococke's *Philosophus Autodidactus*, a transla-
        tion of *Hayy Ibn Yaqzan* into Latin from a manuscript he
        purchased in Aleppo, is published in London. An article
        on Ibn Tufayl appears in *Philosophical Transactions of the
        Royal Society*, indicating the relevance of the Hayy story
        to those interested in scientific methods.

1672   A Dutch translation from Pococke's Latin is published
        as *Het Leeven van Hai ebn Ookdhan* in Amsterdam.

1674   George Keith's *An Account of the Oriental Philosophy*
        translates Pococke's Latin version into English. Keith's
        Woman-Preacher of Samaria is published the same year.
        Both texts circulate among Quakers.

1678   The Quaker Robert Barclay praises Keith's translation
        and acknowledges the influence of Hayy's spirituality in
        his *Apology for the True Christian Divinity*.

1681   Paul Rycaut's English translation of Baltasar Grácian's
        El Criticón is published in London under the title *The
        Critick, one of the Best Wits of Spain*.

1686   Another English translation of Pococke's Latin version
        is printed in London by the Catholic George Ashwell,
        under the title *The History of Hai Eb'n Yockdan, An
        Indian Prince, Or, the Self-Taught Philosopher*.

1688   Aphra Behn's *Oroonoko* is the earliest English novel set in
        the Americas. Henry Neville's *Isle of Pines* also appears,
        telling the story of George Pine's shipwreck on a south
        Pacific island that becomes populated by the offspring
        of Pine and the four women with whom he is stranded.

1690   John Locke's *An Essay Concerning Human Understanding*
        may have been influenced, according to some scholars,
        by Tufayl's *Hayy Ibn Yaqzan*.

1696   *The History of Josephus the Indian Prince* appears to be
        the earliest English work to mimic the *Hayy Ibn Yaqzan*
        plot. The narrative was printed together with Robert
        Greene's *The Pleasant and Delightful History of Dorastus,
        Prince of Sicily, and Fawnia, only daughter and heir to Pan-
        dosto, King of Bohemia*.

1697   The privateer William Dampier publishes the account of
        his circumnavigation of the globe, *New Voyage Round the
        World*, which includes the story of a Moskito Indian who
        lived alone on Juan Fernandez Island in the Pacific after
        being abandoned there by an earlier vessel.

1701   A dialogue between Hayy and Mahmut, the protagonist of Giovanni Marana's *Letters Writ by a Turkish Spy* (Paris 1684; London 1700), appears in the periodical *Memoirs for the Curious; or an Account of What Occurs That's Rare, Secret, Extraordinary Through the World.*

1708   Simon Ockley publishes *The Improvement of Human Reason: Exhibited in the Life of Hai Ebn Yokdhan*, the first English translation directly from Arabic to English. Ockley's edition challenges Keith's Quaker interpretation of the text. Ockley's title indicates the influence of Locke. Hendrik Smeeks publishes, in Dutch, *Description of the Mighty Kingdom of Krinke Kesmes.* Set on an island in the Pacific, this narrative details the transformation of native sun-worshippers in the wake of a shipwreck that leaves a multireligious crew ashore.

1712   Woodes Rogers's *A Cruising Voyage Round the World* includes the first published account of Alexander Selkirk, the Scotsman discovered living alone on Juan Fernandez Island. Selkirk's story is assumed to be Defoe's inspiration for *Robinson Crusoe.*

1719   Daniel Defoe's *The Life & Surprizing Adventures of Robinson Crusoe* is published. *The Adventures, and Surprizing Deliverances, of James Dubourdieu, and His Wife* also appears, a castaway story narrated by Martha Rattenberg, the wife of Dubourdieu. The novel is attributed to Ambrose Evans, and was printed together with *The Adventures of Alexander Vendchurch.* Defoe's sequel, *The Farther Adventures of Robinson Crusoe*, also appears. Alexander Pope refers to Hayy the self-taught philosopher and Alexander Selkirk in a letter to Lord Bathurst.

1720   The anonymously-authored narrative *The Life and Surprizing Adventures of Don Juliani de Trezz* offers a retelling of the Hayy Ibn Yaqzan story. The text claims to be translated from the Portuguese, but no Portuguese equivalent has been found. Defoe's third sequel, *Serious Reflections During the Life and Surprising Adventures of Robinson Crusoe*, appears.

1721   Penelope Aubin publishes the novel *The Strange Adventures of the Count de Vinevil and His Family*, which includes the story of his daughter's shipwreck on a deserted island. Puritan New Englander Cotton Mather refers to

Hayy Ibn Yaqzan in the introduction to *The Christian Philosopher: A Collection of the Best Discoveries in Nature with Religious Improvements.*

1723   Penelope Aubin's novel *The Life of Charlotta Du Pont* appears to be the first castaway novel named for a female protagonist.

1726   *The Voyages and Adventures of Captain Robert Boyle* is published together with *The Voyage, Shipwreck, and Miraculous Preservation of Richard Castleman*, both attributed to W.R. Chetwood. Jonathan Swift publishes *Gulliver's Travels.* A German translation of *Hayy Ibn Yaqzan* by Georg Pritsius is published as *Der von sich selst gelehrte Weltweise.*

1727   Peter Longueville's *The Hermit*, one of the best-known imitators of *Robinson Crusoe*, is published.

1736   The anonymous London-published *History of Autonous* is a more elaborately plotted version of the Tufayl story that focuses on a castaway boy and his father.

1741   Alexander Pope publishes *Memoirs of the Extraordinary Life, Works, and Discoveries of Martinus Scriblerus*, a burlesque romance which might be read as a satire of the Hayy story.

1745   John Kirkby's *The Capacity and Extent of the Human Understanding: Exemplified in the Extraordinary Case of Automathes* is similar to *The History of Autonous* but adds and revises further plot elements. The title explicitly refers to John Locke's essay, and the name of the central figure may refer back to Boyle's manuscript story about Authades.

1754   In *Treatise on the Sensations*, French philosopher Condillac uses the example of a speechless statue to illustrate his ideas of radical sensationalism.

1756   The Puritan John Dove criticizes Robert Barclay's praise for *Hayy Ibn Yaqzan* in his *Plain Truth: Or Quakerism Unmasked.*

1760   "A Remarkable Voyage in the South Sea," a Pacific Ocean castaway story, is published over the course of four issues of *The Edinburgh Magazine.*

1761   The anonymous *Life and Surprizing Adventures of Don Antonio De Trezzanio* largely repeats *The Life and Surprizing Adventures of Don Juliani de Trezz.*

1762   Rousseau's novel *Emile* is published.

1765   Samson Occom writes the first draft of his "Autobiographical Sketch," which responds to allegations by the Boston Commissioners for the New England Missionary Company—apparently designed to sabotage his fundraising efforts—that he was a fake. Occom is believed to be a direct descendant of the Mohegan Indian sachem Uncas.

1767   *The Female American* tells the castaway story of Unca Eliza Winkfield, the genre's first biracial protagonist. The novel is published in London during Occom's English fundraising tour. The anonymous sermon, *A Cry from the Wilderness: or, A Converted Indian's Address to a Xn. Congregation,* parodies Occom's autobiography and appears to have been written in response to his tour.

1768   The second draft of Occom's "Autobiographical Sketch" reveals his mistreatment by white missionaries.

1772   Occom delivers "A Sermon, Preached at the Execution of Moses Paul, an Indian," in New Haven, Connecticut.

1786   Marguerite Daubenton publishes a French castaway narrative featuring a female protagonist, *Zelia Dans Le Désert.*

1789   *Zelia in the Desert* appears in an English translation. Both the French and English editions were printed in London.

1792   Charles Dibdin's *Hannah Hewit; Or, the Female Crusoe,* is one of the best-known female castaway stories.

1800   The anonymous *Life and Wonderful Adventures of Henry Lanson* is published in London, a version of *The Female American* story with a male protagonist who returns to England at the story's conclusion.

1802   *The Life, Voyages, and Surprising Adventures of Mary Jane Meadows* by Isaac Cruikshank is another well-known female castaway novel.

A Note on the Text

There are three very nearly identical editions of *The Female American*. The first was printed in London in 1767, a second in Newburyport, Massachusetts c. 1800, and a third (clearly based on the Newburyport edition) in Vergennes, Vermont in 1814. In preparing this edition, which follows the original London edition, we have relied on a copy of the London text held at the Beinecke Library at Yale University, as well as on photocopy facsimiles of that edition. Comparisons between the London and the later American editions reveal only very minor differences between the three. The two American editions were published under the slightly different title of *The Female American; or the Extraordinary Adventures of Unca Eliza Winkfield*, and both use continuous chapter numbering in place of the London edition's separately paginated two volumes. These two editions also include occasional and minor modifications in spelling, punctuation, and paragraphing. When these changes are significant enough to alter or to clarify the reading or meaning of the text, we have indicated them in footnotes. We have silently corrected very obvious printer's errors but have neither modernized nor regularized spellings, choosing to retain these elements of the original text. We have omitted the title page of volume 2, an announcement by the printers on a rise in rates for circulating libraries that appears at the end of volume 1, and a list advertising other titles available from the printers of this book that appears at the end of volume 2.

The inconsistent and confusing use of indirect discourse in *The Female American* deserves a more extended editorial explanation. All three editions of the novel frequently omit one or more of the sets of quotation marks that would typically distinguish direct from indirect discourse. As described above (p. 24), these omissions become most complicated in the later chapters of the novel. Despite its confusion to readers, we have chosen, for reasons that are explained more fully in the discussion of narrative voice above (pp. 24-25), to preserve this style of the original and to supply clarifying footnotes.

While neither the footnotes nor the appendices are intended to be exhaustive, both are meant to enable readers to consider the novel in a variety of historical, cultural, and literary contexts and to investigate further its relationship to some of the texts, events, and debates with which it was engaged. It is our hope that the number of these sources and our understanding of their role in the production and transmission of this novel will continue to grow as *The Female American* becomes a more widely read and studied text.

THE

Female American;

O R, T H E

ADVENTURES

O F

UNCA ELIZA WINKFIELD.

COMPILED BY HERSELF.

IN TWO VOLUMES.

VOL. I.

LONDON:

Printed for FRANCIS NOBLE, at his Circulating
Library, oppofite *Gray's-Inn Gate, Holbourn;*

A N D

JOHN NOBLE, at his Circulating Library, in
St. Martin's-Court, near *Leicefter-Square.*
MDCCLXVII.

Title page of 1767 London edition. Courtesy of the Beinecke Library,
Yale University.

ADVERTISEMENT.

THE following extraordinary History will prove either acceptable or not to the reader; in either case, it ought to be a matter of indifference to him from what quarter, or by what means, he receives it.

But if curiosity demands a satisfaction of this kind, all that he can receive is only this, that I found it among the papers of my late father.[1]

Upon a perusal of it, I found it both pleasing and instructive, not unworthy of the most sensible reader; highly fit to be perused by the youth of both sexes, as a rational, moral entertainment; and, as such, I doubt not, but that it will descend to late posterity, when, most of its contemporaries, founded only in fiction, will have been long forgotten.

THE EDITOR.[2]

---

1 In both the Newburyport and Vergennes editions of the novel, this sentence reads: "But if curiosity demands a satisfaction of this kind, all that he can receive is only this, that I found it among the papers of a deceased friend."

2 In the Vergennes edition, this advertisement is signed not "THE EDITOR" but "THE AUTHOR."

CHAP. I.

Motives for writing this history; discovery of Virginia; the author's grandfather settles there; he is killed by the natives; his son is taken prisoner, but is saved by one of the king's daughters.

THE following history of my life I never completely related but to one person; and at that time had no intention of committing it to writing: but finding the remembrance of it burdensome to my memory, I thought I might, in some degree, exonerate myself, by digesting the most material events in the form of an history; for which purpose I collected together such loose memorandums as I had occasionally made, which have enabled me to render the following relation more regular and complete than otherwise it could have been, had I been obliged to trust only to the power of recollection: how, and why, I afterwards came otherwise to dispose of it will appear in due time. The lives of women being commonly domestick, the occurrences of them are generally pretty nearly of the same kind; whilst those of men, frequently more vagrant, subject them often to experience greater vicissitudes, many times wonderful and strange. Though a woman, it has been my lot to have experienced much of the latter; for so wonderful, strange, and uncommon have been the events of my life, that true history, perhaps, never recorded any that were more so. However, I shall not endeavour to extort the reader's credence of them, if such my work should ever have any, by solemn professions of veracity; for, perhaps, they may never be read; but if they should, I think the greatest sceptic[1] will allow, uncommon as they are, that they do not exceed the bounds of probability. Here are two ends they cannot fail of answering, rational entertainment, and mental improvement. To proceed then:

The peaceful reign of king James I. of England[2] gave opportunity to the first attempt of the English to make a settlement in the Indies, at a place called, originally, Wingandacoa,[3] part of

Won't beg you to believe her. Doesn't care if believed by reader

Jamestown

---

1 Skeptic.

2 King James succeeded Queen Elizabeth in 1603 and reigned until 1625. The colony of Jamestown was established in 1607.

3 A number of early English explorers to Virginia, including John Smith, report that Wingandacoa is the native name for the country that the English renamed Virginia.

the continent adjoining to Florida, called afterwards Virginia, in honour of our maiden queen Elizabeth, of blessed memory. As this place was first discovered by the great Sir Walter Raleigh, he obtained letters patent to settle a plantation there, *Anno Dom.* 1584. But it was some years after that time before any colony was sent there. The first plantation that proved successful, was began in 1607: at this time a colony arrived there of about an hundred persons, among the conductors of whom was Mr. Edward Maria Winkfield,[1] my grand-father; but as many of these died,[2] a further supply was sent the year after, under the care of captain Nilson; and again more in 1610, 1611, 1612.

In 1618, the settlement was thought of consequence enough to receive a governor from England. A very large colony arrived there two years after; and now the new-comers formed themselves into corporations. The first, and principal town, was honoured with the name of king James. But the happy prospect, with which the new-comers flattered themselves, was unhappily obscured by the native Indians, who came unexpectedly upon them, and massacred three hundred of them;[3] but this loss was soon repaired by a fresh recruit from England.—Thus much for the first peopling my native country.

The plantation which my grandfather first began, and which was the largest and most successful, devolved in a flourishing state to my father, Mr. William Winkfield, of whom I must relate a very extraordinary adventure, as it gave occasion to his growing more suddenly rich than he could have done by an infant plantation, and gave birth to me; and in the consequences of it effected a more happy issue to my future adventures than could otherwise have happened.

---

1 Edward Maria Wingfield was the first president of the Virginia colony. Amid disputes caused in large part by a severe shortage of food, Wingfield was deposed and was succeeded, briefly, by John Ratcliffe and later by John Smith. Wingfield recounts these events and defends himself in his "Discourse on Virginia." Winkfield is a variant spelling of Wingfield.

2 Percy describes these deaths in "Percy's Discourse of Virginia" (see Appendix A2, p. 168).

3 The 1622 massacre of the English colonists at Jamestown was led by Opechancanough, an uncle of Pocahontas. Accounts of the massacre are in Edward Waterhouse's *Declaration of the State of the Colony in Virginia* and John Smith's *Generall History* (see Appendix A3, p. 175).

At the time of the massacre, mentioned above, my grandfather was killed, and my father, with a few more, was taken prisoners[1] by the Indians; and as it was a very dark night, was hurried along many miles before he could perfectly discover any objects: at length the rising sun discovered to his view, at some distance, a large river with a great number of boats on it; into one of these he was forced, and then bound hand and foot. In a little time all the boats were in motion, and for some hours continued to go with great rapidity. My father had now but too much time to reflect on his unpromising situation, and recalling to his mind the words of his elder brother, whom he had left in England, he thought them unhappily predictive.

He was a clergyman, and one of true piety and sound erudition. When his brother, my father, was about to quit England, with their father, to settle in this new discovered country, "My dear brother Bill," said he, "I know too well my duty to my father to remonstrate against any action of his, though in secret I may dread the consequence; but as I am your brother, and your elder, I may presume to give my opinion; may it not be prophetic! We have no right to invade the country of another, and I fear invaders will always meet a curse; but as your youth disenables you from viewing this expedition in that equitable light that it ought to be looked on, may your sufferings be proportionably light! for our God is just, and will weigh our actions in a just scale."

My father at this time was about twenty years old, of a remarkable fair complexion for a man, with brown hair, black eyes, and was well shaped. I should not give a description of his person, but that to it he owed, as it seems, his future preservation. The Indians continued their voyage about four or five hours, when they stopped on the same side of the shore on which they had embarked. As soon as they were landed, my father, with five other English captives, tied one to another, were drove, like sheep, many miles up the country, and then lodged in a cabin till next day; however, in the interim, they were plentifully supplied with dried Indian corn, dried goats flesh, and a kind of small wine, but thick, though well flavoured. They had heard that some of the Indians were men-eaters, and thought these were such, or that they would not have fed them so plentifully

---

1 The word "prisoners" does not appear in the Newburyport and Vergennes editions.

but to render them, as we do hogs, the better food: however, in this they were mistaken.

The next day, soon after sun-rising, my father and his five unhappy companions were brought out of their cabin; their cloaths[1] were taken off, and they placed in a circle formed by a great number of Indians of both sexes, all naked, except a small covering of foliage about their middle, which decently covered the distinction of sexes. This local covering of several of the females was composed of beautiful flowers. The unhappy captives stood amidst this assembly a considerable time, whilst a venerable old man seemed to address them in a pathetic manner, for tears accompanied his words. He was, as my father afterwards learned, their king, and of a very numerous people; and the purport of his long speech was this:

"Men, for I see you have legs, arms, and heads as we have, look to the sun," here he pointed up to that luminary, "he is our god, is he yours? He made us, he warms us, he lights us, he makes our corn and grass to grow, we love and praise him; did he make you?—did he send you to punish us? if he did, we will die, here are our bows and arrows, kill us." Saying this, they all threw their bows and arrows within the circle, between themselves and the captives. Not then knowing their meaning, they stood silent; the king then continued his speech, "Our god is not angry; the evil being who made you has sent you into our land to kill us; we know you not, and have never offended you; why then have you taken possession of our lands, ate our fruits, and made our countrymen prisoners? Had you no lands of your own?[2] Why did you not ask? we would have given you some. Speak." It seems they had no idea that there are more languages than one; therefore taking their silence for a confession of guilt, their king proceeded, "You designed to kill us, but we hurt no man who has not first offended us; our god has given you into our hands, and you must die."[3]

This said, the Indians took up their bows and arrows, whilst

---

1 Clothes.

2 A similar question is raised by the Natives in *The Adventures and Surprizing Deliverances, of James Dubourdieu, and His Wife* (see Appendix D1, p. 237).

3 For reports on the Indians' supposed sun worship, see Appendices A1, p. 164 and A2, p. 168. Defoe also remarks on the Persians' practice of sun worship in *Serious Reflections* (132-34).

others bound my father and his five unhappy countrymen, and cut off the heads of the latter, one after another. My father expected the same fate; but just as the executioner was about to give the stroke, a maiden, who stood by the king, and whose neck, breast, and arms, were curiously adorned with jewels, diamonds, and solid pieces of gold and silver, and who was one of the king's daughters, stroked my father with a wand. This was the signal for deliverance; he was immediately unbound, and a covering, like that the Indians wore, was put round his body, and a kind of chain, formed of long grass, round his neck, of a considerable length, one end of which the princess took hold of, and gently led him along, till she came to a bower composed of the most pleasing greens, delightfully variegated with the most beautiful flowers; a shady defence from the sun, which then shone with uncommon heat. Beneath, was a large collection of leaves, which covered the whole surface of the ground to a great depth; here she made him sit, none present but themselves. She seated herself by him, viewed him with great attention from head to foot, felt his face and hands, but with the greatest modesty. She then arose, and going out returned presently with a cocoa nut shell, and drinking first, presented him the remainder of a liquor of most delicious taste, of the vinous kind; at the same time offering him a basket of various fruits. My father freely accepted of both, and found himself surprizingly refreshed. She then made a sign to him to lie down, and with looks of ineffable tenderness, retired; having first laid her bow and quiver filled with arrows by him, and fastened the door of the bower with a twig.[1]

This tender and extraordinary treatment had so far composed my father's mind, that, joined with the excessive heat of the day, and the wine together, he was so much overcome, that he insensibly fell asleep, amidst his reflections on this strange adventure. When he awoke, he found two Indian slaves fanning and defending him from the flies; which in that country are very hurtful. No sooner did they perceive he was awake, but one of his attendants withdrew, and presently returned, I cannot say with his fair, but with his black deliverer, who, smiling, gently pulled him by his chain, and led him, now willing and fearless,

---

1 Smith's account of his reception by the Queen of Appomatox and his deliverance from captivity by Pocahontas are in Appendix A3, p. 172.

to a neighbouring cabin, greatly distinguished from those about it, both by its largeness and elegance.

Here he again saw the king, before whom he bowed; whilst his patroness presented the end of the chain she held to her father, who with much seeming affability returned it to his daughter. By this act my father understood he gave him as a captive to his daughter, who, immediately breaking the chain from around his neck, threw it at his feet, making a motion to him that he should set his foot upon it, which he having done, she clapt her hands, and cried out, *Hala pana chi nu,* "great peace be to you."

Though my father did not then understand her words, he could not but conceive her actions as declarative of his liberty; for actions are a kind of universal language: he therefore threw himself at her feet, when she in return offered him her hand to rise, and then led him into another cabin, completely furnished after the Indian manner. Here he found the two Indian slaves who had attended him in the bower: these the princess presented to him, and whom by the homage they paid him, he understood he was to consider as his slaves. His cloaths which had been taken from him, together with those of his less happy companions, were brought to him.

The princess continued some hours with him, and they participated of a collation of fruits, whilst the princess continually talked to him, as if he had understood her language. This agreeable society continued several weeks, she visiting him every day, shewing him the neighbouring fountains, woods, and walks, and every thing that could amuse. At last my father began to understand her language, which redoubled all her past pleasures, when, according to the simplicity of the uncorrupted Indians, she declared that love for him, which he had long before understood by her actions.[1]

Though a complexion so different, as that of the princess from an European, cannot but at first disgust, yet by degrees my father grew insensible to the difference, and in other respects her person was not inferior to that of the greatest European beauty; but what was more, her understanding was uncommonly great, pleasantly lively, and wonderfully comprehensive, even of subjects unknown to her, till informed of them by my father, who

---

1 See Appendix A3, p. 173 for Smith's account of the love between John Rolfe and Pocahontas.

took extraordinary pains to instruct her; for now he loved in his turn: and sure he must have had a heart strangely insensible if such great kindness, joined with such perfections, had not had that effect.

They had now lived together six months, and understood each other tolerably, when Unca, for that was the princess's name, proposed their marriage. As she was a Pagan, though my father sincerely loved her, and wished for that union, he could not help shewing some uneasiness at the proposal. This the observant princess instantly saw. "What," cried she, "does not my Winka," so she called him, "love me?" My father caught her in his arms; "Yes, my dear Unca," cried he, "I do, but my God will be angry if I marry you, unless you will worship him as I do." This gave birth to a long conversation, in which, though my father was a very sensible man, and had enjoyed a good education, being very young, he found it not a little difficult to teach another what he yet firmly believed himself, but as we readily believe those whom we love, he was more successful than he expected, and in a little time the princess became convinced of her errors, and her good understanding helped to forward her conversion.[1]

Thus love and religion agreeably divided their time; and so happy was my father with his princess, that he almost forgot his former situation, and begun to look upon the country he was in as his own, nor indeed did he ever expect to see any other again; and he now loved Unca as much as she did him, and was therefore willing to make her and her country his for ever; but an unexpected event soon gave a different turn to their affairs.

the

Power
of love

---

1 For Pocahontas's instruction in Christianity, see Appendix A3, p. 174.

CHAP. II.

The king's eldest daughter conceives a passion for him, which produces
disagreeable consequences, from which he is delivered by.

MY father had never seen any other of the king's daughters since
the day of his deliverance from death, but his dear Unca, till one
day sitting in a wood to shelter himself from the excessive heat of
the sun, the king's eldest daughter approached him. As soon as
my father saw her, supposing she was one of the king's daughters,
he arose to salute her with the profoundest respect. "Winca," said
she, "I have long sought for such an opportunity as this; let us
therefore retire further into this wood, that we may converse with
more freedom." My father, unsuspecting the occasion of this visit,
obeyed, when the princess thus began: "Winca, it is our custom to
be silent, or to speak what we think; we are of opinion that nature
has given us the same right to declare our love as it has to your sex;
know, Winca, then, that I have seen you, and that the oftener I
have seen you the more I love you; I know my sister loves you, but
I am my father's eldest daughter, and as he has no son, whoever
married me will be king after his death."

My father was so much surprized at this unexpected declaration, that he was not able immediately to reply; but as soon as he
was a little recovered, he endeavoured to excuse himself as well
as he could, by pleading his love and prior engagement to her
sister; but it was in vain: all he could say tended but to provoke
her anger. At last, in a rage, not to be described, she cried, "If
you will not love me, you shall die; my sister shall never enjoy
an happiness that I aspire to; nor shall my vengeance be long
delayed; this instant shall put a period to your life." However
menacing these words were, my father was not greatly alarmed,
as they were uttered by an unarmed woman, and which he conceived to be only the effect of passion, and unluckily smiled.
"What!" cried she, "do you scorn my love, deride my power?
know wretch, Alluca can despise love and death at her will." Saying this, she clapt her hands together, and immediately six male
Indians appeared from behind the trees, where they had stood
at some distance unperceived by him. "Seize that white infidel,"
cried she; and in an instant all power of defence or flight was
equally taken from him. She then took a pomegranate-shell out
of a kind of pocket that she wore by her side, and going up to a

poisonous herb, squeezed the juice of it into it; then advancing to my father, "Here," said she, "be mine, or drink this; I offer you love and death; make your choice." "I can love none but Unca," replied he.

She then ordered four of the slaves to hold my father whilst the two others were about to force the poisonous draught into his mouth. "Hold," cried my father, "if I must die, I will drink it myself, I cannot do too much for Unca; she gave me life, and for her sake I will lose it—I drink Unca's health; her love shall make it sweet." He drank it, and I suppose the ministers of his intended death soon left him; for not long after he awoke, as it were from sleep, and found himself in the arms of his dear Unca, when in a languid tone he uttered, "What! do I meet my dear Unca so soon in another world? this was worth dying for." He then sunk again, as into a sleep.

It seems the princess Unca, having missed my father, arrived just after her sister and the slaves had retired, and saw him sink upon the ground. As she was no stranger to her sister's love for my father, her quick apprehension soon suggested what had happened; and as the Indians are remarkable for their knowledge of poisons, and no less so for their skill in antidotes, she instantly sought, and as quickly found, an herb whose salutary efficacy she was well acquainted with. She immediately squeezed the juice of it into his mouth, which soon reached his stomach, and made him eject the poison; but still his eyes were closed; a second dose revived him, and opening his eyes he uttered those words to the princess, just now related. "Heaven be praised," said the princess, "my dear Winka, that I came time enough to save a life dearer to me than my own; suck more of this juice, and you will be entirely recovered." He did so, and was soon able to get up and walk; but with a slow tottering pace, like a man whose brain has been hurt by the fumes of wine. The princess perceived his condition, and as they passed along gathered some flowers, the smell of which quickly dispelled the fumes, and fortified his brain so powerfully, that he was soon perfectly recovered, and his strength and understanding both entirely restored. Having returned the princess ten thousand thanks for thus giving him life a second time, they walked slowly homewards.

During their short walk, my father related to the princess Unca all that had passed between him and the princess Alluca, her sister. When he had finished his relation, the princess replied, "I will take effectual care for your security to-night, where my sister will not be able to discover you, and to-morrow I will consult my father what further measures we shall pursue." She then led him through some bye-paths of the wood, to the hut of an honest Indian, in whom she could confide; here she left him, with a caution not to stir out till her return next day.

Early the next morning the princess Unca, and her father, came to the hut where his daughter had concealed my father. Here a consultation was begun. The king said, "He could no more blame his eldest daughter than he did his younger, for loving my father; that Alluca had conceived an affection for him at the same time that Unca had, and at the instant that she touched him with her wand, Alluca was about to have done the same; that he highly condemned her intention to poison him; yet as she was tenderly beloved by him, as well as Unca, and his heir, he hoped my father would not desire him to inflict any punishment on her, since the loss of her lover would be a sufficient one." My father frankly declared that his regard for him, and his love for Unca, were sufficient motives to induce him to forgive her. The king then proposed that, to prevent all future danger, my father and the princess should be immediately married;[1] and that they should both set out instantly for the place of my father's abode, and that, on his account, he would enter into a treaty of friendship with his countrymen; and added, that he would give him a portion worthy of a princess.

As my father considered marriage as a civil, as well as a religious, ceremony, and found, by their discourse, that their matrimonial ceremonies had nothing in them contrary to his own religion, he very readily consented. An Indian priest was sent for, and the ceremony was soon performed. A proper cabin, or hut, was immediately prepared for the reception of the new-married couple, and they were securely guarded, to prevent further mischief, till such time as the necessary preparations were made for my father's return, with his bride, to his own plantation. In a few days, every thing was ready for their departure. They took an affectionate leave of the old king, and got into a canoe provided for them, attended by several others, in which were several

---

1 Marriages carried out against the wishes of a royal or noble patriarchal figure are common in castaway narratives in the autodidactic tradition (see Appendices B1, p. 180 and B4, p. 196).

Indian maidens to attend Unca, and men slaves for my father, and a considerable baggage, the contents of which my father was then unacquainted with. Taking the advantage of wind and tide, they in a few hours arrived, without any accident, within a small distance of my father's plantation, to which he was heartily welcomed by his neighbours, who never expected to see him again. They were greatly surprised at his extraordinary adventure, and very glad that it proved the means of a friendship between them and the Indians.

My father being again settled with his dear Unca, in his own habitation, they were now married, according to the rights of the church of England, by an English chaplain belonging to one of the men of war that then lay in the harbour. Now they began to examine the presents that the king had made them, and found them to be very valuable, consisting of a great quantity of gold dust and precious stones, and many curiosities peculiar to the Indians. However, my father thought it prudent to conceal the greater part of his riches from the knowledge of his neighbours, not knowing how strong a temptation a display of them might prove, as many of the colony were not only persons of desperate fortunes, but most of them such whose crimes had rendered them obnoxious in their native country.

As my father had persuaded his wife to conform to the European dress, he provided for her as well as he could, till he had an opportunity of procuring cloaths more suitable to her dignity. He took every opportunity that offered to send part of his riches over to England privately, to be there disposed of, and such goods in return to be sent as he wanted; for it seems he had no inclination to leave his habitation, and the thoughts of it were highly disgusting to the princess: but had his own desires been ever so much for a removal, he would have sacrificed them to those of the princess, whom he passionately loved.

My father built him a more elegant house, which was suitably furnished, and his plantation by far the best and largest of any about him. This was a work of time. In the interim, my mother, proving with child from the night of their marriage, was safely delivered of me. I was, a month after, baptized by the name of Unca Eliza. The king, my grand-father, frequently sent a messenger to inquire after his children, who always attended with some present of fruit, flowers, or something more valuable. Thus happily did my father and mother live together, till I was about six years old; during which time they never heard the least news about their sister Alluca: but at this period an Indian brought the news of the old king's death, and that Alluca, still single, was received as queen.

A little after, as my father and mother were sitting in the garden, and I playing at their feet, a slave informed them that two Indians were come from the princess Alluca. As soon as they came into the garden my father was surprised to see that they had each of them a great coat on, contrary to the Indian custom: he had scarce made this reflection before one of them, being come close up to him, pulled a short dagger out of his sleeve, and made a push at him, which most probably would have proved mortal, had not he, by a sudden motion, avoided it. At the same instant my mother gave a loud shriek, when my father, turning his eyes, saw her falling with a dagger in her breast, for the other assassin had been too successful in his murderous attempt. My father caught her in his arms, and received her dying blood and breath together. The slaves, that my mother's shrieks and my cries had brought to us, presently seized the two murderers. One of them, who dearly loved my mother, drew the dagger out of her breast, and plunged it into the heart of him who had assassinated my mother, and was going to have done the same by the other, when my father cried out, as loud as he was able, "Take him alive." He was instantly bound hand and foot, and carried to a place of security.

What is human felicity? How often our greatest pleasures procure us the greatest misery! This moment behold a happy couple mutually endearing themselves to each other, whilst the infant offspring of their loves beholds their joys, partakes of, and adds to them. The next—but let the scene sink into darkness! 'tis too affecting for a daughter's pen to draw.

interracial couples always end in death

CHAP. III.

Death of the Indian queen; Unca and her father embark for England;
provides for his brother; a description of the person and dress of
the female American; her father returns to Virginia; for which she
afterwards sails, where her father dies.

As soon as my mother was buried, and my father a little composed, he called for the surviving assassin, and from him learnt
that the princess Alluca had compelled him and his companion
to be the instruments of her revenge on them, for his having
slighted her love. My father consulted with the rest of the plant-
ers, whether they should deliver the assassin up to justice, or let
him go home. Considering the infant state of the colony, and the
temper of the reigning princess, they thought it prudent to avoid
every thing that might occasion a quarrel with the Indians, and
therefore agreed to give their prisoner his liberty. At his departure, my father charged the slave to tell his queen, that her God,
the sun, had seen the murder she had commanded, and would
revenge it.

It was not long after before my aunt the queen died of grief.
A little before her death, she ordered, that after her decease her
heart should be sent to my father with this message: "Receive a
heart that, whilst it lived, loved you, and had you received it, it
had never been wicked. Forgive my revenge, and let my heart be
buried with you when you are dead; but may the sun give you
many days!" This was accompanied with a very great present of
gold dust, and her bow and arrows, of exquisite workmanship,
for me. The bow, and some of the arrows, I still have.

This renewed my father's grief, which had indeed but little
subsided; therefore to divert his sorrows, and give me a better education, he determined to return to England. Every thing
was accordingly prepared. I was about seven years old when we
embarked, attended by several male and female slaves. We had
a tolerable passage to England, and found my father's brother in
good health. He was, as I before observed, a clergyman, and had
a living in Surry, where he constantly resided, had a wife, one son,
and three daughters, the youngest of them elder than me. He was
exceedingly glad to see his brother, and received me as if I had
been a child of his own. He was an excellent divine, of great piety,
and of uncommon learning, but ill provided for in the church. As

my father was very rich, he gave him five hundred pounds for each of his children, and soon after bought the next presentation to a living of three hundred a year.[1] The incumbent dying soon after, he presented my uncle to it, with a thousand pounds to pay the expence of removing, as he said when he gave it. This occasioned our removal to a pleasant village near Windsor.

If I was kindly entertained by my uncle, I was little less caressed by the neighbours. My tawny complexion, and the oddity of my dress, attracted every one's attention, for my mother used to dress me in a kind of mixed habit, neither perfectly in the Indian, nor yet in the European taste, either of fine white linen, or a rich silk. I never wore a cap; but my lank black hair was adorned with diamonds and flowers. In the winter I wore a kind of loose mantle or cloak, which I used occasionally to wear on one shoulder, or to cast it behind me in folds, tied in the middle with a ribband, which gave it a pleasing kind of romantic air. My arms were also adorned with strings of diamonds, and one of the same kind surrounded my waist. I frequently diverted myself with wearing the bow and arrow the queen my aunt left me, and was so dexterous a shooter, that, when very young, I could shoot a bird on the wing.[2]

My uncommon complexion, singular dress, and the grand manner in which I appeared, always attended by two female and two male slaves, could not fail of making me much taken notice of. I was accordingly invited by all the neighboring gentry, who treated me in a degree little inferior to that of a princess, as I was always called; and indeed I might have been a queen, if my father had pleased, for on the death of my aunt, the Indians made me a formal tender of the crown to me; but I declined it.

My uncle, who gave his daughters the same learned education with his son, desired I might make one of their society. This was very agreeable to my father, and no less so to me, who was very fond of my cousins, and willing to do what they did. I could already speak the Indian language as well as English, or rather with more fluency.

---

1 Presentation is used here in its ecclesiastical sense; in other words, William Winkfield served as a patron for his brother, whom he successfully nominated for a benefice, or ecclesiastical office.
2 See the illustration of Unca Eliza Winkfield which precedes the introduction to this edition; see also Appendices A1, p. 167 and A4, p. 177.

In this manner we lived near a year, happy I should say all of us, but my father, who, as he had no business to do, grew more melancholy: he therefore resolved to revisit the country where he had left the remains of his princess. It was in vain to intreat his stay, my uncle and aunt's remonstrances were lost, and only served to confirm his resolution of returning to his plantation. However, he thought proper to leave me with my uncle, to complete my education. Though I was unwilling to part with my father, I was as much so to leave my cousins, and therefore staid behind pretty contentedly. My father, before his departure, made great preparations for the improvement of his plantation, rather for his amusement, than from a desire of gain.

I continued here till I was eighteen years of age; during which time I made a great progress in the Greek and Latin languages, and other polite literature; whilst my good aunt took care of the female part of my education with equal success. Tawny as I was, with my lank black hair, I yet had my admirers, or such they pretended to be; though perhaps my fortune tempted them more than my person, at least I thought so, and accordingly diverted myself at their expence; for none touched my heart.

Young as I was, I often thought on my dear mother, and honoured her memory with many tears. And as I found it was the custom in England to erect monuments for persons who often were interred elsewhere, I desired my uncle to erect a superb mausoleum in his church-yard, sacred to the memory of my dear mother. It is a lofty building, supported by Indians as big as life, ornamented with coronets, and other regalia, suitable to her dignity. The form is triangular, and on one side is cut an inscription in the Indian language, containing a short account of her life and death. This I drew up and translated into Latin and English, which fills up the two other sides; on the top is an urn, on which an Indian leans, and looks on it in a mournful posture. The whole is surrounded with iron pallisadoes. This I often visited, and here I dropt many a tear.

My father, by this time, begun to think my absence long, and desired my return, which was equally agreeable to me; for though I was pleased with my situation, and the affectionate treatment of my relations, yet I secretly longed to see my native country, of which I retained a perfect idea, but more so to see my father. Every thing being prepared for my voyage, I, with my four slaves, embarked on board a ship for my return home, being then in my eighteenth year. However, my uncle insisted that his son John Winkfield, my cousin, should go with me to take care of me. His regard for me, and desire to see a strange country, made him very glad to accept of the proposal.[1]

During our voyage, my cousin neglected no opportunity to renew his address to me, which he had before begun in England. I gravely told him I would never marry any man who could not use a bow and arrow as well as I could;[2] but as he still continued his suit, I always laughed at him, and answered in the Indian language, of which he was entirely ignorant; and so by degrees wearied him into silence on that head.

I shall not trouble my readers with any particulars of our voyage, and shall only say, that after a tedious and indifferent one, I once more found myself in the embraces of a tender father. The sight of me revived in his memory the remembrance of my dear mother, which drew from him a flood of tears, with which I sincerely joined mine. As soon as these subsided, his transports of joy were as great to see me returned in safety, and so much improved. He received my cousin with great affection, and, on his return home, gave him a bill on England for one thousand pounds sterling; which he might well do, for he was extremely rich. I on my part desired some considerable presents to be sent to my uncle and aunt, and to my cousins, with some of less value to my female acquaintance; together with some natural curiosities of my own country, as birds, shells, &c.

There was one circumstance attending my education, whilst under my uncle's tuition, that, in justice to his memory, I ought not to omit, the religious part; and in this he was as methodical and exact as though I had been to be a divine; nor did he inculcate religion as a mere science; but in such a warm and affecting manner, that whilst his lectures convinced the understanding, they converted the heart, and made me love and know religion at the same time. The happy effects of his pious instructions I have experienced throughout my life; and indeed in one part of it they were not only of the greatest comfort to me, but of the highest use; as will appear hereafter.

---

1 Robinson Crusoe's departure from England is described in Appendix C3, p. 220.

2 See Behn's description of the renowned archery skills of the Native Americans (Appendix A4, p. 177).

But to return to my father: neither his riches, business, nor even my company, whom he most affectionately loved, could cure him of that melancholy under which he laboured from the decease of my mother. This, at length, determined him once more to visit England, that new objects might divert his mind. With this view he soon found means to remove his great wealth to England, and prepared to dispose of his plantation; but by the time he had almost done the former, and had agreed to let his plantation, he grew so bad as to be incapable of removal, and in a few days went to that happiness in another world, which he could not enjoy in this.

CHAP. IV.

Unca buys a sloop, and embarks for England; the captain proposes a match between her and his son; her slaves and attendants massacred, and herself left on an uninhabited island.

HAVING paid my father every funeral honour I could, and having nothing now to attach me to this country, and the bulk of my great fortune lying in England, I determined to embark for that kingdom, and to conclude my days in my uncle's family. But Solomon saith, "The heart of man deviseth his way, but the Lord directeth his going:" and so I found it.[1] I was now in my four and twentieth year. At this time an opportunity offered that favoured my intended voyage. There was a sloop in the harbour, a good sailing vessel, and large enough to carry me, my attendants, and effects. I chose an old captain, who had lately been ship-wrecked, and lost his all, and who wanted to get over to his son in England, to undertake the care of us, and as, a gratuity for his trouble, promised, if we arrived safe in England, to give him the ship, that he might once more be able to follow his occupation.

This proposal he accepted with great joy, and having got together a sufficient number of hands to navigate our vessel, I prepared to embark. Notwithstanding what my father had before sent to England, I had yet a great many valuable goods to take with me, to the amount of near ten thousand pounds. These being safely lodged on board, I followed myself, attended by my two favourite female slaves, who had sailed with me before, and six men slaves, who begged to attend me; though I had offered them their liberty, if they chose to stay behind.

We sailed with the first fair wind, and had not been on our voyage above a day before the captain, willing to lose no time, began to talk to me very freely about marriage. He did not indeed solicit me for himself, but he made strong courtship for his son. I at first answered him with good humour, and told him I hoped he would let me see his son before I determined to have him; and that if he could shoot with my bow and arrows, which then hung by me in the cabin, as well as I could, I would have him, were he ugly or handsome. But I soon found that he was too much in earnest, and I too much in his power: for in a peremp-

---

1 Proverbs 6:18.

tory manner he told me, that if I would not immediately sign a bond to marry his son, on our arrival in England, or forfeit thirty thousand pounds, I should neither see England, nor return to my plantation. I wondered he did not propose himself, but I found afterwards that he was a married man, as he informed me. I did not know law enough then, or else I might have given the bond, and so have avoided the distress that my refusal occasioned, as in equity I might have been released from the penalty; and the readier, as my two female slaves were witnesses to all he said. But as I persisted in my refusal, he grew incensed, and having I suppose gained the ship's crew by promises to assist him, at last told me he was come to a resolution, that as I persisted in my refusal, he was now very opportunely coming to an uninhabited island, where he would leave me to be a prey to wild beasts; and that as I had given him my ship, he would make bold to give himself the cargo. Two of my men slaves happened to come behind him just as he said these words, when one of them caught him in his arms, and the other opening the cabin-window, threw him into the sea. I know not whether I was sorry for this, at that instant; but I soon had occasion to be heartily so, for the consequence was fatal to them. As our ship, at this time made very little way, and the captain could swim, he presently got up to the ship, and being seen by some of the crew, who knew not how he got overboard, a rope was thrown out, and he quickly drawn up. In the mean time, one of the two men slaves went, and brought the other four into my cabin. Soon after the captain, and several of his men, armed with pistols and cutlasses, came into the cabin. The captain advancing up to him who threw him overboard, shot him dead, and now a terrible skirmish began. I indeed got no hurt, which was a wonder, for though no blow was aimed at me, the close[1] of the place exposed me to imminent danger; and the two female slaves got several wounds. My men slaves were unarmed, and therefore soon overcome, three were killed outright, and the others, I suppose, mortally wounded. The poor faithful fellow who opened the cabin-window was hung up alive at the yard-arm, bleeding as he was, there to perish by hunger, thirst, and heat. This touched me more than my own misfortune, I offered the captain a thousand pounds to release him, and to let him be cured of his wounds. "Madam," returned the villain, "where are

---

1 Closeness.

your thousand pounds? all you have on board is already in my possession."—Thus could I only pity, but not relieve.

I now expected my own destiny; and it soon arrived. The captain, who had left the cabin, to dispose of his prisoners, returned, and once more asked me if I would sign the bond? I answered, no; and at the same time desired that my two maids might have some care taken of their wounds. He replied, he had no surgeon, and if they did not grow well soon he should throw them overboard; but if they recovered, he should sell them the first opportunity: he then left the cabin. A few hours afterwards we came to an uninhabited island, where he put me on shore, for nothing that I said could soften his heart. I begged hard for both, or one, of my maids; but all the favour I could obtain, was my bow and quiver of arrows: indeed he gave me a box of clothes; but for these I did not thank him, as I never expected to use them, thinking myself consigned to some wild beast, whose prey I should become.[1]

---

1 Robinson Crusoe's shipwreck is described in Appendix C3, p. 221.

CHAP. V.

*She offers up praise to God; takes refuge in an hermitage, where
she finds a manuscript left by the deceased inhabitant, in which are
instructions how to subsist on the island; reflections on her situation.*

THUS disconsolate, and alone, I sat on the sea-shore. My grief was
too great for my spirits to bear; I sunk in a swoon on the ground:
how long I lay in this senseless state I know not, or whether I
might ever have recovered, had not a wave, brought on by the
rising tide, and which broke over me, awaked me. I arose, hardly
sensible where I was, or what I was doing, and ran to a rising
ground, and here I once again beheld my deplorable condition.
A few minutes recollection brought me to a sense of my duty: for
reflecting within my mind, that as the wicked captain could very
easily have killed, or drowned me, it was a wonder that he should
give me the least chance for life; that I ought therefore to thank
God for this escape, and to commit myself to his providence.
Indeed, in the hour of affliction we are ready enough to pray to
God for help; but are so taken up with a sense of our miseries,
that we forget that we have any mercy to be thankful for. We
should always sing a *Te Deum* before we sigh a litany; for our
sighs will sink before they reach heaven, unless raised thither by
the wind of praise.

Filled with these ideas I fell on my knees, and thanked God,
who had delivered me out of the hand of the wicked, and that now
I was in his only. On this occasion, these words of David came
into my mind; "Let me now fall into the hand of the Lord, for
his mercies are great, and let me not fall into the hands of man."[1]
At the close of my prayers, I solemnly committed myself into the
hands of God. I now arose from my knees with a serenity by no
means to have been expected. During this composure of mind,
I advanced to the highest ground I could see,[2] in hopes I might
discover some place of safety, not considering the improbability
of such a discovery. Though the sun shone very hot, which soon
dried my wet clothes, yet I saw it declining apace; I therefore
kept looking about with eager expectation, when at last I saw, or

---

1   2 Samuel 24:14 and 1 Chronicles 21:13.

2   For a discussion of Crusoe's and similar "monarch-of-all-I-survey"
    scenes, see Weaver-Hightower (2-3).

thought I did, the ruins of a building. I advanced and saw it more distinctly: though it promised what I wished for, an asylum, yet I dreaded to go nearer. I looked, I stopped, I prayed, and then I moved again; thus strangely divided between hope and fear, I still kept going forward, and in an inexpressible agitation got close up to it, almost insensibly.[1]

I was so near now as to perceive a door half open: I listened and heard no noise. Fearful to retire, or to enter, I stood trembling a long time. How long I might have remained in this condition I know not, had not a sudden noise behind me, like the hallooing of a human voice, forced me precipitately to rush in, fearless of the danger within, that I might avoid that which threatened me from without. This double sense of danger deprived me of my senses, and I sunk down in a swoon. As I recovered by degrees, I saw all within the apartment before I was quite sensible enough to be afraid of my situation, and seeing nothing to alarm, I grew quite calm, and observing a kind of great chair, formed of several large and less stones, and the seat covered with a great heap of leaves, I sat down, and rested my weary limbs and agitated spirits.

The sun still shone pretty bright through the holes in the wall, which was of stone, and perfectly discovered every thing within. My fright had deprived me of the thought to shut the door: however, nothing came to hurt or alarm me. Before me was an heap of stones, on which laid a greater, which served as a table, and near enough to lean on. In a large fish-shell that lay on the table I perceived water, which I boldly ventured to drink of, and found myself instantly refreshed. I lifted up my heart to heaven, with thanks, and bespoke its further protection. On my right hand I saw a kind of couch formed, like a table, of a heap of stones, and the flat part, or surface, covered with moss and leaves. I now concluded that this was the habitation of some human being: but this gave me no alarm; for as I had read of hermits, who frequently retire from public life to enjoy their devotions in private, I imagined, from what I saw, that this must be the habitation of such a one, from whom I did not doubt but I should meet with protection and spiritual consolation.[2]

This reflection restored me to such tranquility of mind, that I

---

1 Crusoe's arrival on the island is described in Appendix C3, p. 222.
2 Hermit figures populate castaway narratives; see, for example, Appendices B1, p. 182, B4, p. 202, and D2, p. 243.

rested myself with the pleasing expectation of his return, which, considering it was near night, I thought could not be long. As I now had fresh cause to be thankful, I was so; and found I had spirits enough to sing a short Latin hymn of praise. But still no hermit appeared, and the sun was now set; but the moon was risen, and shone with so much brightness into the cell, that I scarcely missed the greater luminary. As I thus sat waiting, I observed a book lying on the table, which I had not before perceived, which I supposed to be a book of devotion; but on opening it, found it to be a manuscript, in the first leaf of which were these words.

"If this book should ever fall into the hands of any person, it is to inform him that I lived on this uninhabited island forty years; but now, finding the symptoms of death upon me, I am going to retire to another stone room, where I shall lay me down, and, if God pleases, rest for ever from all my troubles."[1]

As this was dated, as to the month and year, tho' without day of the month, I concluded he must be dead, as it was a month ago, and therefore gave over all expectation of seeing the hermit, with the thought of whose presence I had pleased myself. A little lower, in the same page, was added, "If thou shouldest be obliged to stay here any time, there are no wild beasts or noxious animals to injure thee; nor savages, except once a year, on one day, see page of this book, 397.[2] How you may subsist, you may learn from the history of my life."

I immediately turned to the page referred to, and found that it was yet two months to the time of the Indians coming on this island. I now thought I might sleep securely; I therefore shut the door, and fastened it with a heavy stone that lay there, I supposed for that use. Coming back from the door I spied an heap of Indian roots, which I presently knew to be such, and which serve instead of bread. As some of them were yet very good, and had been roasted, being very hungry, I ate heartily, and drank more of the water. As I walked about the room I saw in a nook another shell, which I imagined to be filled with the juice of wild grapes, from the look and taste, and therefore, as I was faint, drank some of it,

---

1   See Longueville's *The Hermit*, Appendix C5, p. 231. Defoe also discusses hermits and solitude in *Serious Reflections* (5-7).

2   This reference to a specific page in the manuscript of the hermit is deleted in the Vergennes edition.

but with caution, as I found it was grown strong with standing. As the moon shone very bright, I took out my Greek Testament, which I always carried in my pocket, it being my custom to read a chapter in it morning and night. I opened accidently in the epistle to the Hebrews, and the first words that offered to my view were these: chap. xiii. Ουμήσε ανω ουδ ' ουμήσε ένκαταλίπω[1] I cannot but say they gave me great comfort, and I thought myself, in that moment, equal to all the difficulties I foresaw I had to encounter with, through the divine protection: though I very well remembered the caution my pious and judicious uncle gave me. "Beware," said he, "of the practice of some enthusiasts of our times, who make the word of God literally an oracle, by opening of it at particular times, and on particular occasions, presuming that where-ever they open, they are to apply the passage to themselves, or to the business they are about; because many have thereby been led into spiritual pride, and others into despair, as they opened on a promise, or a curse; whilst others have but too often, in the same manner, pleaded a warrant from scripture to perpetrate wickedness, or to propagate error.[2] Though," added he, "happy is the christian who by a prudent and rational use of the scriptures procures comfort to his soul. For as the apostle says, Whatsoever things were written aforetime, were written for our learning, that we through patience and comfort of the scriptures, might have hope." Rom. Ch. xv. v. 4.

Having read the whole chapter, and said my prayers, I prepared to take my rest on the stone couch, and laid down in my clothes, with more composure, notwithstanding my dreadful situation, than my wicked captain, I think, could do, though indeed, I believe, a man may sin to such a degree, as to render his conscience quite callous; the most dreadful state a human being can sink into. Sleep soon closed my eyes, and I did not awaken till the sun was up. My spirits cheered by such timely refreshment, and my devotions performed, I quitted my cell, and directed my

---

1 *And be content with such things as ye have: for he hath said, I will never leave thee, nor forsake thee.* This translation of Hebrews 13:5 appears in place of the Greek original in both American editions. The Greek passage printed here follows that of the 1767 edition.

2 Baine (9–10) explains that Defoe never condemned bibliomancy, the practice of "deliberately opening the Bible and relying upon God to direct the fingers and eyes to the appropriate page and verse," although it was generally criticized in his day.

There's a bit of a fortune teller quality to flipping open the Bible and seeing what words first meet your sight.

cf. he addresses this

feet towards the sea-shore, to see what was become of my chest that I had left there the preceding night; little expecting to see it again, because I thought the working of the tide must have washed it into the sea, or have buried it in the sands. After some search, I spied it almost buried indeed in the sands, but was not much better for the discovery, as I was unable to remove it. I therefore returned to my cell, ate some of the Indian roots, and drank a little water, whilst my mind was busied, how I should break open my chest, and so bring away at times what I could not at once. I had indeed a small knife in my pocket, but that was not strong enough to cut through a thick board. I looked round my cell, but found nothing that could assist me. This gave me some concern, for if I could not come at my clothes, I considered that I should soon be very uneasy to myself, and started at the thoughts of going naked; however, for the present, I was obliged to be contented.

But now other cares came into my mind. The roots I fed on were not all of them good, but only a few of them so; and how was I to get more? I did suppose they grew in the island; but I was not fond of rambling. Though the hermit's manuscript assured me there were no inhabitants nor animals to hurt me, yet the thought of wandering alone was terrifying. I might lose my way, and not be able to find my cell again, or not under a long time; and even should I find plants near my habitation, how was I to make a fire to roast them? Other anxious thoughts still pressed upon my mind one after another. At last, I recollected, that in the memorandum I had read the night before, I was informed, that the hermit's manuscript contained instructions how to subsist. This once more cheered my mind; and I now began to give it a careful reading, but not regularly; impatiently looking here and there for those things that most concerned me. It was written in a fair legible hand. I soon found that there was a flint and steel in the cell I was in; that at some distance there was a small river that ran quite through the island; that he made use of the shell of a certain fish for a lamp, in which he burned the fat of goats, and for a wick made use of a particular reed. I then searched to learn how he got goats to supply himself with fat, and, at last, met with this memorandum: "When I first came upon this island, I found plenty of goats, yet having no fire-arms, I was never the better for the discovery, as they were too wild to catch. But observing that they were very fond of a yellow fruit that grows on several of the trees here, and that they were continually watching when any of it fell off to eat it, this suggested a thought, that if I gathered some of it, I might possibly tame them by giving them plenty of it to eat. I accordingly broke down some of the branches, and whilst I held them in my hand, they would follow me up and down like a dog, so that I could catch them when I pleased. I found also that the goats, if I laid plenty of this fruit before them, would let me milk them whilst they fed. I from this time, no more wanted either milk or goats flesh. But as I knew this fruit would not be on the trees all the year, I gathered large quantities of it in the season, and saved them to serve in the other part of the year."

This information gave me great pleasure; I immediately searched and found the steel and flint, and near them dry leaves and touch-wood.[1] I now thought of setting fire to one end of my box, as thinking it better to burn part of my clothes than come at none of them: but however, I declined this method, in hopes of finding some better expedient; but was still very uneasy, lest the tide should remove it into the sea, or bury it out of sight in the sands; but I was obliged to run every risk. A few days afterwards what I wished for was effected by a means that I at first thought would have entirely deprived me of my chest. I was walking near the sea-side, looking at my chest, when I observed the sea to rise, and presently the winds blew very tempestuously. I retreated back enough to observe the storm in safety, which, at last, became very great, and soon saw my chest tossed about by the waves, as though it had been as light as a feather. I expected that every fresh wave would remove it for ever out of my sight; but it was removed further and further on shore, as the sea advanced, till, at last, I saw it no more. I then gave it up for lost, and returned home, for so I now called my cell, very uneasy.

However, the next day, the storm being over the night before, and the sun shining very bright, I again visited the shore, and the spot where the chest had lain, but in vain. But seeing at a distance higher up from the shore some rocks, my curiosity led me to go up to them, not with any expectation of finding my chest, for I had given over all thoughts of it; but climbing up one of them, I found my chest lodged there. I was glad to see it, though the same difficulty still remained, how to open it.

---

1 See Juliani's discovery and use of fire (Appendix B3, p. 200).

Being weary with climbing the rock, I sat myself down to rest. As I was sitting on that side of the rock that declined to the sea, I observed that on the other side of the rock was a very deep descent, at the bottom of which were craggy stones, but level with the rest of the island. I was startled at my nearness to it; however, this suggested something to my mind. If, thought I, I could push the chest down this precipice, the fall might break it; at least, it would be out of the reach of the sea. However, I was afraid to do so, lest I should tumble over with it. But after some consideration, I thought that if I laid myself down on the ground, on the side on which I got up, I might attempt it. I accordingly tried, and with great difficulty moved it, but not immediately; at last, after a great deal of labour, it fell over. The noise it made, when it came to the ground frightened me, though I knew what it was. My next business was to get down the way I came up, and then to find my way to the valley. I did so, but was obliged to go a great deal about. When I was come near to the spot, I found the ground so rugged, that it was with great difficulty, and not without several falls, that I reached the chest, which I found broke into a great many pieces, and it took me up near a whole day to remove the contents; gowns, linen, and many other useful things. All these I conveyed to my cell; not a little pleased that I had, at last, conquered this difficulty, and was now supplied with things that I should have greatly wanted.[1]

But to return to where I left off: having found the steel and flint, I immediately made a trial of them, and they were in very good order. I found three lamp-shells ready prepared; I lighted them, and they burnt very well. My next attempt was to get some goats milk, as I had yet tasted nothing but roasted roots and water; I took a large fish-shell, of which I found plenty ready to my hand. It was not long before I met with the tree with the yellow fruit, and several goats under it, who ran a little way off as I advanced, but not out of sight, but seemed to wait as if they watched me. I found it very difficult to climb the tree; but, at last, got up and broke several boughs off: and as soon as I was down, the goats came to me; I laid the boughs down, and clapt my foot on them, lest the goats should drag them away. I now tried to milk one of them, but very aukwardly [sic], having never done so

---

1   See Appendices C3, p. 222 and C5, p. 231 for other accounts of recovered chests from shipwrecks.

before. However, I got enough to drink then, and to bring home for another time. I repeated this practice till I became very ready at it; and not knowing how soon the fruit might fail, I took care to gather and save a good deal of it.

My next attempt was to kill a goat, as I found I grew weak for want of more substantial food than plants and milk. There was a knife fit for this purpose in my cell, and several others, and forks; but the thoughts of killing shocked me, and I was afraid to kill one whilst the others saw me, lest they should be afraid, and shun me for the future. Having therefore thrown down a good deal of the fruit, with a bough of it, I enticed one of them to follow me till out of the sight of the others; and then, but with great uneasiness to myself, killed it. But a more difficult task was still behind, to skin and cut it up; but as my time was not very precious, I had enough to bestow on it, and, at last, completed my job, though in a very bungling manner. I carried it home, and made a fire, having plenty of wood, and roasting some of it, I made a hearty grateful meal. What I could not eat whilst it was fresh, I salted; for I found plenty of salt on the rocks by the sea-side.

My next care was to provide a new stock of roots, as those I found in the cell were nearly consumed. It was not long before I found plenty; these I roasted on a fire, and laid them up. If I was now rich in provisions, I was quickly more so; for almost every day, looking into the hermit's manuscript book, I learned from thence that there was not only plenty of shell-fish on the shore, all of them wholesome, except the black flesh kind, but that every tide left great numbers of other fishes in the holes and shallows. I soon tasted some of each sort, and found them very delicious; particularly a shell-fish, like what are called oysters in England, and which needed no dressing; others were of the lobster and crab kind; the shells of the latter, being large, were very useful. Besides fish and flesh, I could also help myself to birds of various kinds, particularly some like larks, which I took according to the hermit's direction in this manner. From several of the trees issued a kind of glutinous matter, which I gathered and besmeared the little low brambles and bushes with it, and by that means catched a great many small birds, that used to eat the berries of them.

What a plentiful table was here, furnished only at the expense of a little trouble! This happiness I owed to the misfortunes of another; for had not the hermit made these discoveries, and left the means of my coming at the knowledge of them, how miserable must have been the state of a lonely woman! Doubtless I should soon have perished with hunger! How graciously does the goodness of providence often raise help to the distressed from the misfortunes of others! The hermit who made these discoveries, and by them was supported, had great reason to thank God, and I no less cause to be thankful to the same being who influenced his heart to leave behind him the history of his life, which proved the preservation of mine.

If this reflection gladdened my heart, it was succeeded by one that gave me no less pain: "At last," cried I, "he died!—died here!—what might he not feel for want of some kind friend to ease his sufferings in his last hours! Forty years without human society!—no opportunity offered to restore him to his native, or to any other country!—must this be my fate?" Tears gushed from mine eyes, and sorrow filled my heart. Thus weeping and lamenting I sat, and from time to time exclaimed, Wretched princess! what have I done to suffer thus from human treachery? But at length, a more comfortable view of my condition again presented itself to my mind, and I was consoled: for I again reflected on the great improbability that there was of my finding such a resource in my captivity, as the hermit's book, and how thankful I ought to be. I will take this, cried I, as an earnest of a future deliverance. At this instant, I experienced such an inward persuasion in my mind, that I should escape from this island, that every uneasy thought fled, and left my mind a calm, scarcely to be expressed. I therefore arose, and went cheerfully about my little concerns; but not without having first thanked that God who had given me this consolation.[1]

---

1 Compare to Crusoe's acting "without asking God's blessing" (Appendix C3, p. 221).

CHAP. VI.

*The thoughts of her distress occasion a severe fever; recovers; seeks
comfort in her own reflections.*

As I had now settled my manner of living, I was very easy on
that head, till this reflection destroyed all my peace: 'Tis true,
I am well provided for the present; whilst the summer and fine
weather continue, I can, with little difficulty, or rather amusement, supply myself with fish, flesh, and fowl; but winter no
doubt will come, and how severe that season may prove I cannot foretel. How shall I, during the inclemency of it, procure
the means of subsistence? There will be less plenty of birds; the
gum, which now spontaneously issues from the trees, will then
fail, the sands on the coast being more frequently and violently
agitated, will be unsafe, and my supplies from thence less, perhaps none; the goats will also yield little or no milk; and the rain
perhaps may continue for many days, nay weeks, and confine me
entirely to my cell.—Such were the anxious perplexing thoughts
that agitated my mind; and the fear of the future destroyed the
enjoyment of the present.—I sat dissolved in sighs and tears, and
indulged my melancholy, till the night drew on, when I laid me
down, but not to rest; and so greatly was my mind afflicted, that
it brought on a violent fever, attended with a delirium. I raved,
I cried, I laughed by turns. I soon became so weak, that I was
scarce able to crawl from my bed to get some water, of which I
happened to have plenty. As my thirst was great, I drank freely
of it; but as the fever continued three days, I was now reduced to
my last shell-full of water. I had at this time an interval of sense,
when I found I was too weak to go out of my cell to fetch more,
yet my thirst forced me to drink this; which I did supposing it
would be my last, and that death must be my next potion. I soon
emptied the shell, and as well as I was able, and with as much
resignation as I could, laid me down to die. It was not long before
I fell asleep for the first time since the fever came on me; how
long I slept I could not tell, but awoke in a great sweat, and found
my thirst as great as ever, and to such an intolerable degree, that
I determined, if possible, to attempt going to the river to drink,
though I died in the way; for death itself was more eligible than
the thirst I suffered. With much difficulty I raised myself up, and
got upon the ground; but was obliged to crawl upon my hands

and feet, and to rest very often by the way before I reached the river. Surely deliverance itself could not have given me greater pleasure than the sight of the water; I greedily thought there would be scarce enough to assuage my raging thirst. I laid myself flat on the edge, and whilst I drank, had the additional pleasure of cooling my hands and face.

At length, my thirst was happily allayed; but the river was not dried up. The coolness of the water was so agreeable to my hands and face, that I thought I would wash my feet, as they burnt with no less fierceness. To do this, I was obliged to seat myself on the bank. It was with much labour and difficulty I did so; but had scarce placed myself, when either the bank broke down, or I slipt, and into the water I fell, and plunged all over. Whether the water by its coolness braced my nerves, and gave me strength, or how I know not, but I soon reared my head above the surface, and crawled upon the shore; when my weakness again returned, and I fell all along, unable to stir, expecting to die every moment. At last, I fell into a deep sleep, I suppose for some hours, when I awoke in a violent sweat; I was still thirsty, but not so painfully as before, and even found myself refreshed. I was fearful to have recourse to the river, lest I should fall into it again, when observing a she-goat asleep, very near me, I made shift to creep softly to her, and sucked her dugs, which she happily permitted.[1] This was at first a comfortable relief, but I soon after grew very sick, and vomited violently. But I found that my fever was quite gone off, and that I was no longer thirsty. Reflecting on the great escape I had from drowning, and the favourable change in my health, whereas the mere circumstance of being immersed in the water, in the condition I was, might have proved instant death, I lifted up my heart unto God, and unfeignedly thanked him for his mercy.

I now attempted to get up and crawl to my cell; but found myself too weak to do either. All I could do was, to sit up sometimes a little. The sun, indeed, dried my clothes apace, but its heat was too violent to bear long; I was forced therefore to crawl a little

---

1 Goats or roes play a significant role in a number of castaway fictions, including the stories of Juliani (Appendix B3, p. 198), Josephus (Appendix B1, p. 180), and Robinson Crusoe (Appendix C3, p. 225). See also the role of goats on Juan Fernandez Island, Appendix C1, p. 216 and C2, p. 218.

way off under the shade of some trees that grew on the banks of the river; but this I was long performing, though not above two or three yards off. The shade of the trees protecting me from the sun's scorching beams, and the cool breezes which came upon me from the river refreshing me greatly, I once more fell asleep. When I awaked I was greatly but agreeably surprised to find how much better I was. My clothes were quite dry; and now I hoped I might be able to get to my cell; for I saw the sun was setting: though I was not thirsty, I could have been glad of some more milk, but there was no goat near me; for notwithstanding the milk had made me sick, yet I believe it contributed to my recovery, by clearing my stomach. I once more attempted to crawl home, for I could do no more, and glad was I to do so. At last, I reached my cell, much fatigued and very weak, and greatly in want of some refreshment. I soon recollected there was some of that wine left that I drank of the first day I came, and made shift to reach it, but having no water to mix with it, I drank but a very little of it, and that little was too strong for my stomach to stay in it. Still finding my stomach empty and uneasy, I, at last, remembered my root bread, I cut a slice of it, and soaked it in the wine; I ate sparingly of it, and found it agreed with me, and refreshed me greatly. The rest of it I laid by my couch, and bit a piece of it now and then, for I lay awake most part of the night, but free from both thirst and fever.

Towards morning I slept soundly, and when I awaked I was much surprised to find how my strength was recruited, or rather my weakness abated. I got up, and most heartily thanked God for my recovery, and with the help of two sticks made shift to walk, though slowly. I reached some of the yellow fruit with which I used to entice the goats, and laid it before the door, in hopes, that the goats would see it, for I could not walk in search of them; putting some stones upon the boughs, that they might not drag them away. At last a she-goat came, and I milked her, and drank a large shell of it, with a little bit of my root bread. This agreed extremely well with my stomach; I continued this practice for about a week, once a day, drinking a little wine with water; and thus once more happily recovered my health and my strength to such a degree, that I could now walk about and do my little business; and, in a week more, was as well and almost as strong as before. I now had been upon this place a month; for as I had an Almanack with me, I kept an exact account of time, that

I might be sure to conceal myself on the day the Indians were to arrive, as cautioned by the hermit's manuscript.

Being thus recovered, I could not but reflect that I owed my late sickness to my giving way to those anxious corroding cares that had arisen in my mind concerning my future subsistence; and I could not but condemn my folly, and mourn for the sinfulness of it, and of which, I hope, I heartily repented.

My dear uncle was a great recommender of meditation: "That man," said he, "hardly knows that he is a thinking being, who does not often meditate by himself. It is," said he, "a glorious privilege, and he who practices it will grow wiser and better by an hour's serious meditation than by a month's reading." "We should," continued he, "be often inculcating upon our minds the truths we know, and they will become fixed. We should often rebuke, advise, and console ourselves, and we shall become better men, more prudent, and more contented." I was so strongly convinced of the reasonableness and utility of this practice that I adopted it. And, according to his further advice, used to talk to myself aloud, as the occasion required, as I would to another; and that with all the force of argument, vehemence, and energy of expression I could, or as the nature of the subject required. Upon these occasions I have been frequently surprised to find how my understanding has been convinced, my affections moved, and my will determined. I have assented to a truth I never before believed, wept at the conviction of a fault, and have found a consolation in a time of trouble that I did not expect. On these occasions, it was always my custom to imagine to myself that my uncle was speaking to me; this I thought, as it were, inspired me, and gave an energy to my words, strength to my arguments, and commanded my attention. I have sometimes indulged this reverie to such a degree that I have really imagined, at last, that my uncle was speaking to me.

By reflecting on my late sickness and the occasion of it, I was led into one of these soliloquies; and thus in the imagined person of my uncle did I address myself.

"In vain, I find, are the precepts that I so often inculcated on your mind; they have not reached your heart, and, I fear, are erased from your memory. It was easy in the day of prosperity to hear instructions how to bear adversity, but in the hour of calamity they are forgotten. From the days of your infancy the smiles of providence almost constantly attended you. You were too young at your mother's death long to feel her loss; and that of your father's was the most poignant. Indeed, to be at once deprived of your great affluence, and secluded from human society, are afflictions not of a light weight. But still, could you find no consolation? The dread of approaching winter, in your situation, might alarm; but sure, at your first coming on this island, you had no less reason, surely more so, to be alarmed for your then immediate preservation. Yet what favourable circumstances have intervened! And such as, if properly improved, may prevent the calamities you dread. How preferable is your condition to that of those consigned to slavery for life! forced to bear with accumulated evils, utterly unknown to you! slaves to a tyrant, and the subjects of unrelenting cruelty! Ah, Eliza! would we but compare our sufferings with those of others, where would the wretch be found who would not have something wherewith to console himself?

"How many have voluntarily quitted the advantages of society, to avoid the temptations of it, in a worse retirement than yours?—Thus might I reason with a heathen, and I think, not without success. But is not Unca a christian, or would be such? Receive then the instructions of a higher school, and learn of a better master. Remember him who through sufferings was made perfect, and that the disciple is not to be above his master. Let then your whole life be one continual Ἀφορῶντες εἰς τὴν Ἰησοῦν.[1] The greater your calamities, the greater should be your trust and confidence in God. He who relies most on his providence, glorifies him most. We should never neglect the use of means whilst in our power: but when they fail, we must still look up to him, who needs them not; for when we have done our utmost, we must not despair, as though God's power was cut off with ours. No; at such a time we must commit ourselves and our wants to him, with a firm persuasion that he will help us. If we make him the object of our faith and prayers, we shall become the subjects of his mercy. Remember godliness hath the promise of this life, as well as of that which is to come. But always be mindful that we are to commit ourselves to him by a patient continuance

---

1 *Imitation of Jesus*. The American editions replace the Greek passage with this translation. The Greek passage printed here is consistent with that of the 1767 edition, except that the orthography has been updated.

in well-doing.—No imaginary flights of faith will warrant our confidence in him, nothing will do unless we prove ourselves to be his servants by keeping his commands; for true saving faith always produces good works. Believe and obey; be thankful to God for the mercies you enjoy, and trust in him for those you want. The citizen may be wretched and the solitary happy. Human felicity or misery is confined to no place or circumstance of life. The servant of God is safe wheresoever or howsoever he be. Humble thyself therefore, under the Almighty hand of God, and he shall exalt thee in due time. Let not your care for this present life make you neglect that of a future one. Should your body die here, your soul will not find the way to heaven the more difficult. Though the cloud of affliction now hangs over your head, the sun of mercy behind may dispel it, and once more show his glorious face. Believe, obey, and trust, and be saved, blessed, and delivered."

Thus did I endeavour to fortify my heart, and to learn patience and resignation to the dispensations of providence; nor were my attempts in vain; nor did I ever again suffer such anxious cares as those from which I was just now delivered. Submission or hope, one or both, were ever in a less or greater degree my solace.

CHAP. VII.

Again consults the hermit's manuscript; some account of his life; finds the hermitage to be the temple of the sun; discovers a great number of mummies, and on her return from exploring the temple, perceives the hermit at his devotions.

I HAD not yet read the hermit's manuscript regularly, but here and there, as I hoped to find some necessary and useful directions for my manner of subsistence. But having now pretty well attained this desirable end, I purposed to read it from the beginning regularly through, without omitting any part. But before I begun, for I found it would take up a great while, I once more hastily looked it over, to find when, and what kind of winter I had to expect. I found that it was now but the beginning of the summer, or rather spring, and that I had at least six months certain good weather before me, except some great storms of thunder and lightning. As I had so much time between me and winter, I did not stop now to learn how the hermit provided against that event; but, according to my first intention, assigned a few hours every day to the history of his life.

As I have this manuscript still in my possession, I shall do no more than give a very short view of its contents, though the whole of it would very well deserve to be made public. From this manuscript I learned, that the hermit as I called him, on account of his recluse life, might yet be more properly called so on account of his extraordinary piety. This history of his life is indeed wonderfully extraordinary, highly entertaining, and full of improvement. The first thirty years of his life were unhappily consumed in more than useless follies; in vices that had well nigh brought him to a shameful exit, but ended only in the loss of his liberty, which he very unexpectedly and no less wonderfully regained; if his living the last forty years of his life in this place may be called a state of liberty.

But his residence here proved the happy means of his conversion, of which with great modesty and ingenuousness, he gives an ample account. The manner of his living here was attended with a greater variety of events, than could have been expected from such a solitary situation. His occasional reflections are sensible and pious, useful and pertinent. This cell, as I called it, that I now inhabited, I found to be but one of many others; the ruins, as he rationally conjectured, of some very ancient palace, or rather temple, which he supposed anciently belonged to a very large statue, or image, at a considerable distance from the place of my habitation, and to which the ruins approached, and in part surrounded. This he imagined to have been an ancient idol sacred to the sun, which the Indians adored. For, says he, "Once a year, vast numbers of them come over from the continent in canoes, on the opposite side of the island, and having spent almost the whole day in a kind of devotion to this idol, they then go back again, and never revisit it till the annual return of the same day." The knowledge of which he having learned, he took such effectual care to conceal himself, that he never was discovered, as I afterwards was certainly satisfied. The latter part of his life was uniformly the same to the time that he wrote the memorandum already mentioned, which says, That he was retired from the cell he usually inhabited, to die in some other.

I had not patience to go through the whole history, till I had seen this extraordinary idol. For this purpose, I got up early the next morning, put some roots in my pocket, and a shell to drink out of, that I might have the whole day at my command. I could not, indeed, but have observed before, that there were many other stone rooms besides that which I inhabited; but had never as yet gone into any other excepting two; in one of which I laid up the branches of yellow fruit I gathered for the goats, and the other in which I kept my dried goat's flesh, and some dried fish. Upon searching, I found some uninhabitable, others in as good condition as that I dwelt in, some well lighted with holes on the sides, others dark. But being curious to see if I could discover why this distinction was made, not being far from my cell, I fetched one of my lighted lamps.

The first room I entered, I found surrounded with mummies, like those I have read of in the histories of Egypt, and one of which I once saw in England. At first I started; but instantly recollecting, that I had no cause to fear, I examined them with great attention. They were all placed upright, as close as they could be round the cell, without touching one another. Observing Indian characters upon each of them finely painted, besides various drawings of birds, beasts, insects, and other things, I examined them more nicely. As I understood the Indian languages perfectly, I soon learned that these had been priests of the sun. Each mummy had on it the name of the priest, his age, and the time of his death;

by which I found that most of them had been there at least one thousand years. Leaving this, I went into another, and another, till I had visited a dozen, all filled in the same manner, with the same order of men, all uninjured by time.[1] ⚡

Some other rooms, which were much more spacious, were filled with stone coffins, with just room to pass between, and against the walls they were placed, at a little distance between each, to the height of four coffins. These I supposed had not been embalmed, for as they were all uncovered, I could see no remains of their bodies but the ashes; but at the head of each, lay a kind of coronet. I took up several of them, and imagined they were made of gold, as I afterwards found they were. I suppose, from the make of them, they had been worn upon their heads.

I should have observed that when I was viewing the mummies, I found golden coronets placed upon each of their heads, but of a larger and different make, which showed that they had never been worn, but made on purpose, as I conjectured, for the use to which they were applied. I was very desirous to know who those had been whose ashes only remained, and at last, discovered an inscription on the headstone of each coffin, from which I learned that they had been virgins of the sun, consecrated to the service of the temple. Of these virgins I found in different rooms many hundreds, and several hundreds of the priests. As I continued my search, I found other rooms, but all at a little distance from one another, some not at all injured by time, others a little, and some a great deal. At last, I came to a group of, I believe, about five hundred, of a different form from the rest, and much less. Each of these contained only one mummy, which, upon inspection, I found were the mummies of the high-priests of the sun. These had also a crown of gold on their heads, and suspended on their breasts, a golden figure of the sun, rudely carved in gold. What a collection of mummies and of golden treasure! "But what is this?" cried I, "I had too much gold before to be happy." This reflection gave birth to a sigh; but I soon suppressed its progress; and as I found the day was too far gone to pursue my journey to the idol, I returned ruminating on what I had seen, towards my solitary cell; for such I must still call it, though I might truly say

---

1 European descriptions of Native American embalming and
    mortuary practices in colonial Virginia appear in Appendices A1,
    p. 166 and A3, p. 171.

to my apartment in the palace. I should have mentioned that in each of the dormitories, I found a lamp of gold suspended from the roof, one of these was still burning. This confirmed what I had read of the perpetual lamps of the ancients.[1]

I had indulged myself so long in my rambles among these dormitories, that it was dark before I reached my cell. But what was my astonishment when pushing the door open, I saw in my cell a light! This, at the same instant, discovered to my sight, a venerable old man, with a long beard, kneeling as at his prayers.[2] I concluded, that it must be the ghost of the old hermit. This was too much; and I sunk down in a swoon. My fall, I suppose, alarmed the hermit; for, when I came to myself, I found him sitting by me, supporting me in his arms, being too weak to lift me up. As soon as he saw me revive, "My daughter," said he, "be comforted, you are safe; whatever misfortune may have brought you here, what protection and help a poor feeble old man can give, you may depend on."

Being a little more composed, I got up, and accompanied the old man into the cell; though not as yet thoroughly satisfied whether I conversed with the dead, or the living. In the mean time he brought the shell that had still some wine in it to me; I drank a little of it, and found myself quite recovered, when we entered into discourse. He then drank some himself.

"Holy father," said I, "I thought you had been dead some weeks ago; are you really living, or do I converse with a spirit?" "My daughter," returned the hermit, "I am really a living body, though too weak and faint to live much longer. But how comes it that you speak to me in a manner as if you knew me? I was surprized to see you here, but more so to hear you talk in this manner; and, did not your late swooning convince me that you are a mortal like myself, I should think that I, in my turn, was also discoursing with a spirit."

---

1 Fires and flames that were kept continuously lit are a significant ancient symbol and element in a number of ancient rituals and traditions. This reference to "the perpetual lamps of the ancients" appears to be to the general tradition rather than to a particular use or text.

2 A scene of discovering an older hermit in a cave chamber also appears in Aubin's *Life of Charlotta Du Pont* (see Appendix D2, p. 243). Community castaway stories in particular often include companion figures who serve as guides or advisors to the protagonist.

This gave me occasion to acquaint him with the cause of my coming on the island, and what had passed since, to the time of our meeting.

"Have I then," cried he, "been so happy as to have my misfortunes prove the means of affording assistance to an innocent and unhappy sufferer? Thanks be to God!—I wrote," continued he, "the memorandum of my supposed approaching death, that you have read, and thinking my end to be very near, walked out with a design to go to one of the dormitories belonging, as I find by your information, to the virgins of the sun, in order to clear one of them of the ashes it contained, and lay myself down in it; and there to await my approaching dissolution, which I thought could not then be far off but as I was going thither a kind of delirium seized my brain, and I wandered up and down, unknowing where I went. Though I had intervals of sense, they never continued long enough for me either to find my way back to my cell, or to a dormitory. The only advantage I reaped from them was when I found myself hungry or dry, to gather fruits to eat, and to seek for water. I suppose in my rambles I got to the more remote part of the island. Once indeed I imagined I was very near my cell, and that I thought I saw the figure of a woman standing at the door; upon which I halloed as loud as I could; but it vanished like lightning from my sight. Having to-day the enjoyment of my senses, I at the close of it found my way to my cell; there was just light enough to guide me to one of my lamps, which I lighted, and was kneeled down to say my prayers, when the noise of your fall made me turn round in a start, and I beheld you lying on the ground. This augmented my surprize, and it was some moments before I could recover myself, so as to be able to move to your assistance."

CHAP. VIII.

The hermit dies; the idol of the sun described; discovers a subterranean cell, that leads to the inside of the idol; a terrible tempest.

FINDING the hermit stopped his discourse, I told him, I believed that he really saw me, for that about a month ago, as already related in the foregoing part of my life,[1] the day I was put upon the island, as I stood at the door of his cell, fearful to enter, I then imagined that I heard an human voice calling to me: the fright drove me into the cell; but from that time to this I could never account for it, but concluded afterwards that the noise existed only in my fearful imagination.

During our conversation we refreshed ourselves with some goats flesh and roots, and, now the night being far spent, I persuaded the hermit, after much intreaty, to repose himself on the stone couch, whilst I sat in the chair. The sun was far advanced the next morning, when I found the hermit still reclined on the couch. I thought he might still be sleeping, and went softly out, to get some goats milk for our breakfast, and after my return waited some hours for his awaking; but as he did not stir, I began to suspect he might be dead. At last I persuaded myself to go nearer, and now perceived he was really so. I was sorry so soon to have lost his society, from which I promised myself much solace. As it was impossible for me to remove him, had I been ever so desirous, I immediately set myself to convey every thing out of the room into another, which I found equally convenient; only I had the trouble to gather moss and leaves to lay upon the couch.

When I quitted the room entirely, I pulled the door after me, and with loose stones, of which there were plenty, so closed it up that no creature could enter. The day was now too far spent to renew the searches of the day before; which I therefore deferred till the next day, when I awoke early, and having provided for my subsistence as before, once more visited these solitary ruins. Meeting nothing new I endeavoured to find my way to the idol; which was not very difficult, as the ruins of the buildings continued quite from my first cell to the idol. As I approached nearer to

---

1 The London edition includes a footnote here referring readers back to page 57; in this edition, see p. 66.

it, I found the form of the building to vary much from what I had before seen. The rooms or cells here were much larger than the dormitories; and were I suppose the apartments, some of which were still entire, which the priests inhabited. By all that I could see I concluded that this palace had never been raised higher than one story; which might be the reason that it covered so great an extent of ground.

Now, at the distance of about a mile from the place of my abode, as near as I could calculate, I came near to the idol; and here I suppose the temple began; for I found no more apartments, but the remains of a wall, which had antiently, no doubt, surrounded the idol, and left a large area in the middle. In the center stood this idol. Round it was an ascent of twenty stone steps. The image itself, of gold, greatly exceeded human size: it resembled a man clad in a long robe or vest; which reached quite down to the pedestal-stone or foundation on which it stood, and lay in folds upon it. This image was girt about the waist as with a girdle, and on each breast gathered to a point, fastened as it were, with a button; the neck and bosom quite bear[1] like the manner of women; on the head was a curiously wrought crown, and between the two breasts an image of the sun carved in gold, as was all the rest of it. The right hand supported the figure of a new moon, and the left held a cluster of stars. On the back part of the idol was written in large Indian characters to this purpose, THE ORACLE OF THE SUN. I ascended the steps, and threw a stone at the image, and found it was hollow.[2]

Having now pretty well satisfied my curiosity, I began my walk home again. In my way thither, as I kept a strait way as nearly as the buildings would admit, I struck my foot against something and fell down. I got no hurt; as soon as I was up again, I turned round to see at what I had stumbled, and found it to be a large iron bar. Upon removing the earth, that covered part of it, I discovered a kind of trapdoor of the same metal, of which this was a part, and two strong bolts. I endeavoured, with stones,

---

1 Bare.
2 Harriot describes a Native American oracle in Appendix A1, p. 165. The castaways in "A Remarkable Voyage in the South Sea" also encounter a temple with a "colossal statue of the sun" (Appendix D3, p. 246). See also the amphitheater description in Appendix B6, p. 211.

to force the bolts open, but did not effect it without great labour, and then with equal difficulty pulled the door up, on the inside of which were two other bolts to fasten it within-side. A stone staircase presented itself, I went down a few steps; but as they led me under the earth, I found it too dark to proceed without a light. But my curiosity was so much excited, that I determined to go home, and fetch a light to explore this subterraneous cavity. For this purpose I brought three shell-lamps and my tinder-box.

As soon as I was got to the bottom of the stairs, and had lost all sight of the light above, I sat down one of my lighted lamps; at a further distance I sat down another in the same maner, and with a third and my tinder-box, in case the light should go out, then proceeded. I made use of these three lights to render the passage less terrifying, and that I might be in less danger of being left in total darkness. I found this passage very narrow, capable of admitting only one person to walk abreast, but high enough to admit a person of more than the highest stature. Almost all the way on each side there were a kind of nitches[1] or holes. Upon examining them I found they contained a variety of things, all of gold, of which I knew not the use, besides a great number of rings, bracelets, lamps, and crowns. An immense treasure! a little further I discovered a kind of room, pretty spacious; in this hung up a great many as I supposed, sacred vestments. These were formed of gold wire, or rather of narrow plated gold curiously folded, or twisted together like net work.

I was surprised to find how little they were tarnished; but the place in which they hung was very dry, and had very little air. Among these vestments were some of more extraordinary workmanship and richness. The largest was, as it were, sprinkled over with precious stones, and here and there a large diamond. It appeared to be in the same fashion with that with which the statue of the sun was clothed. By this hung a kind of close vest or cassock of the same make, designed I supposed to be worn under the other, with diamond buttons to fasten it. Near this was a crown of most exquisite make, richly beset with precious stones of various sizes and colours; one on the top particularly large, which emitted from all parts of it a light greater than that of my lamp.

In the same room was a golden staff, or rod, with a small image

---

1 Niches.

of the sun on the top of it. I supposed these two last vestments might have belonged to the high priest; and the staff likewise. In looking over the gold rings, I found one which was set round with precious stones, with a very large one in the middle, which shone with a lustre equal to that on the top of the crown, as I supposed the high-priests wore; this I put on one of my fingers, and two of the richest bracelets, beset with precious stones, on each of my arms.

Having sufficiently satisfied my curiosity with looking at treasures that could yield me no real service, I walked on a little farther, and found another flight of stairs; these I ascended, wondering whither they would lead me. They were very narrow and steep; which I soon found, led me up into the image of the sun. At last I got quite into the body of it, and my head within the head of it. There were holes through the mouth, eyes, nose, and ears of it; so that I could distinctly see all over the island before me, of which the height I was at gave me a great command. I indeed thought I could even behold the sea.

My astonishment was so great at what I had seen, that I exclaimed aloud, "What wonders are here!" As I spoke these words pretty loud, I had scarcely uttered them, before I was almost stunned with the sound of my own voice. This image, particularly the head of it, it seems, was so wonderfully constructed as to increase the sound of even a low voice to such a degree as to exceed that of the loudest speaker: for afterwards saying, in as low a voice as I could, "What a knowledge of mechanics must the ancients have had!" I might, I dare say, have been heard as far as the human voice is commonly heard intelligibly. Nothing therefore could be more natural for me to conclude than that this image was anciently used to give out oracles: I tried to sing an hymn in my usual pitch of voice; but the sound was too much for my ears to bear; and I was obliged to lower my key.

I now thought it time to descend and go home, lest the night should come on me. The extraordinary things that I had seen afforded me a variety of agreeable reflections in my way home, and took off the horror of the gloominess that the approaching evening shed around me. Nor did the thought of walking among the remains of the dead give me the least terror. Having reached my cell, and prepared to take my rest, I was alarmed with a loud clap of thunder, I cannot say terrified, for I naturally love to hear it thunder; there is something awful and great in it, that always composes my mind, raises it above the things of sense, and fills my mind with noble and exalted ideas of God; whose presence I think it, as it were, bespeaks. I bow and reverence: for though sensible that both it and lightning are the effects of natural causes, yet I consider them as under the direction of God; and doubt not that they are sometimes directed to answer some particular ends of providence.

Storms of this kind, that sometimes happen in Europe, are by no means to be compared to those in these parts; and of the latter sort was that which I am now mentioning. The claps of thunder were prodigious loud and long; the lightning almost without intermission. I was fearful that the stone room I sat in might be thrown down, and therefore went out.

But what did I behold! Imagination can scarcely conceive such a total darkness as then covered the earth; as if every particle of light had been annihilated, and primitive chaos had once more resumed its reign; when in an instant the thunder roared, as if the whole earth had been bursting into atoms, whilst the lightning showed the air one entire body of liquid fire, and so illumined the earth, that I knew not which was brighter, that or the air. It was too much to bear; I again sought my cell, and there trembling waited the dissolution of all things, as I indeed then expected.

I suppose this dreadful hurricane might continue two hours, when it gradually expired, or rather seemed to retire, elsewhere, in more low and distant sounds, and all was calm as though it had always been so. I soon became composed myself, and once more retired to rest. But what a new scene presented itself the next morning, when I came out of my habitation to view the effects that the last night might have produced! My way was frequently obstructed by trees torn up with their roots, and scattered here and there, and the earth in many places covered with the bodies of dead birds, goats, &c. and the carcasses of other small animals, whose names I knew not. But when I approached the sea-shore, the objects were changed; but to such as still showed how dreadful the storm had been. The foam, which the agitated sea had thrown on the shore, lay in great quantities intermixed with a prodigious number of dead fish; some of an enormous size. Many of the rocks were rent in pieces, and their broken fragments made an horrid appearance. What a subject of speculation here for a philosopher!

I now turned my steps back to the more inland parts, where I beheld the same havock made among the trees, beasts, and birds, but no hurt done to the remains of the palace; which I suppose owed its security from the general desolation, to the lowness of it. But I must confess I trembled for the statue of the sun, though I knew not why; for what was it to me whether it stood or fell? As soon as I came near enough, I saw it was safe; and was far from being displeased that it was so.

I now returned home, and having thoroughly gratified my curiosity in searching among the ancient ruins and exploring the contents of them, I spent my time in my little domestic concerns, my devotions, and reading the few books that I found in my chest.

CHAP. IX.

Terrified at the annual visitation of the Indians, she intends to conceal herself in the subterranean passage; resolves to convert the Indians; takes her station in the body of the idol.

THE time now drew pretty near when the Indians were to come to pay their annual visit to the idol of the sun.[1] This reflection put me upon thinking how I should secrete myself during that day. I was indeed informed by the hermit's manuscript, that he contented himself with staying within his cell, and forty years had found that precaution sufficient for his concealment; but still I was afraid to follow his example. Perhaps my being a woman made me more timerous. That, thought I, which has never happened may possibly arrive, and if prudence teaches us always to avail ourselves of the best means in our power, I ought rather to secrete myself in the subterraneous passage, a place in which I shall certainly be less liable to be found; and certainly unused by the hermit, only because unknown to him; for I found no mention of it, and most undoubtedly he would not have passed over, in silence, such an extraordinary discovery. The circumstance of the two bolts within-side of the iron door, which opened into the passage, confirmed my opinion in the fitness of this asylum, as by their means I could fasten myself in.

I had no sooner made my fixed determination to retire to this place, but a very strange thought arose in my mind. It was nothing less than this, to ascend into the hollow idol, speak to the Indians from thence, and endeavour to convert them from their idolatry. A bold attempt! not rashly to be undertaken. I weighed this for several days in my mind. As the manner of my education had afforded me an opportunity of learning several of the Indian dialects, so as to speak them with the utmost ease, I thought it very probable they might speak some one of them; and the construction of the image, as before observed, was such, that if they came within any tolerable distance of it, I should discover whether I understood them or not. If the latter, it would remain only for me to be silent; but if

---

1 The islands inhabited by castaways are often paired with a neighboring island, and travel between the two often happens in the pursuit of religious retreat and/or conversion. See Appendix B1, p. 181 and B4, p. 202.

I should understand their language, I thought the extraordinariness of the event, my speaking to them, would appear miraculous, fill them with awe, and prejudice their minds greatly in favour of what I should say to them.[1] I further strengthened my resolution with this reflection, that an attempt to teach the knowledge of the true God to those who know him not, was laudable, and might not want a providential sanction. As to the human means, I knew I was tolerably well principled in the theory of religion, by my uncle's great care, as already mentioned.

With respect to the Indians, I very well knew that they are generally of a docile disposition, and that if you once convince them that your intentions towards them are friendly, no people are more grateful; nor are there any in whom you can, safely, place a greater confidence. Again I considered, that if I should hereafter judge it prudent to discover myself to them, and to go and live among them, that my tawny complexion would be some recommendation. Supposing all this should take place, I thought that though it might not open a way to my return to Europe, yet it might to my living a much happier life, and give me an opportunity of doing abundantly more good, than I had the least reason to think I should ever effect during the whole course of my life. The more I considered the affair, the more resolute I became to undertake it. However, I was determined to give it a very deliberate consideration. Nay, I even made it the subject of my prayers, that if I might become an instrument to promote the knowledge and glory of God, and the salvation and happiness of any of his creatures, I might have his blessing on my endeavours. Surely this was not superstition in one who believes in a particular providence! And of this persuasion shall no man rob me! Certainly he who would divide the belief of a particular providence from religion, destroys that which he should retain. He takes from man that hope which only can support him under the vicissitudes and cares of this life.[2] Let a man be thoroughly persuaded that he is not the subject of divine care, what can support him in the hour of affliction? What can prevent him from seeking relief from the pistol, or the dagger?

---

1 For another account of the use of technology to subdue and convert the Indians, see Appendix A1, p. 164.

2 Defoe reflects on and defends the concept of providence at considerable length in *Serious Reflections* (187-214).

But leaving these reflections to those who are so happy as to think, I return to my history. I reflected that as there were several holes, or openings in the image, I might possibly be seen through them by the Indians, before I might have leisure to judge whether I should address myself to them or not; which might be attended with unforeseen consequences, to my great disadvantage. To come to a certainty as to this material point, I proceeded in this manner: I took one of my gowns, and carried it into the statue, and with other things so stuffed it out, as to make it fast within the idol, and to cover all the holes. I then went out upon the island, and carefully surveyed the statue round, and found, to my great satisfaction, that the several perforations grew narrower as they approached the interior part of the statue, and were so deep that they cast a shadow within themselves, so that upon the nearest approach it was impossible to see into it, without there had been a light within-side; however, at least, I could not distinguish my gown; and the statue was too high for any person to bring his eyes, or even his hands, near to the openings. But for fear this deception might be owing to the gown's covering the holes more closely than my body could, I took it away, and once more went out to make a second observation, and had still the pleasure to find it was impossible to see into the statue at all.

Though this danger was entirely removed, there still remained another. I had discovered, as the reader may remember, that such was the wonderful mechanism of this statue, that the least sound became very audible. The noise I might make then at getting into it might instantly discover me; for it was reasonable to suppose, that the visitants would come as near to their idol as they could; no doubt ascend the very steps leading up to it, and being thus near must needs hear the least noise.

Alarming as this consideration was, it soon subsided. For to avoid the possibility of this event, I determined to place myself in it before their arrival, and to sit perfectly still till their departure, if I should see occasion; or till I spoke, if I should find it proper to do so. The image was very well contrived to favour my purpose; there was in it a convenient seat, and sure footing for my feet; and which also luckily suited my stature, so that when I sat, my face was directly upon a level with the holes; by which means I could, without changing my posture, see every thing that was to be seen through them. Looking in my Almanack I found that the night preceding the Thursday on which the Indians were to come, was the time of full-moon; and that, therefore, they, very probably, would take the advantage of it to set out in the night, to be on the island early in the morning. Nor was my conjecture wrong, as the event proved. I thought, therefore, it would be prudent in me to take up my residence early in the evening.

There were now but three days to come before their arrival, during which, I changed my mind, perhaps, as many times as there are hours in that space. This moment I imagined hundreds of Indians prostrate before me with reverence and attention, whilst like a law-giver, I uttered precepts, and, like an orator, inculcated them with a voice magnified almost to the loudness of thunder. At another time my soul shrunk within me at the imagined noise of their dreadful yell; whilst my imagination painted to me an enraged multitude tearing down, in their fury, branches of trees with which to surround the statue, and to burn me in it.

As one, or other of these thoughts prevailed, I resolved for or against, the undertaking. At last, with more than female resolution, I determined on the attempt, and from that moment fortified my mind, and checked every rising fear. This was on the morning of the preceding day of their coming. Out of the few clothes which I had, I chose those which I thought would make the least rustling, and were the least bulky. I thought one shell-lamp would be sufficient, and that I would put that out, when I came to the foot of the statue, as I should take my tinder-box with me. As I intended to get into the statue at night, and knew not how many hours I might be obliged to continue there the next day, I put a few roots into my pocket, and as I had nothing but shells to take any water in with me, and was afraid I might drop them, and make a noise, I contented myself with some ripe limes and other moist fruits, of which there was plenty on the island. When the evening came on, having first performed some particular devotions on the occasion, I set out, and as soon as I had got low enough down the stairs, I fastened the two bolts of the door after me. I should have observed that before I set out, I concealed every thing I had up and down in holes, which I covered up close with stones, so as nothing could be perceived, that in case any of the Indians should chance to wander into my apartments, they should discover nothing that might prompt them to suppose that any human creature inhabited them.

When I came to the foot of the statue I pulled off my shoes, and left them there, that I might not make any noise with them in changing my posture as I sat. Though my situation was dark within, yet as the moon shone very bright, I had a very agreeable prospect of the island. My mind was too busy to suffer me to sleep; the expectation of the events of the coming day engrossed all my thoughts. I hoped, I feared, I trembled, I prayed. For a moment I resolved to descend, and give up the enterprize; again, much courage revived, and I was a heroine. The consciousness of the purity of my intention, and the goodness of my design, prevailed over every other thought, and I became calm and determined. Whilst I thus sat waiting for the arrival of the Indians, and observing the signs of approaching day, a sudden clap of thunder broke just over my head; the introduction to a more violent hurricane than that which I had lately seen. This was accompanied with an earthquake that shook the whole island, and I expected every moment that I should be swallowed up, or, at the best, that the statue would be overturned with myself in it. I now trembled indeed, and all my courage failed. The storm still continuing, I at last, made shift to descend the stairs; and being arrived in the passage, I sat down on the ground, unable to go far into it.

It was darkness all around me, and I could not find my lamp and tinder-box. The earthquake still continued, as I perceived by the motion of the ground beneath me. I thought it could not be long before I should be buried alive in the earth; and therefore, as well as my disturbed spirits would permit, recommended myself into the hands of God.

CHAP. X.

Finds herself unable to get out of the idol; after despairing of extricating herself forces open the passage; and perceives the earthquake had destroyed her habitation.

In this melancholy situation did I continue for some hours, when I supposed the earthquake was over; for I no longer felt the motion of it. But the thunder still continued, yet with less violence, and the claps were not so frequent. I got up, and once more ascended into the image, saw no appearance of the Indians, and supposed that they would not be able to come at all at that time. Whilst I sat here, I perceived the earth to shake again, and I once more descended into the passage, determined at all events to get out of it, and, if possible, once more, to gain my cell; for I shuddered at the thoughts of being buried alive where I was, which I had but too much reason to fear. I even got over the fear of the Indians coming, and discovering of me, with the hopes that my complexion and the advantage of speaking their language, which I little feared but I should understand, would recommend me to their favour. And with respect to the storm, I might possibly escape without any hurt; and at the worst, I thought it would be better to die by a blast of lightning, or by the stroke of thunder, than to be buried alive in the earth, and very likely be several days in dying.

I should have been glad to have found my lamp; but as I could not, I groped my way as well as I could to the stairs, which led up to the trapdoor, which, having reached, I endeavoured to unbolt; but as the bolts were large and very rusty, they gave me a great deal of trouble and much pain, forced the skin off my hands, and made them very sore and bloody. At last they both gave back, when I pushed the door upwards; but what was my terror at finding it would not give way! I was persuaded that I had unbolted it; and therefore concluded, in my mind, that the earthquake had overturned some of the earth above, and covered it over. It is impossible to describe the agony of my mind; I concluded myself lost, that I was entombed alive, and that I should miserably perish with hunger and thirst. Fear added strength, and I again and again made the utmost efforts to raise the door up, but in vain; I did but increase my pain, and exhaust my strength, till I was unable to make a farther trial.

How dreadful my situation! no other prospect before me but that of a certain lingering death! I sat a long time on the stairs in the most melancholy condition. I endeavoured to pray, but could not; at last I did, when, a little more composed, I got up to look at that light which I never expected to enjoy again with an open freedom. I was satisfied as I crept along, that the earthquake was over. When I was got into the statue, I found that the thunder and lightning still continued. What would I not have given in that moment, to have been exposed to its utmost violence! I most ardently wished for the coming of the Indians, who happily might prove the instruments of my deliverance. But this was rather the wish of despair than a probable event; for how should they know where to find the door, supposing them present and disposed to seek it? Tired with sitting here, or rather with my own tormenting thoughts, I once more, I knew not why, descended into the passage; but what comfort was I to find there? As I got to the bottom of the stairs my foot struck against something, which, upon feeling, I found to be my tinder-box, and by it my lamp. A secret joy spread through my heart. This I instantly checked with this reflection, What comfort, said I to myself, can light afford to such a wretch as I am, doomed to perish in this place? I now upbraided myself with my own folly. Why did I undertake this rash, hazardous enterprize? Could the poor hermit content himself forty years in his lonely cell, and was I so soon weary of it? All the favours of providence are now lost upon me. I might have lived with some degree of comfort, but now must perish miserably. I have by my rashness sinned against the mercy of heaven, and now must die without it.

Thus did I indulge the severest reflections on my own conduct. At last I thought I would once more look at my prison-door, but with no hopes of escape. For this purpose I struck fire, and lighted my lamp, and having reached the door, I carefully examined the bolts, which I thought I discovered to be not quite drawn back; this gave me a little hope. I tried one of them with much pain, for my hands were very sore, and at last it gave back a little; now my hopes were quite revived, and gave me fresh strength to attempt the other, and was again successful, and so happy as to raise the door up. Thus had my mistake procured all this uneasiness to me; and how many of our miseries do often flow from our mistakes? I now once more beheld the open air in freedom, if such can be said of one who was confined in a small island bounded by the sea. I thanked God for my deliverance, and as the day was declining, I intended to make haste to my cell, but found fresh ruins to interrupt my way. Those remains of the palace which I left standing but the day before, were now thrown down; not one had escaped the violence of the earthquake, not even excepting the cell I inhabited. I had reason, indeed, to be very thankful for my confinement in the subterraneous passage, to which, in all probability, I owed my not having perished in my cell. But one misfortune I still sustained, the want of an apartment above ground.

The thoughts of living under-ground were very disagreeable; but no better habitation remained for me. It was well for me, that I had the precaution to remove my few effects out of my cell, which by the fall of it might have been destroyed, but which I found safe where I had deposited them. I took some provisions, and some more lamps and fat, in order to render my dark abode as light as I could, and with an heavy heart returned back to the place I had left but a little while before, not thinking I should ever have made it the voluntary place of my residence, if indeed I may say voluntary; for it was a necessity, not a free choice, that led me thither. Having entered by the door and fastened it, I lighted five other lamps, with that I carried in my hand ready lighted, but these were not sufficient to take off the gloominess of the place. I had no better lodging than the bare ground; for it was too late to furnish myself with leaves.

A melancholy situation this! and scarcely was I able to bear it; but I summoned every thing that could give me comfort, or inspire me with fortitude. Among other things I considered that it was in every respect better than being on the ground above, exposed to the air and other accidents; that here, at least, was a safe retreat; that my distress was neither owing to my own sin or folly; and that, above all, no place is excluded from the presence of God; that his providential eye was still watching over me, and that I was under his protection. Having taken some refreshment, which I greatly needed, and said my prayers, I laid me down in one of the apartments here, already mentioned, with all my lamps burning, and, being tolerably composed in my mind, and very weary and heavy, having had no rest the night before, I fell fast asleep.

The Indians land, and approach the idol; the high-priest interrogates the statue, from which she makes responses, and instructs them in the principles of the Christian religion.

As soon as I awoke I got up, and finding one of my lamps yet burning, I took one of them, walked to the stairs that led up to the statue, which I ascended, and found the sun had been risen for some time, and that it was a very fine calm morning. I had not been here long before I heard a prodigious noise of voices, when looking forwards, I discovered a great number of Indians approaching, at some distance. The noise and sight of them startled me at first; but recovering myself from the surprize, my former intention of speaking to them revived, and I was the more confirmed in my resolution to do so from a consideration of the almost impossibility of living long under ground. Therefore first commending myself to God, and my intention, I waited for a favourable opportunity; in the mean time sitting as still as possible.

There was a great number of them, men, women, and children, who as they drew nearer formed themselves, as it were, into ranks, the oldest men first, then the younger, after these the eldest women, and the youngest; lastly the children, (no infants) boys and girls, the last of which brought up the rear. But I should have observed that the whole body of them was preceded by six old men, their priests, with a very old man at their head, so feeble with age that he was supported by two others. As soon as they had formed themselves in this manner, they came on very slowly, and with a profound silence. This slow march greatly favoured me, and gave me time to be thoroughly composed and fortified. I supposed their reasons were partly reverence, and partly to favour their ancient feeble high-priest; for such he was to the sun. Each of the priests had a small golden image suspended at his breast, and a golden coronet. The high priest the same, only that his coronet was much larger; he had besides a long staff in his right hand, with an image of the sun upon the top of it, also of gold.

Having approached within a few yards of the statue, they all stopt; when the high priest, and the six others, with the whole assembly, very devoutly prostrated themselves to the earth three times: all of them continued prostrate on the ground, except the six priests who each kneeled on both his knees, whilst the high-priest kneeled only upon one. The high priest then begun to sing a kind of hymn, in praise of the sun, as God, joined soon after by the priests, and, lastly, as in a chorus, by the whole assembly. The sound of their voices was so increased by the make of the statue, that I was hardly able to bear it.

I still kept silence; not thinking it as yet a proper time to interrupt them. When this part of their worship was over, they all stood, and the high-priest made an address to the sun, in a very low feeble voice, which yet I could hear very plainly, and to my great joy and encouragement, perfectly understood. The purport of it was to acknowledge him as the author of all things, the support of all, and the giver of all things, with praises naturally resulting from such acknowledgments. Then each of the priests, in his turn, offered up a kind of prayer for long life, health, success in hunting and fishing, &c. The address of the high-priest was truly great and elevated, and a pleasing simplicity and a fervency of devotion ran through the prayers of the priests, which they delivered very distinctly and audibly. When the priests had finished their parts, the whole assembly, which had hitherto observed a profound silence, except in the chorus, begun theirs. A confused disharmonious noise ensued; for each had a petition to offer up, whilst like the priests of Baal, they cried as loud as they could, as if their God was a great way off, or deaf, and could not hear them. In these supplications even the children bore a part.

And now the high-priest begun again, but in a different manner than before, who stood, as did the rest, and very pathetically lamented the long silence of the oracle, and, in a kind of agony, intreated that answers might be again given to them. He ceased at times, when each of the other priests, in his turn, continued the same complaint, and the same intreaties. Every time that one of the priests stopped, the whole company made great lamentations, attended with the most dreadful yells. The seven priests having finished this last part, a general and profound silence ensued.

I now was preparing to speak, thinking I could not have a better opportunity, when the high-priest gave me a much fairer occasion; for, raising his voice, seemingly, as loud as he could, he cried, or asked, in a kind of exultation,

Who is God but the sun?

To whom I immediately replied, in so very loud, yet equally distinct, a voice, that it ecchoed back again from the end of the island,

He who made the sun.

I must acknowledge I trembled when I had done, and was even sorry I had spoken, though truly and properly; yet I rightly concluded that I must proceed—No sooner had I uttered these words, but the lay-assembly leaped up from the ground, as if frantick with joy, and with loud shouts, and strange gestures, expressed the transports they felt, and then all fell prostrate, whilst the priests, with more decency and gravity, profoundly bowed their bodies, three times, to the very earth.

And now the following dialogue commenced between the high-priest and me, the people observing the whole time a solemn silence.

High-Priest. "Who then is that God?"

Answer. "He who always was, is, and ever will be."

High-Priest. "Where does he dwell?"

Answer. "In heaven, though indeed he is present every where; for he filleth heaven and earth with his presence—He sees all things; knows all things; for he made all things, and supports all things, by his power, which is boundless."

High-Priest. "Can we see him?"

Answer. "No; for no man can see God whilst he lives."

High-Priest. "Shall we then see him after we are dead?"

Answer. "Yes; all good men shall see him, and be happy with him; but every wicked man will be banished from his presence, and be miserable."

High-Priest. "Who is a good man?"

Answer. "He who believes in God, who loves and obeys him, and does by every man as he would be done by."

High-Priest. "Who is a wicked man?"

Answer. "He who does not believe in God, love, and obey him; and he who does not do by every one as he would be done by."

Here after a short silence, he continued his questions.

High-Priest. "Are you God?"

Answer. "No."

High-Priest. "Are you the sun?"

Answer. "No; for the sun can neither understand, nor see, nor hear, as I do."

High-Priest. "Who are you then?"

Though I did not mean to impose myself upon them as God, and had declared I was not God, yet I thought it necessary to check this question, judging it as yet too soon to declare myself, and therefore replied,

Answer. "Do not ask; for I will not answer to any questions but as I see proper."[1]

At this instant our dialogue was strangely stopt, and I was greatly surprized to see the whole assembly throw themselves upon the ground, tear, and beat themselves, venting their grief in cries and unintelligible accents, the priests behaving as madly as they. Whilst I beheld this extraordinary change with a concern and surprize that prevented my speaking to them, they all ran away, except the high-priest, who was too feeble, as fast as they could towards the sea-side.

For my own part my ideas were so confused upon this occasion, that I was incapable of thought. What have I said, at last cried I, within myself, that could thus terrify these people? I paused, and as my custom is on all sudden and extraordinary events, endeavoured to withdraw my attention from all outward things, and recollect my mind within me; and now happily I guessed the cause, as the event proved. I had told them I was neither the God I had described, nor the sun, whom they believed to be God, and yet refused to inform them who I was; yet I must have appeared to them to be more than a mere mortal, and recollecting that it was an opinion, common among the untaught Indians, to believe that there are two beings, the one good and the other evil, answering to God and the Devil with us Christians, therefore, from their sudden strange behaviour, I concluded, that they apprehended I must be the latter, the evil being whom they dreaded, and therefore fled.[2] This determined the conduct I was to pursue. I therefore immediately called to the high-priest, who lay on the ground, "Arise, and learn to be wise and happy."

But observing that he continued motionless, and not knowing

---

1   Other uses of the dialogue form for conversion efforts include works by John Eliot and Thomas Wilson. For another account of a Native female speech, see Appendix D1, p. 240.

2   For early English accounts of religious practice among the southern Algonquian, see Appendices A1, pp. 164–65 and A3, pp. 170–71. Defoe's views of North American native religion and his attitude toward conversion are expressed in Appendix C3, pp. 225–26.

but he might be dead, I extended my voice to the highest pitch I could, depending on the mechanism of the statue, for its reaching to the ears of the affrighted multitude; and thus called after them: "Return, I am not the evil being whom ye dread; return and provoke me not, to destroy you, before you can reach your own shore."

I know not whether the casuists may justify this artifice from sin; but to me it appeared expedient, and was successfully adapted to their fears, for they immediately halted, and began slowly to return back. At this instant, perceiving the high-priest to move, I repractised the same artifice on him. "Arise," said I, "and I will neither destroy you, nor the people; but if you would procure my favour, encourage them to return, and to attend to my instructions."

He immediately arose; and turning to the people, beckoned to them to come forwards. This encouraged them to come again to their former station; when he said to them, "The oracle will not hurt you; but he will be heard."

This was as I wished; but, observing the signs of fear still strongly stampt upon them, I thus addressed them:

"Fear not, I am not the evil being; and if you will hearken to me, he shall never hurt you."

These words had the desired effect; they immediately appeared calm and pleased, bowing to the earth with profound reverence. After this the high-priest spoke to me, with a trembling voice.

High-Priest. "Will you protect us from the evil being, that he may not hurt us?"

Answer. "God, who hath all power only, and who is good and gracious, will protect you, and will not suffer the evil being to hurt you."

High-Priest. "But must we not pray to the evil being not to hurt us?"

Answer. "No; you must pray to God only."

High-Priest. "Must we not pray to the Sun?"

Answer. "No; for he was made by God, to give you light and heat, and has no understanding."

High-Priest. "Will he not be angry then, and leave us in the dark."

Answer. "No; look at that tree on your right hand, you know it grows, bears leaves and fruit; do you think it can see, or hear, or understand?"

High-Priest. "I don't know."

Answer. "Can it move about from place to place, as you do?"

High-Priest. "I believe not?"

Answer. "I told you before that God made all things; the sun is one of those things which he hath made by his great power, and hath fixed it in the air, but it cannot move from place to place, by any power that it hath in itself, as you can, but is moved as God pleases. It can neither see, hear, speak, nor think as you can, who therefore art a more excellent creature than the sun, and therefore must not worship him, for he was made for your use, any more than you should worship that tree, because it does you good by bearing fruit for you to eat: nor must you worship any other creature you see, for the same reason; because they are all made by God for your use, and he hath given them to you."

High-Priest. "Did God send you to teach us?"

Answer. "He brought me hear,[1] and I will teach you."

As it was now high noon, I thought they might want to refresh themselves, and therefore said, "You may now eat and drink, and then I will speak to you again." The whole assembly then bowed themselves, with great reverence, three times to the ground, and then sat down to eat and drink.

I was myself very glad to have a little time, to consider how I should proceed on this extraordinary occasion. Whilst I took some refreshment myself, I reflected very deliberately upon this important business I had undertaken, and prayed to God that I might be the means of instructing them in the truth, and bring them, happily, to the knowledge of Christianity. But as this affair required a very mature deliberation, I thought it would be best to dismiss them at this time, and order some of them to come again the next week. As soon then as I found that they had finished their repast, I said to the high-priest, "I would have you now, all of you, return home, and you the priests, and as many of you as will, may come here again this day week, but not before, upon pain of my displeasure, and then I will instruct you further."

Upon this they all set up a shout of joy, and having made their obeisances as before, returned back to the shore, in a reversed order from that they came in; for now the children walked first,

---

1 Here.

the grown people next, and the priests last, carrying the high-priest with them.

End of VOL. 1.[1]

---

1 The London edition contains a notice, printed between the first and second volumes of the text, issued by some proprietors of circulating libraries to explain that subscription rates for lending books will be increased. The note, titled "Reputable Circulating Libraries," is dated 8 November 1766.

VOLUME TWO

CHAP. I.

Our heroine traverses the island; description of an uncommon animal,
with her thoughts thereon.

I HAD matter enough to employ my thought during this interim, to reconsider what I had said, and what method I should pursue for the future with these people. Besides, I had some domestick cares upon my hands: I now set about preparing a better convenience for my rest by night, and busied myself the remainder of the day, as soon as I perceived the people were gone off the island, with gathering leaves and other things to make my bed, which at last I made pretty tolerable. The next day I removed all the things I had concealed into the subterraneous apartments, bestowing some in one and some in another. I found it necessary also to provide myself with more fat, that I might now want light, and indeed with some meat; for these purposes I was obliged to kill a couple of goats, a task always disagreeable to me. As my habitation was very gloomy and melancholy, I spent what leisure time I had; in walking up and down the island. In these few days, I saw more of it than I had in all the time I had been upon the island. I found it well watered with little rivulets, and vast variety of trees, many of which bore different kinds of fruits. Those which I perceived had been pecked by birds I tasted, and found some of them very delicious.

Among the various kinds of birds I found one sort exceeding beautiful. It was about the size of a large parrot; its feathers delightfully variegated with the colours of the rain-bow, those of its tail spreading like those of the peacock; but not near so large, nor numerous. Of the four-footed animals I saw one of a most extraordinary kind. It was of the size of a large dog, as to its body, but its legs, which were very long, were by no means proportioned to the bulk of this strange animal, being so slender as to bend under him, insomuch that it could move only with the utmost slowness. I wondered within myself how this creature could either defend, or provide for itself, but observing it more closely, I took notice that its eyes were uncommonly large, for an animal of that size, projecting far from the head, and so frightful as to excite fear in me; and I should have fled from it, only that I perceived it could not overtake me, had I walked ever so slow. The mouth of it was no less dreadful; it kept the lips of it almost constantly drawn asunder, which showed two horrid rows of sharp, but short teeth.[1]

It was at this time labouring to get into a kind of pasture. I determined to watch its motions, thinking it might be seeking its prey; for I did not doubt but that the goodness and wisdom of providence, which had thus wonderfully provided for its security, had doubtless taken no less care for its support. It was a long time in getting to the place it seemed designed to reach. As it walked or rather limped along, several animals passed it, many much bigger than itself, who no sooner saw it than they ran from it, as if afraid of being destroyed by it. I took notice that as any of these approached him, he rowled[2] his eyes, which encreased their fierceness, at the same time showing his teeth.

At length he got into the grass, and then laid himself down, extended as if dead. I came up to him behind, for his looks were too terrifying to face him, and sitting down at some distance, was resolved to watch, that I might discover whether he chose this place merely for rest, or with some other view. He soon changed his posture a little, so that I could perceive that his eyes were shut, and his lips closed; I therefore concluded that he was going to sleep; however, I still continued in my place. The hair on his body was very thick and long, perhaps five or six inches; the extremities of every cluster of them formed a kind of bunch, or small tuft, as large as an hasel-nut. Having sat about a quarter of an hour, I saw a great number of field-mice come up to him, who presently began to nibble at these tufts, the animal continuing to lie still; but after a very considerable number of mice had thus employed themselves, he got up, and shook himself violently, when, to my great astonishment, I found these mice, some way or other so fastened and secured to these tufts, that very few of them could disengage themselves. And now, his neck being very long, he turned his head, and devoured them very greedily, one after another. I dare say that in a few minutes, he ate near three hundred of them; for his body was almost covered with them.

My curiosity was amply gratified, if an human being may say so, of the sudden destruction of such a number of innocent ani-

---

1 See the domesticated lion-like animals described in Appendix D1, p. 238.
2 Rolled.

mals; but the divine being has been pleased to permit animals to support themselves by devouring one another. I say permit; for I cannot think that it was the original design of the Almighty, that animals should at all destroy one another. I suppose it rather to be one of the unhappy consequences of the general corruption of nature. I know it may be replied, that some animals seem by their make to be designed to subsist on animal food only, and are accordingly provided with teeth and claws, unadapted for feeding on herbage, or fruits, and with stomachs evidently made for digesting animal substances; whilst those parts in animals who eat no animal food, are quite differently formed. I know and grant this; but yet my opinion is not by this concession destroyed. For it is highly reasonable to suppose, that these kind of creatures were so formed to prey upon dead animals, that by their feeding upon them, they might remove what would otherwise be an hurtful nuisance, in more senses than one. However, it is not my intention, here, to display the naturalist; otherwise I think, though a woman, I should gain the laurel from an Aristotle or a Pliny, were they to oppose me on this subject.[1]

But to return to the event which gave rise to this digression, I should be very glad if I could inform the reader, and especially myself, by what means these mice were entangled by, or fastened to, the tufts of hair, so as not be enabled to disengage themselves, no not even when the creature shook himself so violently, which, one would naturally think, was a circumstance in their favour. However, since I am upon this subject, which at least is pleasing to myself, and I think no ignoble contemplation for an ingenuous mind, I will hazard my own conjecture upon the occasion. As we know, by the assistance of the microscope, that the hairs of animals are pervious, or hollow, and that they are pervaded by

---

1 Among his other works, the Greek philosopher Aristotle wrote
several biological treatises, including *The History of Animals*, *On
the Parts of Animals*, *On the Progression of Animals*, and *On the
Generation of Animals*. Pliny, a Roman naturalist, wrote *Historia
Naturalis*. For the ancients, laurel symbolized victory and merit.
Although she claims not to be a naturalist, Unca Eliza is following
here in the footsteps of Hayy Ibn Yaqzan and subsequent
autodidact castaways, who spend their solitary time on the island
observing and learning from the natural world. See Appendix B1,
p. 181 and B3, pp. 189–90. By contrast, Juliani dominates and
controls the animals on his island (Appendix B4, pp. 199–200).

some kind of liquid matter, for their growth and nourishment, perhaps that with which the hairs of this animal are filled and nourished may be of a more extraordinary glutinous kind, and as the tufts formed by the extremities of these hairs are pretty big, a large quantity of this glutinous matter being lodged there, the nibbling of the mice breaking the hairs, this glutinous matter may so fasten the hairs to the inside of their mouths, as to render it exceeding difficult for them to disengage themselves, at least soon enough to prevent their being devoured: and I think the shaking of the animal must doubly contribute to their danger; because this motion prevents them from fixing their feet against his body, which would assist them in disengaging their mouths from the tufts, and being thus in a hanging state, their fear may make them bite the tufts the closer, upon the motion of the beast, and thereby render them a still easier victim: so that nature seems to have endowed him with this artifice the more effectually to secure his prey.[1]

---

1 Descriptions of unusual flora and fauna, or rarities, characterize New World travel narratives as early as Columbus. In early castaway narratives, animals tend either to be used and mastered by the human occupant of the island (Appendix B4, p. 198) or to be a source of physical and spiritual knowledge (Appendix B3, p. 189) or even companionship (Appendix C2, p. 219).

CHAP. II.

The Indians return to the island; she continues her instructions, and commands them to return weekly.

THUS did I busy or amuse myself, and indeed I cannot imagine to myself any situation in which a thinking being, free from pain of body, and great anxiety of mind, cannot divert itself. I can always find something, from without or within myself, for my amusement. Often have I been diverted with watching the flights of a fly, or the excursions of a spider, till my mind has been so filled with the display of the infinite wisdom of the Creator, in the formation of his works, as to elevate my mind to the most exalted adoration. Nor does darkness deprive me of my mental amusements: in this state I can reflect on those things that I have seen, heard, or read of. The recollection of these sets my busy imagination at work, and I am pleased, nay, I am happy; and darkness has no horrors for me.

How miserable must those be who complain for want of amusement! How wretched such a state! What! want matter for thought? Can a thinking being, such as man is, say thus? Look round, is not all nature about thee teeming with subjects well adapted for thy contemplation, happily prepared for thy entertainment? But whither will my thoughts carry me? my province is not that of a philosopher, but historian. And if my reader has travelled thus far with me, I doubt not but he is impatient to hear again of my late visitors, perhaps more so than I was. Nor do I wonder that events so extraordinary should attract his attention; and if ever they should be published in any country, I doubt not but they will soon be naturalized throughout Europe, and in different languages, and in succeeding ages, be the delight of the ingenious and inquisitive; and that some future bold adventurer's imagination, lighted up by my torch, will form a fictitious story of one of his own sex, the solitary inhabitant of a desolate island.[1] Such imaginary scenes, like

---

1 "Our authoress here seems to please herself, with the thoughts of the immortality of her history, and to prophesy of that of Robinson Crusoe, which only is inferior to her own, as fiction is to truth"— *Author's/"Editor's" note.*

those of a play, may have a temporary effect, but not permanent, like the real ones of mine.[1]

At length the appointed morning came, against whose advent I took care to be ready placed within the statue. Having waited a short time, I saw only the seven priests advancing towards me. I wondered not to see them followed by any of their people, and thought it very odd. When they were come up pretty near, they stopt, and having made their accustomed obeisances, stood silent, I supposed waiting till I spoke. After I had reflected a little on this occasion, I begun. "Why has none of the people attended you?"

High-Priest. "It is our business to instruct the people, and if you will please to teach us, we will inform them accordingly."

Answer. "Why?"

High-priest. "Because we live by teaching them, and if you only should teach them, they will not give us those good things which they now do."

Answer. "But I will not teach you only; I will teach them also. Nor need you fear losing your subsistence. I will take care it shall be continued. Hear me then, and if you fear me, observe my command. Let one of you go and fetch some of the people; and let the rest of the priests wait here till the others return."

The peremptory manner in which I uttered these words, seemed to affect them much. They made their usual obeisances; and then the high-priest answered, "that they were very ready to comply with my commands; but that it would rather take up too much time, to go back to their countrymen, and return again the same day, to make any convenient stay afterwards, to hear my instructions; but that if I pleased they would return home, and attend me, with some of the people, in the morning."

To this I agreed, and accordingly they immediately withdrew, having taken a respectful leave.

As soon as they were gone, I descended into my subterraneous

---

1 In an apparent attempt to deflect anticipated criticisms that this novel is an imitation of Defoe's *Robinson Crusoe*, the author has the narrator Unca Eliza Winkfield retroactively accuse Defoe of imitation; Winkfield boldly "predicts" that her story will be adopted, fictionalized, and masculinized by a "later" writer. This same charge accusing Defoe (as well as of the author of the Hayy Ibn Yaqzan story) of plagiarism appeared in an earlier castaway narrative (Appendix B4, p. 195).

apartments, took some refreshments, and spent the remainder of the day in providing some necessaries, and rambling about the island. The next morning, I took care early to place myself in the statue. Nor had I waited very long, before I perceived the priests coming forward, with a considerable number of the people with them. The usual ceremonies past, I began to discourse upon the nature and attributes of the Deity, from what are usually called the principles of natural religion; though I believe, strictly speaking, all religion to be revealed.[1] I stopt at every convenient pause, two or three minutes, that I might not weary their attention, and give them opportunity to reflect, as it were step by step, upon what I said.

As I was well acquainted with the manners of the Indians, I adapted my discourse to their own way of reasoning, and avoided all such terms, and modes of speech, as are intelligible only to Europeans. When I had discoursed near three hours in this manner, I desisted, desiring them to take some refreshment, with which I saw they had provided themselves, and that afterwards I would call to them; and then the priests, or any of the people, might ask what questions they should please concerning what I had delivered. I ordered them to retire to some distance from where they were. This I did, that I might not be heard, as I intended to withdraw for a little time out of the statue, to take some refreshment myself.

As soon as I had taken my place as before, I called to my audience, who respectfully returned to their former station. I repeated the leave I had given them, to ask any questions relative to my discourse. All the priests, in their turns, asked me several pertinent and sensible questions; to which I replied as well as I was able and I believe to their satisfaction. But observing that the laity still kept silence, I endeavoured to encourage them to propose their questions also, and was answered, by some, "We know nothing; our priests know all; teach our priests, and they

---

1 Keith offers a strong defense of female preachers (Appendix B2, p. 185). By beginning her instruction with natural religion, Winkfield appears to be following the program set out by the Society for the Propagation of the Gospel in Foreign Parts (SPG) for converting Indians (see, for example, *A Collection of Papers*, ix). The SPG, founded in 1701, was dedicated to advancing the Church of England abroad through missionary work. Defoe discusses natural and revealed religion in *Serious Reflections* (186-87).

will teach us." From this I concluded, that the priests had dealt in private with them, and had forbid their asking any questions, that they might preserve their superiority among them.[1]

I therefore addressed myself to them with some sharpness, reminding them of what I had told them before, "that I would not teach them only, but that I would teach the people also."

Upon this the priests submissively bowed, and declared their readiness to obey my commands. I then proceeded, as well as I could, further to explain what I had delivered in the fore part of the day; and concluded with telling them, I should be ready to continue my instructions to them, for that I had much more to say, once a week, provided the priests would attend that day week, and so on, with as many of the people as should choose to come; but as the high-priest was very aged and infirm, he might come, or not, as he pleased. To this the high-priest said he would conform. I then told them they might return home as soon as they pleased; and it was not long before they all quitted the island.

---

1 Crusoe's religious instruction to Friday likewise includes warnings against "priestcraft." See Appendix C3, p. 226.

CHAP. III.

Perplexed in what manner to act, she ascends the idol, addresses the Indians, and informs them, that a person shall come to instruct them in the knowledge of the true God.

I NOW once more found myself left to my little occupations, and to my own thoughts. I soon, and easily, fulfilled the demands of the former; but not so those of the latter. I had engaged in an affair that required the utmost attention, and not the smallest abilities. This latter reflection startled me. What an arduous attempt? thought I, and was abashed; would I had never engaged! but how can I desist? This was as difficult to answer, as how to go on. As I knew something of the manner of the Indians, I did not doubt of their docibility;[1] but I was very suspicious of the priests. I foresaw they would never easily suffer themselves to become useless to the people, and nothing less could be the consequence of my instructing them.[2] And supposing this to be got over, how was I to proceed to continue teaching them from the statue, if I hoped to make any tolerable progress, as it would render their attendance more frequent than might be convenient to them? and in the wet season they could not come at all; and further, how could I, with any possible degree of comfort, continue to live under ground even in the summer? and in the winter I should be entirely confined under ground. This last thought affected me so much, that I saw the absolute necessity of going to live among the Indians, whatever my success in teaching, or reception, might prove. I determined to trust in providence for a discharge of the first; and no less to rely on its protection, as to my personal security. Though I had thus determined the part I was to take, there yet remained a great difficulty, how to introduce myself among them. They might at present conceive of me as more than mortal, reverence me, and pay an implicit faith to all my teachings; but how would their opinion of me change, when they should discover me to be a mere mortal, a

---

1 Docility.
2 Questions about the usefulness of priests are implicitly raised by the stories of autodidact castaways who gain knowledge through solitude and observation of the natural world, rather than instruction from a religious authority. See, for example, the story of Josephus in Appendix B1, p. 179.

destitute stranger, even needing their support! What credentials had I to support the novel doctrines that I was to introduce? How was I to combat old opinions, handed down from father to son, received with reverence, and, no doubt, maintained with obstinacy? What advantage would not all these difficulties give the priests over me, among an ignorant and deluded people? and what might not exasperated bigotry prompt them to? nay, I knew not, but they might even think it necessary and right to destroy one who should dare to deny the deity of the sun, and expose the absurdity of their religion.

These were discouraging reflections, and the more I considered them, the more I was intimidated; and I heartily repented that I had ever spoken to them, and again was irresolute as to going among them. Thus was I distracted whether I determined to stay, or go; to stay was attended with certain evils; to go, too probably, with very great ones. Miserable wretch! cried I, what shall I do? tears succeeded; and I could think no more, with any coherence. As soon as I was a little composed, I had recourse to my usual consolation, prayer; and now my mind was calm, I could view the difficulties before me without terror, and distinguish between positive and real dangers.

I concluded to trust providence, in adopting that course, which, upon the most mature consideration, should appear to have the fewest difficulties, and the most advantages on its side. It was to go among the Indians; the manner thus; not to acquaint them in the least with my condition, that they might not conceive any prejudices against me on that account, and that by keeping them ignorant who I was, or how I came to them, I might preserve a superiority over them, sufficient to keep them in awe, and to excite their obedience: yet I determined to speak no untruth. Accordingly, when the day of their return arrived, and the priests, and a great many of the people were present before the statue, I thus addressed them:

Oracle. "Be attentive, and hear! You are a people ignorant of the knowledge of the true and only God, who made heaven and earth, and every thing therein; you are also ignorant of that worship, which God expects from his creatures; and of that happiness, which he will bestow upon all those who worship him according to his holy will.

"This his holy will he hath revealed to many thousands of men and women like you, who live in other parts of the earth, and now you also may know his holy will and be happy.

"God hath been pleased to send into the world, from time to time, holy men, and sometimes women, to instruct mankind in the knowledge of him; and at last his son, to instruct them more fully.

"But forasmuch as mankind had by their great wickedness offended God, of whom you are a part, he would have punished them with a very grievous punishment; but his son, who loved them, came down upon earth and was made a man, and offered himself up a sacrifice to his father, that mankind might be forgiven, reconciled unto his father, and be made good people, by believing and doing as he taught them.

"He was, whilst upon earth, attended by certain persons, called his disciples, who wrote the history of his life. This history, with the writings of the holy men, who lived before his coming into the world, and the writings of his disciples, designed to teach all men, you shall have for your instruction.

"With respect to teaching you the holy religion of the son of God from this place, it will be too inconvenient to you to come here as often as necessary; and during the rainy seasons, every year, it will be impossible for you to come at all.

"Therefore, that you may not want that instruction, which is necessary to your happiness here, and after you are dead, you shall be taught in this manner.

"A person shall come to you, like yourselves, and that you may be the less fearful or suspicious, that person shall be a woman, who shall live among you as you do.

"She shall bring with her the holy writings I have been speaking of, and shall teach all of you, especially your priests, who shall instruct you after her departure, the knowledge of the true God, and the way to be happy for ever.

"You must be sure to show the greatest respect to her, do every thing that she shall command you, never ask who she is, from whence she comes, or when, or whether she will leave you. Never hinder her from coming to this island when she pleases, nor follow her hither without her leave. You must all believe, and do as she shall instruct you, and never presume to come to this island without her leave, or do any thing that she forbids.

"But I do not want to force her among you: if you do not choose she should come, speak, and she shall not come; and I will be dumb for ever."

Answer. "Let her come! let her come! let her come! and we will love and obey her."[1]

This was the cry of all, with a noise in my ears like that of thunder; whilst they showed every outward sign of joy. As soon as all were again silent, I once more addressed them.

Oracle. "Hear me then, let as many of you as please come here three days hence, two hours after the sun is risen, and you will see her sitting upon these steps, drest like the high-priest of the sun. Receive her with great respect, and conduct her to your country, and remember all I have said."

I now was silent, when the whole multitude shouted,

Answer. "We will meet her! we will meet her!"

This important business of the day being thus concluded, they all returned home, and left me not a little pleased at the happy expedient I had devised to procure myself a favourable retreat among the Indians, and a high probability of success in my future teachings.

It now only remained to prepare for my departure. The day before the return of the Indians I collected together all my clothes, and the few books that I had; but had no chest to put them in, having broken that when I tumbled it down from the rock. I considered how to supply this want, and at last concluded to tie them up as well as I could with twigs, having no cords. Having first chosen such things as I intended to make my appearance in, I wrapt my bundle up in one of the priest's golden vestments, and put in two others. The last evening I spent in particular prayers upon the ensuing occasion.

---

1 This cry calls to mind the original seal of the Massachusetts Bay Colony, which represents an Indian who, echoing the Macedonian's appeal to Paul in Acts 56:9, cries "Come over and help us."

CHAP. IV.

Apparels herself in the richest manner and waits the approach of the Indians; acquaints them she was sent by the oracle; presents them with rings, and partakes of a repast.

WHEN the expected morning came, I awoke by day-break, drest myself in white, and, over all, put on the high-priest's vestments, that I had found upon my first searching of the subterraneous apartments. These were a kind of cassock, or vest, formed of gold wire, or rather of small narrow plated gold, curiously folded, or twisted together, like net-work, which buttoned close with diamonds. Over this I put on, formed of the same materials, and in the same manner, a gown, sprinkled all over with precious stones, and here and there a large diamond. On my head I placed a crown of most exquisite make, richly beset with precious stones of various sizes and colours; one on the top particularly large, which emitted from all parts of it a light greater than that of either of my lamps. In my right hand I held a golden staff, or rod, with a small image of the sun on the top of it. On one of my fingers I wore the ring, and on each arm a rich bracelet, all which I found at the same time I discovered all these other things.[1]

I had made myself a kind of wicker basket, which I filled with a great number of gold rings, all from the same repository. When I first discovered all these treasures, I then little thought they would ever prove of any real use to me. Nor did I now thus adorn myself from pride; but I thought the extraordinary appearance that they would give me, might procure me a more favourable reception. The rings I designed for presents. I should have mentioned that, besides the fine ring that I put on, when first I found the rings, I put one upon each of my fingers.

When I left my subterraneous dwelling, I not only bolted the door, but covered it over with earth. Being come to the statue I sat down on the biggest step, in all my finery, the crown on my head, my staff in my right hand, and on my left stood my

---

1   Compare with the castaway Juliani's response to gold (Appendix B4, p. 200) and Crusoe's (Appendix C3, p. 223). For a similar description of a temple to the sun decorated in gold and pearls, see Appendix D3, p. 246.

twig-basket; at some distance lay my bundle, which, being wrapt up in one of the gold vestments, glittered, as the sun shone very bright.

Thus I sat, with my bow and arrows hung over my shoulders, waiting for the important interview, my mind not a little agitated between hope and fear. However, I very solemnly recommended myself and my undertaking to God; and then endeavoured to fortify my mind so that on the approach of the Indians I might not discover the least symptom of fear; for I knew on this much depended.

I had sat near an hour before they approached; but at last saw them advance in the same order as at their first coming. At the first sight of them my heart leapt, and every limb trembled, and for a moment I wished myself within my subterraneous habitation. But as they advanced slowly, I had time enough to recover myself, and, before they came near enough to distinguish my countenance, I believe it was sufficiently steady.

As they came near, led by the high-priest and the others, they bowed almost to the ground at every step; I still kept my seat looking firmly at them. When they were come near enough to hold a conversation, they halted, and the priests and all the company, who were about two hundred, without any children, prostrated themselves to the ground; I then arose, and extending my golden rod towards them said, "Arise."

They did so; when, observing that they held a profound silence, I thus addressed them, with as much affability as I could; yet with an air of superiority.

"I suppose you are come to invite me to reside in your country?"

To this the high-priest answered, "Yes;" which was presently ecchoed throughout the whole multitude.

I then desired the high-priest to sit down at my right hand, which he did, not without some mannerly reluctance; I then placed the other priests on the steps a little lower on the right and left hand.

Sitting with the priests in this manner, I again addressed them:

"I suppose most of you were here three days ago, and heard, or know, what was then delivered from above," pointing up to the statue. "In consequence of what was then promised you, and to which you who were then present agreed, I am come to live among you, at least for some time, and to instruct you; observe what was then enjoined you.

"You must obey my commands, observe my instructions, never ask who I am, from whence I come, or whether, or when, I will leave you.

"Though if at any time you should desire me to quit your country, you may tell me so, and I will leave you. And further, you are never to oppose my coming here, as I shall do from time to time, nor any of you presume to follow me hither.

"If you will faithfully observe these things, I will come and live with you, acquaint you with the holy books of God, instruct you in the knowledge of God, and in the ways of his religion; which will make you happy for ever."

Here I paused; when the high-priest arose up with great reverence, and having bowed three times, almost to the ground, said, "Holy woman, we heard, with great attention what the oracle said, and when we returned into our country we called, the next day, all our countrymen together, and told them every thing that the oracle had delivered. Our countrymen rejoiced to hear the good news, and all desire you will come and live among them; they will love you, obey all your commands, and will make you their queen, for our king is lately dead, and as he had no children, we have not as yet chosen a new king. Will you therefore go home with us, and be our queen?"

Answer. "I thank you for your kind offer; but I will not be your queen, therefore you may choose whom you please. But, as you desire it, I will come and live among you, and will be only your instructor."

I had scarcely finished my answer, before the whole company made the greatest acclamations of joy, crying out,

"Come! Come! Come! and make us happy."

I arose up, and, after their manner, made three respectful bows to them; which were returned with new acclamations of joy.

As soon as all were silent again, I sat down, and taking out of my twig-basket two of the best rings, I presented them to the high-priest, and to each of the priests two others, near in goodness to those of the high-priest's; when, finding that I had a sufficient number of rings, I desired the people to come to me one by one, and I presented each with a ring, which they all received with great expressions of joy.

I soon found that they were confounded in their ideas about me, and conceived of me, as one more than mortal; for the high-priest, with great reverence, asked me if I ever ate and drank?

I chearfully replied "Yes; and if you have brought any provisions, I will eat and drink with you." At this he seemed both pleased and surprised. He then called to some of the people, who came forwards, bringing a kind of wicker baskets. The contents of them were dried fish, goats flesh, and other animal food, various kinds of fruit, dried corn, and a liquor like wine.

Before I began to eat, I stood up and said grace, at which they seemed much surprised. Then the priests and I took a comfortable repast together; whilst the people sat down, and did the same, we all observing a profound silence during the whole time. When we had finished, I again surprised them with returning thanks, according to the manner of christians.

The high-priest, hearing me conclude with the name of Jesus Christ, asked me very submissively who he was? I answered the son of God, of whom he had heard three days ago; that he had offered himself up a sacrifice to his father, for mankind; therefore we ought to praise God in his name, and in his name to ask for whatever it is lawful for us to desire: but of this, added I, I shall speak to you more fully hereafter.

But move on that later.

CHAP. V.

*She embarks with the Indians for their country; expounds the
scriptures to them, and translates the Bible and Common Prayer into
the Indian language. Visits her island.*

WHILST these things past, I considered, that as I was entering
upon an affair of the utmost importance, it would be highly
necessary to commence with prayer. I was indeed sensible that
it would be, in a great measure, very unintelligible to the Indians, yet I could not be satisfied with the omission, and thought I
might pray in such a manner as that they, at least, would understand that I was desiring God to do them good. I therefore stood
up, and told them, I would pray to God to be good to them, and
that they were all to kneel down, as I did. But that they might
not think I prayed to the statue, I got up to the top of the steps,
and there kneeled down, with my back to the statue, and my face
towards the people; and endeavoured to level my language, as
well as I could, to their understandings; whilst the whole multitude showed great attention.

As I could sing very well, having learnt whilst I was in England, and had composed several hymns in the Indian language,
as soon as I had done praying, I stood up and sung. It is not to be
expressed how the whole multitude were affected, showing every
decent expression of joy. I now told them I was ready to attend
them to their own country. On this they set up a shout of glad-
ness. I desired that some body would carry my bundle. I then set
out in company with all the priests, followed by the multitude to
the sea-side, where I saw a great number of canoes. I entered into
one of them, and immediately the whole company entered into
theirs. During our little voyage, I could not help reflecting upon
the bold undertaking in which I had engaged; nor was I without
my fears. But in my heart recommending myself to providence, I
reassumed my courage, and fortified my mind.

When we approached the destined shore, it was covered
with the natives, who, when I landed, respectively prostrated
themselves to the earth. I, in return, bowed my body to them.
I observed that they viewed my address with particular attention; whilst the priests conducted me to a little town full of small
huts or cottages, into one of the best of which I was desired to
enter. This, by the preparations that had been made, I supposed

was designed for my residence. Here I found half a dozen Indian maids appointed to attend me, who, on my entrance, kneeled before me, till I ordered them to arise. These presented me with dried fish and flesh, fruits and flowers, and different liquors, as appeared from the look of them; for I took nothing but some fruit, of a kind, different from any I had seen upon my own island; for I was still on an island, though much larger. After I had been here some time, with the priests, I expressed my desire to be left alone, and that I should be glad to see the priests the next morning.

How greatly was my situation changed! From a solitary being, obliged to seek my own food from day to day, I was attended by a whole nation, all ready to serve me; and no care upon me but how to discharge the important business of an apostle, which I had now taken upon me. To this purpose, besides my daily instructing the priests in the knowledge of Christianity, I once a week taught the people in public; who I found very ready, and tolerably capable, to receive my instructions.[1]

As to the priests, I had expected much difficulty with them, and no little opposition; but was very agreeably surprized. They were very attentive, quick of apprehension, fond of instruction, and very ready to give me what assistance they could in teaching the people. The use I made of them was this; I mean the young priests, for the high priest was mostly confined at home, by the infirmities of his great age. The use, I say, I made of the young priests was to teach the children, and young people, the church of England's catechism: for as I had found a Common Prayer Book, among the few books that were in my chest, I translated the catechism into the Indian tongue, with a short and plain comment upon it; this I taught the priests to read, who afterwards made the children get it by heart. And as I had a Bible, I, at my leisure, translated that also, beginning with the plainest parts first, till I had finished the whole.[2]

I from time to time read the Bible in public to them, and,

---

1 Compare to the change in Crusoe's role on the island following his encounter with Friday and others; Appendix C3, p. 227.

2 John Eliot's complete translation of the Bible into Algonquian was printed in 1663. As a Puritan, however, he would not have sanctioned use of the Anglican Book of Common Prayer, much less translated it.

as I was able, explained it. I cannot but say I found myself very happy, among these plain, illiterate, honest people. There was nothing that they could do to please me, but they did it; and often expressed their hope, of my never leaving them. I found the manner of introducing myself among them was highly serviceable to me: for though, in every respect, they could not but observe that I was like them; yet it was easy to discover, that they conceived me more than a mere mortal. However, I did not think it my duty, any more than my interest, to undeceive them, as this opinion secured to me that respect and authority which were necessary for me to preserve, in order to carry on the great work among them, in which I was engaged.[1]

I sometimes amused myself in shooting with my bow and arrows, in which I exceeded any of them. But even this circumstance, trifling as it was, raised their opinion of me. In the summer season, I now and then went to visit my old island; but whenever I did so, I always ordered the Indians who rowed me over, to wait with the canoe by the sea-side; or to return home and fetch me in the evening, whilst I roamed about at my own pleasure.

When the same time returned next year, at which season they used to visit the oracle, the priests asked me, in the name of the people, if they should go to visit the oracle. I answered by no means, for that they would never more hear any answers from it.

I passed near two years very agreeably among them; in which I not only finished the translation of the Bible, as well as that of the Catechism, but indeed of most of the prayers in the Common Prayer-Book. I also had made a great progress in instructing the people; whom I happily brought off from their idolatry, to the knowledge of the true God, and to a tolerable idea of the christian religion. We now regularly observed the Lord's day, according to divine appointment. Though I had no right to administer the sacrament of the Lord's supper, yet I was well satisfied, that under the circumstances we were in, I might baptize. But I never did so, till I was well satisfied that the party had a tolerable notion of the christian religion, and earnestly desired to be baptized.

---

1 Alain-René Lesage's *Chevalier de Beuchêne* (1732) also incorporates an American Indian utopia and the character of a female missionary.

I could not help making one observation, and that a very just one. I remembered when I was in England, that I used to look into some of the deistical writers in my uncle's study. These writers laboured to prove, that Christianity was repugnant to plain uncorrupted reason. Yet I found this assertion intirely false; for, here a people, who had no other guide but their reason, no sooner heard Christianity plainly and firmly expounded to them, but they soon embraced it. And I am fully persuaded that whenever any unprejudiced person tries the religion of Christ by his reason, though he may find it in some measure above his reason, he yet will not find it contrary to it, and that it is worthy of his assenting to it.

But to continue my history. In the beginning of the third summer of my being here, not having been for a long time at my old island, on account of the late rainy season, answerable to winter in Europe, I ordered some Indians to row me thither, early in the morning. I told the Indians they might return back, and come again in the evening.

Every time I made this visit, I always went into my subterraneous apartments, to get some rings to distribute among the Indians. I suppose they wondered how I came by them, but never asked me. And, that they might have no suspicion that I brought them from the island, I never gave them any on my return to them; but always a few days before I intended a visit to my old habitation.

CHAP. VI.

Lands on her island, ascends the idol, perceives two Europeans approach the statue, one of whom she finds to be her cousin. Speaks to them from the oracle, and after several interrogations discovers herself.

As soon then as I was landed I walked to the iron door, which I always left covered with earth, and fastened after me, as soon as I had struck a light. I commonly ascended into the oracular statue, and used to sit there sometimes to view the island. I did so this time; but how greatly was I surprised, when looking forward I saw some men advancing towards me! I soon perceived that they were Europeans, and, as well as I could conjecture, at the distance they were from me, Englishmen.

I supposed that they belonged to some ship, that had either cast anchor off the island, upon some occasion, or other, or were shipwrecked; nay, thought I, they may be pirates. Whatever might be the cause of their landing, I had much to fear.

Indeed I was safe where I was; but how was I to get home? and to stay long in such a place I could not. My next fear was for the poor Indians, who would come in the evening, and not finding me by the shore, as usual, would no doubt come upon the island, in search of me, and be taken for slaves. Nor might the evil stop thus; their country might be discovered, and probably invaded, and numbers of the people be carried away into slavery, and other injuries committed. Thus did my busy imagination create, as in a moment, evils that happily never came into existence: for these strangers soon came forwards, as I supposed, to view the statue, and being come near enough to be heard, one of them said to another, "We have indeed found a strange thing; what can this huge statue be designed for?"

"I know not," replied one who stood by him, "nor can I take pleasure in any discovery in a place where, no doubt, my dear cousin was starved to death or devoured by beasts."

These words, and the voice, alarmed me. "Sure," cried I within myself, "he speaks of me, and it is my cousin Winkfield."

As he came nearer, I thought more certainly it was he. I listened attentively to their conversation, in hopes to hear something that might confirm my suspicion. They stood still, I suppose, to examine the statue, when as often as one of them spoke, I was the more confirmed, by hearing and seeing him, that it was my uncle's son.

"But how," cried I, "should he come here? how know I was left on this island?"

These reflections destroyed my first suspicions, and my former fears began to revive; when he who I supposed was my cousin, said, "Let us stand here no longer; but as this seems undoubtedly to be an uninhabited island, let us continue our search, and perhaps we may yet find the bones of my dear Unca Winkfield; and by burying them pay the last, and only, respect we can to her unhappy memory; for if some beast destroyed her, he hardly ate her bones."

I heard these last words, including my name, too distinctly any longer to doubt, whether the speaker was my cousin, or not, and perceiving the company, was walking away cried out, "Winkfield, stay!"

At these words my cousin started violently, and turning round, as they all did, said to his companion, "Surely, Charles, I was called!" "No doubt," replied his companion Charles, "but it must be some of our companions who called you; for this island is uninhabited: we have been over it enough to see its bounds."

Mr. *Winkfield.* "No, Charles; it was too loud a voice to be human. Did not you hear it, gentlemen?" *speaking to his company.*[1]

Company. "Yes, indeed; and it was like thunder."

The joy of finding my cousin raised my spirits, and I was determined to indulge an adventure which promised much pleasure, and continued as follows.

Mr. *Winkfield.* "Sure it must be the spirit of my dear cousin! My father, who you know is far from being superstitious, has often said, he believes, that upon very important occasions, departed spirits are suffered to appear again: O that I could hear the voice again!"

Unca Winkfield. "Is your father alive?"

Mr. *Winkfield.* "Hark! it speaks again, like thunder! amazing!—shall I answer? Yes I will. I hope so, he was alive a few months ago."

One of the company. "This is strange, indeed! But it may be dangerous to stay; you know not with whom you may be conversing, it may be an evil spirit, and may hurt us. I have heard of such; let us go."

Another of the company. "I think the same; and never heard

---

1 At this point, the narrative begins to shift toward the mode of dramatic dialogue.

that any departed spirit, if it did return upon any particular occasion, spoke with as thundering voice as this. Besides, look at that statue, it brings to my mind the oracles that we read of in ancient history; and, to my apprehension, the voice seemed to come from thence; and, perhaps, it may be true, as we have read, that devils speak from such kind of statues."[1]

Mr. Winkfield. "You speak with reason; but, I think, I could be almost content to speak to the devil to hear news of my cousin."

Charles. "Fie, talk not so; let us commit ourselves to God, and wait a little to hear if it will speak again, and listen if the sound comes really from the statue; but do not speak any more to it."

I could not help being much diverted at their fears; but unwilling yet to discover myself, I however determined to dissipate their terrors; and beginning a midnight hymn of my uncle's composing, which my cousin had set notes to, and taught me to sing, they started when I begun; but as soon as my cousin distinguished the tune, and understood the words, he was calm, and made a motion to the company to be silent, and when I had done, said,

"An evil spirit would not sing such holy words. My father composed them, and I taught my cousin to sing them."

One of the company. "This is not to be accounted for; yet we read that Satan can transform himself into an angel of light."

Mr. Winkfield. "Away! I have no fears; I will speak to it.— Does my cousin Unca live?"

Unca. "She lives, and is happy."

Mr. Winkfield. "Perhaps, in heaven."

Unca. "No; she lives upon earth."

Mr. Winkfield. "Shall I ever see her?"

Unca. "You may."

Mr. Winkfield. "But when and where?"

Unca. "Here; and that soon too."

Mr. Winkfield. "Let me see her then."

Unca. "You shall, if you will do one thing."

Mr. Winkfield. "I will do any thing that"—

Charles. "Stop, be not rash; ask what you are to do before you promise. I am myself not without my suspicions."

Mr. Winkfield. "I was going to say, I would do any thing not unworthy of a christian."

---

1 See McMurran for a discussion of the novel in the context of contemporaneous debates and discussions about oracles.

Charles. "I am satisfied."

Mr. Winkfield. "If I may see my cousin I will do any thing not unworthy of a christian."

Unca. "What I shall require is worthy of a christian."

Mr. Winkfield. "Propose it then."

Unca. "It is only to continue all of you where you are, and do you sing your favourite hymn, and before you have done you shall see Unca. It begins,

"Whilst thus the sun illumes our sphere,
And bids the earth bring forth,
O spirit, deign in me to rear
Fruits of superior worth."

Mr. Winkfield. "I will do it—But who, or what, Charles, can this invisible being be, who seems thus intimately to know me?"

Charles. "I know not—but its request is innocent and pious; therefore begin."

As this hymn was a pretty long one, I knew it would give me sufficient time to carry my design into execution; which was to go out of my subterranean passage, drest in my priestly habits, and with my staff and crown; for in this manner I always came upon these insular visits. As they stood, it would be impossible for them to see me ascend from the earth. I pleased myself much with the surprize they would be in, to see me in a dress of which they could form no expectation, nor conceive the meaning of. I must mention one circumstance more, which contributed not a little to surprise them.

I had found among my clothes a small parcel of brass wire, which I had to mend my cages, in which I was carrying over some curious birds to England. After I came to live among the Indians, I made a strange kind of musical instrument. It was a long narrow box, made of thin wood, with holes cut in it, and several pieces of brass wire, placed in a particular manner. This I used to place in a tree, and when the wind blew properly upon it, it would send out certain soft pleasant notes.[1]

---

1 "By this description, and the use to which she applied her invention, it seems to have been of the same kind with that we now call Æolus's harp."—*Author's/"Editor's" note.* Aelous's harp, or the Aeolian harp, is a musical instrument played by the wind as it blows across the instrument, vibrating its strings.

I had a mind to try what effect it would have in the statue. I found out a method to fix it, opposite to the mouth, withinside of the statue, and when the wind sat right to blow into it, the sounds were very delightful, and might be heard I believe almost over the whole island. After I had made this discovery I always brought it with me, and placed it in the statue, and, if the wind stood properly, I was greatly entertained with its melodious sounds, as I walked up and down.

As I found the wind sat full against the statue, I placed the instrument before it, and heard it play with a loudness that I could not have borne long. This no doubt could not but give my visitors a new alarm; yet, from the nature of it, was less terrifying than my speaking had been, with such a magnifying voice, as the mechanism of the statue occasioned: and indeed they were greatly alarmed, which gave birth to the following dialogue, just as my cousin began to sing, as I was afterwards informed.[1]

Mr. Winkfield. "Ha! how sweet, but strange are these sounds!"

Company. "Astonishing beyond conception!"

One of the company. "This can be no human artifice; the loudness of it exceeds the power of art. I wish we were safe aboard our ships. I never was credulous; but henceforth I shall believe every fairy tale, if I escape this adventure; which I much fear."

Mr. Winkfield. "Let us be men, at least, and reflect that we are come in an honest cause. I own these appearances are very extraordinary: but they may portend good as well as evil. Must every supernatural event terminate in evil? Why may not the interruption of the usual course of things be as well for good as hurt?"

Charles. "True—Let us construe the omen in our favour, and be composed, and let Mr. Winkfield sing the hymn he promised."

Their conversation was so earnest, that they did not perceive me advancing, taking a slope till I got behind them, though at some distance, just as my cousin began his hymn. I stood still till he had done, in hopes they would see me before I walked up quite close to them; for I was afraid of alarming them too much. As

---

1 Compare to the description of beautiful and enchanting music that issues from the island in the narrative of Dubourdieu and his wife (Appendix D1, p. 236).

soon as my cousin had finished his hymn, and all, looking at the statue, had stood silent some minutes, my cousin exclaimed,

"I have sung the hymn, but where is Unca?"

As he said these words, I moved gently towards the left, and then walked forwards, till I came upon a line with them. The musick still sounding, I then stopped, holding my staff so that the image of the sun, on the top of it, prevented a full view of my face. Presently, he who was called Charles saw me; when starting aside, he cried,

"Bless me! what is that?"

Upon this all turned and saw me, to their great surprize. They stood still and silent like mutes. I now bowed my staff as saluting them, and exposed my face to their full view, not very far from them, when my cousin, in his turn, exclaimed,

"It is my cousin's face! but can it be her?"

Unca. "It is."

Mr. *Winkfield.* "And living too?"

Unca. "Yes, cousin, and living too;" and smiling, added, "but have you forgot all your gallantry, and must I make the first advance?"

Having said this, I began, slowly, to step forward, when one of the company cried out,

"Nay, if you all have a mind to stay till the devil comes to you, I will not;" and ran away as fast as he could.

I still kept slowly moving on, whilst my cousin, and the rest, stood amazed, half leaning back, as if in doubt whether to stay or run after their companion. Their great amazement confounded me. I was at a loss what to say or do. I stopt short, and all of us stood silently gazing, them at me, and I at them. At last recovering from the confusion their great surprize had thrown me into, I addressed my cousin in these words:

Unca. "Dear cousin Winkfield, be not so much alarmed, I am really your cousin Unca Eliza Winkfield."

Mr. *Winkfield.* "You indeed appear to be such; but the strange things which I have seen and heard to-day, and your no less extraordinary appearance, scarce leave me sufficiently master of my senses to form a right judgment of what I see and hear."

By this time I was got close up to him, for he stood like a statue, and giving my hand said,

"Cousin Winkfield, be composed, and satisfied, that it is your cousin Unca who speaks to you."

He then took me in his arms, embraced and kissed me, and as soon as his transports, at finding me, a little subsided he said,

"But, pray my dear Unca, what mean the huge statue; the monstrous voice, loud like thunder, that talked to me and sung; this loud musick, which I still hear; the strange rich dress I see you in, and how have you subsisted in this strange uninhabited place? or say whether it is not the abode of invisible spirits, who have wrought the wonderful things I have heard, and whether they have not been your guardians? and whether—"[1]

Unca. "Stop, dear cousin; you have asked too many questions, and such as cannot be answered in a hurry: and I have, on my part, my questions to ask you, for your appearance here is very surprizing to me. How you should know of my being here is what I cannot conjecture. But of these things we will talk together at our leisure, when you are more composed."[2]

---

1 This representation of an enchanted island filled with strange sounds is reminiscent of Shakespeare's *Tempest*.
2 Scenes of the rescue of other castaways from their islands can range from relief to regret; see Appendices B1, p. 184, B4, p. 202, B5, p. 206, and C3, p. 227.

CHAP. VII.

One of the company, terrified at Unca's appearance, runs to the ship, and makes such a report to the crew, that they refuse to take them on board.

BY this time the company, being pretty well satisfied that I was a mortal, which at first they doubted of, came up to us, and wished us joy on our unexpected happy meeting. We thanked them, and I assured them, they need not be under any uneasiness; for that they were perfectly safe where they were: for however extraordinary what they had heard and seen might appear to them, the whole was the effect only of natural causes. They were too mannerly to contradict what I said; but I could easily perceive that they did not believe me. However, I left them to their suspicions for that time.

My cousin now briefly informed me, that one of the gentlemen in company, whom he called captain Shore, the very day I was left on this island, took my ship and the captain of it prisoner; and had sent him to England to be tried: that captain Shore, coming to England, at my cousin's request, consented to bring him over in search of me; as he thought, from the account that the captain had given him, he could find the island, as he happily had. He added, the ship now lies at anchor, on the part of the island behind the statue, or whatever it is, and if you please I will conduct you on board; for by this time they will expect us to dinner, and I reckon are not a little uneasy about what may have befallen us; for I suppose our companion has made a dreadful report.

I answered that I was entirely at his disposal for a few hours. "For a few hours!" returned he briskly, "why, must my dear Unca and I ever part again? You talk strangely; and once more make me almost doubt the reality of what I see and hear."

"Yes, we must part for a little," answered I, "but I will soon satisfy you on that head. But let us pass on; I attend you."

As we walked along I told him, that I had come over on a visit to the island that morning, and that at night I was obliged to return back to the island on which I had lived above two years; or otherwise my friends there would be under great uneasiness at my absence. Thus we went on talking, till we came to the shore, when my cousin was greatly surprised at not seeing the boat.

"I ordered the boat," said he, "to wait for me here; and though Mr. Lock[1] in his fright might take it to go on board, he should have sent it back, and there has been time enough for its return."

Upon which captain Shore took a glass out of his pocket to look at the ship, which rode at anchor, some distance off. "Bless me," said he of a sudden, "what do I see! they are preparing to set sail. Sure the crew have not mutinied." He then called to them as loud as he could, and waved his handkerchief. He then said, "They made a signal that they see me." In a little time after he saw the boat coming. It soon appeared; but as it came near to the shore, the sailors it seems heard the musick from the statue, as the wind blew directly off from the island; this, together with my tawny complexion, and strange dress, so terrified them, that they stopped rowing, and would come no nearer; when one of the sailors said,

"Mr. Lock said right, this is certainly some inchanted island, and I would not row a stroke nearer if it was for the king."

Second Sailor. "Nor I; for I hear the devil's bagpipes playing as loud as thunder."

Third Sailor. "Aye; and don't you see that she-devil there wrapt in gold?"

Fourth Sailor. "I suppose she is the devil's wife, and this is their wedding-day, which makes her so fine and have so much musick."

Fifth Sailor. "I don't fear all the devils in hell, for I am a good catholic; I have crossed myself, and prayed to St. Patrick. But the devil shan't catch me ashore for all that."

Sixth Sailor. "I wish though I had her devilship's gold crown and gown, I would go no more to sea."

Fifth Sailor. "You fool, if you had them in your hand, they would all turn to dust."

We were obliged to hear this strange dialogue before captain Shore could put in a word. At last, with much ado, he made them hear him; but neither threats nor fair words could prevail

---

1 Reilly (271-73) has convincingly suggested that the character Lock (whose name is later spelled Locke) is a reference to the philosopher John Locke (1632-1704) whose *Essay Concerning Human Understanding* may have been influenced by *Hayy Ibn Yaqzan* (Russell).

upon them to come nearer the shore, whilst I stayed there. One of them said, that Mr. Lock came on board in a terrible fright, and said, he had seen a monster as tall as the moon, that it talked and sung louder than thunder, and that if he had not run away, a she-devil would have run away with him; and as one of our men was rowing him back, they said, they saw a hundred devils fly away with you all into the air, whilst they saw a great devil playing upon the bag-pipes, and he said, that for that matter he played much better than ever he heard a Scotchman in his life.

We therefore called a council, and had agreed to sail directly, if captain Shore had not called to us.[1]

As soon as the sailor had done talking, I told my cousin that I would leave them, that they might go on board their ship, and try to undeceive the crew, and that I would meet him the next morning at the steps. My cousin was much concerned at this unexpected sudden separation; but it appeared absolutely necessary, and there was no time for deliberation; for the men threatened every moment to row back to the ship.

1　This sentence belongs to the spoken account in the preceding paragraph, delivered by one of the sailors on board the ship. The "we" refers therefore to the ship's crew. Like the paragraph before it, there is no use of quotation marks either to indicate spoken discourse or consistently to differentiate speakers from each other.

CHAP. VIII.

Mr. Winkfield left on shore; and after relating what passed between him and the ship's company, Unca and he retire in the evening to the other island.

THUS I left them, lamenting my own folly for not having discovered myself in a less alarming manner. As soon as I was got out of sight, the sailors set up a shout of joy, whilst I pensively walked on to my subterraneous apartments. I hastened up into the statue, to remove the occasion, which had had no little effect in the late unlucky incident. Here I sat musing on what might be the consequences of this affair. They may perhaps, cried I, murder my cousin, or force him to return back immediately, and not suffer him to go aboard again; or, if they do, may sail away, and take him with them. Better had it been never to have seen him again, than thus to prove the occasion of his death, or of new vexation to myself. I might have concluded my life with ease and pleasure among the Indians; but if I see him no more, I shall have laid a fresh cause for uneasiness as long as I live, and drag out the remainder of my life in misery; a burden to myself, and useless to all around me. What, continued I, is human life? As a wave destroys in a moment the wave that preceded it, so often does the arising moment the joys of the last; never more to return. Thus destroyed, perhaps, is all my past happiness! The sun, which in the morning saw me happy, now beholds me mourning; shedding tears which perhaps must flow, till death stops the current. Nor shall mine flow alone; an aged father, with his afflicted consort, may mourn a lost son, and curse the hour in which they first knew me, the unhappy means of bringing their gray hairs with sorrow to the grave.

I had taken no refreshment, since I came upon the island, in the morning; and my grief was too great to let me think of any, till at last, fatigued with weeping and fasting, I grew faint. I then thought I would leave the place, and take some refreshment; but not till I had sought comfort of him who only can give it. Now finding my mind more composed, and having determined to banish every anxious thought, till I saw what the returning day might produce (for I purposed to come again the next morning) I made haste to get above ground.

I did so, and was walking to the place where I had put some

provisions, till I might want them, when I found part of the evils that my mind foreboded but too true; for who should I see walking solitarily along towards the statue, but my poor cousin! He did not see me till I called to him.

"Cousin Winkfield," said I, "what have my fears proved true? will they not receive you on board?"

Mr. *Winkfield.* "No; but be not alarmed, my dear Unca, captain Shore will soon be here again, and if, in the mean time, I can be with you I shall be happy."

Unca. "But will not your father and mother be alarmed at your delay?"

Mr. *Winkfield.* "They will not: for as I supposed it would be uncertain how long I might be searching for you, if I ever found you, I desired two years absence."

Unca. "I am so far satisfied. But relate what happened after I left you on the shore."

Mr. *Winkfield.* "As soon as you had left us, the sailors waited till you was got out of sight, and then set up a great shout, which possibly you heard."

Unca. "I did hear it, and from that moment was filled with fears, lest they should murder you, or leave you on shore, as they have done."

Mr. *Winkfield.* "Weep not for me, my dear Unca, for to live with you I should be contented if he never returns."

Unca. "I feel the tenderness of your expression. But my manner of living, length of time hath rendered agreeable to me; but it would be very disgusting to you. Rather may you soon return to your native country, be happy and leave me"—

Mr. *Winkfield.* "Stop, dear cousin! nor talk of leaving you; I never can, nor"—

Unca. "Hold, this is the language of a lover, ill suited to the present time and circumstances. The day wears away apace, and I must soon leave this island. Let us consider how you are to be disposed of. In the interim, will you partake of such mean fare as I have here? for, I suppose, you have had no refreshment since morning any more than myself."

We then walked to where I had stored my provisions, and there sat down to our repast. I now desired him to continue his relation.

Mr. *Winkfield.* "I said the sailors shouted when you were out of sight, and instead of rowing up to us, as we expected, boldly told the captain, that they had sworn before they set out, not to bring me on board; being determined never to sail in company with, a man, who, as Mr. Locke told them, had talked and sang songs with the devil: and had it not been for us, you know, captain, said one of them, he would have brought a she-devil on board with him, and as soon as she was on board, to be sure captain, she would have sunk the ship, and flown away with us all—No, no, good captain, we are bad enough, indeed; but we won't keep the devil company neither; nor any of his cronies.[1] He may go after her devilship if he pleases, if he can catch her; for I saw her fly into the air. Did you not, Jack?"[2]

Jack. "Yes, that I did. And she has left a terrible stink of brimstone behind. Don't you all smell it?"

All. "Smell it! aye to be sure; do you think we have no noses?"

Captain Shore was in a great passion. He told them "they were mutineers, and, he supposed, wanted to run away with the ship." To this they replied,

"No, no, captain, though we don't like the devil's company, we are honest fellows; we don't want to run away with the ship; that would be going to the devil another way, and I warrant he would trim us for using his lady so ill. You are our captain, and we will take you on board, if you please; but Mr. Winkfield is only a passenger, and we are not obliged to take him."

Finding there was no good to be done with them, I whispered the captain that I would stay on shore all night, at all events; but desired he would come to me in the morning, and let me know if he had brought them to reason. However, as I had not spoken to the sailors, I was willing to try what I could do with them. "Gentlemen," said I, "you are really under a great mistake; that gentlewoman, whom you call a she-devil, is my cousin. She was three years ago left upon this island by a rogue of a captain, who ran away with her ship."

---

1 Baine (50-51) surveys Defoe's beliefs on devils and she-devils in particular.

2 Although this paragraph begins in Mr. Winkfield's own voice, by this point he is speaking in the voice of sailors. The dialogue that follows does not always distinguish clearly between John Winkfield's voice and the voices of others whose speech he is recounting for Unca Winkfield. It must therefore be read as a kind of dialogue within a dialogue.

Sailor. "Well, Sir, if she is not a devil, I suppose she is a witch, and that is as bad; and that made the captain set her on shore. And pray was that tall monster who sung and played upon the bag-pipes your cousin too? You know, Sir, we heard him play ourselves, and the devil could not play louder."

Mr. *Winkfield.* "I was confounded at this question, not knowing myself how to account for what I had heard. They saw my confusion, and laughed: I therefore once more told the captain I would leave them, and hoped to see him in the morning. So we shook hands, and parted; he looking at me with great concern. I remembered you said, you should not leave this place till night. I was therefore walking up to the statue, in order to wait there some time, in hopes of seeing you thereabouts; if not, I intended walking up and down in quest of you; but as I was going thither, I had the pleasure of hearing you call me."

Unca. "I am very glad you found me so soon, for the sun is declining apace; and if you had missed me you would have passed an uneasy night. For though there is here nothing to hurt you, you could not know that. But as we have done eating, let us go down to the sea-side, where a canoe will soon be ready to carry us where you shall pass the night in safety. In the morning we will return here, and I hope we shall see the captain, and hear that matters are made up on board. And as I suppose you are impatient to know what has happened to me since I was put upon this island, and to know the meaning of the extraordinary things that you have seen and heard, I will inform you as we go along."

CHAP. IX.

They return in the morning to see whether the captain had brought the crew to obedience; but find they had forced him to sail back to Europe.

WE now walked down to the sea-side, where two Indians waited with my canoe. They seemed surprised at the appearance of a stranger, especially of a white man, as having never seen one before. I quickly spoke chearfully, and told them, that he was a relation of mine, who was come to see me. They seemed very well satisfied, and asked no questions, as they were used to pay an implicit regard to every thing I said. During our short voyage I made a brief relation of every thing that had befallen me from my first being put upon the island to the time of my cousin's arrival. He listened with an attention little short of astonishment.

"What a series," cried he, "of amazing providences! I will learn their language, and end my days in carrying on the great work you have so wonderfully begun amongst them; for never shall I be able so successfully to fulfil the duties of my function as among a plain, uncorrupted, honest people as these I find are; for since I saw you, Unca, I have entered into holy orders."

Unca. "The novelty of what you have heard, has heated your imagination, and hurried you into a resolution, that in your calmer moments you will retract. Besides, what will your parents say to their only son's becoming a voluntary exile?"

Mr. *Winkfield.* "They are too good to oppose so pious a resolve. What a glorious harvest do I see! I will return, and ask their leave. I know I shall obtain it. And then I shall have but one thing more to ask, and that is, Unca's hand for ever, in return for my heart, which she has long had—What says my dear cousin?"[1]

Unca. "That we must land," returned I, very gravely, "for we are upon the shore, and the Indians waiting for us."

I saw he was chagrined at this unexpected answer so foreign to his question; when, rising up, I gave him my hand to conduct me on shore, which he squeezed, as if he meant to punish it for the mortification my tongue had given him. It was a fine moon-

---

1 Robinson Crusoe's eventual marriage is referred to in Appendix C3, p. 229. Earlier castaway narratives tended to conclude not with marriage, but with continued isolation (see Appendices B1, pp. 184–85 and B4, pp. 202–03).

light night, and there were a great many Indians waiting for my return. Seeing a stranger with me, they looked as if in doubt or fear, whether they should come up to me as usual. Perceiving their condition, I called to them with that air of affability with which I always spoke to them, telling them I had brought a relation with me, who had come a great way to see me.

Their usual joy at my presence now revived, and they came up to us, shewing my cousin the same respect commonly paid to me. They attended us to my hut. I desired two of the priests to sup with us, that no offence might be given by being alone with a man: though such was the chaste simplicity of their manners, and their high opinion of me, that I believe the precaution was unnecessary; for suspicion reigns most in guilty hearts, and chiefly with regard to those we think meanly of. My cousin was pleased with his repast, though but the second time he had ever partaken of such kinds of provisions. The priests, who had learned a little English of me, were mightily pleased whenever they understood a word that my cousin said, and most highly so as often as they could make themselves understood. When it was time to go to rest, the priests took care to provide a proper place for my cousin.

We were up the next day very early, breakfasted, and then set out for the island. During our voyage, the night before, I was the chief speaker; but now, in his turn, my cousin briefly told me how he came to know where I was; of which hereafter.

Nor did he omit any opportunity in the course of his narration to give me to understand, that he had all along preserved that affection for me that he had formerly professed. But as often as he dropped such expressions, I took care to show no particular regard to them, but only a general attention to the thread of his discourse.

When we had reached the island I ordered the Indians not to return as usual, not knowing what sudden occasion I might have for them; but strictly charged them not to advance a foot forward into the island, nor to row to any other part of it. My cousin and I now crossed the island to the place where we expected the boat to come to. We sat and walked up and down here, by turns, till noon, but saw no boat. We then took some of the provisions we had brought, and dined. In short, we passed the whole afternoon, till it was time to think of returning home, without seeing any signs of a boat: we therefore feared the crew had mutinied, and run away with the ship, and may be murdered the captain and the other passengers; at least, that they would not suffer the captain to come on shore again. The evening being far advanced, we were obliged to return home, not a little chagrined at our disappointment.

My concern, indeed, arose upon my cousin's account, for had the ship arrived I would not have gone away in it, being determined to live and die amongst my dear Indians.[1] Nor, indeed, was it his intention to have gone home in her, but to have sent word to his parents that he had found me, and was determined to live and die with me; which, however, as often as he mentioned it, I most strongly opposed.

My cousin insisted upon his going without me the next morning, to which I was forced to agree; but was greatly surprised to see him return before noon. "What means this quick return?" cried I; "I cannot conjecture the occasion."

Mr. *Winkfield*. "It seems," said he, "as if providence, though by a somewhat adverse stroke, designs that I shall carry my resolution to teach the Indians into practice, and spend my days with my dear Unca, whether she will or no; for as I drew near, this morning, to the part of the shore where we yesterday waited for the boat, I saw, as I thought, several chests, and casks, and such, indeed, they were: and when I came up to them, I beheld a stick fixed in the ground, to the top of which was tied a letter. This I took, and found it directed to me. Here it is.

"Sir,
"I solemnly assure you, that I have done every thing in my power, both by threats and promises, to induce the crew to let me fetch you on board; but in vain: so deeply has Mr. Locke's foolish reports wrought upon their superstitious minds; for which indeed he is now very sorry. All that I can obtain is, that they will carry all your goods, and put them on shore by break of day, to-morrow, provided they see nothing of your cousin, as I hope they will not, and that you may at least have your goods, which no doubt you will want. As the men were only hired to come here, they insist upon returning to Europe. Please God I arrive safe there, I will give your father and mother the best account I

---

1 Compare to the fate of Crusoe's island and its inhabitants; see Appendix C3, p. 228.

can. As your cousin has found means of subsisting, I hope you will too. I intend to come again in search of you next year; for it will be impossible to come sooner. I remember your cousin said her residence was on another island, where I suppose you will live also.

"If I am so happy as to live to come again, I will set up an high pole, in some conspicuous part of the island with a streamer; so that if you come from time to time to look for me, you will be sure to know when I am arrived; but you must not expect me much short of a year hence. But as I know not at what part of the island I may be obliged to cast anchor, or at what distance from it, when I arrive, I will place a small piece of cannon on the shore nearest to where the ship may lie, that if you come whilst we are on board, you may by firing it, give notice of your being upon the island. I most heartily wish your cousin and you health and happiness, and hope we shall meet again; nor to that end shall any thing be wanting that may be in the power of,

Sir, &c. &c."

I was heartily sorry at reading of this; but my cousin smiled, and said he should now live with me whether I would, or not. "I am," added he, "only uneasy for my father and mother; but I know when they are assured that you are living, and that we are together, their concern will be greatly lessened, and they will comfort themselves with the pleasing hope of hearing of us both next year. And it is in your power, my dear Unca, greatly to add to their pleasure, by enabling me to acquaint them, that you have become their daughter. Let us then be united in the glorious work you have begun; teach me the Indian language, and I will join the glorious task you have commenced, and tread, with you, the path that leads to glory and happiness by well doing. One motive for my seeking you was, that, if we should meet, we might be for ever united. Consider one thing more, that if you refuse me, we cannot enjoy those hours of privacy together, I at least shall wish for, without offence to those around us; at least I know your delicacy will be hurt by them."

This last remark had some weight with me, yet I declined a direct answer; for though I loved him as a friend and relation, I had never considered him as a lover; nor any other person. It appeared to me, indeed, as if it must be as he would have it, yet the reflection gave me no pleasure; for though the Indians, I believed, would not entertain any ill suspicions of my conduct, yet I could not satisfy myself with the reflection of being much alone with a man, as it hurt my modesty. However, postponing the matter for further consideration, my immediate care was to provide a sufficient number of canoes, the largest that could be got, to fetch my cousin's baggage.[1]

---

1 Martha Rattenberg, who eventually marries her fellow castaway James Dubourdieu, similarly resists his proposal before agreeing to it (see Appendix D1, p. 235–36).

CHAP. X.

Embark their effects for the inhabited island. Mr. Winkfield marries his cousin, and proceeds in the work of conversion. He relates by what means he came to the knowledge of her being in that part of the world.

No, boy

THE next morning my cousin set out with a sufficient number of canoes, and brought all his things over. Besides a proper stock of clothes for himself, and some useful books, he had, as if certain of finding me living, and the naked inhabitant of a desolate island, brought over apparel for me. The linen indeed was very acceptable to me, as I now began to be in great want of it.

I was very much pleased to see a basket with about a dozen live fowls, cocks and hens; with these the island was soon stocked, and were very pleasing to the Indians, who had never seen any before. But what were these to the many other things the Indians had never seen before, at which they wondered, and were delighted with? a gun and the surprising effects of gunpowder, a telescope, and many other European curiosities, and without which indeed they were sufficiently happy![1] However, the sight of these raised in them an high opinion of my cousin, next to that they had for me.

I passed my time happily enough, before my cousin's arrival, but more so afterwards; for from his presence I enjoyed a new advantage. We now had divine service every Lord's day; which my cousin performed in English, and I was interpreter, till he had learned the Indian language, which he did much sooner than could have been well expected; and at last preached in the Indian tongue. I had now the great pleasure of once more enjoying all the ordinances of the church, and the constant company of a religious and sensible companion, to whom, through his constant importunity, I was at last obliged to give my hand, about two months after his arrival.[2] We first married ourselves according to

---

1 See Appendix A1, p. 164. This novel ascribes a kind of nostalgic dimension to the Indians' existence prior to their encounter with European technology that is not present in the original sources and that reflects the emergence of primitivism, romanticism, and the figure of the noble savage.

2 The anti-romantic character of the Winkfields' marriage bears contrasting to contemporaneous English novels such as Richardson's *Pamela* (1740). The double ceremony, performed in two religious traditions, resembles that of her parents and also that of Martha Rattenberg and James Dubourdieu (Appendix D1, p. 236).

the church rites, the high-priest acting as father, who died about a week after. We were also married according to the custom of the Indians, that they might the more perfectly be satisfied, their form having nothing in it contrary to our religion.

From the time of my cousin's settling here, or rather my husband, as I must now for the future call him, the Indians were properly baptized, married, and many of them, at their earnest desire, admitted to the Lord's supper. My husband and I spent much of our time in teaching the christian religion to the children; he the boys and I the girls; so that, what with catechising, and his preaching twice a week, we had greatly the appearance of a christian country. The natural simplicity and purity of the Indian manners greatly accelerated this work.

Being now more at leisure, I desired my husband to recount to me at large, what he had at first but briefly told me of, concerning his learning where I was, and of the captain who had robbed me, and set me on the uninhabited island. It was thus:

"There came one day," said my husband, "a sea-faring man to my father, who enquired of him if he had not a niece at Virginia of the same name with himself. To this my father replied, that he had a brother, and niece, at that place, if they were not come away, for that he had expected them some months, his brother having sent over great part of his effects, which he had received, and who had informed him by letter, that he and his daughter would soon follow; but, added he, do you, Sir, know any thing of them?"[1]

"Yes, Sir," replied the stranger: "your brother, I am sorry to inform you, died just as he was about to set out for England."

Mr. *Winkfield senior.* "I am very much concerned to hear of my dear brother's death—But as to my niece, does she intend to come over to England, or to continue there? perhaps she has sent you with orders concerning her effects."

Stranger. "As to your niece, I do not come from her. I never was at Virginia in my life, nor did I ever see her: yet I have some

---

1 Again, Winkfield Jr.'s account of previous events is presented as a series of dialogues within a dialogue that makes it difficult to distinguish speakers from each other. In the following account, John Winkfield Jr. tells a story heard by his father, the minister Winkfield Sr., who tells a story told by an unnamed stranger who is the captain of a merchant ship, who tells a story told by a pirate, who is revealed to be Captain Shore.

news to acquaint you with concerning her; but which I am sorry to say will give you much concern."

Mr. *Winkfield senior.* "Indeed, after hearing of the death of my brother, I shall be still farther grieved to hear of any affliction that may have befallen my dear niece but God's will be done: pray let me hear it, whatever it is."

Stranger. "I shall be ready to give you all the information that I can about her. But as I cannot do so in a few words, I must beg your patience, whilst I relate to you circumstantially all the particulars that I know.

"I am, Sir, a captain of a merchant-ship. As we were sailing from the West-Indies for this my native country, we met with a sail, which fired a gun for us to bring to. This alarmed us; for as it was a time of peace, I feared it might be a pirate, as indeed it proved; but happily one from whom we received not the least injury, as you will hear.

"We were, in no wise, capable of defending ourselves, the pirate being a ship of force: we, therefore, were obliged to suffer them to come a-board us. As soon as the captain got upon deck, he addressed himself to me in these words:"

Pirate. "Be not alarmed: I am, indeed, a pirate, but design no hurt to you. I come on board only to ask a favour, which you can easily grant, if you, as I see you are my countryman, are bound to England; if not, I will return to my own ship, and leave you unmolested to pursue your own course."

Merchant Captain. "I am bound, Sir, for England, and if I can render you any service there, will readily and faithfully do it."

Pirate. "If you please, I will go into your cabin with you, and there open my business more fully."

Merchant Captain. "According to his request, captain Shore, (for that he told me was his name) and his mate, and I, retired into my cabin, when he soon resumed his discourse in this manner."

Captain *Shore.* "I was a few years ago, as I find you are, a merchant captain; but having very bad success, I proposed to my mate, here, to turn pirate, to which he consenting, we broke our intentions to the crew, who too readily agreed to our proposal. However, we all resolved never to commit a murder, and rather quit our prey than kill any, if we could not otherwise get master of them: and this resolution we have happily kept to this moment. We have been very successful in our robberies. But not daring to put into any port in these parts, and as little to return to England, we sought for, and found, a small uninhabited island, where we stored our treasures, and at times resided. This was very privately situated, and where we were in no danger of being discovered, and lay very convenient to put to sea from, and retreat to, as we saw occasion.

"The last prize we made was in this manner. Discovering a small ship, we, as usual, made what sail we could till we came pretty near to her, and then fired a gun for her to bring to. As she was a ship of no force, and we had our guns out ready to fire upon her, she immediately surrendered. As soon as we came on board, we saw an Indian hanging up alive, and bleeding at the yard-arm. I asked the captain the meaning of this cruel treatment. He replied, that he was a very wicked fellow, and had thrown him over-board, and that he and five others of his countrymen had conspired to murder all the crew, and run away with the ship; but that he and his men had overpowered and killed the five others. Though this seemed very plausible, such things often happening at sea, yet I could not help observing a confusion in the countenance of the captain, which destroyed the credit of his story. Naturally abhorring cruelty, and suspecting something bad, I ordered the Indian to be immediately taken down, and his wounds to be dressed. Being determined to make what enquiry I could into this affair, I ordered the captain, and the poor Indian to be carried, for indeed he could not walk, to go down into the cabin with me and my mate: and here a dismal scene presented! the floor and wainscot of the cabin all smeared with blood, and two female Indians wounded and bleeding, who seemed to start with horror at the sight of the captain. Having imposed silence on the captain, I ordered the women to give me an account of what had happened, which, as well as their fright and weakness would permit, they did; and the poor Indian, in a few words, not being able to speak much, confirmed what the women had said: but the captain absolutely denied their relation, and appealed to the crew, who confirmed his denial.

"But suspecting the captain to be guilty"—

Here Mr. Winkfield senior interrupted him somewhat peevishly. "Pardon me, Sir," cried he, "you are very prolix. I am confounded, and want to know what all this has to do with my niece; the part of the world, the slaves alarm me; let me know the worst at once: was my niece murdered, Sir, on board this ship?"

Merchant Captain. "No, Sir, she was not, and may be yet living for ought I know to the contrary."

Mr. *Winkfield senior.* "*May be yet living!* you talk mysteriously. I thought you came to tell me news about her, and you only say *she may be yet living*—I abhor suspense; if you know anything concerning her, tell it me at once."

Mr. *Winkfield junior.* "Honoured Sir, don't be in such a hurry, you will offend the gentleman, and we may never come to the perfect knowledge of this affair."[1]

Merchant Captain. "Sir I take no offence, I attribute your father's interruption to his concern for his niece, but cannot give him the information he wants, except in the manner I was going to do it. If it be agreeable, I will proceed."

Mr. *Winkfield senior.* "I am of a warm temper, Sir, the subject is very interesting, and in affection I know no difference between my niece and my daughter; I hope therefore you will excuse my rude interruption, and be pleased to proceed in your own way."

Merchant Captain. "I am satisfied. I left off I think, with saying that notwithstanding the captain's denial of what the Indians accused him of, and though backed by his crew, that captain Shore still thought him guilty."

Mr. *Winkfield senior.* "You did, good Sir, what am I next to hear? poor Unca!"

Merchant Captain. "I was determined, said captain Shore, to come to the bottom of this affair, and therefore made every inquiry that I could. The account the Indians gave me was this, that their mistress's name was Unca Eliza Winkfield; that her father, a very rich man, had lately died at Virginia; that she was coming over to England to an uncle, her father's brother, a clergyman; that she had great riches on board the ship; and that the ship also was her's, which she had promised to give upon her arrival in England to the captain, who took care of it for her, and who was a poor broken man; that the captain would have forced her to sign a bond, to marry his son upon their arrival in England, where he lived; that upon her absolute refusal to sign this bond, he threatened to put her upon some uninhabited island. Saying this in the hearing of her male-slaves, who loved

---

1 Here Winkfield Jr. is recounting his own words delivered in the earlier context of the conversation between his father and the merchant captain.

her dearly, he who had been hanged up at the yard-arm, and another, threw the captain out of the cabin window into the sea; but that swimming to the ship, he was taken up again, when at the head of his men he came into the cabin, murdered five of the male Indians, and hung the sixth up at the yard-arm, intending there to let him die; and then put their mistress upon a desolate island, and was proceeding to sail away with the ship and all their mistress's effects."

the Story Summed up

CHAP. XI.

Continues his relation. Some account of captain Shore, who resolves to leave off his piratical practices.

"Having heard this relation," continued captain Shore, "I immediately searched among the goods on board, and found sufficient proofs that they belonged to Mrs. Winkfield.

"However, I was determined, if possible, to make the captain confess his guilt: looking therefore very sternly, I gave orders that my men should take and hang him up at the yard-arm, where the poor Indian had lately hung, and there to remain till he should confess his crime, or die; when he, seeing my command was going to be carried into execution, immediately acknowledged his crime, and, falling down at my feet, besought my pardon. No, cried I, if the innocent could find no mercy, the guilty shall not. You was[1] deaf to the cries of the injured Mrs. Winkfield, and I will be deaf to yours; you shall be hanged.

"At the instant I uttered this command these words of Scripture came strong upon my mind, suddenly like lightning, *Thou are inexcusable, O man, whosoever thou art, that judgest: for wherein thou judgest another, thou condemnest thyself for thou that judgest doest the same things. And thinkest thou this, that thou shalt escape the judgment of God?*[2] I was so sensibly struck with these words, that I started up, as in a fright, from my seat. What, cried I to myself, am I doing? is such a wicked wretch as I am a proper person to set in judgment upon another? I have not murdered indeed, but how many robberies have I not committed? My heart was changed, as it were in a moment, I saw my own wickedness, abhorred myself, and repented. But concealing my confusion, as well as I could, from those about me, I turned about to the captain, and said, I will not take upon myself to execute the sentence upon you that your crimes deserve; but I will take care to have you and your men sent to England, there to be tried by the laws of your own country.

"I then ordered that he should be secured, and all his men, and to make the best of our way with both ships to our island. When we arrived there, I ordered all possible care to be taken

---

1 Were.
2 Romans 2:1-3.

of the three Indians. But the poor Indian who had been hung up, died in a few days. Whilst he lived, he greatly lamented the fate of his mistress, and almost his last words were, *Pray hang the wicked captain.* As to the females they soon recovered, their wounds being but slight.

"The day after we reached our island, I told my mate what had passed in my mind the day before; and that I was determined to leave off the evil course I had unhappily engaged in, at all events. He seemed much affected with what I said, and, after pausing some time, answered, But how shall we be able to extricate ourselves? Where go to live with safety?

"To this I replied, that I was determined to save my soul, if I could not my body, and would sooner get, by some means or other, to England and be hanged, than continue the life I had led. For I considered the words that came into my mind yesterday as no less than the words of God. To this my mate replied, I am not a little affected with what happened to you yesterday, and do pray that I may be enabled to follow you in so good a resolution; and may God give to us both, *a repentance not to be repented of.* But what shall we do with our men?[1]

"I answered, I have not been without my thoughts concerning them. You know they all love me much, and are not such wicked men as most of their profession commonly are. And I have at times heard them lament their long absence from their families, and now and then express some dislike at the unhappy way they are in. I intend therefore to talk to them, and to propose a way by which possibly we may all obtain our pardon, and return again to our own country.

"Accordingly the same evening I called them all together, and, my mate being present, thus addressed them:

"My dear countrymen!
"I once was so unhappy, and so wicked, as to persuade you to join with me in the evil course, which we have but too successfully followed for some years. What distress, by our robberies, have we brought upon many innocent persons? But how much greater distress will come upon us, unless we most seriously repent of our sins? You know what happened, yesterday, on board the ship,

---

1 Cf. Appendix C3, p. 228, in which Crusoe leaves several criminals behind on his island.

we took. Whilst I was, in presence of some of you, reproving that wicked man, my own conscience smote me with these words of holy writ, *Thou are inexcusable, O man, whosoever thou art, that judgest: for wherein thou judgest another, thou condemnest thyself: for thou that judgest doest the same things. And thinkest thou this, that thou shalt escape the judgment of God?*

"From that moment it was, I hope, given me to repent, and I am determined to break off my sins, let the event be what it will. As I once led you into the ways of sin, happy should I be, if I might recover you to the paths of virtue. Consider, though we have hitherto escaped the vengeance of man, we cannot escape that of God. Nor, indeed, can we in all probability, to the end, escape the justice of man. The wretch who yesterday no doubt gloried in his success over an innocent, helpless woman, before night fell into our hands, and has lost his liberty, and the riches for which he damned his soul. Let his fate be a warning to us before the like befalls us: I have thought of a method by which we may very probably escape the punishment due to our crimes, do a noble piece of justice, and have an opportunity, if God shall please to bless it, to repent.

"It is to keep the prisoners we took yesterday close confined on board their own ship, and to secure that and the treasure in it, and to draw up the whole account of this affair to send it to the injured lady's uncle in England, acquainting him that if he will apply to king James, and procure a pardon for us, that we may return to England, upon condition that we bring the captain and all his crew there, that they may suffer for their crimes, and deliver up to the lady's uncle the ship and all effects on board. This no doubt will be complied with. To carry this scheme into execution, is to stop the first small ship that we may meet with going to England; I will tell the captain our situation, and desire him to take me on board, and set me down on the coast of Holland or France, as maybe most convenient, where I may wait in safety, whilst he carries my letters to England, and till I can receive the conditional pardon and a passport for myself and you to return to England in a convenient limited time; which, as soon as I receive, I will hire a small sailing-vessel, and make what haste I can to you, that we may once more see our native country. As we have always divided among ourselves what we have taken, if I reach England, I will publish my return, with an offer to restore the effects I have unjustly taken, to such persons as can satisfy me that I robbed them, though I should have nothing left. For if I don't do so, I shall doubt the sincerity of my own repentance; for there can be no true repentance without restitution. As to you, I must leave it to your own consciences, whether you will follow my example, or not. But God grant you may! Consider what I have said, and may God direct you, and tomorrow give me your answer.[1]

"They accordingly came to me the next morning, when they all expressed their hearty consent to my proposal. Though I could not but observe, that this unanimity of opinion proceeded from different motives; in some it arose only from fear of being caught and hanged, in others, from a desire of enjoying their ill gotten wealth: but I had the pleasure to find that a few were touched with what I had said, and seemed to manifest signs of repentance.

"I answered, that since they were come to this resolution, our immediate business was to watch for the opportunity, and that when it offered, I told them, that they must be sure to continue upon the island till I should return, unless I staid so long as to give them good reason to conclude, that some accident had happened to me. This they all most solemnly promised to do.

"And now, Sir, said captain Shore, speaking still to me,[2] the wished-for opportunity offers, if you please to afford it; but I lay you under no restraint; for though I wish you may grant my desire, you are at your liberty. If you have any reason to object to it, you are welcome to pursue your voyage in peace and safety; for I will not offer the least injury to you, or any with you."

"For my part, answered I, I am very ready to give you all the assistance in my power, towards carrying so good a resolution into action, and as I have some business to transact upon the coast of France, I can very conveniently land you there, and when I arrive in England will diligently and faithfully execute what commission you shall please to give me."

"Well then," replied captain Shore, "I will go on board my

---

1 Captain Shore's speech to his crew concludes here; with the following paragraph we return to his conversation with the merchant captain, who of course is telling this story to the Winkfields in England.
2 The "me" here is the merchant captain.

own ship, and get together such things as I want, and return to you, that we may proceed upon our voyage. In the mean time, Sir, in order to remove any bad impressions that your crew may have conceived of me, be pleased to inform them that I did not stop you as a pirate, but only to request the favour of a passage to France. I promised I would do so;[1] and accordingly did; and they were all well satisfied.

"As soon as captain Shore returned on board with his baggage, we set sail, and when we arrived upon the coast of France, I there left him, and, being myself[2] returned safe to England, have waited on you. And here, Sir, continued the strange captain to my[3] father, is a letter from captain Shore to you, bills of parcels of the goods on board your niece's ship, and some other papers belonging to your niece."

Story within a story

---

1 The "I" of this sentence is the merchant captain; the "I" of the previous sentences in this paragraph is Captain Shore.
2 This "myself" is the merchant captain.
3 This "my" is Winkfield Jr., although the sentence he is recounting here is in the voice of the merchant captain.

CHAP. XII.

After captain Shore had obtained a pardon for himself and crew, he returns in search of Mrs. Winkfield. Fate of the captain who left her on the uninhabited island. They resolve to settle their affairs in England, and live with the Indians. Conclusion.

"My father and I heard this wonderful relation with great attention and surprise; but still mourned for you, my dear Unca, being ignorant of your fate. However, we proceeded to bring the captain to justice. The case was laid before the king and council, together with captain Shore's petition, on behalf of himself and people. I got the conditional pardon granted, having three years allowed to bring home the ship and crew, with a proper passport.

"As soon as captain Shore received notice of this, he came home to England, in order to hire a ship to carry him back to his people.

"Whilst he was making the proper preparations for his voyage, we were much together. I asked him, as he was well acquainted with those parts where my cousin had been left upon some island or other thereabouts, whether he thought it improbable to discover the island.

"He answered, I know those parts extremely well, and I doubt not, that if the captain[1] will give me the best account of the situation of the island that he can, but that I should be able to find it out.[2] This gave me great pleasure. Well then, said I, if my father and mother will give their consent, I will go along with you in quest of her.

"It is not impossible, added I; but she may be yet living. I have read of as surprising deliverances; at the worst we may find her bones, and pay the last honours to her dear unhappy memory: and here, my dear Unca, I wept indeed!

"My father and mother consented with pleasure, and as soon as every thing was settled, and ready, we sailed. We had a speedy and prosperous voyage to the captain's island; where

---

1   I.e., the captain who abandoned Unca Eliza Winkfield and whom Shore hung from the yard-arm.

2   The "I" of this sentence is Shore; the "me" and "I" of the following two sentences are spoken by Winkfield Jr.

he and the pardon he brought were highly welcome. I there saw the wicked captain, who robbed you. He gave captain Shore a very clear account of the situation of your island. We staid here no longer than till your ship and the captain's were ready to sail for England with your treasure, and the prisoners all under his mate's command. We promised to follow them soon, to our native country. We then set sail for your island, and happily discovered it; but, what was a much happier discovery, found you alive and well."

Thus my husband ended his extraordinary relation;[1] full of a wonderful series of providences. At length the time arrived to expect the return of captain Shore; and now my husband went twice every week over to the island for three months; but no appearance of any ship. But at last as he approached the shore one morning, he saw a streamer playing in the air; he knew the signal, and rejoiced. But walking to the place where he first landed out of the ship that brought him, he saw no cannon, nor any body upon the island; he continued walking along the shore, yet saw no ship. At last he spied a cannon; having always a tinder-box ready about him for the expected occasion, he struck a light, and fired the cannon. It was not long before he saw a boat making for the shore, and soon discovered that captain Shore was one of the company. They were very glad to see each other. It seems captain Shore had arrived but the day before, when he set up the flag, and having waited all day, left the cannon ready charged before he returned on board. My husband went on board the captain's ship, and dined with him, when they agreed that captain Shore should come with my husband to our island, and spend three days with us. We[2] were both very glad to hear that our father and mother were all well, and our sisters. We desired captain Shore to relate the particulars that had happened from the time he left the island, which he did, as follows:

Captain Shore. "I shall pass over the unimportant accidents that occurred during our voyage. Upon our arrival in England, I found all your family well. They were amazingly surprised to hear of Mrs. Winkfield's being alive. And the thought of your

---

1 Here the text returns to the first-person narrative of its heroine.
2 The narration here shifts to the plural first person; it does not revert again to the singular first person of Unca Eliza Winkfield until the final paragraph of the text.

being together made them easy as to their not seeing their son again with me, as they expected. But when I told them of the strange things that I had seen and heard on the island, they were confounded. I know not, said your father, what to make of these things; they exceed human comprehension. Surely your fears and surprise made you to imagine things to exist that really did not. May be so, returned I, willing to drop a subject, that I myself did not understand, and which if insisted on, might have given great uneasiness.

"I should have returned much sooner here, continued captain Shore; but as my ship, and Mrs. Winkfield's were both arrived a week before me, I was obliged to stay till the cargoes were landed, and what belonged to Mrs. Winkfield committed to your father's care.[1] Besides, I was obliged to attend the trial of the captain and the crew, who were found guilty upon their own confession.[2] The captain, and three of his men, were hanged at Execution-Dock, and afterwards hung in chains; the rest of the crew were transported for life.[3] As soon as this was over, I, and my men, took out our pardons in due form. They afterwards went where they pleased. Several persons, who I had robbed at sea brought in their claims, all which I fully answered. These things settled, I set out in Mrs. Winkfield's ship, and arrived safe at your first island."

In return to captain Shore's relation, we acquainted him with every thing that we had done in his absence, and satisfied his curiosity about the wonderful things that he had met with upon the island. When we had finished our account, the captain

---

1 Thus William Winkfield's New World fortunes, inherited from Unca Eliza's Indian mother, are transported to the Old World and into patriarchal hands. The economic fate of earlier castaways ranges from Crusoe's extraordinary wealth (Appendix C3, p. 229) to the explicit renunciation of any wealth or attachment to material possessions (see Appendix B5, p. 207 and Appendix D1, p. 237).

2 That is, the captain and crew who abandoned Unca Eliza Winkfield and killed or wounded her slaves.

3 Execution Dock, located in East Wapping, was one of several sites in and outside of London where hangings took place. The bodies of those convicted of particularly aggravated crimes were sometimes hung in chains for public display after they were executed. Criminals who escaped hanging were often transported, that is, banished to foreign lands and sentenced to indentured labor.

expressed great surprise and satisfaction at what had happened, and added, "Since what has befallen me, I shall not like to reside in England, nor any more to be concerned in worldly affairs; therefore if you think me a true convert, let me join in your society. We replied, that we had no doubt of his sincerity, and should be very glad of his company."

We now agreed captain Shore and my husband should return together to England, that my husband might take a final leave of his relations, receive his parents blessing, and settle half of his and my fortune upon his sisters, and leave the rest for charitable uses, and bring over such books and things as might be useful to us in our retirement. But we first determined to go upon my island, to collect all the gold treasure there, to blow up the subterraneous passage, and the statue, that the Indians might never be tempted to their former idolatry. When all this was done, and the golden treasure put on board, the captain and my husband set out upon their voyage.[1] They arrived safe in England, saw our father and mother, who consented to their son's request, and gave him their blessing. As soon as my husband had sold his golden treasure, and settled his affairs, and bought a large library of books, and many kinds of goods and linen, he and captain Shore once more returned to me. We ordered the sailors to unload their cargo upon my first island, and to leave us a large boat for the more convenient conveying our goods to the other island, where we lived. We did not suffer the sailors to come any farther upon the island, than just to land the goods, that no discovery of our habitation might be made. As we never intended to have any more to do with Europe, captain Shore and my husband ordered a person who came for that purpose, to return to Europe with the ship, by whom, for my father and mother's satisfaction, I sent over these adventures.

FINIS.[2]

---

1 This destruction and plunder is reminiscent of Cortés's conquest of Mexico. McDowell (309) suggests that the representation of Indians in *The Female American* combines North American with South American sources.

2 The 1767 London edition contains a final list of other titles sold by the printers of this novel.

Appendix A: The Colonial Americas and Its Native Peoples

[English writings about the colonial Americas depicted the struggles and possibilities of settlement in the New World and described its Native inhabitants. Thomas Harriot's *Briefe and True Report*—first published in 1588 (but reprinted in 1590 with engravings by Theodore de Bry)—provided detailed descriptions of southern Algonquin religious practice and the region's potential commodities. George Percy's narrative of the group of Virginia settlers led by Edward Maria Wingfield indicates the difficulties faced by the English and their dependence on the Native Americans. Although Wingfield wrote his own account of the disputes that afflicted the group and led to his overthrow, his "Discourse" did not appear in print until 1845, while Percy's 1606 "Discourse" was included in Samuel Purchas's widely circulated travelogue *Hakluytus Posthumous; or Purchas His Pilgrimes* (1625). John Smith gained recognition in England as the author of a number of travel narratives, the most famous of which was his *Generall History of Virginia* (1624). This account contained his last and most elaborate version of the Pocahontas story, as well as descriptions of Algonquian culture, politics, and religion. Aphra Behn's novel *Oroonoko* (1688), set in Surinam, is the earliest novel in English about the Americas and emphasizes the prelapsarian innocence of the Native Americans and the corrupting effects of their contact with Europeans.]

1. From Thomas Harriot, *A Briefe and True Report of the New Found Land of Virginia*, drawings by Theodore de Bry, 1590

Some religion they haue alreadie, which although it be farre from the truth, yet beyng at[1] it is, there is hope it may bee the easier and sooner reformed.

They beleeue that there are many Gods which they call *Mantóac*, but of different sórtes and degrees; one onely chiefe

---

1 As.

and great God, which hath bene from all eternitie. Who as they affirme when hee purposed to make the worlde, made first other goddes of a principall order to bee as meanes and instruments to bee vsed in the creation and gouernment to follow; and after the Sunne, Moone, and Starres, as pettie goddes and the instruments of the other order more principall. First they say were made waters, out of which by the gods was made all diuersitie of creatures that are visible or inuisible....

They thinke that all the gods are of humane shape, & ther[e]fore they represent them by images in the formes of men, which they call *Kewasowok* one alone is called *Kewás*; Them they place in houses appropriate or temples which they call *Mathicómuck*; Where they woorship, praie, sing, and make manie times offerings vnto them. In some *Machicómuck* we haue seene but on[e] *Kewas*, in some two, and in other some three; The common sort thinke them to be also gods....

And this is the summe of their religion, which I learned by hauing special familiarity with some of their priestes. Wherein they were not so sure grounded, nor gaue such credite to their traditions and stories but through conuersing with vs they were brought into great doubts of their owne, and no small admiratiõ[1] of ours, with earnest desire in many, to learne more than we had meanes for want of perfect vtterance in their language to expresse.

Most things they sawe with vs, as Mathematicall instruments, sea compasses, the vertue of the loadstone in drawing yron, a perspectiue glasse whereby was shewed manie strange sightes, burning glasses, wildefire woorkes, gunnes, bookes, writing and reading, spring clocks that seeme to goe of themselues, and manie other thinges that wee had, were so straunge vnto them, and so farre exceeded their capacities to comprehend the reason and meanes how they should be made and done, that they thought they were rather the works of gods then of men, or at the leastwise they had bin giuen and taught vs of the gods. Which made manie of them to haue such opinion of vs, as that if they knew not the trueth of god and religion already, it was rather to be had from vs, whom God so specially loued then from a people that were so simple, as they found themselues to be in comparison of vs. Whereupon greater credite was giuen vnto that we spake of concerning such matters.

---

1 Admiration.

Manie times and in euery towne where I came, according as I was able, I made declaration of the contentes of the Bible; that therein was set foorth the true and onelie GOD, and his mightie woorkes, that therein was contayned the true doctrine of salutation through Christ, with manie particularities of Miracles and chiefe poyntes of religion, as I was able then to vtter, and thought fitte for the time. And although I told them the booke materially & of itself was not of anie such vertue, as I thought they did conceiue, but onely the doctrine therein cõtained;[1] yet would many be glad to touch it, to embrace it, to kisse it, to hold it to their bre[a]sts and heades, and stroke ouer all their bodie with it; to shewe their hungrie desire of that knowledge which was spoken of. (25-27)

XXI.
Ther Idol Kiwasa.

The people of this cuntrie haue an Idol, which they call KIWASA: yt[2] is carued of woode in lengthe 4. foote whose heade is like the heades of the people of Florida, the face is of a flesh colour, the brest white, the rest is all blacke, the thighes are also spottet with whitte. He hath a chayne abowt his necke of white beades, betweene which are other Rownde beades of copper which they esteeme more then golde or siluer. This Idol is placed in the temple of the towne of Secotam, as the ke[e]per of the kings dead corpses. Somtyme they haue two of thes[e] idoles in theyr churches, and somtine[3] 3. but never above, which they place in a darke corner wher they shew terrible. Thes poore soules haue none other knowledge of god although I thinke them verye Desirous to know the truthe. For when as wee kneeled downe on our knees to make our prayers vnto god, they went abowt to imitate vs, and when they saw we moued our lipps, they also dyd[4] the like. Wherfore that is verye like that they might easelye be brongt[5] to the knowledge of the gospel. God of his mercie grant them this grace.

---

1 Contained.
2 It.
3 Sometimes.
4 Did.
5 Brought.

"Ther Idol Kiwasa," engraving by Theodor de Bry from Thomas Harriot, *A Briefe and True Report of the New Found Land of Virginia*, 1590. Courtesy of the Library of Congress.

XXII.
The Tombe of their Werowans or Cheiff Lordes.

The[y] builde a Scaffolde 9. or 10. foote hihe as is expressed in this figure vnder the tõbs[1] of their Weroans, or cheefe lordes which they couer with matts, and lai the dead corpses of their weroans theruppon in manner followinge. First the bowells are taken forthe. Then layinge downe the skinne, they cutt all the flesh cleane from the bones, which the[y] drye in the sonne, and well dryed the[y] inclose in Matts, and place at their feete. Then their bones (remaininge still fastened together with the ligaments whole and vncorrupted) are couered a gayne with leather, and their carcase fashioned as yf their flesh wear not taken away. They lapp eache corps in his owne skinne after the same in thus handled, and lay yt in his order by the corpses of the other cheef lordes. By the dead bodies they sett their Idol Kiwasa, wher of we spake in the former chapiter: For they are persuaded that the same doth kepe the dead bodyes of their cheefe lordes that nothinge may hurt them. Moreouer vnder the foresaid scaffolde

---

1 Tombs.

some on[e] of their preists hath his lodginge, which Mumbleth his prayers nighte and day, and hath charge of the corpses. For his bedd he hath two deares skinnes spredd on the grownde, yf the we[a]ther bee cold hee maketh a fyre to warme by withall. Thes poore soules are thus instructed by nature to reuerence their princes euen after their death. (71-73)

The trwe picture of a women Picte II.[1]

The woemen of the pictes aboue said wear noe worser for the warres then the men. And wear paynted after the manner followinge, hauinge their heads bear, did lett their hairre flying. Abowt their Showlders wear painted with griffon heades, the lowe parts and thighes with lion faces, or some other beaste as yt commeth best into their fansye,[2] their brest hath a maner of a half moone, with a great stare,[3] and fowre[4] lesser in booth the sides, their pappes[5] painted in maner of beames of the sonne, and amõg[6] all this a great litteninge[7] starre vppon their brests. The saids[8] of som pointes or beames, and the hoolle bellye as a sonne, the armes, thighes, and leggs well painted, of diuerses Figures: The[y] dyd also carye abowt theyr necks an ayern[9] Ringe, as the men did, and suche a girdle with the soorde hainginge, hauinge a Picke or a lance in one hande, and twoe dardz in the other. (78)

2. From George Percy, "Percy's Discourse of Virginia," 1625

Captaine Newport being gone for England, leaving us (one hundred and foure persons) verie bare and scantie of victualls,

---

1 The second of two drawings of Picts. The first one depicted a man; this one depicts a woman with an ornately tattooed body and carrying spears and a sword.
2 Fancy.
3 Star.
4 Four.
5 Paps, or breasts.
6 Among.
7 Lightning.
8 Sides. Harriot is describing the tattooed designs of sunbeams on .the sides of women's bodies.
9 Iron.

furthermore in warres and in danger of the Savages. We hoped after a supply which Captaine Newport promised within twentie weekes. But if the beginners of this action doe carefully further us,[1] the Country being so fruitfull, it would be as great a profit to the Realme of England, as the Indies to the King of Spaine, if this River which wee have found had beene discovered in the time of warre with Spaine, it would have beene a commoditie to our Realme, and a great annoyance to our enemies. The seven and twentieth of July the King of Rapahanna, demanded a Canoa which was restored, lifted up his hand to the Sunne, which they worship as their God, besides he laid his hand on his heart, that he would be our speciall friend. It is a generall rule of these people when they swere by their God which is the Sunne, no Christian will keepe their Oath better upon this promise. These people have a great reverence to the Sunne above all other things at the rising and setting of the same, they sit downe lifting up their hands and eyes to the Sunne making a round Circle on the ground with dried Tobacco, then they began to pray making many Devillish gestures with a Hellish noise fo[a]ming at the mouth, staring with their eyes, wagging their heads and hands in such a fashion and deformitie as it was monstrous to behold....

The fourth day of September died Thomas Jacob Sergeant. The fift[h] day, there died Benjamin Beast. Our men were destroyed with cruell diseases as Swellings, Fluxes, Burning Fevers, and by warres, and some departed suddenly, but for the most part they died of meere famine. There were never Englishmen left in a forreigne Countrey in such miserie as wee were in this new discovered Virginia. Wee watched every three nights lying on the bare cold ground what weather soever came warded all the next day, which brought our men to bee most feeble wretches, our food was but a small Can of Barlie sod in water to five men a day, our drinke cold water taken out of the River, which was at a floud verie salt, at a low tide full of slime and filth, which was the destruction of many of our men. Thus we lived for the space of five moneths in this miserable distresse, not having five able men to man our Bulwarkes upon any occasion. If it had not pleased God to have put a terrour in the Savages hearts, we had all per-

---

1 Percy is urging those investors back in England ("the beginners of this action") to continue to fund and support ("further") the fledgling colony.

ished by those vild[1] and cruell Pagans, being in that weake estate as we were; our men night and day groaning in every corner of the Fort most pittifull to heare, if there were any conscience in men, it would make their harts to bleed to heare the pittiful murmurings & out-cries of our sick men without reliefe every night and day for the space of sixe weekes, some departing out of the World, many times three or foure in a night, in the morning their bodies trailed out of their Cabines like Dogges to be buried: in this sort did I see the mortalitie of divers of our people.

It pleased God, after a while, to send those people which were our mortall enemies to releeve us with victuals, as Bread, Corne, Fish, and Flesh in great plentie, which was the setting up of our feeble men, otherwise wee had all perished. Also we were frequented by divers Kings in the Countrie, bringing us store of provision to our great comfort.[2]

The eleventh day, there was certaine Articles laid against Master Wingfield which was then President, thereupon he was not only displaced out of his President ship, but also from being of the Councell. Afterwards Captain John Ratcliffe was chosen President....

William White (having lived with the Natives) reported to us of their customes in the morning by breake of day, before they eate or drinke both men, women and children, that be above tenne yeeres of age runnes into the water, there washes themselves a good while till the Sun riseth, then offer Sacrifice to it, strewing Tobacco on the water or land, honouring the Sunne as their God, likewise they doe at the setting of the Sunne. (416-19)

3. From John Smith, *The Generall Historie of Virginia*, 1624

The next day came divers[3] Boats, and in one of them the Kings Brother, with forty or fifty men, proper people, and in their behaviour very civill; his name was Granganameo, the King is called Wingina, the Country Wingandacoa. Leaving his Boats a little from our Ships, he came with his trayne to the poynt:

---

1 Wild.
2 Percy's account makes it clear how dependent the English settlers were for survival upon the Native Americans.
3 Diverse; various.

where spreading a Matte he sat downe. Though we came to him well armed, he made signes to us to sit downe without any shew of feare, stroking his head and brest, and also ours, to expresse his love. After he had made a long speech unto us, we presented him with divers toyes, which he kindly accepted. He was greatly regarded by his people, for none of them did sit, nor speake a word, but foure, on whom we bestowed presents also, but he tooke all from them, making signes all things did belong to him....

... my selfe with seaven more went twenty myle into the River Occam, that runneth toward the Cittie Skicoack, and the evening following we came to an Ile called Roanoak, from the harbour where we entred 7. leagues; at the North end was 9. houses, builded with Cedar, fortified round with sharpe trees, and the entrance like a Turnpik. When we came towards it, the wife of Granganameo came running out to meete us, (her husband was absent) commanding her people to draw our Boat ashore for beating on the billowes, other she appoynted to carry us on their backes aland, others to bring our Ores into the house for[1] stealing. When we came into the other roome, (for there was five in the house) she caused us to sit downe by a great fire; after tooke off our clothes and washed them, of some our stockings, and some our feete in warme water, and she her selfe tooke much paines to see all things well ordered, and to provide us victuall....

... This discovery was so welcome into England that it pleased her Majestie to call this Country of Wingandacoa, Virginia, by which name now you are to understand how it was planted, disolved, renued,[2] and enlarged.... (64-65, 66, 68)

There is yet in Virginia no place discovered to be so Savage, in which they have not a Religion, Deere, and Bow, and Arrowes. All things that are able to doe them hurt beyond their prevention, they adore with their kinde of divine worship; as the fire, water, lightning, thunder, our Ordnance, peeces,[3] horses, etc. But their chiefe God they worship is the Devill. Him they call *Okee,* and serve him more of feare then love. They say they have conference with him, and fashion themselves as neare to

---

1 In his edition of Smith, Barbour inserts [fear of] here (66).
2 Renewed.
3 Pieces, or weapons.

his shape as they can imagine. In their Temples they have his image evill favouredly carved, and then painted and adorned with chaines of copper, and beads, and covered with a skin, in such manner as the deformitie may well suit with such a God. By him is commonly the sepulcher of their Kings. Their bodies are first bowelled, then dried upon hurdles till they be very dry, and so about the most of their joynts and necke they hang bracelets, or chaines of copper, pearle, and such like, as they use to weare, their inwards they stuffe with copper beads, hatchets, and such trash. Then lappe they them very carefully in white skins, and so rowle them in mats for their winding sheets. And in the Tombe which is an arch made of mats, they lay them orderly. What remaineth of this kinde of wealth their Kings have, they set at their feet in baskets. These Temples and bodies are kept by their Priests....

Upon the top of certaine red sandy hils in the woods, there are three great houses filled with images of their Kings, and Devils, and Tombes of their Predecessors. Those houses are neare sixtie foot in length built arbour-wise, after their building. This place they count so holy as that but the Priests and Kings dare come into them; nor the Salvages dare not goe up the river in boats by it, but they solemnly cast some peece of copper, white beads, or *Pocones* into the river, for feare their *Okee* should be offended and revenged of them....

To divert them from this blind Idolatry, we did our best endevours, chiefly with the Werowance of Quiyoughcohanock, whose devotion, apprehension, and good disposition, much exceeded any in those Countries, who although we could not as yet prevaile, to forsake his false Gods, yet this he did beleeve that our God as much exceeded theirs, as our Gunnes did their Bowes and Arrowes, and many times did send to me to James Towne, intreating me to pray to my God for raine, for their Gods would not send them any. And in this lamentable ignorance doe these poore soules sacrifice themselves to the Devill, not knowing their Creator; and we had not language sufficient, so plainly to expresse it as make them understand it; which God grant they may.... (121-22, 125)

At last they brought him[1] to Meronocomoco, where was Powha-

---

1 Smith, taken captive, referring to himself in third person.

tan their Emperor. Here more then two hundred of those grim Courtiers stood wondering at him, as he had beene a monster; till Powhatan and his trayne had put themselves in their greatest braveries. Before a fire upon a seat like a bedsted, he sat covered with a great robe, made of Rarowcun[1] skinnes, and all the tayles hanging by. On either hand did sit a young wench of 16 or 18 yeares, and along on each side the house, two rowes of men, and behind them as many women, with all their heads and shoulders painted red; many of their heads bedecked with the white downe of Birds; but every one with something: and a great chayne of white beads about their necks. At his entrance before the King, all the people gave a great shout. The Queene of Appamatuck was appointed to bring him water to wash his hands, and another brought him a bunch of feathers, in stead of a Towell to dry them: having feasted him after their best barbarous manner they could, a long consultation was held, but the conclusion was, two great stones were brought before Powhatan: then as many as could layd hands on him, dragged him to them, and thereon laid his head, and being ready with their clubs, to beate out his braines, Pocahontas the Kings dearest daughter, when no intreaty could prevaile, got his head in her armes, and laid her owne upon his to save him from death: whereat the Emperour was contented he should live to make him hatchets, and her bells, beads, and copper; for they thought him as well of all occupations as themselves. For the King himselfe will make his owne robes, shooes, bowes, arrowes, pots; plant, hunt, or doe any thing so well as the rest....

Two dayes after, Powhatan having disguised himselfe in the most fearefullest manner he could, caused Captaine Smith to be brought forth to a great house in the woods, and there upon a mat by the fire to be left alone. Not long after from behinde a mat that divided the house, was made the most dolefullest noyse he ever heard; then Powhatan more like a devill then a man with some two hundred more as blacke as himselfe, came unto him and told him now they were friends, and presently he should goe to James towne, to send him two great gunnes, and a gryndstone, for which he would give him the Country of Capahowosick, and for ever esteeme him as his soone Nantaquoud. So to James towne with 12 guides Powhatan sent him. That night they quar-

---

1 Racoon.

terd in the woods, he still expecting (as he had done all this long time of his imprisonment) every houre to be put to one death or other: for all their feasting. But almightie God (by his divine providence) had mollified the hearts of those sterne Barbarians with compassion....

Powhatan and his Dutch-men brusting[1] with desire to have the head of Captaine Smith, for if they could but kill him, they thought all was theirs, neglected not any opportunity to effect his purpose. The Indians with all the merry sports they could devise, spent the time till night: then they all returned to Powhatan, who all this time was making ready his forces to surprise the house and him at supper. Notwithstanding the eternall all-seeing God did prevent him, and by a strange meanes. For Pocahontas his dearest jewell and daughter, in that darke night came through the irksome woods, and told our Captaine great cheare should be sent us by and by: but Powhatan and all the power he could make, would after come kill us all, if they that brought it could not kill us with our owne weapons when we were at supper. Therefore if we would live shee wished us presently to bee gone. Such things as shee delighted in, he would have given her: but with the teares running downe her cheekes, shee said shee durst not be seene to have any: for if Powhatan should know it, she were but dead, and so shee ranne away by her selfe as she came....

Long before this, Master John Rolfe, an honest Gentleman, and of good behaviour, had beene in love with Pocahontas, and she with him, which thing at that instant I made knowne to Sir Thomas Dale by a letter from him, wherein hee intreated his advice, and she acquainted her brother with it, which resolution Sir Thomas Dale well approved: the brute of this mariage came soone to the knowledge of Powhatan, a thing acceptable to him, as appeared by his sudden consent, for within ten daies he sent Opachisco, an old Uncle of hers, and two of his sons, to see the manner of the mariage, and to doe in that behalfe what they were requested, for the confirmation thereof, as his deputie; which was accordingly done about the first of Aprill: And ever since wee have had friendly trade and commerce, as well with Powhatan himself, as all his subjects....

I have read the substance of this relation, in a Letter written by Sir Thomas Dale, another by Master Whitaker, and a third

---

1 Bursting.

by Master John Rolfe; how carefull they were to instruct her in Christianity, and how capable and desirous shee was thereof, after she had beene some time thus tutored, shee never had desire to goe to her father, nor could well endure the society of her owne nation: the true affection she constantly bare her husband was much, and the strange apparitions and violent passions he endured for her love, as he deeply protested, was wonderful, and she openly renounced her countries idolatry, confessed the faith of Christ, and was baptized....

During this time, the Lady Rebecca, alias Pocahontas, daughter to Powhatan, by the diligent care of Master John Rolfe her husband and his friends, was taught to speake such English as might well bee understood, well instructed in Christianitie, and was become very formall and civill after our English manner; shee had also by him a childe which she loved most dearely, and the Treasurer and Company tooke order both for the maintenance of her and it, besides there were divers persons of great ranke and qualitie had beene very kinde to her; and before she arrived at London, Captaine Smith to deserve her former courtesies, made her qualities knowne to the Queenes most excellent Majestie and her Court, and writ a little booke to this effect to the Queene....

The small time I staid in London, divers Courtiers and others, my acquaintances, hath gone with mee to see her, that generally concluded, they did thinke God had a great hand in her conversion, and they have seene many English Ladies worse favoured, proportioned and behavioured, and as since I have heard, it pleased both the King and Queenes Majestie honourably to esteeme her, accompanied with that honourable Lady the Lady De la Ware, and that honourable Lord her husband, and divers other persons of good qualities, both publikely at the maskes and otherwise, to her great satisfaction and content, which doubtlesse she would have deserved, had she lived to arrive in Virginia.

The Treasurer, Councell and Companie, having well furnished Captaine Samuel Argall, the Lady Pocahontas alias Rebecca, with her husband and others, in the good ship called the *George*, it pleased God at Gravesend to take this young Lady to his mercie, where shee made not more sorrow for her unexpected death, than joy to the beholders, to heare and see her make so religious and godly an end. Her little childe Thomas Rolfe therefore was left at Plimoth with Sir Lewis Stukly, that desired the keeping of it....

Having occasion to send to Opechankanough about the middle of March, hee used the Messenger well, and told him he held the peace so firme, the sky should fall or he dissolved it; yet such was the treachery of those people, when they had contrived our destruction, even but two daies before the massacre, they guided our men with much kindnesse thorow[1] the woods, and one Browne that lived among them to learne the language, they sent home to his Master; yea, they borrowed our Boats to transport themselves over the River, to consult on the devilish murder that issued, and of our utter extirpation, which God of his mercy (by the meanes of one of themselves converted to Christianitie) prevented, and as well on the Friday morning that fatall day, being the two and twentieth of March, as also in the evening before, as at other times they came unarmed into our houses, with Deere, Turkies, Fish, Fruits, and other provisions to sell us, yea in some places sat downe at breakfast with our people, whom immediately with their owne tooles they slew most barbarously, not sparing either age or sex, man woman or childe, so sudden in their execution, that few or none discerned the weapon or blow that brought them to destruction: In which manner also they slew many of our people at severall works in the fields, well knowing in what places and quarters each of our men were, in regard of their familiaritie with us, for the effecting that great master-peece of worke their conversion; and by this meanes fell that fatall morning under the bloudy and barbarous hands of that perfidious and inhumane people, three hundred forty seven men, women and children, most by their owne weapons, and not being content with their lives, they fell againe upon the dead bodies, making as well as they could a fresh murder, defacing, dragging, and mangling their dead carkases into many peeces, and carying some parts away in derision, with base and brutish triumph. (150-52; 198-99; 245-46; 251; 258; 261-62; 294)

4. From Aphra Behn, *Oroonoko*, 1688

This Adornment, with their[2] long black Hair, and the Face painted in little Specks or Flowers here and there, makes 'em a

---

1 Through. This 1622 massacre is referenced in *The Female American* (p. 46).
2 The female narrator is describing the natives of Surinam in the West Indies.

wonderful Figure to behold. Some of the Beauties, which indeed are finely shap'd, as almost all are, and who have pretty Features, are charming and novel; for they have all that is called Beauty, except the Colour, which is a reddish Yellow; or after a new Oiling, which they often use to themselves, they are of the Colour of a new Brick, but smooth, soft and sleek. They are extreme modest and bashful, very shy, and nice[1] of being touch'd. And though they are all thus naked, if one lives for ever among 'em, there is not to be seen an undecent Action, or Glance: and being continually us'd to see one another so unadorn'd, so like our first Parents before the Fall, it seems as if they had no Wishes, there being nothing to heighten Curiosity; but all you can see, you see at once, and every moment see; and where there is no Novelty, there can be no Curiosity.... And these People represented to me an absolute *Idea* of the first State of Innocence, before *Man* knew how to sin: And 'tis most evident and plain, that simple Nature is the most harmless, inoffensive and vertuous Mistress. 'Tis she alone, if she were permitted, that better instructs the World, than all the Inventions of Man: Religion wou'd here but destroy that Tranquillity they possess by Ignorance; and Laws wou'd but teach 'em to know Offence, of which now they have no Notion. They once made mourning and fasting for the Death of the *English* Governor, who had given his Hand to come on such a day to 'em, and neither came nor sent; believing, when a Man's word was past, nothing but Death cou'd or shou'd prevent his keeping it: And when they saw he was not dead, they ask'd him what Name they had for a Man who promis'd a thing he did not do? The Governor told them, Such a Man was a *Lyar*, which was a Word of Infamy to a Gentleman. Then one of 'em reply'd, *Governor, you are a Lyar, and guilty of that Infamy.* They have a native Justice, which knows no Fraud; and they understand no Vice, or Cunning, but when they are taught by the *White* Men.... (3-4)

With these People, as I said, we live in perfect Tranquillity, and good Understanding, as it behoves us to do; they knowing all the places where to seek the best Food of the Country, and the means of getting it; and for very small and unvaluable Trifles, supply us with that 'tis impossible for us to get.... And then for

---

1 Sensitive.

shooting, what they cannot take, or reach with their Hands, they do with Arrows; and have so admirable an Aim, that they will split almost an Hair, and at any distance that an Arrow can reach: they will shoot down Oranges, and other Fruit, and only touch the Stalk with the Dart's Point, that they may not hurt the Fruit. So that they being on all occasions very useful to us, we find it absolutely necessary to caress 'em as Friends, and not to treat 'em as Slaves, nor dare we do other, their numbers so far surpassing ours in that Continent. (4-5)

Appendix B: Ibn Tufayl and Autodidactic Castaways

[Ibn Tufayl's *Hayy Ibn Yaqzan* has served as a template for many later English castaway narratives. Written originally in Arabic in the 1160s, it was translated into Latin by Edward Pococke in 1671 under the title *Philosophus Autodidactus*. Others translated the text into English from Pococke's Latin, including George Keith's *An Account of the Oriental Philosophy* (1674) and George Ashwell's *History of Hai Eb'n Yockdan, an Indian Prince, Or, the Self-Taught Philosopher* (1686). Keith published a tract defending female preachers the same year as his translation, and both texts circulated in Quaker circles. Finding these translations (and their religious interpretations) unsatisfactory, Simon Ockley translated the text directly from Arabic to English in 1708. Many writers borrowed the plot of Tufayl's narrative from these English translations, often altering the text by changing names and settings and by adding or revising plot elements. This resulted in works such as *The History of Josephus, an Indian Prince* (1696), *The Life and Surprizing Adventures of Don Juliani de Trezz* (1720), *The History of Autonous* (1736), and *The History of Automathes* (1746). Despite their differences, these texts all feature the island castaway as a self-taught autodidact and generally conclude with the arrival on the island of a hermit who discovers the solitary philosopher. Depending on the text, the castaway's return results either with his integration into society or with his decision to self-exile to the island again after finding society to be a lost cause. These texts often emphasize inward discovery over external conquest of the natural world, are set in the Indian Ocean, and constitute a literary history often overshadowed by that of Robinsonades (see Appendix C, p. 220).]

1. From *The History of Josephus the Indian Prince*, 1696

Amongst some *Indian* Islands, near or under the Equinoctial Line, it is said there was a Desart-Island, of pretty large Circumference, scituate in a pleasant and temperate Air; and not far from it was another Island, which did abound with most Necessaries for Life, and well stockt with Inhabitants. The King, or Prince that govern'd it is said to be of a Proud and Jealous Temper, and having a very beautiful Sister, he kept a strict Eye over her; not suffering her to Marry, because he thought none of his Country good enough for her Husband; but having a Kinsman called Josephus, the placing her Affections on him, privately marries him unknown to the said Prince her Brother: By whom proving with Child soon after Marriage, bore a Son, and fearing the Birth of the Child and her Marriage shou'd be discover'd to her Ambitious Brother, and after the Babe had taken to suck, resolves to put him in a little Wooden-Chest; and being attended with some of her Servants and faithful Friends, carries him close nailed up to the sea-shore in the Night-time, resolving to recommend him to the Mercy of God and the Waves, rather than divulge the Matter to her proud Brother; and putting up her Prayers to Heaven for the Preservation of the Infant, by his merciful Assistance, Guard, Direction and Government, she took her sorrowful leave of it, committing the Chest to the Sea; the Waves began to swell with the Tide, and the same Night convey'd it on Shore of the first mentioned Desart-Island: This happened to be in a time of the year when the Tides were very great, which swell'd the Water so high, that it overflowed the adjacent Shore, so that the force of the Flood cast the little Chest into a shady adjacent Grove thick set with Trees very pleasant, and sheltered from Wind and Weather; Rain nor Sun in its Flowing or Ebbing no way molesting it. Soon after the Water Ebbing, the Chest wherein the Child was, remain'd in the same place the Flood cast it; the Wind and Water heaping up the Sands, stopt the passage up to the Grove that the Waters could not reach it; and withal the Chest being driven into the Grove, had its Nails drawn and loosened by its Motion, and the Chest broke open; so that the Child therein awaking, fell a crying, and lying at the edge of the Shore, which being heard by a Roe[1] who had just lost its Fawn by an Eagle which had carry'd it away, she thinking it had been that Fawn, came to the Chest, and with her Claws getting loose one of the Boards, got the Child out, and gave it her Dug to suck, and constantly afterwards came to it, cover'd it and kept it from harm; and in short, having plenty of Milk, and mightily taken with it, the Child grew strong under such tender

---

1 A gazelle or deer.

Nursing, there being no ravenous or hurtful wild Beast in all the Island. Thus with her Milk she suckled it to two year old, when having got its teeth, and beginning to use its Feet, by degrees it followed the Roe, who conducted it to Fruit-bearing Trees, and fed it with the ripe Fruits that fell therefrom, and broke with her Teeth for it what was too hard for it ... constantly herding with the rest of the Deer, insomuch, that they always company'd with them; and the Child could so well imitate their Voice, as hardly to be distinguished from theirs: Likewise he could exactly repeat whatsoever Voice he heard from any Bird, or other brutish Creature; but chiefly used the Voice of the wild Deer, whether in crying out for help, or calling to them to draw near, or keep farther off. And thus he lived amongst them as one of them; and now being about 7 years old, he began to observe that others had Horns, and were of a different Shape and Make from himself; that they had Hair and Tail to cover their privy Parts, he began to be ashamed of his own Nakedness, and so sowed[1] broad Leaves together to hide it; making himself a Girdle of Palm-Tree Leaves and Rushes to girt about him, he likewise made him a Staff to beat off any of the Deer that opposed him, ... he at length found a dead Eagle, with whose Skin, Wings, Feathers and Tail he made a shift to cover himself before and behind, which kept him warm, and frighten'd the rest of his Company; so that none of the wild Beasts durst come near him, except the Roe his Nurse, who never forsook him ... when she grew old he brought her the very best and pleasantest Fruits to eat, till at length she dy'd, which he was much amazed and troubled at, not knowing what Death meant, and calling to her in the same Voice as he used, when she always (at hearing) answer'd; he cryed out as loud as he could, but perceived no Motion in her, so that he began to look in her Eyes and Ears, but all was in vain; and having viewed all her Body, and finding no hurt or blemish, cut her open to the very Heart, searching and examining the occasion; till at last he was forced to give over and leave her.... (65-68)

It is reported, there was an Island not far from that wherein Josephus was born, which Island it is said, a certain Sect of People betook themselves to live in, who had one of the pious Prophets

---

1 Sewed.

of old for their Patron or Author[1].... In this Island, you must know, two pious and virtuous Men were born, true lovers of what is good, the one *Salaman* by Name, and the other *Asal*, who adhered to this Sect after the best and most perfect manner, daily observing all its Precepts, and doing such Acts as were required by it: For the same purpose they contract[ed] a mutual great Friendship; and among several other Passages contained in the Law of that Sect, their Enquiry was made into the Descriptions, or Attributes of the Deity and his Angels; as also of a Resurrection and future Rewards and Punishments. Now whilst busie in such Scrutinies and Enquiries, *Asal* search'd further into the very inmost Nature of Things, and into the Mystical Senses of Words, being very diligent about Explaining and Interpreting them: His friend *Salaman* chiefly observ'd the outside and visible part of the Law as it at first sight appeared, abstaining from all curious Interpretations, Examinations, and Speculations of Matters. They were both of them diligent observers of all External Works required by the Law, making their Reason a Rule whereby to act, constantly fighting and contending against their unruly Passions and inordinate Affections: But whereas that their Law seem'd to Encourage Men to affect Solitude, or a Solitary Life, as if Happiness and Salvation consists in such a State; as also again on the other-side, seemed to exhort Men unto Civil Acquaintance and Fellowship, and apply themselves to Humane Society, as a means to drive away Evil Thoughts, and banish that Diversity of Opinions in the Mind: But the Difference of their Opinions in that Matter grew so great, that they parted upon it. Now whereas *Asal* had heard of that Island which we have already mentioned that *Josephus* was bred up in, and withal knowing the Fertility and Conveniences of it, and its healthful temperate Air, which wou'd make such a suitable Retirement as he wish'd for, resolved to go thither and withdraw from all Humane Society for the rest of his Life; and having gathered all his Substance together, hires a Ship with part of it to carry him to that Island, giving the rest in Charity to the Poor, and taking leave of his old Friend *Salaman*, to Sea he went, and the Ship arriving in a short time at the

---

1   The following events transpire decades after the death of the roe, during which time Josephus has gained both extensive empirical knowledge and great spiritual understanding, and has retreated to live in a cell.

said Island, as soon as they could get him on Shore they left him and departed. Thus *Asal* was left alone in the Island, serving and magnifying God, and meditating on his glorious Name and Attributes, having neither his Mind nor Thoughts interrupted or disturbed: When he was Hungry he took of the Fruits of the Island, or of what he got by Hunting, in which State he continued a while, enjoying the greatest Pleasure and Tranquility of Mind imaginable, from the uninterrupted Conversation he had with his Lord; daily experiencing his Favours and good Providence in supplying him with the Necessaries of Life to his greatest Comfort. Now thus exercised was *Josephus* in his high and Heavenly Speculations, that he went not out of his Cell above once a Week to get his Food, which was the Reason that *Asal* did not so soon see him; for having walked round the bounds of the Island, and perceiving no Footsteps of any Person, his Joy was much encreased at it, obtaining his desire of a Solitary Retirement, which he had sought after so earnestly. But at last it fell out so, that *Josephus* went out of his Cell for Food, and *Asal* being near it, they happened to espy one-another: As for *Asal*, he doubted not but the Person he saw was one that had devoted himself to a Solitary Life like himself, and therefore was afraid, by meeting him or being made known to him, he shou'd disturb him in that State and Condition of Life: But as for *Josephus*, he knew not what to make of the sight of *Asal*, being he was of a different Shape from the other Creatures he had seen before; and withal by his being clad with a black Coat made of Hair and Wool, which he took for some Natural kind of covering,[1] stood a long time wondering what it shou'd be, upon which Asal turns about and fled least he should divert his Attention in what he seemed so busied; ... In the mean while, *Josephus* draws nearer, unperceived by *Asal*, till he could hear his Reading and see his humble Gesture, and the knocking of his Breast, which Voice seemed pleasant, having never seen nor heard the like before from any Animal; then observing the form of his Body, see it the same Shape of his own, and that his Coat was not his own natural Skin, but borrowed somewhere, like as his own was; therefore being desirous to be acquainted with him, drew yet

---

1 This encounter—in which Josephus misrecognizes Asal's black coat as his skin—seems to have been rendered by Defoe into a racial identity in the character of Friday.

nearer, till *Asal* perceiving it, betook himself to his Heels, but *Josephus* pursued him (being swift of Foot) soon overtook him, seized him and held him that he could not get from him. Now *Asal* seeing him clothed with the hairy Skins of Beasts, and the Hair of his Head so long, that it covered great part of his Body, and that he was so swift of Foot and so strong of Body, was very much afraid of him, and sought to appease him, gently stroaking him, adding kind and humble Entreaties....

Then *Josephus* desired him to let him know from whence he came, and his Condition of Life; which *Asal* describing to him, and the Island from whence he came; that amongst the Inhabitants was a Religious Sect, explaining their Laws touching a Divine World of *Paradise*, and the Fire of *Gehenna*, of a Resurrection of Mankind, and their Judgments, and Accounts of all their Actions: All which *Josephus* very well knowing already, thought agreeable with what he had seen in his sublime Contemplations, therefore thought him a Messenger from God; believing and owning what he had now said to be Truth. Then asking him of the Precepts deliver'd by God's Messenger, *Asal* declar'd them to him; namely, Prayer, Alms, Fasting, and suchlike External Works, which *Josephus* believ'd true, and embraced....

... Now *Salaman*, *Asal*'s Friend, was Sovereign of this Island,[1] who thought Humane Society the best, and Solitude unwarrantable, therefore *Josephus* began to unfold the Mysteries of Wisdom to them; and when in his Discourse he advanced but a little beyond what was settled and rooted in their Minds, they withdrew from him, abhorring his Doctrine; conceiving an inward Hatred against him, though seemingly they honored and respected him (as being a Stranger) in respect of his Companion *Asal*. But *Josephus* perceiving his Advice to be lost on them, that their chiefest delight was in what they at present possest, chusing their Lusts for their God, gathering the empty, worthless, trifling Vanities of the World, and that neither Reproof nor Advice could Influence them, but wou'd obstinately adhere to their own Sentiments, excepting a very few of them. After a courteous Leave taken of their Prince *Salaman* and the Islanders, he and *Asal* returned to their Desart-Island as soon as they could, whither (when they were safe gotten) *Josephus* betook himself to his for-

---

1 Josephus and Asal have traveled together to the neighboring island to bring their spiritual discoveries to its inhabitants.

mer sublime State of Speculation; and *Asal* (as far as he could attain) followed his Example, both worshipping God there, till Death seized them both. (71-75, 77-78)

2. From George Keith, *The Woman-Preacher of Samaria; A Better Preacher, and more Sufficiently Qualified to Preach than any of the Men-Preachers of the Man-made-Ministry of these Three Nations*, 1674

Come hither all you Men-Preachers, of a *Man-made Ministry*, in the three Nations; whether Conformists, or Nonconformists unto the present way of the Ministry, and Worship in these Nations Established by a Humane Law, who cry out against Womens Preaching, and Speaking, and say, Women ought not to Preach, There should not be Women Preachers, They should keep them to the Affairs within the House, and not meddle with our holy Function. Behold, a Woman-Preacher! the Woman of *Samaria* (*John* 4) who may be a Example unto you all; and the best of you, and most Learned and Qualified of you all, have need to learn of her how to Preach. This Woman of *Samaria* may be your School-Mistress to teach you to Preach; and it were good for you to learn of her, who though being dead, yet speaketh unto you. Verily, she is a witness for God, unto the true way of Ministry, and Preaching, against you all, and against all your false and invented ways. Oh for shame let alone your crying out against Women-Preachers; while you are short, exceedingly short of this Woman-Preacher of *Samaria*; and, first of all, learn the true silence, and to have that mouth in you stopped, which God hath never opened; that the true mouth which is of his opening, you may come to witness, or else for ever to be silent.... (1)

3. As concerning her Call, (as was said) she had it not from Men, and indeed we read not of any outward Call she had from Christ; but certainly he who taught her inwardly, called her also inwardly, by his Holy Spirit; yea, so powerful was her inward Call, and the motion of the Spirit of Christ within her, that it caused her to make hast, she tarried not to carry home her water pot, for it is said expressly, *she left her water-pot, and went into the City, and said unto the Men, Come, see a Man*, &c.... They did not despise her because she was a Woman, they did not say unto her (as many now say) thou art a Woman, thou should not Preach;

... I say, these Men, they neither upbraided her with her being a woman, nor secondly, with her being unlearned; nor thirdly, that she wanted her Call, and was idle, or medled with a business that did not concern her; they did not say unto her, Go home to your wheel, and your Spinning, and such like words, as men commodly[1] now say to Women Friends,[2] whom the Lord hath taught and Called by his Spirit to testifie of him, as he did this Woman of *Samaria*. Nor fourthly, did they upbraid her with the place, as men commonly also now do, who wonder, and gaze, and mock, and scorn, if they see or hear any speak any thing of Christ in the streets; O, say they, this is not the Church, go to Church, if ye would Preach, this is not a fit place to Preach in. (7-8)

5. She preached Christ freely, as she had freely received, so she freely gave; She did not begin to Contract, or Covenant, or bargain with them before hand, for monie, or for any Worlds good; she said not unto them, what money or Hire will ye give me, and I will preach Christ unto you? Nay, nay, she was not of such a Mercinary Spirit, she was more Noble; far unlike the preachers of the *Man-made-Ministry* in these daies, whether Episcopal, or Presiterian,[3] as well as *Popish*, where all is done for money, no money, no preaching, as the old proverb is, *No penny, No Pater Noster*.... (10)

6. Though she was a woman, yet she was not afraid to bear Testimony of Christ, she did not call them, to whom she preached into a Cellar, or Vault under the ground, or some private place, but opening, and publickly she preached him to a great company, so many heard and believed because of her saying, and yet no doubt there was a hazard so publickly to confess him, and own him in that day.... (11)

7. Also it is observable, the pithy and effectual way of hear[4] reasoning, by Question, or Interrogation, which implyeth both a strong affirmation, and a clear inference or induction from the premises, leaving it as it were unto themselves to judge, or conclude, *Is this not the Christ, who has told me all that ever I did?* this cannot be a meer man, this cannot be only a Prophet, this must

---

1 Commonly.
2 Women who were Quakers, or members of the Society of Friends.
3 Presbyterian.
4 Her.

be the Christ, seeing he hath told me all that ever I did. How effectually doth she reason, as she was taught by the Spirit of Christ in her, though she never learned the Art of Logick. (12)

3. From Simon Ockley, *The Improvement of Human Reason, Exhibited in the Life of Hai Ebn Yokdhan*, 1708

Frontispiece to Simon Ockley's *Improvement of Human Reason* (1708), depicting Hayy in animal skins and a philosopher (perhaps Asal) ascending the steps of a temple or mosque flanked by the figures of Avicenna and Averroes. Courtesy Department of Special Collections, Stanford University Libraries.

The Design of the Author is to shew, how Human Capacity, unassisted by any External Help, may, by due Application, attain to the Knowledge of Natural Things, and so by Degrees find out its Dependance upon a Superior Being, the Immortality of the Soul, and all things necessary to Salvation....

I was not willing (though importun'd) to undertake the translating it into *English*, because I was inform'd that it had been done twice already; once by Dr. *Ashwell*, another time by the *Quakers*, who imagin'd that there was something in it that favoured their Enthusiastick Notions. However, taking it for granted, that both these Translations were not made out of the Original *Arabick*, but out of the *Latin*; I did not question but they had mistaken the Sense of the Author in many places....

And lest any Person should, through mistake, make any ill use of it, I have subjoin'd an *Appendix*, the Design of which the Reader may see in its proper place. (Preface)

3. They say, that there lay, not far from this our Island, another Great Island very fertile and well peopled; which was then govern'd by a Prince of a Proud and Jealous Disposition: he had a Sister of exquisite Beauty, which he confin'd and restrain'd from Marriage, because he could not match her to one suitable to her quality. He had a near Relation whose Name was *Yokdhân*, that courted this Princess, and Married her privately, according to the Rites of Matrimony then in use among them: it was not long before she prov'd with Child, and was brought to Bed of a Son; and being afraid that it should be discovered, she took him in the Evening, and when she had Suckled him she put him into a little Ark which she closed up fast, and so Conveys him to the Sea shore, with some of her Servants and Friends as she could trust; and there with an Heart equally affected with Love and Fear, she takes her last leave of him in these Words, *O God, thou form'dst this Child out of nothing, and didst Cherish him in the Dark recesses of my Womb, till he was compleat in all his parts; I, fearing the Cruelty of a Proud and unjust King, commit him to thy Goodness, hoping that thou who art infinitely merciful, will be pleas'd by thy gracious Providence to protect him, and never leave him destitute of thy Care....*

22. Upon this the whole Body[1] seem'd to him a very incon-

---

1 Following the death of the roe, he dissects her body in order to locate and remove the source of its defect, before realizing that she could not be revived.

siderable thing, and worth nothing in respect of that Being, he believed once inhabited, and now had left it. Therefore he applied himself wholly to the consideration of that Being. *What it was? and how it subsisted? what joyn'd it to the Body? Whether it went, and by what passage, when it left the Body? What was the Cause of its Departure, whether it were forc'd to leave its Mansion, or left the Body of its own accord? and in case it went away Voluntarily, what it was that rendred the Body so disagreeable to it, as to make it forsake it?* And whilst his Mind was perplext with such variety of Thoughts, he laid aside all concern for the Carcass, and threw it away; for now he perceiv'd that his Mother, which had Nurs'd him so Tenderly and had Suckled him, was that *something* which was departed: and from it proceeded all those Actions by which she shew'd her Care of him, and Affection to him, and not from this unactive Body; but that the Body was to it only as an Instrument or Tool, like his Cudgel which he had made for himself, with which he used to Fight with the Wild Beasts. So that now, all his regard to the Body was remov'd, and transferr'd to that by which the Body is govern'd, and by whose Power it moves. Nor had he any other desire but to make enquiry after that....

26. ... he began to think that the Substance which was departed from the Heart of his Mother the Roe, was, if not the very same with it, yet at least of a Nature very much like it. He was confirm'd in his Opinion, because he had observ'd in all Animals, that as long as they liv'd, they were constantly warm without any Intermission, and as constantly Cold after Death. Besides he found in himself, that there was a greater degree of Heat by much in his Breast, near that place where he had made the Incision in the *Roe*. This made him think that if he could dissect any Animal alive, and look into that Ventricle which he had found empty when he dissected his Dam the *Roe*, he might possibly find it full of that Substance which inhabited it, and so inform himself whether it were of the Substance with the Fire, and whether it had any Light or Heat in it or not. In order to [determine] this he took a Wild Beast and ty'd him down, so that he could not stir, and dissected him after the same manner he had dissected the *Roe*, till he came to the Heart; and Essaying the left Ventricle first, and opening it, he perceiv'd it was full of an Airy Vapour, which look'd like a little Mist or white Cloud, and putting in his Finger, he found it hotter than he could well endure it, and immediately the Creature Dyed. From whence he

assuredly concluded, that it was that Moist Vapour which communicated Motion to that Animal, and that there was accordingly in every Animal of what kind soever, something like it upon the departure of which Death follow'd....

27. The way which he us'd in this Enquiry was the Dissection of all sorts of Animals, as well Living as Dead, neither did he leave off to make an accurate Enquiry into them, till at length he arrived to the highest degree of Knowledge in this kind which the most Learned Naturalists ever attain'd to.[1] (28-29, 49-50, 53-55)

Hayy on the island, from Ockley's *Improvement of Human Reason*. Courtesy Department of Special Collections, Stanford University Libraries.

---

1 These animal dissections reappear in literary history in H.G. Wells's *The Island of Dr. Moreau* (1896) in which a castaway discovers experiments in vivisection and animal-human hybrids on a remote island. This scientific element is present in *The Female American* largely in the chapter where Unca observes and describes an unusual animal (pp. 109-12).

"Appendix: In which the Author's Notion concerning the Possibility of a Man's attaining to the true Knowledge of God, and Things necessary to Salvation, without the Use of external Means, is briefly consider'd."

1. Tho' the preceeding History, upon the account of the lively Image and Representation which it gives of unspotted Virtue, unfeigned Love of God, and Contempt of the Things of this Life, does very well deserve to be read: So, as it contains several things co-incident with the Errors of some Enthusiasts of these present Times, it deserves to be consider'd. Upon which Account, I had no sooner suffer'd my self to be perswaded to undertake the Translation of this Book, than I determin'd to subjoin some Reflections upon such part of it as seem'd to me most worthy of Consideration. Lest otherwise, that Book, which was by me design'd for the Innocent, and not altogether unprofitable Diversion of the Reader, might accidentally prove a means of leading some into Error, who are not capable of judging aright; and of confirming others in their Mistakes, who, through their own Weakness, or the Prejudice of a bad Education, have the Misfortune to be led out of the way. And I was the more willing to do it, because there has been a bad Use made of this Book before....[1]

2. I shall pass over the greatest part of them, as not being likely to do any harm; and confine my self chiefly to the Examination of this Fundamental Error of my Author, viz,[2] That God has given such a Power or Faculty to Man, whereby he may, without any external Means, attain to the Knowledge of all things necessary to Salvation, and even to the Beatifick Vision it self, whilst in this State: In doing which I shall still have regard to the Errors reciev'd concerning these things in the present Age.

3. In order to this I shall examine the Ways and Means by which the People of God in all Ages, came to the Understanding

---

1 Ockley refers here to the Quakers and to George Keith's 1674 translation of *Hayy Ibn Yaqzan* into English. Ockley's edition takes pains to insist that the book does not support Quaker ideas of direct revelation.

2 Ockley includes a note here that refers readers to sections 84 and 85 of his text.

of his Will. Now 'tis evident, from the absurd Notions which the ancient Heathens had of the Deity, and their Idolatry, that Mankind was so far degenerated and deprav'd, that they had lost the true Knowledge of God, and of his Attributes, and consequently were ignorant of their Duty towards him; for which reason, God was pleas'd, out of his infinite Love and Mercy towards Mankind, to send at sundry times *Prophets*; that is, Men who were inspir'd by the *Holy Spirit*, and had the Will of God *immediately* reveal'd to them; to the end that they might instruct others how to serve him (the ancient Tradition reciev'd from our first Parents, and those good Men which succeeded them, being now almost worn out, and over-grown by the increasing Wickedness of the World) and thereby avoid those Judgments which would otherwise infallibly overtake them, if they continu'd in Impenitence and Disobedience.

4. This was the Means which the Generality of the People of God had to know his Will. They receiv'd it from the *Prophets*, who had it *immediately* from God. So that the Difference of their Knowledge consisted in the Manner of their receiving of it, not in the Things receiv'd, which were the same both to the *Prophets* and the *People*. Only the *Prophets* receiv'd it *immediately*, but not the *People*: for then consequently they would all have been Prophets, which it is plain they were not....

12. To begin therefore with our Blessed Saviour himself. It is evident that he never recommended any such way of worshipping God, as is contended for by the *Mysticks*, nor promis'd to reward the most sincere of his followers with the *Vision of God* whilst in this State.... He let them know, that, contrary to their Expectation, his Kingdom was not of this World; but that his Business was to bring Men out of Darkness to Light, and from the Bondage and Slavery of Sin, to the Liberty of the Sons of God. He taught them to abandon all ungodly Lusts, and to set their Hearts upon Things above; assuring them, that if they continu'd in his Love, they should be rewarded with everlasting Happiness. And lest his Disciples, and those Churches which should be planted by their Ministry, should be destitute of necessary Encouragement and Assistance, he assures them in most endearing Terms, of his Love towards and Care over them....

17. Since it is not foreign to the Matter in hand, the Reader

will, I hope, pardon me if I digress a little, to shew why we cannot reasonably expect Prophets now. And it seems to me, that there are several Reasons to be given why there should be Prophets during the time of the Mosaical Dispensation, rather than after the Gospel had taken Root. For, the Promises made to the *Jews* having Relation to their possessing the Land of *Canaan*, God was pleas'd to send them Prophets to quicken their Memories, and keep them in mind of their Duty, that thereby his Judgments might be averted from them; (and especially, because of the prevailing Idolatry of those Times; for after they were well fix'd in the Practice of the True Religion, and out of that Danger, we find no Prophets;) and we find that most of the Ancient Prophecies tend that way. But now we are quite upon another Bottom; we are taught, that *we have here no continuing City; that, when these Tabernacles shall be dissolv'd, we have a Habitation not made with Hands, eternal in the Heavens.* That we are to *set our Minds on Things above, not on Things on the Earth*; that we are to *deny our selves, and take up our Cross and follow Christ*; that, *through many Tribulations we must enter into the Kingdom of Heaven*, and many Passages to the same Effect. So that to have Prophets foretelling future Events, relating to the Welfare and Preservation of our Temporals, or the contrary, seems not so proper for a People, whose very Profession supposes them to have laid aside all Solicitude concerning them. Again, before the Coming of Christ, God's Will was but imperfectly reveal'd; and it was necessary that there should be Fore-runners to prepare the way against his Coming, and raise the Expectation of him in the People, that they might be the better prepar'd to receive him. But after he was once come, ... I say, after God had, by this glorious Person, manifested and reveal'd his whole Will to us, and declar'd whatsoever he requir'd to be believ'd and done by us, whilst in these Mortal Bodies; there was no longer need of Revelation to those who had receiv'd the most perfect one that could be deliver'd. So that all those Reasons being remov'd, which were to be given for a Succession of immediately inspired Prophets before the Coming of Christ; it is altogether groundless, to say no worse of it, to expect any now he is come. (167-69, 181-82, 187-89)

Hayy with the hermit Asal on the island, from Ockley's *Improvement of Human Reason*. Courtesy Department of Special Collections, Stanford University Libraries.

4. From *The Life and Surprizing Adventures of Don Juliani de Trezz; Who was Educated and Lived Forty-five Years in the Island of Malpa, an Uninhabited Island in the East-Indies*, 1720

The following Papers, when they were first presented to the World, were receiv'd with such Applause as scarce any thing of this Nature ever met with.

They were Originally wrote in the Portuguese *Language, from when they were very speedily Translated by the* Sieur Moulin, *into the* French *Tongue.*[1]

---

1   There is no evidence of such a prior Portuguese or French version
    of the story.

Whether they are Authentick, or not, I cannot say; but it is allowed by all Hands, that the Probability is altogether observed throughout the whole Piece.

This History has certainly been known to some few of our Countrymen, who have made so good an Advantage of it, as to furnish us with two Pieces very nearly akin to this. The first of these was Hai Ebn Yokdan, *or the self-taught Philosopher; which, tho' pretended to be Translated from the* Arabick, *was certainly little better than a Paraphrase upon this History. The next was the late History of* Robinson Crusoe; *which plainly shows its Author had his first Hints from hence*[1].... (Preface)

When we consider the strange variety of Fortune which attends us in this World, we should be very cautious of being too elated when under her Smiles, or too dejected when under her Frowns: For Joy and Calamity, since they tread so near on each other's heels, ought mutually to partake of each other's Colour....

An Instance of this my Reader will find in the following Relations, which for its Truth and surprizing Accidents, had certainly been long since published, had it not been scooped by Plagiaries, to supply the far most valuable part in some late Fabulous and Romantick Histories.[2]

It happened in the Year 1510, that the *Portuguese* became Masters of the Island of *Goa* in the *East Indies*;[3] which by its pleasant Situation, and the many Advantages it promised to the Traders in its Produce and Commodities, invited many of the *Portuguese* Gentlemen (who had either by Gallantry, Debauchery, or ill Fortune, lessen'd their Patrimony) to go over and settle there. Among others, *Don Carlos Juliani* (the fourth Son of *Count Juliani*, who

---

1 Like *The Female American* (p. 113) does, this book claims to be the original from which Defoe's novel was copied. The George Ashwell translation of Ibn Tufayl's narrative, titled *The History of Hai Eb'n Yockdan, an Indian Prince, Or, the Self-Taught Philosopher*, appears to be the text referred to here as an imitation of the presumed Portuguese original to *Don Juliani*.

2 Another insistence that Defoe and others have copied this story, despite the fact that this one postdates the publication of *Robinson Crusoe*.

3 Goa was an early major trading center on the western coast of India, and it became the center of Portuguese India after it was captured in 1510.

so remarkably signalized himself in the Defence of his Country against the Kings of *Spain*) having consumed the major part of his Substance, went over to settle there. He was now near Fifty Years of Age, and had bury'd his Wife, who left three Sons and one Daughter to be provided for out of the small remains of his tattered Fortune. These Children he transported to *Goa* with himself, they being by Natural and Artificial Endowments, (of which both Nature and their Father had been almost prodigal towards them) very likely to restore their decay'd Family to its pristine State, and flourishing Condition.

The *Portuguese*, being extravagantly Superstitious, had taken great care to build Monasteries, and Nunneries, as looking upon Religion and Piety to be the most ready Road to success in whatever they should undertake; and for that Reason, always caressed the Fryars, and gave them the most free access, and hearty welcome to their Houses. Among others of the Clergy, who frequented *Don Juliani*'s House, there was one *Garcias*, a Youth of the most comely Stature and Deportment, much more addicted to Gaiety than Religion; and who had for that Reason, very much turned his Mind to courtly Accomplishments, and the Study of Mankind. This *Garcias* soon saw and felt the Charms of *Juliana*, the Daughter of this *Don Carlos Juliani*, who had every thing that might recommend her to a Man of his nice Taste. He found he had the most burning Passion for her, and was therefore resolved to gain her Affections: But knowing the Danger and Difficulty there would be in an Intrigue of this nature, if managed at her Father's House; he thought he might attack her with much more conveniency, and less danger, if he could but get her to take the Order of a Nun.... On the other hand *Garcias*, who had now gained great lengths in the Opinion of *Donna Juliana*, had put Notions into her Head, of the vast Pleasure and Diversions she would meet in that religious Life; whose Austerities were nothing but Cloaks to conceal the most exalted Transports of Pleasure and Diversion. *Donna Juliana* had too good an Opinion of *Garcias*'s taste for Pleasure, as well as his Honesty, to doubt any thing which he affirmed; so that she with the greatest willingness imaginable consented to her Father's Order, to prepare her self for the Initiation. So strangely credulous is Woman when she is once prepossessed with a good Opinion of her Author or Adviser.

... *Garcias* knowing it to be now intirely out of her Power to return Home, soon took an Opportunity to acquaint her with the Passion he had so long entertained for her, and how far that was his Motive, for giving her his Advice to take up the Veil: She could not but be somewhat surprized at the hearing this piece of Treachery; but the Love she had for him, and a Constitution not a little inclined to Love, joyn'd to the Impossibility of returning, pleaded so hard in his Favour, that he soon obtained his pardon, with the intire Possession of the lovely *Juliana*. He now enjoy'd the greatest Happiness this World could afford him full Eighteen Months, without ever considering what must be the Effect of so freely enjoying the most transporting Passion: When the unfortunate *Juliana* finding her self with Child, gave her self up entirely to Grief and Dispair. But *Garcias* knowing the Severity of the Inquisition, thought continually of Schemes to preserve his beautiful *Juliana* and himself from its Jaws. He at last perswaded her to send word to the Abbess that she was very ill, and that she would be removed into the Infirmary ... where she lay till the time of her Delivery, which was of a fine Boy.

Juliana would very willingly have brought up her Boy, but *Garcias* resolutely advised that it should be thrown into the Sea; for if by any ill Accident, it should chance to be discovered to the Inquisition, they were both sure to pay for it with their Lives. This made the affrighted *Juliana* consent to what her *Garcias* had proposed: whereupon she dressed her self in a Disguise, which he had provided for her and stole out of the Monastery the same Way that *Garcias* used to come to her.[1] She had provided an Ark fit to keep out Water, in which, having suckled the child she put it; and conveyed it to the Sea-shore, where with a Heart raging with Grief and Fear, she put it into the Sea; taking her last leave of it in these Words:

O God thou form'dst this Child out of nothing and hast cherished him in the dark Recesses of my Womb, till he was compleat in all his Parts; I fearing the Cruelty of the severe and unjust Laws, commit him to thy Goodness, hoping that thou who art infinitely Merciful, will be

---

1 The use of disguise to escape detection is a common feature of the castaway narratives and novels that developed and circulated after *Hayy Ibn Yaqzan*, including Unca's own masquerade as/within the idol.

pleased by thy gracious Providence, to protect him, and never leave him destitute of thy Care.[1] She spoke and let go her hold....

The Wind and Tide, by the divine Direction, bore the Ark to an Island about Seven Leagues off from *Goa*; but tho' so near, and known to the *Indians*, was intirely uninhabited, because, having attempted thrice to land there, their Ships had been staved against the Rocks; for which Reason they had then intirely laid aside all thoughts of ever settling a Colony in it. Upon this Island it was that Providence, and the Waves, cast the Ark; where the Tide going out, it left it very dry; and the Wind rising, blew a heap of Sand against it, sufficient to secure it from the next Tides. (1-7)

When he was now arrived to about the Age of Fourteen, and proved himself to be the Master of the Island by his Staff;[2] he began (as it was but natural he should) to look above those Creatures which he had subjected to him, insomuch, that he was very uneasy at his being obliged to lye and eat in common with them. But could contrive no means of separating himself from them, but by getting up into a Tree; and this was too dangerous, for he found that when he had endeavoured to Sleep there, he had very near fell down, so that he only made use of the Tree to sit in by Day, whence he could, with much Pleasure and Pride, see whole Troops of his Subjects, which were not long since his Superiours. But as to his sleeping amongst them, he could not nevertheless brook it, because it put him upon a level with them whom he now knew he was Master of....

His Pride taking away all Tenderness and Softness, and his Appetite prompting him to it, he now made no scruple of killing a Fawn, or (when Fawns were not to be found) a Deer, to satisfy an Appetite which was now grown large and luxurious. He had now got Staves much more bulky and long than formerly he was strong enough to manage: Upon the Ends of which he used to

---

1 These words of the mother sending her infant to sea are identical to those in Ockley's translation (p. 188), although the story preceding it has been changed considerably in this version.

2 The staff is a tree bough that he smoothed and then used to "attack the Wild Beasts, assaulting the Weaker sort, and defending himself from the Stronger. By this means he began to know his own Power" (11-12). This version of the story emphasizes the castaway's increasing desire for mastery.

stick the Horns of the Wild Cows, of which he had found several in the most woody part of the Island. These Horns he had made excessively sharp by scraping the Ends of them with his Flint-stones; so that by his own Strength, and the length of his Staves, and sharpness of the Horns, he could very easily kill the Deer at his pleasure. When there was now nothing that seemed wanting to gratify his Luxury, he was really nearer want; for the Deer, what with seeing him kill their Companions, and what with having been often gored by him, were grown so very shy of him, that they always fled if either they saw him, or heard him coming towards them....

... He now began to have such a Love for his Horses, that he could think nothing too good for them; for it was by the use of them that he regain'd his almost lost Soveraignty over the Beasts; so that he was desirous they should eat of every thing that he eat of, and lye as he did; for which Reason he soon built them a House bigger than his own, and laid great Quantities of Palm Leaves for them to lye on. But when he came to offer them some of his Venison, they refused it; and rather chose to feed on the Herbage which he had gathered for them before.... He soon caught a very fat Buck, which he had lamed by running him through the Right fore leg, (which Leg he afterwards broke short in two, to prevent his making his escape) and laying him upon his Horse, carry'd him to his Cabbin alive; where he cut his Throat, and let him bleed into great broad flat Shells, to prevent his Cabbin being bloody. After this, he cut him open, and offered several pieces of the Flesh to his Horse; but the Horse snorted, and would not touch it. At last considering that he had not drank for some time, and that he might perhaps drink the Blood, he held one of the large Shells full of Blood, which the Beast immediately lick'd up.... After this he try'd him as to the Flesh again, and finding he eat it as before; he offered him some Herbage, but the Horse refused it, chusing rather to live on the Flesh.... This [carnivorous] kind of Diet agreed so perfectly well with his Horses, that they could run longer and swifter, than any of the Wild Horses; so that he had them now as much under his Command as the Deer themselves....

The success he had met with in this Enquiry[1] had so far

---

1   The reference is to the knowledge he has gained from dissecting the roe and other animals.

increased his Curiosity, that he could scarce see any Thing, but he must know its Nature, till he grew to the highest Perfection in Speculative as well as Physical Knowledge, always Reasoning with the greatest strictness and exactness, unassisted Human Reason is capable of.

But as his Knowledge increased, so did his Wants grow more numerous also. He every Day saw new Grievances, and new Causes for Complaint: It was Distraction to him to see any Thing which he could not be Master of, so as to view it narrowly, and to try what Force his Fire would act with towards it; for whatever he met with, after handling it for some time, he always put it into the Fire....

... He also gathered up all the Gold Dust he could find, and lay'd it in his Cabbin, in order to make any Thing which he might hereafter have Occasion for; and at the same time brought home the largest and smoothest Stones he could find, together with Pebbles proper for his Designs, by which means he made himself, not only a more beautiful, but also a more useful Set of Tools; for he by degrees improved himself so far in Hammering of his Mettle, as to bring it to an Edge so as to cut like a Sword. By which means he still gain'd a greater Command over the Deer, and other Wild Beasts; for his Horns would often gore them, and yet they would get out of sight; whereas he had now learned the way of Hamstringing them, by cutting them with a Machine which he had fixed to the Tops of his Staves in the room of the Horns.... (13-14, 18-19, 20-22, 32-33, 35)

He had observed that the hollow Shells of Nuts would swim, and bear up a considerable Weight in the Water: Now this Quality of Swimming he entirely attributed to its being Hollow, because he had observed that his Golden Cups, though by much too heavy to swim when solid, yet when he had cast and beat to a sufficient Hollowness, they would always swim: Hence he thought he might reasonably conclude, that it was not impossible for him to make some thing which might be large enough, and hollow enough to swim, tho' he himself were in it. The Possibility of effecting this Design joyn'd to the earnest Desire he had to extend (if possible) his Limits and Power, made him always very uneasy till he had set about this Project....

As he was one Day sailing pretty near the Shoar, he heard a prodigious Noise at Sea, which was equally loud as Thunder;

but not continuing so long, he satisfied himself that it was not Thunder, but something which he had never before heard.

Being of a Temper equally bold and curious, he resolved to run to the Shoar, and see what it could be which could make so great a Noise; when he came to the Sea-side, he saw, at a very great distance, two Things, from which he saw flashes of Fire rise before he heard the Noise. He immediately leap'd into his Boat, and row'd himself towards them, with as much Expedition as the Wind (being full against him) would permit. He soon came near enough to have a full View of them. He found them so prodigious large, and the Noise and Fire so very terrible, that he thought it much the best way, to lye off at a good distance from them; for he concluded them to be two terrible Animals, who breathed Smoak, and threw Fire at each other, and that they were fighting for each others Life.[1] ...

He staid within his Cabbin all that Evening, and the next Day, not daring to go near the Shoar: But the third Day he mounted one of his Horses, and went to see what was become of the Monster. When he came to the Shoar, he met with the most agreeable Surpize imaginable: For the Tide was far gone out, and had left the Strand cover'd with Ten thousand things; which he admired not only as they were such things as he had never seen but also as he saw they would most of them be of service to him.

The Ship which was Stranded being a large *English East India* Merchant Ship, which, when she found she could neither conquer, nor save herself by Flight, had sunk herself rather than fall into the Hands of the Pyrates, who had engaged her....

The Tide was now coming in, and he had saved what he thought the most valuable of the Goods, when he began to look about the Shoar, where he saw under the Rocks a Body intirely (as far as he could see) like his. This Sight, tho' it was very surprising, was nevertheless very welcome to him, because it satisfied him as to what he had much doubted, *viz.* whether or no there were not more than one of his Shape, as well as that of other Creatures....

All this while he had many Uneasinesses about the Man which he had found upon the Shoar: For as the Melancholy which had seized him, went off, it left a very great Desire in him of meeting such another Creature alive, who might be a Companion

---

1 Here the castaway misinterprets as animals two ships engaged in battle offshore.

for him, and perhaps be very assisting to him, in making many Conveniences which he found he very much wanted. (52, 60, 62, 63, 66)

For as the Island of *Goa* grew more populous, so the Number of Religious Sects multiplied likewise among them: Among the rest, there were many Mendicants, whose whole Subsistance depends upon the accidental Charity of those who please to relieve them, by giving them the Fragments and Offals: Among these there are some who choose rather to lead an Hermitical Life, devoid of all the Pleasures of Society; and others who think it sufficient Penance to live by begging only....

Among the former Sect of these Mendicants, there happened to be one *Sebastian*, who was resolutely bent upon leading the most retired Hermitical Life he could possibly contrive. In order to which, having got Intelligence that there was an uninhabited Island, which the Ships passed by in their Eastern Voyages, he agreed with a Captain of a Vessel to endeavour to set him ashoar on this Island....

Juliani in the mean time was wholly employed at the other End of the Island, in building his House; so that *Sebastian* did not meet with him.

But *Juliani*, as we before observed, being obliged to leave his Building till the next Summer, now roving through all Parts of the Island, they soon spy'd each other.

Sebastian, for his part, did not in the least doubt but it was some religious Person, who, for the sake of a solitary Life, had retired into the Island as he himself had done; for which Reason he thought it not in the least proper to speak to him lest he should spoil his Meditation.

Juliani, on the other hand, was over ravished with Joy, to think that he had found what he so long wished to see, a Creature like himself....

When they were landed,[1] *Sebastian*'s Friends came about him, and he gave them an Account of *Juliani*, and how he had lived: So that the People flock'd to him on all sides, and admired and reverenced him.

Nor were the Religious less pleased at his profound Sense and

---

1 At this point, Sebastian and Juliani have been transported by ship from the island to Goa.

Judgment; for they very speedily initiated him into their Order, being in the Fifty third Year of his Age; where he enjoys Ease, Plenty, and Respect. (69, 70, 71, 77-78)

5. From *The History of Autonous, Containing A Relation how that Young Nobleman was accidentally left alone, in his Infancy, upon a desolate Island; where he lived nineteen Years, remote from all Humane Society, 'till taken up by his Father,* 1736

My Father's Name, says he, is *Eugenius* the chief of one of the most ancient Houses in this Kingdom, whose Ancestors for several Hundred Years have born the Title of Dukes of *Orthotimia.* At Twenty-five Years of Age he was married to a young Lady called *Paramythia*, of Quality nothing inferior to himself. This Couple lived together in all the Felicity of a married State for Seven full Years, before they had any Issue; at the End of which Time, I was born to them. But, such is the Uncertainty of all worldly Happiness, my Birth seemed to be the Birth of their Sorrows, and few joyful Days befell them afterwards.

About the same Time a Rebellion was raised by certain discontented Lords, who lived in our Neighbourhood, which, by the timely Care of his present Majesty was suppressed, 'ere it got to any considerable Height. Among those who were taken into Custody, as the principal Fomenters of this Insurrection, to the great Surprize of all who knew his Loyalty, my Father was one. This fell out through the underhand Dealings of some ill designing Persons, who cou'd not brook the high Esteem he was in with his Prince, but sought all Occasions to work his Overthrow. And so effectually did they bring their Ends about, by the Advantage which this Opportunity gave them, that by a Decree of the Senate, he was sentenced to Banishment and had all his Estate forfeited, against whatever the King himself cou'd do to prevent it, who was fully persuaded of his Innocence. Thus we see upon what slippery Grounds all humane Grandeur is fixed. They who obtain the most exalted Stations are continually push'd at by them beneath, and the higher Men are, still the more uncertain are they to stand, and the greater Danger of their Fall. Whereas they who are more lowly set are secure from such Mischances, being out of the Reach of Envy, and not so subject to the Changes and Caprices of Fortune.

Upon this unjust Sentence, my Father accompanied with his beloved Consort, who was resolved to live and die with him, was in a short Time constrained to take shipping, and with heavy Hearts bid adieu to their native Country, being only attended with a Servant Man and a Maid. And this was the first Taste of their approaching Sufferings: A sad Prelude to a much sadder Conclusion. They carried along with them me their Issue, who at that time had scarce reached twelve Months old, and was nourished at my Mother's Breast; it being a Reproach in our Country for Persons of the highest Rank to neglect nursing their own Children, unless upon Occasions of the most apparent Necessity.

We had not sailed long upon the unconstant Deep, 'ere we were assaulted with a most furious Storm, which lasting for three whole Days drave us upon an unknown Coast, where the Ship beat with such Vehemence upon the Sand, that she was expected every Moment to fall in Pieces. In this Extremity all that cou'd, except my Father and Mother who concluded it safest to stay by the Ship, got into the Boat hoping to reach the Land; but full dearly did they pay for their Rashness, for every Soul perished in the Attempt, being swallowed up in the boyling Waves. Whereas had they staid behind, they had without Doubt been preserved with us. For the Vessel being strongly built endured the Violence of the Tempest till the Ebb left her dry upon the Sand, and gave us an Opportunity of arriving safe upon the Shore.

But small was the Comfort of this unfortunate Couple from this Deliverance: For the Place on which they were cast proved to be an uninhabited Island, so that they were for some Time obliged to take up their Lodgings with me under the open Air; and we must all inevitably have perished with Famine, had it not been for the Helps we received from the Ship, which, as Heaven order'd it, both satisfied our present Hunger, and enabled us to provide for the Future....

In this Manner lived this disconsolate Pair. Their Food chiefly consisted of Herbs and Roots, and their Drink was limped Water, with which they were supplied from a small Brook running close by the Door of their Cottage. Their greatest Satisfaction was in Devotions and Spiritual Exercises, the usual Resort of Persons in Affliction.... Thus it happen'd with my Parents; till now they had never truly experienced the Vanity of this World, and till now they had never been truly serious in the Business of the other, for their Direction in which they were happily supplied with a Bible found in the Ship. That Divine Book they deservedly look'd upon as the greatest Blessing which Heaven had granted them in their Solitude; and their frequent Meditations therein helped to make their Condition more easy. It shew'd them that true Happiness was only to be had by placing their Affections and Desires upon such Objects as were of the same Duration with their immortal Souls, and no such being to be found in this World, they were therefore to seek them in another. It convinced them that Religion was to be prefer'd before every Thing else in Life, and when they reflected upon the wretched Coldness they had formerly shewn for the Worship of God, while they had the happy Opportunities thereby of regularly performing those sacred Rites, which were instituted by Christ as Means of Grace, they cou'd not but highly condemn themselves....

And the Consequent of these Reflections was a perfect Reconciliation to their present Condition. They now look'd upon themselves to be as sufficiently supplied with all the real Necessaries of Life as ever, tho' not in so splendid a Manner. Their homely Fare went down with as good a Relish, as when they were entertain'd with more costly Dishes; and their Sleep was as sweet upon their Beds of Moss, as what they formerly enjoy'd upon those of Down: The Reason was because they now eat and slept only to satisfy Nature and not Luxury. It is true they had not now the same Advantages of Society, but this was balanced to them, when they considered that they had so much less of Vanity and Impertinence. In fine, they began to look upon this Change as so far from being an Evil, that they blessed God for using such a Means to bring them to a true Knowledge of themselves, and were in the highest Degree thankful for the many Conveniences Providence had furnished them with in this desolate Place, the Want of any one of which wou'd have made their Condition much worse.... (3-11)

The Loss of his beloved Consort put a Stop to my Father's growing Felicity, and in Spite of all his Fortitude, for some Time reduced him to a State more disconsolate than ever. The Thoughts of her sweet Fellowship came ever and anon into his Mind, and as often as he looked upon me, my innocent Smilings, as ignorant of my own Loss, drew Showers of Tears from his Eyes. One Day laden with these sad Reflections, as he was looking out to Sea, he imagin'd he discover'd Land not far off, which upon a stricter Examination he found to be true. And so far was he now out of Love with his Solitude, that he studied how he might get himself transported thither with me, at all Adventures, in Hopes of finding some of his own Species to converse with. While he was big with these Thoughts, recollecting the Ship's Boat which lay still upon the Beach, he went directly to her....

At the Sight of this,[1] he stood for some Time with his Eyes and Hands lift up to heaven like a Statue, and then recovering himself cried out in the most pitiful Manner, *O! my Infant! my Infant!* wringing his Hands and beating his Breast; and, so far had he now forgot all Bounds of Moderation, even cursing the Hour of his Birth, which had brought him into such a World of Misfortunes....

In this Condition lived my Father and I for near nineteen Years, he in one Island, and I in the other. But in the End, Heaven found out a Means for our Deliverance, and my Father saw himself put into a Capacity of once more visiting his native Country; and what was least of all expected, obtain'd another Sight of me.

The Accident fell out thus. One of his Majesty's Ships of War in Pursuit of the Enemy came up with these Islands, which were three in Number. They first put ashore in the Island where my Father resided; and notwithstanding his ragged Disguise, he was known to most of the Officers, who cou'd scarce tell how to express the Joy they conceiv'd at so unlook'd for an Accident, and that Fortune had put it in their Power to do Service to one, for whom they had so great an Esteem.

They had not staid many Hours on this Island, 'ere they returned with my Father on Board, and treated him according to his Dignity. But before they pursued their Voyage homewards, the Captain in Compliance to my Father's Request, accompanied him into the other Island, that he might once more visit the Remains of his beloved Consort, and Child, before he took his final Adieu of the Place.

Here my Father to his Surprize, found so great an Alteration in and about his former Cottage, that he cou'd scarce discern it

---

1 His father has traveled by boat to the nearby island, with the intent of returning later that day to the first island where he has left his son, but is stranded when the boat washes away in a storm.

to be the Place it was. A Proof to him that it must since have been occupied by some later Inhabitant; of which, they were all sufficiently convinced, when to their great Astonishment they beheld a naked Youth coming out of the Woods, and mingling boldly among them, as one desirous of their Acquaintance; but all the while silent. My Father was presently sensible that this must be his Son, who had by some extraordinary Means been thus preserved; and my near Resemblance to him bespoke no less to the whole Company. And overcome with Transport at this unexpected Sight, he ran towards me, clasped me in his Arms, and was for some Time not able to speak for the Overflowings of his Joy: I in the mean Time shewing no less Tokens of Affection, after my mute and unpolished Manner; as if secretly acquainted with the Nearness of our Relation. After these mutual Endearments were over, my Father taking his last Farewell of my Mother's Tomb, beckoned of me to follow him with the rest of the Company to the Ship, which I readily and joyfully obey'd, like one unwilling by any Means to be separated afterwards from him.

After all Things were in Readiness, we hois[t]ed Sail for *Epinoia*, where in a short Time we safely arrived, to the Wonder of every one who saw us. The general Notion had been, that we were cast away in our Transportation to Banishment, which was no small Affliction to the King, and most of his Subjects: My Father's Innocence of what he was maliciously accused, being soon after made clear to the World.

The News of his Return was therefore most joyfully received by his Majesty, who determined to make him all possible Amends for his past Sufferings; in Consequence of which, all his Estates, and the Profits of them, ever since his Banishment, were faithfully restored, and the highest Court Preferments were offer'd him. But these last he modestly refused, as being quite out of Love with a Life of Splendor and Noise, and chose rather to pass the Remainder of his Days in Privacy and Retirement....

And herein I much surpassed his Expectation; for when I became capable of expressing my Thoughts to my Tutors; to their great Amazement, they found me more like a Philosopher than a Savage; having attain'd as just a Notion of many important Truths, by my own Reflections alone, as if I had learn'd them from the Mouth of a *Plato* or *Aristotle*. I guessed the Manner of my own Original from that of other Creatures, and from the Works of the Creation I inferr'd the Being of the Creator. The utter Incapacity of Thought in Matter, as such, instructed me in the Independance of these one upon another; and from hence I gathered the natural Incorruptibility of the thinking Principle. I learn'd a Sort of Arithmetic peculiar to my self, and my Necessities taught me to perform several Problems in Geometry: In fine, within three Years I was sent to this University, where I have now continued about twice that Term and am just about to make my Return. (14-15, 17, 21-24, 26-27)

6. From John Kirkby, *The Capacity and Extent of the Human Understanding; Exemplified In the Extraordinary Case of Automathes; a Young Nobleman, who was Accidentally left in his Infancy, upon a desolate Island, and continued Nineteen Years in that solitary State, separate from all human Society*, 1745

One Morning, after I had been diverting myself with the Organ, I went up to the highest Terrace behind my Bower; and there walked for some time to and fro, repeating the Tune in my Mind to which that Instrument was set.[1] While I mused thus within myself, I heard a Melody at a great Distance, as I thought, up in the Air directly over my Head; which, for Sweetness and Solemnity, as much exceeded the Music of my Organ, as I esteemed that above the mere Whistling of the Wind among the Trees. I looked wishfully upwards to see what might be the Occasion of this wonderful Harmony, which gave me a sensible Delight, beyond any thing I ever had felt; but, after all my earnest Gazing, I could see nothing but the blue Sky over me, from whence I imagined it to proceed. I was entertained with this ravishing Music, from the same Place, for more than an Hour, which seemed to me to consist of a Number of human Voices, divided into a nigher and more distant Chorus, answering each other alternately, by a continual Variation into still new Modulations. At length these two Choruses seemed to meet and unite all their Voices together, descending much nearer to me with a Melody much louder, and,

---

1 This description of the musical enchantment on Automathes's island may be a source for the description of the strange music heard on Unca's island by those men who arrive with her cousin near the conclusion of *The Female American* (p. 133).

if it was possible, much more harmonious; but, for the great-est Part, in very different Tones. Beside the *Vox humana*, in all its different Notes, was now added to this heavenly Concert, at proper Periods, the Softness of the Harp, the Viol, and Flute, with the Majesty of the Trumpet, the Clarion, and deep-toned Cymbal; but all to infinitely greater Perfection than any thing I ever afterwards heard from the same Instruments in the Hands of Man. At the Hearing of this last, I was quite transported out of myself with ecstatical Raptures; and I seemed as if nailed to the Ground where I stood; till I perceived the Harmony move off towards the middle Parts of the Island, and in a little time it went quite out of my Hearing....

But my ill Opinion of Mankind was yet much increased, when I became acquainted with the many Murders and Bloodsheds, which they committed upon one another, since the Beginning of the World.[1] This I thought was the highest Instance of the exceeding Degeneracy of human Nature, and put Men below the most savage Brutes. And when I came afterwards to read the many dreadful Judgments of God upon Mankind, especially in that of Drowning the old World, in the Burning of *Sodom* and *Gomorrah*, and in the Extirpation of the seven Nations by the Sword of the Children of *Israel*; I could not but look upon all these, as no less signal Instances of the Divine Compassion towards their miserable State, than of Justice upon them for their Wickedness. For to have continued such Monsters of Iniquity longer upon Earth, I concluded would only have been giving them an Opportunity to heighten their Crimes; and, conse-quently, both to increase their own Misery, and bring infinite Numbers after them into the same wretched Circumstances.

And thus I have given you a brief History of my Life, and the Manner of my Attainment of Knowledge from my Infancy, till the Time of my Entrance into human Society; which happened towards the End of my Twenty-first Year, after I had continued in the Island about 19 Years and 10 Months; and it is now near 11 Years since. Through all which, I would have it well observed, that I attribute those Acquirements no more to the Effect of my

---

1 This is the conclusion of Automathes's narration of his story to those who have discovered him living in island solitude; these men have just shared with him a description of the society in which they live.

own Capacity alone, than if I had the most complete Education which the World could afford. For I have all the Reason in the World to believe, that if I had been left entirely to myself, after my Father's Departure from me, I should have been little better than my dumb Companions. From whence I cannot but conclude, *That Man, by Nature, depends as much after his Birth upon the Care and Instruction of others, to bring him to act agreeably to his rational Character, as he before depended upon the Action of others to give him his Birth.* And, if so, I think it may easily be made appear, *That all Nations of Men, how distantly soever placed from each other, do actually derive their Education from a* supernatural Original; *and that ever since their first Appearance in the World.* Which I take to be as clear a Proof of the Certainty of Divine Revelation as can be required, when it is demonstrated, *That not only the Knowlege which is peculiar to Christianity, but even that which is necessary to distinguish Men outwardly from mere Brutes in human Shape, could possibly be derived in no other Way, than originally from God himself, in a Manner equally extrinsic to pure Nature.* (213-15, 232-34)

The next Morning, betimes, *Automathes*, with two other young Gentlemen of his Acquaintance, set out with us; each of us being provided with a very good Horse, upon which we mounted, when we had crossed the River: And as soon as we had ascended the Top of the Hill on the other Side, which reached to a considerable Height, *Automathes* shewed us at a Distance the *Amphitheatre*, which his Father had spoken of, without giving any further Description of it, to make our Surprize the more agreeable. What he called an Amphitheatre, then seemed to be nothing but a long high Mountain, about twenty Miles before us; which appeared through a Spy-glass to be mostly covered with Trees....

But how agreeably were we surprised at the Sight, which now presented itself! Here we stood some time contemplating upon what we saw. The Mountain appeared in the Form of a circular verdant Bank, or Terrace, of exactly the same Height, making the same regular bending Descent inwards, with the Ground upon which we stood; in such sort, that a green Trench, or Valley, just below us, of about forty Perches over, extended itself like an inner Border quite round the whole Circuit; and the interior Limb of this Valley was all along edged with a kind of Rampart, or Bulwark, or solid Rock of a crimson Colour, which reached above the Height of a Man on Horseback. But what mixed this delightful Scene with a kind of pleasing Horror was an amazing Precipice, which shewed itself on the opposite Side, falling down directly below the rocky Rampart, to such a Depth as made the Head turn giddy....

This Precipice was, doubtless, the most stupendous Work of Nature, which could be found upon the Face of the whole Earth; and, had it not been, that each Part of it was of a Size too monstrously enormous, and beyond all Possibility of being any way conceived manageable by human Art, we must necessarily have concluded the Whole to be the Effect of that.... But, still, the most astonishing Thing was the intermediate Space between the Cornice and Surface; the Ground of which was of a light Blue, and could not but be much higher than the Dome of *St. Peter*'s Church at *Rome*. Upon this, as a Field, there seemed carved an innumerable Multitude of grotesque Figures in *Basso Relievo*, all in their natural Colours, which made one of the most magnificent Appearances I ever saw.

This prodigious Wall inclosed a circular Space of Ground perfectly level, of about four Miles Diameter, upon which grew nothing but Grass, affording a most delightful Verdure; and our new Acquaintance, dismissing the Shepherd's Boy with a Reward for his Trouble, soon found us a Way into it, after the following Manner: We remounted our Horses, and, after we had rode some Distance along the Trench, we came to the Mouth of a large Cave, in which ten Men might ride abreast, and seemed to be cut out of the Rock. Here we descended gradually for above a Mile under Ground upon a fine gravelly Road, having always sufficient Light thro' the Crevices of the Precipice on our Lefthand, which served as so many Windows. When we came to the Bottom, we spent a considerable Time in riding about, and viewing the monstrous Figures,[1] which appeared on every Side of the shocking Precipice which surrounded us: But we had the best Prospect from the Centre; the whole Group seeming chiefly to consist of Trees, Woods, and Houses, with Beasts, Serpents, and Fowls of the strangest Shapes, and here-and-there an huge Giant in Armour....

And now we took a different Route down the Mountain for our Return, in a Road less frequented; but, before we were descended half-way, we found ourselves stopped by the Fall of a great Num-

---

1 Carvings of figures into the rocks.

ber of tall Trees, occasioned by a furious Hurricane, which had happened there some Days before. This obliged us to seek our Way through the unfrequented Woods; where, afer we had travelled some Distance, we were surprised with the loud Shrieks and Cries, as we thought, of a Woman suffering some Violence pretty near, in the thickest Part of the Wood: This made us all immediately quit our Horses, leaving them with three of our Company; our three Guides, with their drawn Swords, followed by myself, and the rest, making our Way through the Thickets, as directed by the Voice, with what Expedition we could, to rescue the Person whom we supposed in Distress. The Cry still continuing, we presently came to a little Opening, in which we discovered a kind of Tent, or Pavilion, from whence it seemed to proceed. Into this we rushed, and to our great Surprize, found a young Lady sitting upon a Couch, to which she was fast tied with Cords from the Middle downwards; but we could perceive never a Soul near her. At this piteous Spectacle one of *Automathes*'s young Companions, named *Eustathes*, immediately knowing who she was, dropped his Sword, and ran to her Assistance, embracing her with the utmost Tokens of Tenderness and deep Affliction: And, as soon as she discovered her Deliverer, she cried out, O! my *Eustathes*! and swooned away in his Arms, being quite overcome with the sudden Torrent of Joy, which broke in upon her. We quickly cut asunder the rude cords by which this Fair-one was confined, and used our utmost Endeavours to bring her to herself; which, in a short time, we had the Pleasure to see effected. In the mean time, we especially, who were Strangers, wondered among ourselves to what this odd Adventure would tend; but our Wonder was much increased, when we came to understand, that this young Lady was no other than *Eustathes*'s espoused Wife; whose Marriage together, according to the Custom of the Country, was, within a few Days, designed to be consummated. Her Name was *Dorothea*, the only Daughter of a Widow Lady, who lived about one Quarter of the Distance between this Place and the House of the *Eugenius*, some Miles out of the Road. Her Affections, it seemed, had been placed upon *Eustathes*, even from her Childhood, and were not to be removed by all the Efforts, which were afterwards made by another young Cavalier, named *Phlegon*, who loved her even to Distraction, and, consequently, bore all the Hatred to *Eustathes*, which is too common in like Cases against an over-powerful Rival: And they were not without violent Suspicions, that all this was done by some villainous Contrivance of *Phlegon*, since they were not unacquainted with the Wickedness of his Disposition, and knew this secret Recess to stand upon his Ground, at scarce half an Hour's Ride from his House....

And in the very Moment, while *Eustathes* and *Dorothea* were expressing their Gratitude for this signal Instance of the Divine Care over them, they had so full a Confirmation how nearly they were escaped from the very Brink of Ruin, as made their Hearts to tremble; for *Automathes*, casting his Eyes through the Trees, observed *Phlegon* himself at some Distance, making towards us on Foot all alone; which we doubted not was to take Possession of his innocent Prey, and perpetrate his villainous Designs upon her. This we all fairly beheld, and waited with Silence, till we should have him within our Reach; but before this could happen, either through some Discovery he made of us, or our Companions with the Horses, he thought fit to make his Escape, with the utmost Precipitancy, thro' the Woods; where we thought it not worth our Time to pursue him. (275-83[71], 285[273][1])

---

1 In the original, the pages are misnumbered and begin with 265 on what should be 276. The misnumbering continues until the end of the book. The brackets contain the misnumbered pages, for ease of reference to the original.

Appendix C: Isolated Castaways

[The best-known island shipwreck tales feature an isolated castaway, and the most popular of these is undoubtedly Daniel Defoe's *Robinson Crusoe* (1719). It has long been supposed that Defoe's hero was based on the historical figure of Alexander Selkirk, who was discovered living alone on Juan Fernandez Island in the Pacific by Woodes Rogers. Rogers describes this account in his 1712 narrative, and it was further popularized by Richard Steele, who wrote an essay on Selkirk in 1713 for the newspaper *The Englishman*. Selkirk's story, however, was preceded not only by multiple versions of the Hayy Ibn Yaqzan narrative but by William Dampier's 1697 account of finding a Moskito Indian living alone on Juan Fernandez Island, where he had been abandoned by his ship's crew three years earlier. Defoe's *Robinson Crusoe*, which moves the island to the Atlantic, was followed up by two sequels, including *Serious Reflections During the Life and Surprising Adventures of Robinson Crusoe* (1720). Meanwhile, novels such as Peter Longueville's *The Hermit* (1727), the story of Phillip Quarl's survival in isolation for 50 years, became one of the most popular castaway imitations to follow in the wake of *Crusoe*. These fictional and nonfictional accounts tend to stress the ingenuity and survival skills of men living in isolation.]

1. From William Dampier, *New Voyage Round the World*, 1697

March the 22d 1684, we came in sight of the Island, and the next Day got in and anchored in a Bay at the South end of the Island, and 25 Fathom Water, not two Cables length from the Shore. We presently got out our Canoa, and went ashore to see for a *Moskito Indian*,[1] whom we left here when we were chased hence by three *Spanish* Ships in the Year 1681, a little before we went to *Arica*;[2]

---

1 The Moskito Indians are a Central American nation from the region of what is now Honduras and Nicaragua. Dampier is here referring to his crew's earlier transportation of this Indian to Juan Fernandez Island, which Dampier calls "*John Fernando's* Isle" (65).
2 Port city in northern Chile.

Capt. *Watlin* being then our Commander, after Capt. *Sharp* was turned out.

This *Indian* lived here alone above three Years, and altho' he was several Times sought after by the *Spaniards*, who knew he was left on the Island, yet they could never find him. He was in the Woods, hunting for Goats, when Captain *Watlin* drew off his Men, and the Ship was under sail before he came back to shore. He had with him his Gun and a Knife, with a small Horn of Powder, and a few Shot; which being spent, he contrived a way by notching his Knife, to saw the Barrel of his Gun into small Pieces, wherewith he made Harpoons, Lances, Hooks and a long Knife, heating the pieces first in the Fire, which he struck with his Gunflint, and a piece of the Barrel of his Gun, which he hardned; having learnt to do that among the *English*. The hot pieces of Iron he would Hammer out and bend as he pleased with Stones, and saw them with his jagged Knife; or grind them to an edge by long labour, and harden them to a good Temper as there was occasion. All this may seem strange to those that are not acquainted with the Sagacity of the *Indians*; but it is no more than these *Moskito* Men are accustomed to in their own Country, where they make their own Fishing and Striking Instruments, without either Forge or Anvil; tho' they spend a great deal of Time about them.... With such instruments as he made in that manner, he got such Provision as the Island afforded; either Goats or Fish. He told us that at first he was forced to eat Seal, which is very ordinary Meat, before he had made Hooks: but afterwards he never killed any Seals but to make Lines, cutting their Skins into Thongs. He had a little House or Hut half a Mile from the Sea, which was lin'd with Goats Skin; his Couch or Barbecu[1] of Sticks lying along about two foot distant from the Ground, was spread with the same, and was all his Bedding. He had no Cloaths left, having worn out those he brought from *Watlin*'s Ship, but only a Skin about his Waste.[2] He saw our Ship the Day before we came to an Anchor, and did believe we were *English*, and therefore kill'd three Goats in the Morning, before we came to an Anchor, and drest them with Cabbage, to treat us when we came ashore. He came then to the Sea-side to congratulate our safe Arrival. And when we landed, a *Moskito Indian*, named

---

1 A rack of sticks for drying meat.
2 Waist.

Robin,[1] first leap'd ashore, and running to his Brother *Moskito* Man, threw himself flat on his face at his feet, who helping him up, and embracing him, fell flat with his face on the Ground at *Robin*'s feet, and was by him taken up also. We stood with pleasure to behold the surprize, and tenderness, and solemnity of this Interview, which was exceedingly affectionate on both Sides; and when their Ceremonies of Civility were over, we also that stood gazing at them drew near, each of us embracing him we had found here, who was overjoyed to see so many of his old Friends come hither, as he thought purposely to fetch him. He was named *Will*, as the other was *Robin*. These were names given them by the *English*, for they had no Names among themselves; and they take it as a great favour to be named by any of us; and will complain for want of it, if we do not appoint them some name when they are with us: saying of themselves they are poor Men, and have no Name....

Goats were first put on the Island by *John Fernando*, who first discovered it on his Voyage from *Lima* to *Baldivia*; (and discovered also another Island about the same bigness, 20 Leagues to the Westward of this.) From those Goats these were propagated, and the Island hath taken its Name from this its first Discoverer, who when he returned to *Lima*, desired a Patent for it, designing to settle here; and it was in his second Voyage hither that he set ashore three or four Goats, which have since by their increase, so well stock'd the whole Island. (65-66, 67, 68)

2. From Woodes Rogers, *A Cruising Voyage Round the World*, 1712

We sent our Yall ashore about Noon, with Capt. *Dover*, Mr. *Frye*, and six Men, all arm'd; mean while we and the *Dutchess* kept turning to get in, and such heavy Flaws[2] came off the Land, that we were forc'd to let fly our Topsail-Sheet, keeping all Hands to stand by our Sails, for fear of the Wind's carrying 'em away: but when the Flaws were gone, we had little or no Wind. These Flaws proceeded from the Land, which is very high in the middle of the Island. Our Boat did not return, so we sent our Pinnace with the Men arm'd, to see what was the occasion of the Yall's

---

1 Possibly a source for the name of Defoe's castaway protagonist.
2 A wind squall or brief storm.

stay; for we were afraid that the *Spaniards* had a Garison there, and might have seiz'd 'em. We put out a Signal for our Boat, and the Dutchess show'd a *French* Ensign. Immediately our Pinnace return'd from the shore, and brought abundance of Craw-fish, with a Man cloth'd in Goat-Skins, who look'd wilder than the first Owners of them. He had been on the Island four Years and four Months, being left there by Capt' *Stradling* in the *Cinque-Ports*; his Name was *Alexander Selkirk* a *Scotch* Man, who had been Master of the *Cinque-Ports*, a Ship that came here last with Capt. *Dampier*, who told me that this was the best Man in her; so I immediately agreed with him to be a Mate on board our Ship. 'Twas he that made the Fire last night when he saw our Ships, which he judg'd to be *English*. During his stay here, he saw several Ships pass by, but only two came in to anchor. As he went to view them, he found 'em to be *Spaniards*, and retir'd from 'em; upon which they shot at him. Had they been *French*, he would have submitted; but chose to risque his dying alone on the Island, rather than fall into the hands of the *Spaniards* in these parts, because he apprehended they would murder him, or make a Slave of him in the Mines, for he fear'd they would spare no Stranger that might be capable of discovering the *South-Sea*. The *Spaniards* had landed, before he knew what they were, and they came so near him that he had much ado to escape; for they not only shot at him, but pursu'd him into the Woods, where he climb'd to the top of a Tree, at the foot of which they made water,[1] and kill'd several Goats just by, but went off again without discovering him. He told us that he was born at Largo in the County of *Fife* in *Scotland*, and was bred a Sailor from his Youth. The reason of his being left here was a difference betwixt him and his Captain; which, together with the Ships being leaky, made him willing rather to stay here, than go along with him at first; and when he was at last willing, the Captain would not receive him. He had been in the Island before to wood and water, when two of the Ships Company were left upon it for six Months till the Ship return'd, being chas'd thence by two *French South-Sea* ships.

He had with him his Clothes and Bedding; with a Firelock, some Powder, Bullets, and Tobacco, a Hatchet, a Knife, a Kettle, a Bible, some practical Pieces, and his Mathematical Instruments

---

1 Urinated.

and Books. He diverted and provided for himself as well as he could; but for the first eight months had much ado to bear up against Melancholy, and the Terror of being left alone in such a desolate place. He built two Hutts with Piemento Trees, cover'd them with long Grass, and lin'd them with the Skins of Goats, which he kill'd with his Gun as he wanted, so long as his Powder lasted, which was but a pound; and that being near spent, he got fire by rubbing two sticks of Piemento Wood together upon his knee. In the lesser Hutt, at some distance from the other, he dress'd his Victuals, and in the larger he slept, and employ'd himself in reading, singing Psalms, and praying; so that he said he was a better Christian while in this Solitude than ever he was before, or than, he was afraid, he should ever be again. At first he never eat any thing till Hunger constrain'd him, partly for grief, and partly for want of Bread and Salt; nor did he go to bed till he could watch no longer: the Piemento Wood, which burnt very clear, serv'd him both for Firing and Candle, and refresh'd him with its fragrant Smell....

After he had conquer'd his Melancholy, he diverted himself sometimes by cutting his Name on the Trees, and the Time of his being left and Continuance there. He was at first much pester'd with Cats and Rats, that had bred in great numbers from some of each Species which had got ashore from Ships that put in there to wood and water. The Rats gnaw'd his Feet and Clothes while asleep, which oblig'd him to cherish the Cats with his Goats-flesh; by which many of them became so tame, that they would lie about him in hundreds, and soon deliver'd him from the Rats. He likewise tam'd some Kids, and to divert himself would now and then sing and dance with them and his Cats: so that by the Care of Providence and Vigour of his Youth, being now but about 30 years old, he came at last to conquer all the In conveniences of his Solitude, and to be very easy. When his Clothes wore out, he made himself a Coat and Cap of Goat-Skins, which he stitch'd together with little Thongs of the same, that he cut with his Knife. He had no other Needle but a Nail; and when his Knife was wore to the back, he made others as well as he could of some Iron Hoops that were left ashore, which he beat thin and ground upon Stones. Having some Linen Cloth by him, he sow'd himself Shirts with a Nail, and stitch'd 'em with the Worsted of his old Stockings, which he pull'd out on purpose. He had his last Shirt on when we found him in the island. (71-72, 73)

3. From Daniel Defoe, *Robinson Crusoe*, 1719

Being the third Son of the Family, and not bred to any Trade, my Head began to be fill'd very early with rambling Thoughts: My Father, who was very ancient, had given me a competent Share of Learning, as far as House-Education, and a Country Free-School generally goes, and design'd me for the Law; but I would be satisfied with nothing but going to Sea, and my Inclination to this led me so strongly against the Will, nay the Commands of my Father, and against all the Entreaties and Perswasions of my Mother and other Friends, that there seem'd to be something fatal in that Propension of Nature tending directly to the Life of Misery which was to befal me.

My Father, a wise and grave Man, gave me serious and excellent Counsel against what he foresaw was my Design. He call'd me one Morning into his Chamber, where he was confined by the Gout, and expostulated very warmly with me upon this Subject: He ask'd me what Reasons more than a meer wandring Inclination I had for leaving my Father's House and my native Country, where I might be well introduced, and had a Prospect of raising my Fortunes by Application and Industry, with a Life of Ease and Pleasure. He told me it was for Men of desperate Fortunes on one Hand, or of aspiring, superior Fortunes on the other, who went abroad upon Adventures, to rise by Enterprize, and make themselves famous in Undertakings of a Nature out of the common Road; that these things were all either too far above me, or too far below me; that mine was the middle State, or what might be called the upper Station of *Low Life*, which he had found by long Experience was the best State in the World, the most suited to human Happiness, not exposed to the Miseries and Hardships, the Labour and Sufferings of the mechanick Part of Mankind, and not embarass'd with the Pride, Luxury, Ambition and Envy of the upper Part of Mankind....

It was not till almost a Year after this that I broke loose, tho' in the mean time I continued obstinately deaf to all Proposals of settling to Business, and frequently expostulating with my Father and Mother, about their being so positively determin'd against what they knew my Inclinations prompted me to. But being one Day at *Hull*, where I went casually, and without any Purpose of making an Elopement that time; but I say, being there, and one of my Companions being going by Sea to *London*, in his Father's Ship, and prompting me to go with them, with the common Allurement of Seafaring Men, *viz.* That it should cost me nothing for my Passage, I consulted neither Father or Mother any more, nor so much as sent them Word of it; but leaving them to hear of it as they might, without asking God's Blessing, or my Father's, without any Consideration of Circumstances or Consequences, and in an ill Hour, God knows.... (3-4, 7)

The last Time of these two had well near been fatal to me; for the Sea having hurried me along as before, landed me, or rather dash'd me against a Piece of a Rock, and that with such Force, as it left me senseless, and indeed helpless, as to my own Deliverance; for the Blow taking my Side and Breast, beat the Breath as it were quite out of my Body; and had it returned again immediately, I must have been strangled in the Water; but I recover'd a little before the return of the Waves, and seeing I should be cover'd again with the Water, I resolv'd to hold fast by a Piece of the Rock, and so to hold my Breath, if possible, till the Wave went back; now as the Waves were not so high as at first, being nearer Land, I held my Hold till the Wave abated, and then fetch'd another Run, which brought me so near the Shore, that the next Wave, tho' it went over me, yet did not so swallow me up as to carry me away, and the next run I took, I got to the main Land, where, to my great Comfort, I clamber'd up the Clifts of the Shore, and sat me down upon the Grass, free from Danger, and quite out of the reach of the Water....

I walk'd about on the Shore, lifting up my Hands, and my whole Being, as I may say, wrapt up in the Contemplation of my Deliverance, making a Thousand Gestures and Motions which I cannot describe, reflecting upon all my Comerades that were drown'd, and that there should not be one Soul sav'd but my self, for, as for them, I never saw them afterwards, or any Sign of them, except three of their Hats, one Cap, and two Shoes that were not Fellows....

After I had solac'd my Mind with the comfortable Part of my Condition, I began to look round me to see what kind of Place I was in, and what was next to be done, and I soon found my Comforts abate, and that in a word I had a dreadful Deliverance: For I was wet, had no Clothes to shift me, nor any thing either to eat or drink to comfort me, neither did I see any Prospect before me, but that of perishing with Hunger, or being devour'd by wild

Beasts; and that which was particularly afflicting to me, was, that I had no Weapon either to hunt and kill any Creature for my Sustenance, or to defend my self against any other Creature that might desire to kill me for theirs: In a Word, I had nothing about me but a Knife, a Tobacco-pipe, and a little Tobacco in a box, this was all my Provision, and this threw me into terrible Agonies of Mind, that for a while I run about like a Mad-man; Night coming upon me, I began with a heavy Heart to consider what would be my Lot if there were any ravenous Beasts in that Country, seeing at Night they always come abroad for their Prey.

All the Remedy that offer'd to my Thoughts at that Time, was, to get up into a thick bushy Tree like a Firr, but thorny, which grew near me, and where I resolv'd to set all Night, and consider the next Day what Death I should dye, for as yet I saw no Prospect of Life ... and having cut me a short Stick, like a Truncheon, for my Defence, I took up my Lodging, and having been excessively fatigu'd, I fell fast asleep, and slept as comfortably as, I believe, few could have done in my Condition, and found my self the most refresh'd with it, that I think I ever was on such an Occasion....

When I came down from my Appartment in the Tree, I look'd about me again, and the first thing I found was the Boat, which lay as the Wind and the Sea had toss'd her up upon the Land, about two Miles on my right Hand....

... and having consider'd well what I most wanted, I first got[1] three of the Seamens Chests, which I had broken open and empty'd, and lower'd them down upon my Raft; the first of these I fill'd with Provision, *viz.* Bread, Rice, three Dutch Cheeses, five Pieces of dry'd Goat's Flesh, which we liv'd much upon, and a little Remainder of *European* Corn which had been laid by for some Fowls which we brought to Sea with us, but the Fowls were kill'd; there had been some Barly and Wheat together, but, to my great Disappointment, I found afterwards that the Rats had eaten or spoil'd it all; as for Liquors, I found several Cases of Bottles belonging to our Skipper, in which were some Cordial Waters, and in all about five or six Gallons of Rack,[2] these I stow'd by themselves, there being no need to put them into the Chest, nor no room

---

1   From the boat which he has boarded by means of a raft.
2   Arrack, a distilled alcoholic drink.

for them ... it was after long searching that I found out the Carpenter's Chest, which was indeed a very useful Prize to me, and much more valuable than a Ship Loading of Gold would have been at that time; I got it down to my Raft, even whole as it was, without losing time to look into it, for I knew in general what it contain'd.

My next Care was for some Ammunition and Arms; there were two very good Fowling-pieces in the great Cabbin, and two Pistols, these I secur'd first, with some Powder-horns, and a small Bag of Shot, and two old rusty Swords....

My next Work was to view the Country, and seek a proper Place for my Habitation, and where to stow my Goods to secure them from whatever might happen; where I was I yet knew not, whether on the Continent or on an Island, whether inhabited or not inhabited, whether in Danger of wild Beasts or not: There was a Hill not above a Mile from me, which rose up very steep and high, and which seem'd to over-top some other Hills which lay as in a Ridge from it northward; I took out one of the fowling Pieces, and one of the Pistols, and an Horn of Powder, and thus arm'd I travell'd for Discovery up to the Top of that Hill, where after I had with great Labour and Difficulty got to the Top, I saw my Fate to my great Affliction, (*viz.*) that I was in an Island environ'd every Way with the Sea, no Land to be seen, except some Rocks which lay a great Way off, and two small Islands than this, which lay about three Leagues to the West.

I found also that the Island I was in was barren, and, as I saw good Reason to believe, un-inhabited, except by wild Beasts, of whom however I saw none, yet I saw Abundance of Fowls, but knew not their Kinds, neither when I kill'd them could I tell what was fit for Food, and what not; at my coming back, I shot at a great Bird which I saw sitting upon a Tree on the Side of a great Wood, I believe it was the first Gun that had been fir'd there since the Creation of the World; I had no sooner fir'd, but from all the Parts of the Wood there arose an innumerable Number of Fowls of many Sorts, making a confus'd Screaming, and crying every one according to his usual Note; but not one of them of any Kind that I knew: As for the Creature I kill'd, I took it to be a Kind of a Hawk, its Colour and Beak resembling it, but had no Talons or Claws more than common, its Flesh was Carrion, and fit for nothing. (45-53)

I observ'd, that the two[1] who swam, were yet more than twice as long swimming over the Creek, as the Fellow was, that fled from them: It came now very warmly upon my Thoughts, and indeed irresistibly, that now was my Time to get me a Servant, and perhaps a Companion, or Assistant; and that I was call'd plainly by Providence to save this poor Creature's Life; ... I slowly advanc'd towards the two that follow'd; then rushing at once upon the foremost, I knock'd him down with the Stock of my Piece; I was loath to fire, because I would not have the rest hear; though at that distance, it would not have been easily heard, and being out of Sight of the Smoke too, they wou'd not have easily known what to make of it: Having knock'd this Fellow down, the other who pursu'd with him stopp'd, as if he had been frighted; and I advanc'd a-pace towards him; but as I came nearer, I perceiv'd presently, he had a Bow and Arrow, and was fitting to shoot at me; so I was then necessitated to shoot at him first, which I did, and kill'd him at the first Shoot; the poor Savage who fled, but had stopp'd; though he saw both his Enemies fallen, and kill'd, as he thought; yet was so frighted with the Fire, and Noise of my Piece, that he stood Stock still, and neither came forward or went backward ... at length he came close to me, and then he kneel'd down again, kiss'd the Ground, and laid his Head upon the Ground, and taking me by the Foot, set my Foot upon his Head; this it seems was in token of swearing to be my Slave for ever....

But that which astonish'd him most, was to know how I had kill'd the other Indian so far off, so pointing to him, he made Signs to me to let him go to him, so I bad[2] him go, as well as I could, when he came to him, he stood like one amaz'd, looking at him, turn'd him first on one side, then on t'other, look'd at the Wound the Bullet had made, which it seems was just in his Breast, where it had made a Hole, and no great Quantity of Blood had follow'd, but he had bled inwardly, for he was quite dead; He took up his Bow, and Arrows, and came back....

He was a comely handsome Fellow, perfectly well made; with straight strong Limbs, not too large; tall and well shap'd, and as I reckon, about twenty six Years of Age. He had a very good

---

1 "Savages" who are pursuing another "savage" who has escaped from them.
2 Bade.

Countenance, not a fierce and surly Aspect; but seem'd to have something very manly in his Face, and yet he had all the Sweetness and Softness of an *European* in his Countenance too, especially when he smil'd. His Hair was long and black, not curl'd like Wool; his Forehead very high, and large, and a great Vivacity and sparkling Sharpness in his Eyes. The Colour of his Skin was not quite black, but very tawny; and yet not of an ugly yellow nauseous tawny, as the *Brasilians*, and *Virginians*, and other Natives of *America* are; but of a bright kind of dun olive Colour, that had in it something very agreeable; tho' not very easy to describe. His Face was round, and plump; his Nose small, not flat like the Negroes, a very good Mouth, thin Lips, and his fine Teeth well set, and white as ivory. After he had slumber'd, rather than slept, about half an Hour, he wak'd again, and comes out of the Cave to me; for I had been milking my Goats, which I had in the Enclosure just by: When he espy'd me, he came running to me, laying himself down again upon the Ground, with all possible Signs of an humble thankful Disposition, making a many antick Gestures to show it: At last he lays his Head flat upon the Ground, close to my Foot, and sets my other Foot upon his Head, as he had done before; and after this, made all the Signs to me of Subjection, Servitude, and Submission imaginable, to let me know, how he would serve me as long as he liv'd; I understood him in many Things, and let him know, I was very well pleas'd with him; in a little Time I began to speak to him, and teach him to speak to me; and first, I made him know his Name should be *Friday*, which was the Day I sav'd his Life; I call'd him so for the Memory of the Time; I likewise taught him to say *Master*, and then let him know, that was to be my Name....

During the long Time that *Friday* has now been with me, and that he began to speak to me, and understand me, I was not wanting to lay a Foundation of religious Knowledge in his Mind; particularly I ask'd him one Time who made him? The poor Creature did not understand me at all, but thought I had ask'd who was his Father; but I took it by another handle, and ask'd him who made the Sea, the Ground we walk'd on, and the Hills, and Woods; he told me it was one old *Benamuckee*, that liv'd beyond all: He could describe nothing of this great Person, but that he was very old; much older he said than the Sea, or the Land; than the Moon, or the Stars: I ask'd him then, if this old Person had made all Things, why did not all Things worship him; he look'd very grave, and with a perfect Look of Innocence, said, *All Things do say O to him*: I ask'd him if the People who die in his Country went away any where; he said, yes, they all went to *Benamuckee*; then I ask'd him whether these they eat up went thither too, he said yes.

From these Things, I began to instruct him in the Knowledge of the true God: I told him that the great maker of all Things liv'd up there, pointing up towards Heaven: That he governs the World by the same Power and Providence by which he had made it: That he was omnipotent, could do every Thing for us, give every Thing to us, take every Thing from us; and thus by Degrees I open'd his Eyes. He listned with great Attention, and receiv'd with Pleasure the Notion of *Jesus Christ* being sent to redeem us, and of the Manner of making our Prayers to God, and his being able to hear us, even into Heaven; he told me one Day, that if our God could hear us up beyond the Sun, he must needs be a greater God than their *Benamuckee*, who liv'd but a little way off, and yet could not hear, till they went up to the great Mountains where he dwelt, to speak to him; I ask'd him if ever he went thither, to speak to him; he said no, they never went that were young Men; none went thither but the old Men, who he call'd their *Oowacakee*, that is, as I made him explain it to me, their Religious, or Clergy, and that they went to say *O*, (so he called saying Prayers) and then came back, and told them what *Benamuckee* said: By this I observ'd, That there is *Priestcraft*, even amongst the most blinded ignorant Pagans in the World; and the Policy of making a secret Religion, in order to preserve the Veneration of the People to the Clergy, is not only to be found in the *Roman*, but perhaps among all Religions in the World, even among the most brutish and barbarous Savages.

I endeavour'd to clear up this Fraud, to my Man *Friday*, and told him, that the Pretence of their old Men going up the Mountains, to say *O* to their God *Benamuckee*, was a cheat, and their bringing Word from thence what he said, was much more so; that if they met with any Answer, or spake with any one there, it must be with an evil Spirit: And then I entred into a long Discourse with him about the Devil, the Original of him, his Rebellion against God, his Enmity to Man, the Reason of it, his setting himself up in the dark Parts of the World to be Worship'd instead of God, and as God; and the many Strategems he made use of to delude Mankind to his Ruine; how he had a secret access to our Passions, and to our Affections, to adapt his Snares so to our Inclinations, as to cause us even to be our own Tempters, and to run upon our Destruction by our own Choice....

My Island was now peopled, and I thought my self very rich in Subjects;[1] and it was a merry Reflection which I frequently made, How like a King I look'd. First of all, the whole Country was my own meer Property; so that I had an undoubted Right of Dominion. *2ndly,* My People were perfectly subjected: I was absolute Lord and Law-giver; they all owed their Lives to me, and were ready to lay down their Lives, *if there had been Occasion of it,* for me. It was remarkable too, we had but three Subjects, and they were of three different Religions. My Man *Friday* was a Protestant, his Father was a *Pagan* and a *Cannibal,* and the *Spaniard* was a Papist: However, I allow'd Liberty of Conscience throughout my Dominions: But this is by the Way. (202-06, 216-17, 241)

I was at first ready to sink down with the Surprize. For I saw my Deliverance indeed visibly put into my Hands, all things easy, and a large Ship just ready to carry me away whither I pleased to go. At first, for some time, I was not able to answer him[2] one Word; but as he had taken me in his Arms, I held fast by him, or I should have fallen to the Ground....

Then I took my Turn, and embrac'd him as my Deliverer; and we rejoyc'd together. I told him, I look upon him as a Man sent from Heaven to deliver me, and that the whole Transaction seemed to be a Chain of Wonders; that such things as these were the Testimonies we had of a secret Hand of Providence governing the World, and an Evidence, that the Eyes of an infinite Power could search into the remotest Corner of the World, and send Help to the Miserable whenever he pleased....

After these Ceremonies past, and after all his good things were brought into my little Apartment, we began to consult what was to be done with the Prisoners[3] we had; for it was worth con-

---

1 Crusoe and Friday earlier discovered a group of natives visiting the island and preparing to feast on two prisoners they held captive: one was a Spaniard and the other turns out to be Friday's father. By this point, the two have killed the natives and set their two prisoners free.
2 The captain of an English ship that earlier arrived on shore after a mutiny. The captain has at this point recovered control of the ship.
3 Members of the ship's crew who mutinied against the captain and who have been captured by Crusoe and the captain.

sidering, whether we might venture to take them away with us or no, especially two of them, who we knew to be incorrigible and refractory to the last Degree; and the Captain said, he knew they were such Rogues, that there was no obliging them, and if he did carry them away, it must be in Irons, as Malefactors to be delivered over to Justice at the first *English* Colony he could come at; and I found that the Captain himself was very anxious about it.

Upon this, I told him, that if he desir'd it, I durst undertake to bring the two Men he spoke of, to make it their own Request that he should leave them upon the Island: *I should be very glad of that*, says the Captain, *with all my Heart*....

When the Captain was gone, I sent for the Men up to me to my Apartment, and entred seriously into Discourse with them of their Circumstances, I told them, I thought they had made a right Choice; that if the Captain carry'd them away, they would certainly be hang'd. I shewed them the new Captain, hanging at the Yard-Arm of the Ship,[1] and told them they had nothing less to expect.

When they had all declar'd their Willingness to stay, I then told them, I would let them into the Story of my living there, and put them into the Way of making it easy to them: Accordingly I gave them the whole History of the Place, and of my coming to it; shew'd them my Fortifications, the Way I made my Bread, planted my Corn, cured my Grapes; and in a word, all that was necessary to make them easy: I told them the Story also of the sixteen *Spaniards* that were to be expected; for whom I left a Letter, and made them promise to treat them in common with themselves[2]....

And thus I left the Island, the Nineteenth of *December*, as I found by the Ship's Account, in the Year 1686, after I had been upon it eight and twenty Years, two Months, and 19 Days; being deliver'd from this second Captivity, the same Day of the Month,

---

1 The leader of the mutiny has been killed and is hanged to serve as an example to the other crewmembers. The remaining mutineers agree to stay on the island since they would face a similar punishment if they returned to England. Crusoe leaves them with instructions on how to survive on the island.

2 The Spaniard (and Friday) earlier departed for the mainland with plans to find and bring back to the island his 16 countrymen who were living there as castaways among the natives.

that I first made my Escape in the *Barco-Longo*, from among the *Moors* of *Sallee.*

In this Vessel, after the long Voyage, I arriv'd in *England*, the Eleventh of *June*, in the Year 1687, having been thirty and five Years absent. (273-78)

I was now Master, all on a Sudden, of above 5000 *l. Sterling* in Money, and had an Estate, as I might well call it, in the *Brasils*, of above a thousand Pounds a Year, as sure as an Estate of Lands in *England*: And in a Word, I was in a Condition which I scarce knew how to understand, or how to compose my self, for the Enjoyment of it....

I was now to consider which Way to steer my Course next, and what to do with the Estate that Providence had thus put into my Hands, and indeed I had more Care upon my Head now, than I had in my silent State of Life in the Island, where I wanted nothing but what I had, and had nothing but what I wanted: Whereas I had now a great Charge upon me, and my Business was how to secure it....

In the mean time, I in Part settled my self here; for first of all I marry'd, and that not either to my Disadvantage or Dissatisfaction, and had three Children, two Sons and one Daughter: But my Wife dying, and my Nephew coming Home with good Success from a Voyage to *Spain*, my Inclination to go Abroad, and his Importunity prevailed and engag'd me to go in his Ship, as a private Trader to the *East Indies*: This was in the Year 1694.

In this Voyage I visited my new Colony in the Island, saw my Successors the *Spaniards*, had the whole Story of their Lives, and of the Villains I left there....

Besides this, I shar'd the Island into parts with 'em, reserv'd to my self the Property of the whole, but gave them such Parts respectively as they agreed on; and having settled all things with them, and engaged them not to leave the Place, I left them there.

From thence I touch'd at the *Brasils*, from whence I sent a Bark, which I bought there, with more People to the Island, and in it, besides other Supplies, I sent seven Women, being such as I found proper for Service, or for Wives to such as would take them: As to the *English* Men, I promis'd them to send them some Women from *England*, with a good Cargoe of Necessaries, if they would apply themselves to Planting, which I afterwards perform'd. And the Fellows prov'd very honest and diligent after they were master'd, and had their Properties set apart for them. I sent them also from the *Brasils* five Cows, three of them being big with Calf, some Sheep, and some Hogs, which, when I came again, were considerably encreas'd. (285-86, 305-06)

4. From Daniel Defoe, *Serious Reflections During the Life and Surprising Adventures of Robinson Crusoe*, 1720

If we take the north part of America, exclusive of all the country which the Spaniards possess, and which they call the empire of Mexico, and exclusive too of what the English and French possess on the coast and in the two rivers of Canada and Mississippi as above, which indeed are but trifles, the rest of that country, which, as far as it has been travelled into, is found exceeding populous, is a great deal larger than all Europe ... —I say this vast continent, full of people, and no doubt inhabited by many millions of souls, is all wrapt up in idolatry and paganism, given up to ignorance and blindness, worshipping the sun, the moon, the fire, the hills their fathers, and, in a word, the devil.

As to the thing we call religion, or the knowledge of the true God, much less the doctrine of the Messiah and the name of Christ, they not only have not, but never had the least intimation of it on earth, or revelation of it from heaven, till the Spaniards came among them; nay, and now Christians are come among them, it is hard to say whether the paganism is much abated except by the infinite ravages the Spaniards made where they came, who rooted out idolatry by destroying the idolaters, not by converting them....

Let but an open door be made for the preaching of the word of God, and the ministers of Christ be admitted, if they do not spread Christian knowledge over the face of the earth the fault will be theirs. Let but the military power reduce the pagan world, and banish the devil and Mahomet from the face of the earth, the knowledge of God be diligently spread, the word of God duly preached, and the people meekly and faithfully instructed in the Christian religion, the world would soon receive the truth, and the knowledge of Divine things would be the study and delight of mankind. (221-22, 227)

5. From Peter Longueville, *The Hermit*, 1727

About forty Paces further, he finds a Chest in a Clift of the Rock, which had been wash'd up there by the Violence of the late Storm: Heavens, said he, more fatal Effects of Fate's Cruelty and Man's Temerity! Was the Sea made for Men to travel on? Is there not Land enough for his rambling Mind to rove? Must he hunt after Dangers and put Death to Defiance? What is the Owner of this the better for it now? Or, who can be the better in a Place so remote, and the Access to it so difficult, being not to be approach'd, but on the Wings of Providence, and over the Back of Death? Now, was this full of massy Gold, or yet richer Things, I thank my God, I am above the Use of it; yet I'll take it Home, it was sent here by Providence; perhaps for the Relief of some so necessitated and destitute; so goes to lift it, but could not, therefore was oblig'd to fetch his Hatchet to beat it open, that he might take away what was in it by degrees; so having taken as much of the Sail-Cloath as he could conveniently carry, with the few Oysters he had got, he went Home and fetch'd the Tool, wherewith he wrench'd the Chest open, from which he took a Suit of Cloaths and some wearing Linen, these, said he, neither the Owner, nor I, do want, so laid them down, the next Thing he took out, was a Roll of several Sheets of Parchment, being blank Indentures and Leases; these, said he, are Instruments of the Law, and often apply'd to Injustice; but I'll alter their mischievious Properties, and make them Records of Heavens Mercies, and Providence's wonderful Liberality to me; so instead of being the Ruin of some, they may chance to be the reclaiming of others: At the Bottom of the Chest lay a Rundlet[1] of Brandy, a *Cheshire* Cheese, a Leather Bottle full of Ink, with a Parcel of Pens, and a Pen-Knife; as for these, said he, they are of Use, the Pens, Ink, and Parchment have acquip'd me to keep a Journal, which will divert and pass away a few anctious Hours; as for the Cheese and Brandy, they will but cause me new Cares, before I had 'em, I wanted 'em not; now, the Benefit and Comfort I shall find in them (when gone) will make me hanker after them most; I wish I had still been without 'em, but now they are here, it would be a Sin to let them be lost, I'll take them Home, and only use them

---

1 Unit of measurement. A rundlet is a fourteenth of a tun, or slightly less than a hogshead.

at my need, which will both make them hold out the longer, and me grow less fond of them.

So by Degrees takes Home the Chest, and what was in it; and now having Materials to begin his Journal, he immediately fell to Work, that, for want of other Books, he might, at his Leisure, peruse his past Transactions, and the many Mercies he had receiv'd from Heaven; and, that after his Decease, whoever is directed there by Providence, upon reading his wonderful Escapes in the greatest of Dangers, his miraculous Living, when remote from human Assistance, that in the like Extremity they might not despair: Thus begins, from his being eight Years old (as well as he can remember he heard an old Aunt of his say) to the Day of his being Cast-away, which happen'd on the 10th of *July* 1675, being then twenty eight Years of Age, resolving to continue it to his Death. (182-84)

Appendix D: Castaway Communities

[In 1719, the same year that *Robinson Crusoe* was published, *The Adventures and Surprizing Deliverances of James Dubourdieu, and His Wife* also appeared. This narrative is recounted by a woman and features not a lone man surviving on an island but a group of castaways who strive to recreate some semblance of society on their island. Many of the texts in this tradition—such as Penelope Aubin's *The Life of Charlotta Du Pont, an English Lady* (1723) and W.R. Chetwood's *The Voyages and Adventures of Captain Robert Boyle* (1726)—consist of multiple plots and subplots involving forced marriages, pirates, and shipwreck. Rather than assert dominance over the natural world and create a kingdom on an island, these castaways often forge communities where they construct civilization in isolation. While the stories of DuPont and Dubourdieu are set in the Atlantic world, the latter was printed together with the castaway story of Alexander Vendchurch, set largely in the Pacific. Similarly, one serialized account published in 1760 followed the fate of a supposed 1597 Spanish expedition from Panama that wrecks in the Pacific while in search of riches. The voyagers visit an island of Indians who worship a sun idol, live in a subterranean cavern on another island, and discover a strangely unsatisfying utopia before returning later that year to Acapulco.]

1. From [Ambrose Evans], *The Adventures and Surprizing Deliverances, of James Dubourdieu, and his Wife: Who were taken by Pyrates, and carried to the Uninhabited-Part of the Isle of Paradise*, 1719

I told you just now of our retreat into the thicket, to avoid the rage and lust of the pirates;[1] but having staid there the next day 'till near noon, without hearing any thing of them, it was agreed to send one of our party out to gain intelligence how things stood, and Monsieur Dubourdieu proffer'd himself to be the man; he

---

1 The story is narrated by Dubourdieu's wife, Mrs. Martha Rattenberg (whose name, the novel explains, did not change upon marriage, in accordance with French tradition).

return'd again in a little more than an hour, full of amazement, and telling us that we might all quit our lurking place, since our enemies, in all probability, were no more, but swallow'd up, ship and all, in the earthquake that we felt something of last night, or were overwhelm'd with that vast quantity of earth that had risen up and cover'd all that part of the island where they were, and reach'd even as far, within a few furlongs, as our last settlement. Upon his assurances, full of thanks for our escape, we all came out into the open country, and went back to see the strange revolution in our little world; and were stricken with unspeakable terror and wonder at the sight we beheld, finding that all the country, from our settlement to the sea, had entirely chang'd its face; and that in the night, in the midst of those terrible noises which we heard, the sea or earth had thrown up prodigious mountains for twelve miles together; that is, from the most *Westerly* point of those rocks. We saw at our coming hither, even six miles beyond the main land of the island to the *West*, by which jetting out into the sea there was form'd a sort of a haven, or calm road, protected against all winds but the *West* and *Northwest*; that from the height of these mountains, in all probability, there had tumbled down such vast quantities of earth, as to have cover'd all the low-land, and part of the sea, for betwixt three and four miles broad, and so rais'd the surface by an easy ascent up to the mountains themselves.

We view'd all this so long, that we were almost stupid with the confusion which it gave us; blessing our good fortune that had made us fly so far from this dangerous neighbourhood; and tho' the pirates and their Ladies were a parcel of most profligate wretches, we could not but pity their terrible fate, which had so on a sudden sunk them in the midst of their sins; but our own proper fears soon banish'd these considerations, and made us think of removing to some other settlement, farther from this direful place; but since we could not presently carry away our effects, we were content to go only with our hammocks some few miles from it, 'till we had fix'd upon a convenient situation....

Mr. *Walker*, his Lady, and the old Gentlewoman could speak no *French*, nor could the *Frenchmen* at first speak any *English*, but in time they came to speak it intelligibly; 'till when, most of the conversation run thro' my hands, I being interpreter to them all, tho' they were every one full of the complaisance, so usual in those of that nation; yet *Monsieur Dubourdieu* discover'd a more than ordinary civility to, and care of me, nor did he at last make any scruple of declaring, that he had a peculiar love for me.

One day when the men were gone out for provisions, or a walk, and we women were left alone, Mrs. *Walker* discover'd a very great uneasiness at her present condition, and express'd her fear that she would never get from this place. I did what I could to comfort her, and told her, that I thought our present state something better than that of our first parents after the Fall, they being more solitary for several years together, since there was no other people in the world but themselves, nor could expect any 'till their children were grown up fit for conversation; but we were a pretty jolly company, and were not without hopes we might be deliver'd by the chance arrival of some ship. True, said she, but that is very uncertain, since I find, that the pirates themselves, who are us'd to these seas, knew nothing of this island; so that there is more probability of the decrease than the increase of our company. Oh, Madam, said I, as long as you live, I hope we shall every now and then increase by a little one from you, since I find, at last, an instance of it from your being with child. That will be but slow work, interpos'd Mrs. *Wright*, unless you add to the number of our breeders, by marrying *Monsieur Dubourdieu*, who has long express'd his love for you.[1] I would fain have diverted the discourse, but the old Gentlewoman went on; you find, said she, that he is the only person among the six men whom you can make choice of for a husband; the three joyners hear,[2] are, by their own confession, marry'd men; and the two priests, you know, according to their Religions, can have no wives: Nor, said I, is *Monsieur Dubourdieu* like to have one in me, he is too much a stranger to me to entertain any such thoughts about him, and I have suffer'd too much already, by being credulous of the professions of mankind.

This was the sum of that day's discourse, which Mrs. *Walker* told her husband, and in that, the rest of the company; as soon

---

1   This concern with island reproduction follows in the tradition of the popular narrative *The Isle of Pines*, published in 1688 by Henry Neville. The book tells the story of George Pine, who is shipwrecked in the Pacific and survives along with four women, three white and one black. When the island is discovered by visitors many decades later, it has been populated by the hundreds of offspring Pine fathered with these women.

2   Here.

as they came to us, *Monsieur Dubourdieu* return'd them thanks for their good offices, and desir'd earnestly that they would renew them, nor give over 'till they had vanquish'd my obstinacy: They perfectly comply'd with his desire, nor would let me alone; 'till having had sufficient experience of his good temper, and verily believing that I should have better fortune with him, than I formerly had, either with the *English* or *Irishman*; in the beginning of the third year, I consented to become his wife, and the ceremony was perform'd by the elder of the two priests, who could speak the best *English*, and who was forc'd to satisfy me, in performing it over again, according to my *Common-Prayer Book*.[1] ...

The priest, and Mr. *Dubourdieu*, went daily out a walking, either to the sea side Westward, to see if they could discover any ship, or sometimes to the North-west hill on the same errand, but it was long before they ventur'd upon the new hill that was risen upon the South-west part; but at last seeing it all over green, they went up to the top of it, and from its height look'd out for ships, but to no purpose; this being too far for a day's walk, without a great fatigue, they would not venture to stay long for fear of frightening us by their absence, without letting us know of it beforehand; but they agreed to go on purpose to stay a day or two, in order to search it from one end to the other; accordingly, in about a week's time, they went, and return'd in three days after, giving us this account; That the hill thrown up in the night, was about twelve miles long, and three miles in the declivity; that going to the most easterly part of it, they came within ten foot of the mountainous rocks that were there before; that being there by day break, they heard the most harmonious musick, both vocal and instrumental, that could be imagin'd on this side heaven: The priest, who had been in *Italy*, and present at all the performances of both voices, and musick, which were eminent in that country, declar'd, that they were all insipid and flat, in comparison of what he had now heard; and they both told us, it seem'd to them to pass on like a procession, tho' it was of some hours continuance. (51-52, 54-55, 59-60)

---

1   This episode recalls the reluctant marriage of Unca Eliza Winkfield to her cousin.

From thence we were re-conducted to our lodging, but our masters[1] then ventur'd to come closer to us, and every day endeavour'd, with abundance of diligence, to instruct us in their language; and when we could understand them tolerably well, they seem'd very inquisitive to know what we were? When we came? And how we got thither? In all which we endeavour'd to give them what satisfaction we could, with that little part of their language which we understood; but being at last good masters of it, we gave them an account of our country, religion, and manners, and also of our voyage to that place. We had much ado to make them understand what a ship was, and how it was possible for us to pass so many worlds of seas as should take us up near seven months in our passage, and that without seeing land once in all that time; but they seem'd amaz'd not only at so strange a passage where no tract could direct them, but that men should venture their lives in so small a machine so far from their own country. They frequently ask'd us what could be the motive to so hazardous an undertaking? And said that surely we inhabited some miserable climate, that we should chuse to fly from it thro' so many dangers.

We did all we could to make them understand that it was in pursuit of gain and riches for which we did this; but we could by no means make them comprehend what gain and riches were. They ask'd us whether we wanted food in our own country, and were forc'd on that account to seek it abroad? We told them it was not that, but the earnest desire of having more than what was absolutely necessary, that made us venture so far, since large possessions and great abundance did not only gain the respect and veneration of those who had not the same advantage, but even an authority over them. This likewise seem'd to puzzle them, for they could not form an idea of any pleasure and fascination that there should be in those things; but to give them the better notion of it, we proceeded to give them an account of our manners and condition: That envy, malice, ambition, avarice and lust, rul'd absolutely in our parts of the world; and that he who was not in some measure a slave to any of them, was look'd upon either as contemptible, or indeed very miserable.

I find, said one of them, that you are the number of the children

---

1 The castaways have at this point discovered a remote society of native peoples and are being questioned by this community.

of wrath, of which we have an obscure traditionary account, tho' we could scarce believe it, 'till your words now confirm the fact. Oh! wretched generation, with whom reason has so little power, and passion so much. How happy are we, who want nothing that's necessary to life, nor have any desire or wishes for what we do not want.

After some of these conversations we were admitted to more liberty, and allow'd a greater freedom of going among the natives in general, at least in those parts which were not far from our first lodgings, whither we were every night conducted and guarded with our *Lyons*. I call them *Lyons*, not that they were really so; but because their heads and manes were more like *Lyons* than any other creature I know of; but by their temper and condition they might rather be call'd dogs, tame and domestick animals, and were much more terrible in their aspect than in their nature: As for their food, they liv'd not upon flesh, but upon the fruit and herbage of the country, and therefore their teeth were not made like those of *Lyons*, or dogs, or any other voracious animal; they were mighty tractable and obedient to the beck of their masters, and were bréd so, that they every day went their rounds about the hills; by which means we first fell into their custody. We saw several other animals, both birds, and four-footed beasts, tho' none of them like any we have in our parts of the world; they were all tame, and would come to the hand....

By a frequent conversation, I found that the people of this place had no form of government among them, but liv'd like that colony of the Sidonians, mention'd in the book of Judges; that is, without magistrates, or any rule, which might contradict the inclinations of every particular or individual. And indeed there was no occasion for magistrates, when there was no ground for contention; there being no property among them, but a perpetual and uninterrupted course of a perfect love of one another. What the earth produc'd was a sufficient stock, plentifully to provide for their subsistence; and their cultivation of these products was so far from being laborious to them, that it was only their exercise and diversion....

I could not observe that they made any difference of days, or distinguish'd *Sunday* from the rest; but upon our mentioning that we set apart one day in seven, as a day peculiar for the service of God, which we therefore call the Lord's day, they cry'd out, in a sort of a wonder, Why is not every day the day of the Lord, and dedicated to his service either in prayer, or such duties and exercises as he has ordain'd? But when we said we did it in commemoration of God's resting from his labour, after he had in six days created the heavens and the earth, and all things in them; they stopp'd their ears, and cry'd out, Blasphemy; esteeming it so, in calling whatever God did, labour; and expressing it in such a manner, as if tir'd with his foregoing work he wanted rest, like man, to refresh himself. We were at last admitted to their conversation after dinner, and there, to the whole company, gave an account of the customs, laws, manners and vices of our part of the world; particularly of our wars, and the many thousands slain in battle, with the vast devastations and desolation which the ambition of princes brought upon their people, all which seem'd to strike them with the utmost horror: However, this was the occasion that we were sent from tribe to tribe round the whole island, and oblig'd to each tribe in several particular and general assemblies to rehearse the same account, and always met with the same horror and detestation in every one of our audiences. This progress of ours took up the rest of the time that we staid among them; but before we were permitted to go away, there was a general assembly of the elders of all the tribes, at which were present likewise many of the younger sort; the place in which this assembly was held was about the middle of the Island, where, in a spatious plain, there arose a magnificent building, if I may call that a building whose walls were all vegetables, for they were composed of several lofty trees set at convenient distances, the spaces between each being fill'd up with smaller plants, which being interwoven, each within the other, seem'd a sort of a green wall which did not rise up to the roof, but left several openings like windows to let in both the air and the light; the roof being form'd out of branches of the tall trees seem'd supported by them as by so many pillars; the roof of this was much the same with that I describ'd; and here likewise was such another ampitheatre, tho' much larger, and capable of holding a far greater number of people. In the midst of this there grew another lofty tree, whose branches spread far and wide, and help'd to compleat the canopy that kept off the sun and weather from incommoding the assembly. Beneath this middle tree, there was a bank all rais'd up behind it to such an eminence that it overlook'd the audience, and from it were made such speeches as were address'd to the whole company; and here it was that we were to have our audience of leave, as I may call it;

and where my good friend the Priest had like to have spoil'd all by an untimely zeal for propagating the Gospel among them; for being mounted upon this eminence, after he had given thanks for the human[1] treatment we had met with among them, he went on, and first prais'd their happiness in their knowledge of the true God, as well as in the place of their abode, and the strength and fineness of their reasoning; but, said he, there is still one thing wanting to render your felicity compleat; that is, to hinder its expiring with your life, for I do assure you, there are much greater blessings in the eternal kingdom of God, which can only be obtain'd by the means of Jesus Christ. In return therefore of all our obligations, and in obedience to the dictates of my conscience, I shall offer you another religion, which is yet in some measure built on that which you already profess. Here the audience would not let him proceed any farther, and one of the eldest of the company spoke thus to him. Stranger, let not thy ignorance of what we believe, put thee upon a fruitless trouble to waste our time in hearing what can never have any agreeable effect among us; therefore before you proceed, hear an account of our religion, and then if you can offer any thing better you shall have leave to speak. Upon this we were ordered to descend and stand among the audience; and a young virgin of about fifteen, was commanded to mount the eminence in our room, and thence to give an account of their religion. They did this for two ends; first, to shew how well their young ones were instructed; and next by way of contempt, by putting so young a creature to open the argument against us. When she was got up, bowing her self, and putting one knee to the ground, she implor'd heaven to enable her to speak in such a manner as was agreeable to the importance of what she had to utter. *O Assa*, (which by interpretation signifies Thou Being without a name) 'tis thou whom we adore, thou who hast produc'd, by thy infinite power and wisdom, all things that fill the universe; thou who art infinite and every where; thou who dost by thy providence sustain every thing that is, and which only and wholly subsists by and in thee; thou who hadst no beginning, but didst give beginning to every thing else, to thee are all our prayers and our praises due and daily paid, as our eternal benefactor and source; and to thee be praise for evermore. (76-80, 84-88)

---

1 Humane.

2. From Penelope Aubin, *The Life of Charlotta Du Pont, An English Lady*, 1723

I believed something new and diverting would be welcome to the Town, and that the Adventures of a young Lady, whose Life contains the most extraordinary Events that I ever heard of or read of, might agreeably entertain you at a time when our News-Papers furnish nothing of moment. The Story of Madam Charlotta du Pont, I had from the Mouth of a Gentleman of Integrity, who related it as from his own Knowledge. I have join'd some other Historys to hers, to imbellish, and render it more entertaining and useful, to incourage Virtue, and excite us to heroic Actions, which is my principal Aim in all I write; and this I hope you will rather applaud than condemn me for.... (v-vi)

According to the Resolution taken in the Morning, *Charlotta* and the rest[1] walk'd to the Rock in the Evening, and getting up to the top of it, saw from thence the black Man standing at the entrance of his Cave, with a white Woman who seem'd to be very young and very handsom[e]; she had a *Molotta* Child in her Arms about a year old, her Gown and Petticoat was made of a fine Silk. Don *Mendenta* call'd to them in *French*, at which the Man look'd up; and *Charlotta* spoke in *English* to the Woman, desiring her to come up and speak to her; on which the Blackamoor push'd the Woman in, and returning no answer, shut the door upon himself and her. Don *Mendenta* and the rest concluded, that they fear'd being discovered; so they all descended the Rock and went to the Door, resolving to force it open if they could not gain entrance otherwise ... they broke open the Door with much difficulty, and entering, went thro a narrow Passage in the Rock, so strait that but one Person could go a-breast; at the end of which they came into some strange Rooms fashion'd by Nature, tho cleans'd of Moss and loose Stones by labour: Into these Light enter'd by the Holes that were in some places open thro the top of the Rocks; but some part of the Caves, or Caverns (for they were scarce fit

---

1 Charlotta, the daughter of a French father and an English mother, is sold to a ship captain by her stepmother. The ship is attacked by pirates and is rescued by a Spanish ship carrying Don Mendenta, son of the Governor of St. Domingo. That ship wrecks and leaves the group stranded on a near-deserted island. Here they discover an interracial couple living in exile on the island.

to be call'd Rooms) were very dark. In the biggest Room was a Lamp burning, and here they saw two Chests lock'd, and on a Shelf some Platters and Bowls made of Calibash-shells, with two or three wooden Spits; and some Sticks were burning in a corner of the Room, in a place made with Stones pil'd round, and opening in the front like a Furnace, on which stood a Pot, wherein something was boiling.... At last they heard a Child cry, and following the sound of the Voice, went thro a narrow Turning on the right Hand, which brought them to a Place where a Door was shut, before which lay a terrible Bear: Don *Mendenta*, who was the foremost, carrying the Lamp in one hand, and his Sword in the other, being presently more apprehensive of *Charlotta*'s danger than his own, she being next behind him, ran at the Bear, designing to kill it, if possible, before it could rise; but was stop'd by the sound of a human Voice which came from that Beast, saying, "For Heaven's sake, spare my life, and I'll do all you'll have me." At these words the Negro came out of the Bear's Skin, and threw himself at *Mendenta*'s Feet, who took him up ... And now they were all cheerful, and the Negro being told, that they wanted nothing but his assistance, to carry one of them to any of the adjacent Islands that was inhabited to get them some Provisions, and hire a Vessel to carry them to the Island of St. *Domingo*, he readily promis'd to do it....

"And now I have acquainted you with all my unhappy Story,[1] and must implore your Assistance to persuade *Domingo* to leave this Place, and take us with you, or else help me to escape from him; tho I would now willingly consent to be his Wife, having Treasure sufficient to purchase us a good Settlement in any Place. If he be ever found by any body from *Virginia*, my Father will surely put him to death, but *Domingo* will [illegible] first; and to live thus is worse than Death." Here she wept, and *Charlotta* embracing her, promis'd never to part with her. "No, my dear *Isabinda*, said she, we will part no more; *Domingo* shall be

---

1   This is the conclusion of the narrative of Isabinda, the daughter of a white Virginia planter who was kidnapped by Domingo, an African prince (and Muslim) enslaved on her father's plantation who is in love with her. The boat on which the two escape from Virginia had earlier wrecked on the same deserted island where Charlotta and the other castaways find them. At this point, Isabinda and Domingo have a child together and wish to marry; later, Isabinda also converts to Islam (99).

carry'd hence to the Place we are bound to, where he may safely and lawfully possess you; since you now love, as I perceive, and have forgiven him his Crime in getting you, we will assist him to be happy. The selling human Creatures, is a Crime my Soul abhors; and Wealth so got, ne'er thrives. Tho he is black, yet the Almighty made him as well as us, and Christianity ne'er taught us Cruelty: we ought to visit those Countrys to convert, not buy our Fellow-creatures, to enslave and use them as if we were Devils, or they not Men." Don *Mendenta* join'd with her in opinion; and the Captain and all agreed to have them marry'd, and take them along with 'em.... (79-82, 88-89)

I was two Days and Nights acrawling to this ruinous Place,[1] into which I enter'd to rest my self, being quite spent. I had a Bottle of Wine, and some Bread and Meat ty'd up in a Cloth in this little Basket, in which I us'd to gather Fruit for the Table. After I had eat and slept here, I begin to consider what to do; if I enter'd the City, I should run the risk of being taken up perhaps and examin'd, and so be sent to Prison for a Runaway, or sent back to my Master, which was almost as bad: so a thought came into my Head, that if I could find means to subsist and live conceal'd in this Place, I might have some fortunate opportunity of finding where you were. Then I began to view the Place more narrowly, and found this Door: I descended into the Vault, but it was so dark I could not discern what was in it, but groping about, I thought I heard a Groan, and turning my Head, discern'd the glimmering of a Lamp on one of the inner Rooms: I enter'd it, tho in some disorder, and there I saw one of the most dismal Objects that ever Eyes beheld, it was an aged Man dress'd in this coarse Coat that I have on, his Beard reached to his Waste, his Bones appear'd ready to start thro his parched shrivel'd Skin, his Eyes were sunk, his Voice fail'd, and he seem'd to be in the last Agonies of Death, as indeed he was. I could hardly recollect my Spirits, I was so mov'd at this dreadful Sight. He fix'd his Eyes upon me, and seem'd desirous to speak to me. In the Name of

---

1 One of many embedded stories in the novel, this one tells of Catherina's and Angelina's escape from captivity in Algeria by dressing as eunuchs. During their escape, they find stairs to an underground chamber, where they discover a hermit who turns out to be Catherina's lost husband.

Jesus, said I, what are you that are thus come to dwell amongst the Dead? That Name, said he, is sweet indeed; speak it again, dear Christian, and comfort my departing Soul. At these Words charity made me haste to give him some of my Wine, of which he swallow'd but a little with much difficulty; yet that a little reviv'd him, and I beg'd him to get down some more. In fine, he was so refresh'd, that I hop'd I should have sav'd his Life, but was deceiv'd....

... since Providence has been so merciful to bring you hither, you shall take up with this sad Being some few days, till I can procure such a Disguise for each of you as I have on, and colour your Faces like mine, which will wash off again;[1] and then I'll provide some better place near the Sea-side for us to dwell in, till God is pleas'd to send some Ship to carry us off from this sad place. The rich Vests and Turbants[2] you have on would surely betray us; we will take the Jewels off, and hide them in the Vault among the dead Bones, where none will seek them, and to-morrow I will buy two Coats, and Boots, with Flannel to make you long Tunicks to your Heels, to keep you warm, and hide your fine Linen underneath; your Heads shall be cover'd with Flannel-Hoods, like Cowls, with Straw-Hats. This resolv'd on, they sat down, and eat thankfully of the Scraps he had brought home. Thus with a good Conscience, Men may live contented, nay be even happy in the most miserable Circumstances. A Charnel-House now entertains these two Ladies, who are better pleas'd to eat Scraps, and lie on Straw and the cold Stones, than dwell in a fine Palace, and sleep on Beds of Down with infamy....

... They charg'd their Fire-Arms,[3] and crept along the Shore till they came to a Hut, into which they enter'd, and found two Savages, a Woman, three Children, and an *European* Man, as his Complexion shew'd, asleep; they seiz'd the Savages, but for the white Man, who appeared to be of a great Age, he arose and embraced them, crossing himself; and lifting up his Hands as a Man over-joy'd, he spake to them in the *Latin* Tongue, desiring

---

1 Here the two women pursue their escape by swapping their Islamic disguises for hermit ones.

2 Turbans.

3 Charlotta's lover, Belanger, has been left ashore on the Oroonoko River along with some Spaniards who were unable to return to the ship before it departed. There he discovers a monk who has lived among the local Indians.

to know who they were and whence they came. The *Spaniards* afraid to speak the true Cause of their coming thither, said they were come on Shore in their Boat in search of fresh Water, and being set upon by the Savages, had been detained there whilst the Boat went off; those they left in it being as they suppose frighted away by the Noise of their Guns. Then the old Man spoke to the *Indians* in their Tongue, and they immediately fell at the *Spaniards* Feet, kissing them, and bowing down their Heads in token of Obedience. The old Man told *Belanger* that he had liv'd twenty Years in that Country; that he was a *Benedictine* Monk, born at *Valladolid* in *Spain*, and thence sent to *Peru*, from whence he had travel'd to this Place by land; that he had learn'd the Language of these Savages, and living amongst them, gain'd their Esteem, and converted many to Christianity; that these poor Savages were some of them, with whom he chose to live, being very honest People; that he would undertake they should supply all their Wants, and be very serviceable to them; that the Savages they had fought with were the Enemies of the Prince that govern'd that part of the Country, and us'd frequently to invade him, and carry off some of his People, whom they eat, as his Subjects did them; but that now he had persuaded a great many from doing it, and pretty well broke them of those barbarous Customs. Then he desir'd the *Spaniards* to sit down with him, and take some Refreshment without fear. After which he said he would conduct them to a place where they might live securely, till he could find means to procure their Return to the Island of *St. Domingo* or *Virginia*, offering to be their Guide to *Cartagena*, from whence they might get Shipping to either Place. (154-55, 160-61, 204-05)

3. From "A Remarkable Voyage in the South Sea," *Edinburgh Magazine*, March-June 1760

Perhaps the following relation of a voyage, full of uncommon events, and accounts of a strange people, may not be thought unworthy a place in your Magazine. It is faithfully extracted from the writings of Mr. John Northey, an old navigator, who lived in the sixteenth century; an age when discoveries were made the reigning taste, and every adventurer hoped to acquire, in an unknown land, treasures equal to those extracted from the mountains of Peru.

The author of these papers was many years in the Spanish service, and in 1597 made the voyage of which I now send you an extract....

It being determined by the president of Panama, and other great officers, to attempt the making some discoveries in the South seas, Don Juan Hamel, captain of the St. Christopher, was sent on this expedition, in which I served in quality of master....

Great care was taken in supplying the ship with every necessary for the voyage; and on Monday the 4th of April 1597, we left the road of Panama, and steered to the westward, through that immense tract of waters, called by the Spaniards the Pacific ocean....

But on our landing they returned, and received us with all the marks of satisfaction and astonishment, considering us probably as beings of a nature superior to themselves. The monarch approached us with the most submissive gestures, and conducted us to his palace, which was a large, but low structure, and resembled in some measure the Indian buildings in Mexico. Here we were entertained with maize and pulse;[1] dressed in the Indian manner, and a kind of liquor resembling in taste the wine extracted from the palm-tree.

After our repast, the Cacique conducted us to the temple of the sun, which stood near his palace; it was a very large structure, being about one hundred and sixty paces long, and sixty wide. At the end opposite to the entrance, was a colossal statue of the sun, indifferently executed, and his head encircled with rays extending to the opposite walls of the temple. The walls were near forty feet high, and the roof, instead of tiles, covered with mats of reeds, resembling the carpets of the Moors. The walls on the inside were covered with beautiful shells and pearls, intermixed with beads of gold, which reflected the rays of the sun in a very pleasing manner. The image of the deity was dressed in a scarlet robe covered with pearls, and about its neck hung a string of gold beads, intermixed with the most beautiful pearls I ever beheld. (March 1760: 131-33)

Nothing now was talked of but the immense riches we should soon be masters of, and some had even determined on the manner in which they would dispose of their share when they

---

1 Beans.

returned to New Spain. But let mortals from hence learn not to flatter themselves with acquiring what possibly may never be in their power, nor fix their minds on what they have not in their possession; lest, like us, they feel the cruel reverse of fortune, and the golden prize which glitters in the eyes of their imagination should prove only the phantom of a waking dream. (April 1760: 190)

How restless is the mind of man! Never satisfied with its present condition, but continually longing for what it cannot enjoy! We might have spent the remainder of our days in peace and security, in this lovely valley; for nature had here provided every thing necessary for our subsistence, even without our own labour and toil. We were at a distance from the bustle and noise of the world; and had nothing to fear either from the open force of a declared enemy, or the secret attempts of a pretended friend. Ambition, which has so often deluged the world with the blood of its inhabitants, and turned fruitful kingdoms into arid wastes, was a stranger here; nor had we any thing to apprehend from the invenomed tongue of envy. But we considered ourselves as banished from the human species, and debarred the pleasure of social life. (June 1760: 288)

Appendix E: Reviews of The Female American

[Only two brief notices of *The Female American* appeared when the novel was first published in 1767, both in English journals devoted to literary reviews. There are no extant reviews of either the 1800 or 1814 editions and apparently no reviews of any of the three editions of the novel appeared in America.]

1. *The Monthly Review; or, Literary Journal,* vol. 36, 1767

A sort of second *Robinson Crusoe*; full of wonders; and well calculated to make one sort of readers *stare*. (238)

2. *The Critical Review; or, Annals of Literature,* vol. 23, 1767

Mrs. Unca Eliza Winkfield is a most strange adventurer, and her memoirs seem to be calculated only for the wild Indians to whom she is so closely allied. We could therefore have wished, as well for her sake as our own, that this lady had published her adventures at the Fall of Niagara, or upon the Banks of Lake Superior, as she would then, probably, have received the most judicious and sincere applause from her enlightened countrymen and princely relations, and have saved us six hours very disagreeable employment. (217)

Works Cited and Recommended Reading

Primary Sources

Ashwell, George. *The History of Hai Eb'n Yockdan, an Indian Prince, Or, the Self-Taught Philosopher*. London, 1686.

Aubin, Penelope. *The Life of Charlotta Du Pont, an English Lady*. London, 1723.

———. *The Life of Madam de Beaumount, a French Lady* and *The Strange Adventures of the Count de Vinevil and his Family*. 1721. Ed. Josephine Grieder. New York: Garland, 1973.

Barclay, Robert. *An Apology for the True Christian Divinity*. London, 1678.

Behn, Aphra. *Oroonoko*. 1688. New York: Norton, 1973.

[Chetwood, W.R.]. *The Voyages and Adventures of Captain Robert Boyle … to Which Is Added the Voyage, Shipwreck, and Miraculous Preservation of Richard Castleman*. London, 1726.

A Collection of Papers, Printed by Order of the Society for the Propagation of the Gospel in Foreign Parts. London, 1706.

The Critical Review; or, Annals of Literature. By A Society of Gentlemen. Vol. 23. London, 1767.

Dampier, William. *Memoirs of a Buccaneer: Dampier's New Voyage Round the World, 1697*. Mineola, NY: Dover, 1968.

Defoe, Daniel. *Robinson Crusoe*. 1719. Ed. J. Donald Crowley. Oxford: Oxford UP, 1972.

———. *Serious Reflections During the Life and Surprising Adventures of Robinson Crusoe*. 1720. New York: Thomas Crowell & Co., 1903.

Dibdin, Charles. *Hannah Hewit; or, the Female Crusoe*. London, 1792.

Dove, John. *Plain Truth: Or Quakerism Unmasked*. London, 1756.

Eliot, John. *A Late and Further Manifestation of the Progress of the Gospel amongst the Indians in New-England*. London, 1655.

———. *John Eliot's Indian Dialogues: A Study in Cultural Interaction*. Ed. Henry W. Bowden and James P. Ronda. Westport, CT: Greenwood P, 1980.

[Evans, Ambrose.] *The Adventures and Surprizing Deliverances, of James Dubourdieu, and his Wife*. London, 1719.

Gracián y Morales, Baltasar. *The Critick.* Trans. Paul Rycaut. London, 1681.

Harriot, Thomas. *A Briefe and True Report of the New Found Land of Virginia.* 1590. New York: Dover, 1972.

The History of Autonous. London, 1736.

The History of Josephus the Indian Prince. London, 1696. Bound with Robert Greene, *The Pleasant and Delightful History of Dorastus.* 65-78.

Keith, George. *An Account of the Oriental Philosophy, from Pococke's Latin.* London, 1674.

———. *The Woman-Preacher of Samaria; A Better Preacher, and more Sufficiently Qualified to Preach than any of the Men-Preachers of the Man-made Ministry of these Three Nations.* London, 1674.

Kirkby, John. *The Capacity and Extent of the Human Understanding: Exemplified in the Extraordinary Case of Automathes.* London, 1745.

Lennox, Charlotte. *The Life of Harriot Stuart.* 1751. Madison: Fairleigh Dickinson UP, 1995.

Lesage, Alain-René. *Aventures du Chevalier de Beauchêne.* 1732. Paris: Impr. De LeBlanc, 1910.

The Life and Surprizing Adventures of Don Juliani de Trezz. London, [1720].

The Life and Surprizing Adventures of Don Antonio de Trezzanio. London, 1761.

The Life and Wonderful Adventures of Henry Lanson. London, [1800].

Longueville, Peter. *The Hermit.* 1727. New York: Garland, 1972.

Mather, Cotton. *The Christian Philosopher.* 1721. Ed. Winton U. Solberg. Urbana: U of Illinois P, 1994.

The Monthly Review; or, Literary Journal. Vol. 36. London, 1767.

Occom, Samson. *The Collected Writings of Samson Occom, Mohegan.* 1748-90. Ed. Joanna Brooks. Oxford: Oxford UP, 2006.

Ockley, Simon. *The Improvement of Human Reason, exhibited in the Life of Hai ebn Yokdhan.* London, 1708.

Percy, George. "Percy's Discourse of Virginia." 1606. *Hakluytus Posthumous or Purchas His Pilgrimes.* By Samuel Purchas. 1625. Vol. 18. Glasgow: James MacLehose and Sons, 1905. 403-19.

Pococke, Edward. *Philosophus Autodidactus.* London, 1671.

"A Remarkable Voyage in the South Sea." *Edinburgh Magazine* (March-June 1760). 131-33; 189-92; 231-33; 288-91.

Rogers, Robert. *Ponteach; Or the Savages of America.* 1766. Ed. Tiffany Potter. Toronto: U of Toronto P, 2010.

Rogers, Woodes. *A Cruising Voyage Round the World: The Adventures of an English Privateer.* 1712. Santa Barbara: Narrative P, 2004.

Rowlandson, Mary. *The Sovereignty and Goodness of God*. 1682. Ed.
Neal Salisbury. Boston: Bedford Books, 1997.

Rowson, Susanna. *Reuben and Rachel; or, Tales of Old Times*. Boston, 1798.

Seaver, James. *A Narrative of the Life of Mrs. Mary Jemison*. 1824. Ed.
June Namias. Norman: U of Oklahoma P, 1992.

Smith, John. *Generall History of Virginia*. 1624. In *The Complete Works
of Captain John Smith*. Vol. II. Ed. Philip Barbour. Chapel Hill: U
of North Carolina P, 1986. 3-475.

Smith, William. *An Historical Account of the Expedition Against the Ohio
Indians*. Philadelphia, 1765.

Tufayl, Ibn. *Ibn Tufayl's Hayy Ibn Yaqzan: A Philosophical Tale*. Trans.
Lenn Evan Goodman. Chicago: U of Chicago P, 2009.

Waterhouse, Edward. *A Declaration of the State of the Colony in
Virginia*. 1622. New York: Da Capo P, 1970.

[Wilson, Thomas.] *An Essay Towards an Instruction For the Indians*.
London, 1740.

Wingfield, Edward Maria. "A Discourse on Virginia." In *The
Jamestown Voyages Under the First Charter 1606-1609*. Vol. I. Ed.
Philip Barbour. Cambridge: Hakluyt Society at Cambridge UP,
1969. 213-34.

Secondary Sources

Aland, Barbara, et. al. *The Greek New Testament*. Stuttgart: Deutsche
Bibelgesellschaft, 1993.

Aravamudan, Srinivas. "East-West Fiction as World Literature: The
Hayy Problem Reconfigured." *Eighteenth-Century Studies* 47.2
(2014): 195-231.

Armstrong, Nancy and Leonard Tennenhouse. *The Imaginary
Puritan: Literature, Intellectual Labor, and the Origins of Personal Life*.
Berkeley: U of California P, 1992.

Attar, Samar. *The Vital Roots of European Enlightenment: Ibn Tufayl's
Influence on Modern Western Thought*. Lanham, MD: Lexington
Books, 2007.

Baine, Rodney M. *Daniel Defoe and the Supernatural*. Athens: U of
Georgia P, 1968.

Bannet, Eve Tavor. *Transatlantic Stories and the History of Reading,
1720-1810: Migrant Fictions*. Cambridge: Cambridge UP, 2011.

Baroud, Mahmoud. *The Shipwrecked Sailor in Arabic and Western
Literature: Ibn Tufayl and His Influence on European Writers*. London:
I.B. Tauris, 2012.

Ben-Zaken, Avner. *Reading* Hayy Ibn-Yaqzan: *A Cross-Cultural History of Autodidacticism*. Baltimore: Johns Hopkins UP, 2011.

Blackwell, Jeannine. "An Island of Her Own: Heroines of the German Robinsonades from 1720 to 1800." *The German Quarterly* (1985): 5-26.

Bowen, Scarlet. "Transatlantic Anglicanism in *The Female American*." *Eighteenth Century: Theory and Interpretation* 53.2 (2012): 189-207.

Brophy, Elizabeth Bergen. *Women's Lives and the 18th-Century Novel*. Tampa: U of South Florida P, 1991.

Brown, Laura. *Ends of Empire: Women and Ideology in Early Eighteenth-Century English Literature*. Ithaca: Cornell UP, 1993.

Burnham, Michelle. *Captivity and Sentiment: Cultural Exchange in American Literature, 1682-1861*. Hanover: UP of New England, 1997.

Castiglia, Christopher. *Bound and Determined: Captivity, Culture-Crossing, and White Womanhood from Mary Rowlandson to Patty Hearst*. Chicago: U of Chicago P, 1996.

Cross, Arthur Lyon. *The Anglican Episcopate and the American Colonies*. Hamden, CT: Archon Books, 1964.

Demos, John. *The Unredeemed Captive*. New York: Knopf, 1994.

Dharwadker, Aparna. "Nation, Race, and the Ideology of Commerce in Defoe." *The Eighteenth Century* 39 (1998): 63-84.

Dugaw, Diane. *Warrior Women and Popular Balladry 1650-1850*. Cambridge: Cambridge UP, 1989.

Ekhtiar, Shelly. "*Hayy ibn Yaqzan*: The Eighteenth-Century Reception of an Oriental Self-Taught Philosopher." *Studies on Voltaire and the Eighteenth Century* 302 (1992): 217-45.

Green, Martin. *The Robinson Crusoe Story*. University Park: Pennsylvania State UP, 1990.

Hassan, Nawal Muhammad. *Hay bin Yaqzan and Robinson Crusoe: A Study of an Early Arabic Impact on English Literature*. Baghdad: Al-Rashid House for Publication, 1980.

Heilman, Robert Bechtold. *America in English Fiction 1760-1800*. 1937. Repr. New York: Octagon Books, 1968.

Hulme, Peter. *Colonial Encounters: Europe and the Native Caribbean 1492-1797*. London: Routledge, 1986.

Hunter, J. Paul. *The Reluctant Pilgrim: Defoe's Emblematic Method and Quest for Form in Robinson Crusoe*. Baltimore: Johns Hopkins UP, 1966.

Joseph, Betty. "Re(Playing) Crusoe/Pocahontas: Circum-Atlantic Stagings in *The Female American*." *Criticism: A Quarterly for Literature and the Arts* 42.3 (2000): 317-35.

Kolodny, Annette. *The Land Before Her: Fantasy and Experience of the American Frontiers 1630-1860*. Chapel Hill: U of North Carolina P, 1984.

Madsen, Peter. "The Strange Fate of the Self-Taught Philosopher in England." *Islam in European Literature*. U of Copenhagen. <Complit.ku.dk/islamineuropeanliterature/workingpapers/dokument3>

Marouby, Christian. "Utopian Colonialism." *North Dakota Quarterly* 56.3 (1988): 148-60.

McDowell, Tremaine. "An American Robinson Crusoe." *American Literature* 1 (1929-30): 307-09.

McKeon, Michael. *The Origins of the English Novel 1600-1740*. Baltimore: Johns Hopkins UP, 1987.

McMurran, Mary Helen. "Realism and the Unreal in *The Female American*." *Eighteenth Century: Theory and Interpretation* 52.3-4 (2011): 323-42.

"No More Separate Spheres!" Special issue ed. by Cathy N. Davidson. *American Literature* 70.3 (1998).

Nordius, Janina. "'Thus Might I Reason with a Heathen ...': The Gothic Moment in *The Female American*." *NJES: Nordic Journal of English Studies* 7.2 (2008): 1-18.

Novak, Maximillian E. *Defoe and the Nature of Man*. Oxford: Oxford UP, 1963.

Owen, C.M. *The Female Crusoe: Hybridity, Trade and the Eighteenth-Century Individual*. New York: Rodopi, 2010.

Pastor, Antonio. *The Idea of Robinson Crusoe*. Watford, UK: Góngora P, 1930.

Reilly, Matthew. "'No Eye Has Seen, or Ear Heard': Arabic Sources for Quaker Subjectivity in Unca Eliza Winkfield's *The Female American*." *Eighteenth-Century Studies* 44.2 (2011): 261-83.

Russell, G.A. "The Impact of the *Philosophus Autodidactus*: Pocockes, John Locke and the Society of Friends." In *The "Arabick" Interest in the Natural Philosophers in Seventeeth-Century England*. Ed. G.A. Russell. Leiden: E.J. Brill, 1994. 224-65.

Sayre, Gordon. T*he Indian Chief as Tragic Hero: Native Resistance and the Literatures of America, from Moctezuma to Tecumseh*. Chapel Hill: U of North Carolina P, 2005.

Seidel, Michael. *Robinson Crusoe: Island Myths and the Novel*. Boston: Twayne, 1991.

Slotkin, Richard. *Regeneration through Violence: The Mythology of the American Frontier, 1600-1860*. Middletown, CT: Wesleyan UP, 1973.

Spengemann, William C. *A Mirror for Americanists: Reflections on the Idea of American Literature*. Hanover, NH: UP of New England, 1989.

Stevens, Laura M. "Reading the Hermit's Manuscript: *The Female American* and Female Robinsonades." *Approaches to Teaching Defoe's Robinson Crusoe*. Ed. Maximillian Novak and Carl Fisher. New York: Modern Language Association of America, 2005. 140-51.

Thompson, Carl. "The *Grosvenor* Shipwreck and the Figure of the Female Crusoe: *Hannah Hewit, Mary Jane Meadows*, and Romantic-Era Feminist and Anti-feminist Debate." *English Studies in Africa* 51.2 (2008): 9-20.

Vaccaro, Kristianne Kalata. "'Recollection ... Sets My Busy Imagination to Work': Transatlantic Self-Narration, Performance, and Reception in *The Female American*." *Eighteenth-Century Fiction*: 20.2 (Winter 2007-08): 127-50.

Watt, Ian. *The Rise of the Novel: Studies in Defoe, Richardson, and Fielding*. Berkeley: U of California P, 1957.

Weaver-Hightower, Rebecca. *Empire Islands: Castaways, Cannibals, and Fantasies of Conquest*. Minneapolis: U of Minnesota P, 2007.

White, Michael. "Reading and Rewriting: The Production of an Economic *Robinson Crusoe*." *Southern Review* 15.2 (1982): 115-42.

Wingfield, Jocelyn R. *Virginia's True Founder: Edward-Maria Wingfield and His Times 1550-c. 1614*. Athens, GA: The Wingfield Family Society, 1993.

Wolfe, Stephen. "Unifying Misnomers: Unca Eliza Winkfield's *The Female American*." *American Studies in Scandinavia* 36.2 (2004): 17-34.

from the publisher

A name never says it all, but the word "broadview" expresses a good deal of the philosophy behind our company. We are open to a broad range of academic approaches and political viewpoints. We pay attention to the broad impact book publishing and book printing has in the wider world; we began using recycled stock more than a decade ago, and for some years now we have used 100% recycled paper for most titles. As a Canadian-based company we naturally publish a number of titles with a Canadian emphasis, but our publishing program overall is internationally oriented and broad-ranging. Our individual titles often appeal to a broad readership too; many are of interest as much to general readers as to academics and students.

Founded in 1985, Broadview remains a fully independent company owned by its shareholders—not an imprint or subsidiary of a larger multinational.

If you would like to find out more about Broadview and about the books we publish, please visit us at **www.broadviewpress.com**. And if you'd like to place an order through the site, we'd like to show our appreciation by extending a special discount to you: by entering the code below you will receive a 20% discount on purchases made through the Broadview website.

Discount code: **broadview20%**

Thank you for choosing Broadview.

Please note: this offer applies only to sales of bound books within the United States or Canada.

The interior of this book is printed on 100% recycled paper.